Two coup

by the

in…

The Baby Connection: Twins!

Two children – twice as much joy!!

Also available

The Baby Connection

featuring

The Baby Bargain by Peggy Nicholson

Little Girl Lost by Marisa Carroll

The Baby Connection: Twins!

DEBRA SALONEN
ANNA ADAMS

Harlequin Mills & Boon Limited, Eton House,
18-24 Paradise Road, Richmond, Surrey TW9 1SR

ISBN: : 978 0263 86595 0

024-0408

Harlequin Mills & Boon policy is to use papers that are natural, renewable and recyclable products and made from wood grown in sustainable forests. The logging and manufacturing processes conform to the legal environmental regulations of the country of origin.

Printed and bound in Spain
by Litografia Rosés S.A., Barcelona

My Husband, My Babies

DEBRA SALONEN

In memory of Kyle Woodrow Gray.

We miss you, sweet boy.

CHAPTER ONE

November 23, 2000
Thanksgiving

SAM O'NEAL GRABBED his younger brother by the collar of his sage-green brushed-cotton shirt and pressed him up against the weathered siding of the Old Bordello Antique Shop. "Jenny won't look me in the eye," he growled, after making sure no one was near. "Why does your wife run out of the room every time I walk in?"

Josh tried to shrug but was handicapped by the two foil-covered plates of turkey and trimmings that he carried like a circus juggler. Sam had one, too, in his left hand. In his right—the one at his brother's throat—was a grapefruit-size pink ball labeled Rosemarie. Ida Jane Montgomery—Josh's wife's eighty-something great-aunt who had raised Jenny and her two sisters—had insisted Sam and Josh use her so-named 1972 pink Cadillac to make their deliveries and pick up the other guests who were joining the family for Thanksgiving dinner.

"The old coots deserve some dignity," she'd told Sam as she pressed the hideous key bob into his hand. "Can you see those ladies trying to climb into your big fancy pickup?"

Josh rolled his chin away from Sam's fingers. "Jen's just getting used to the idea of being pregnant. It wasn't easy talking her into it, you know,'' he said, his voice slightly strangled.

Sam released his grip but didn't move away. He kept his voice low. ''What do you mean *talk her into it?* I thought it was her idea.''

Josh's color rose to clash with the key bob. ''The in vitro was her idea. I'm the one who pushed to use your sperm.'' He winked in a manner so typically Josh that Sam backed off. His brother knew all too well how to get around Sam's common sense.

When Josh had first broached the idea of Sam's donating sperm so Josh and Jenny could conceive, Sam had flat out refused, but Josh was...well, Josh. And when the three of them met in the office of the fertility counselor three weeks ago, Jenny, Josh's wife of ten years, had seemed guardedly enthusiastic. ''If Sam's okay with this, then I am, too,'' she'd said.

Sam had returned home to think about the idea. He couldn't come up with any real objection. The recurrent phrase in his mind was ''Why not?'' After all, the chance of his getting married and having kids of his own seemed remote.

''So why is she avoiding me?'' Sam asked again.

Josh eased sideways to put some distance between them. ''You're imagining things. She's just busy with all these preparations. You know how organized she is.

''And if you and I don't get these plates delivered and pick up the old girls—excuse me, the town matrons—we'll be dining on hot tongue and cold shoulder instead of turkey.'' He shuffled toward the wide steps leading to the parking lot.

Sam followed, mindlessly squeezing the pink ball to ease his trepidation. Something was wrong. He felt it. But Josh was right. This was Jenny's big day. The first

Thanksgiving in ten years that the Sullivan sisters were celebrating together. And at some point in the festivities, Josh would make the big announcement that Jenny was pregnant.

However, they'd unanimously decided that the role of Sam's sperm in the Petri dish would remain a secret. He'd made the commitment and signed the necessary papers. He was going to be an uncle not a father. And if that felt a little weird, he'd learn to live with it because—bottom line—he'd do anything for Josh. Always had. Always would.

THE ARTIST IN HER made Jenny Sullivan O'Neal yearn to capture every single nuance of the moment. The *Sullivan Sisters' Thanksgiving,* she named the imaginary piece.

She took a second to memorize the way Kristin's strawberry-blond hair glistened in the light, and the odd combination of Andi's Marine Corps camouflage pants and pumpkin-orange sweater that somehow worked.

Their first reunion in ten years.

Kristin—the youngest of the Sullivan triplets—stirred the gravy with one hand then dashed to the corner of the oak buffet where she was assembling a salad. A "will-o'-the-wisp," Ida Jane used to call her. Kristin had left home right after high school to stay with family in Ireland where she'd worked as a companion to their uncle's aged grandmother. Later, Kris and two of their Irish cousins, Moira and Kathleen, moved to Wisconsin where she became certified in massage therapy. Although she'd migrated back to the West Coast, she seldom made the seven-hour drive from southern Oregon to Gold Creek, their hometown in the historic gold rush corridor of the Central Sierras in California.

''Ida Jane is getting older,'' Kris was saying, shaking her head. ''So she's a little forgetful and makes a few mistakes. Are you suggesting it's something more serious? Like Alzheimer's?'' she added, lowering her voice.

''No. Not exactly. I don't know. But I think her business is in trouble,'' Jenny said, moving with care around the clutter of her great-aunt's kitchen. Ida Jane's idea of decorating was to fill every available nook and cranny with hodgepodge, from cobweb-laced pinecones in a battered copper urn to chipped vases stuffed with dusty peacock feathers and dried weeds. Jenny worried that the jumble might trip the eighty-one-year-old woman, but Ida loved her ''junque,'' as she called it. Thankfully, so had the collectors who'd visited her antique shop, the Old Bordello, over the years.

The name of the shop reflected the original use of the turn-of-the-century Victorian building. The front half housed Ida's antiques; the second floor and rear section provided the home where Ida had raised Jenny and her sisters. Until recently, the store had been fairly successful. But something had changed. That was one reason Jenny had pushed for this reunion. There was a second reason, too.

Andrea, who'd shortened her name to Andi when she was seven, repeatedly plunged a potato masher into the crockery bowl resting in her lap. ''Ida Jane Montgomery is the most astute businesswoman I've ever known. If her profits are down, then it has to be due to something else. Maybe she needs a new marketing angle.''

On leave from the marines, Andi was seated cross-legged on the butcher-block countertop between the old-fashioned stove and the even more old-fashioned refrigerator.

''I was thinking about it on the plane,'' Andi continued. ''You said foot traffic is sluggish and Ida refuses to have anything to do with the Internet.'' She took a breath. ''What if we went with some kind of advertising ploy—like a ghost?''

''What ghost?'' Kristin asked. ''This place isn't haunted.''

Andi shrugged. ''Maybe not, but it's got history. It used to be a bordello. And I swear I remember Ida telling us a story about a young prostitute who was murdered in one of the upstairs bedrooms. That sounds spooky enough.''

Jenny shook her head. ''She just said that to keep us out of Grandma Suzy's stuff.'' The triplets' grandmother, Suzanne Montgomery Scott, a tragic soul who'd been in and out of mental institutions, had passed away decades earlier, leaving behind a daughter, Lorena. Lori and her Irish-born husband had returned to Gold Creek to give birth, when tragedy struck. A car accident claimed Mick Sullivan's life first, then—after an emergency cesarean section to deliver the triplets—took his wife's, as well.

Andi put a finger into the bowl and popped some potato into her mouth. Chewing, she said, ''Doesn't matter. I think the story has just the right combination of tragedy and mystery to attract antique hunters and curious skeptics.''

Jen agreed. ''I like the idea, Andi. When can you come back to implement it?''

Her sister stiffened. ''Move back here?''

The inflection she gave the last word left no doubt in Jenny's mind that Andi wanted nothing to do with Gold Creek. She thought she understood Kristin's antipathy toward the town—people had unfairly labeled her a screwup—but Andi had always kept her reasons for leaving home to herself.

"Yes," Jenny said bluntly, giving both her sisters a look they'd understand. "Ida Jane isn't getting any younger. She needs our help."

As she pried the cornmeal muffins from the speckled enamel tin, she told them, "Warren Jones stopped me on the street a couple of weeks ago and told me we'd better do something before our aunt loses the bordello. But when I asked to see her books, Ida told me to mind my own business."

Andi made a grumbling sound. "Warren Jones has always been a worrywart."

Jenny agreed, but if Warren, who'd filed Ida Jane's income tax returns ever since his father, Walter, retired three years earlier, was worried, then they owed it to their aunt to find out what was going on.

After Jenny transferred the muffins to the warming basket, she brushed back several strands of deep-auburn hair that had escaped from the lapis clip at the nape of her neck. "All I'm saying is that we need to stay on top of the situation. Remember Sandy Grossman…Grimaldo?"

Jenny noticed the way Kristin threw herself into opening a can of ripe olives. Her exaggerated disinterest in the conversation made Jenny wonder if her sister might still harbor feelings for her old boyfriend, Donnie Grimaldo. "Sandy's mother got hooked on bingo and lost everything. Sandy didn't discover how bad it was until Poopsie was facing eviction."

Andi pitched the potato masher into the sink then hopped down from the countertop. She scraped the fluffy white potato into a serving bowl, added a dollop of butter and covered the dish with a plate. "Ida Jane's no gambler. How many times has she repeated the cautionary tale of her father losing the Rocking M in a poker game?''

Kristin, who'd driven down from her home in Ashland that morning, nodded. ''For years I was afraid to buy a lottery ticket for fear I might turn into a gambleholic.''

Andi opened the oven door and leaned down to pull out the golden–breasted turkey. ''So we'll talk before Kris leaves. No problem. Is that the only reason you pushed for this reunion, Jen?'' She heaved the enamel roasting pan to the counter then whipped about to face her sisters.

A tremor fluttered in Jenny's belly. She knew it wasn't the baby. They'd only received confirmation of the success of the procedure on Tuesday. ''Well, there is one other thing, but I thought I'd wait to make the announcement at dinner.''

Andi and Kristin glanced at each other. The two hadn't been on good terms since high school, but they still seemed to be able to communicate without words. ''Tell us,'' Andi ordered.

''Josh and I are pregnant.''

''Told you so,'' Kristin said smugly.

''You knew?'' Jenny sputtered. ''How?''

''Lucky guess,'' Andi said sourly. ''It's not like you haven't wanted to be a mother forever. What I can't figure out is why you're not shouting out the news from the upstairs porch.''

Because we cheated.

''We've been seeing a fertility specialist,'' she admitted, her words tumbling over each other. ''We used in vitro. There was a chance it wouldn't take.'' But it did take. *I'm going to be a mother. Of my brother-in-law's child.*

Andi left the turkey to rest and walked to Jenny's side. She looped a slim, muscular arm around her shoulders and squeezed. "I understand. You're Jenny Perfect. You shouldn't need technology and Petri dishes to make offspring. But, hey, sometimes even the best of us need help."

The teasing might have stung if Jenny hadn't heard it a million times. Her sisters had nicknamed her in kindergarten when she'd brought home her first report card: all S's and O's—Satisfactory and Outstanding. No N's—Needs Improvement. Unfortunately, the name had stuck.

Just last week, Gloria Harrison Hughes, author of "Glory's World," a local "news" column in the weekly *Gold Creek Ledger,* had reported:

> Jenny O'Neal, the Sullivan triplet better known as Jenny Perfect, will host her sisters and select friends at a Thanksgiving dinner at her great-aunt Ida Jane Montgomery's home. This reporter can't help but wonder how long it's been since the Sullivan triplets have been together. Isn't it a shame when family is torn apart by poor judgment?

The dig had infuriated Jenny, but Josh had cajoled her into laughing at the vindictive woman who held Kristin responsible for her son's premature departure from high school. "Gloria Hughes is a small-town, small-minded harpy," he'd stated. "Everyone knows she got the job because her brother owns the paper. Nobody pays any attention to her column."

Jenny knew that wasn't true, but there wasn't anything she could do to change Gloria's mind. She'd tried.

She stuck out her tongue at her sisters, knowing it was the expected response, then walked to the pantry to retrieve the folding stool. Kristin and Andi laughed, and peripherally Jenny saw them exchange a look that she remembered well from their teen years.

Triplets shared a dynamic wholly different from twins. Much of the time they were a threesome—''Our Sullivan Girls,'' the people of Gold Creek called them, partly because many of the townsfolk felt they'd lent a hand in raising the orphaned triplets. But factions arose, too. Sometimes one combination, sometimes another.

Kristin finished preparing the garnishes then slithered a second can of jellied cranberries onto a ruffled crystal dish that had belonged to their mother. Earlier they'd culled some turkey and fixings for Ida's housebound friends. Josh and Sam were due back any minute from their taxi duties.

Chewing on a stalk of celery, Kris tilted her head and asked, ''Why in vitro? You're young, healthy. Why didn't you and Josh just try harder? Isn't that half the fun?''

''We've been trying to get pregnant ever since we got married, Kris. The fertility clinic finally determined that Josh has some problems left over from his bout of testicular cancer when he was twelve.''

Kristin's expressive face showed concern. ''I'd forgotten about that. Is there a problem?''

Jenny shook her head. ''No. He's fine. He's been cancer free for nearly fifteen years. But unfortunately, the treatment affected his ability to make viable sperm.'' *Like he doesn't. Period.* ''So, it came down to in vitro or adoption.''

Jenny plopped open the wobbly oak, A-frame stool beside the sink and gingerly climbed up to reach the overhead cupboard. ''Frankly,'' she continued, poking through the clutter to hide her nervousness, ''I favored adoption. There are a lot of kids out there who need a family, but Josh felt strongly about carrying on the O'Neal family genes.''

The O'Neal family genes. Saying the words made her feel like a fraud. The genes in question were Sam's not Josh's. But Jenny was determined to honor her husband's wish that this be kept between the three of them. ''If it ever becomes an issue, for health reasons or whatever, you can tell your sisters, but you know as well as I do that the only way to keep a secret in a small town is to seal your lips,'' he'd argued.

''And I'd appreciate it if you keep this—the in vitro part—to yourselves,'' Jenny added. ''Josh says it doesn't bother him, but you know how guys are.''

Andi, who'd been in charge of carving the turkey since age eight—the year she'd taken up fencing—sharpened the carving knife on a whetstone. ''Having lived in testosterone-ville for the past four years, I can attest to that. Men can be very strange when it comes to things having to do with the penis.''

Jenny thought she detected a certain edge of bitterness in her sister's tone, but she didn't have a chance to question it because the dining-room door suddenly opened and Sam O'Neal walked in.

''Deliveries made, dowager queens present and accounted for,'' he said with a lazy, John Wayne–style salute.

Jenny turned back to hunting down the gravy boat she knew was lurking somewhere in the cluttered cupboard. She told herself she wasn't deliberately trying not to look at her brother-in-law.

''We're just about ready,'' she mumbled, stretching to the far corner where she spotted the vessel. Unfortunately, the stool—an antique like everything else in her aunt's home—chose that instant to wobble. Jenny reached for the cupboard door again, but it swung out of reach. She would have fallen if not for Sam's quick action. He wrapped his arms around her thighs to steady her. His chin was level with her womb.

The intimacy, given their situation, made Jenny react poorly. She yelped and tried to squirm out of his hold, which resulted in her losing her footing.

"Hold on a sec," Sam murmured, trying to keep her from toppling backward.

Before she could blink, she was safely on the ground, gravy boat clasped to her breast. Sam gave her a puzzled look. "Are you okay?"

Jenny felt her cheeks fill with color; she knew her sisters were watching. "Fine, thanks," she said, quickly turning toward the sink. "I have to wash this."

Sam closed the overhead door then moved a foot or so to rest his backside against the counter. Casually dressed in what looked like a new camel-colored shirt and black jeans and low-heeled boots, he seemed remarkably at ease. As he chatted casually with her sisters, it occurred to Jenny that she really didn't know Sam very well at all, even though he'd been a part of her life for ten years.

Jenny watched him surreptitiously. He was a big man—six inches taller and forty pounds heavier than his brother. In his youth, he'd been a movie stuntman and even put in a few years on the rodeo circuit. At thirty-nine, he still possessed a restless, untamed quality that made the town matchmakers eager to find him a wife. To Jenny, he'd gone from enigmatic brother-in-law to raw bone of contention in less than a month.

Jenny knew Sam was not to blame. It wasn't his fault that his virility was an affront to her, considering what her poor, beloved husband had been going through. It just wasn't fair.

"I asked, 'How is the book coming?'" Sam turned slightly to face her.

Darned if his casual attitude didn't irritate Jenny, too. It was as if he thought they could all go back to life as usual now that the deed was done. Jenny knew otherwise. She knew nothing would ever be the same again. Everything had changed the moment the decision was made to use Sam's sperm to impregnate her egg.

"It's not," she muttered, attacking the fragile gravy boat with a woven plastic scrubber.

"What book?" Kristin asked. "The last I heard you were a fourth-grade teacher."

"Jenny's a gifted artist and writer, too," Sam said. "I saw some of the watercolors she did for a children's book last summer."

"Cool," Andi said. "Maybe you could do a book on our ghost, too."

Jenny ignored their banter. Her book project was a dream, and Josh had promised her the summer off to work on it, but knowing Josh, something would come up.

"I plan to work on the text this summer," Jenny said, not liking the testy edge to her tone, "but we all know June through August is Ida Jane's busiest season. But, if Andi moves back after her enlistment is up…hint, hint."

When Sam asked Andi about her plans, Jenny tuned out the conversation. Her sister would do what her sister would do—that was Andi. "Willful and stubborn as the day is long," Ida always said.

Instead, Jenny pictured how she'd begged Josh to consider choosing a donor from the impressive list their fertility counselor had provided. But Josh had pleaded, sweet-talked and pressured her into believing this arrangement would be better than using an anonymous donor.

''This is a win-win scenario, Jenny,'' he'd argued. ''Even though we had different fathers, Sam is my closest blood relative. My *only* relative besides Mom.''

Jenny knew Josh was sensitive about the fact his mother hadn't married his father. Diane claimed that the reason she gave her second son Sam's surname was to make things easier for Josh, but Jenny wasn't sure she believed that.

''This way we get a child that's at least *part* me, and Sam can feel good knowing the O'Neal line isn't going to die. That's more important to him than you think,'' he'd quickly added, anticipating Jenny's reply.

She and her sisters had long speculated about why such a virile, handsome man as Sam O'Neal didn't have a wife and children. Josh attributed his brother's decision to remain single to Sam's teenage marriage and subsequent annulment. Although Jenny didn't know the details, Josh maintained that Sam was ''once burned, twice shy.''

Sam's love life is not my problem, Jenny reminded herself. *What I need to figure out is how to treat him in light of his magnanimous donation.*

When she reached for the cotton towel her aunt kept hanging under the cupboard, Sam beat her to it. ''Here,'' he said. His deep voice sounded strained.

Jenny accepted the cloth with a forced smile. ''Thanks.'' Their fingers touched briefly, just enough to make her insides flutter in a way she didn't recognize. She quickly stepped back and nearly tripped over the dilapidated stool.

Suddenly angry, and very close to tears, she kicked its slightly askew leg. ''Would somebody please throw that damn thing away before we end up with a lawsuit on our hands?''

The kitchen door swung open and a blond head popped in, a video camera to one eye. ''What's that? Did I hear my wife use profanity? Lord have mercy. Jenny Perfect cussed.''

Jenny saw Sam slip out of the range of fire, as if he could read her temper brewing. This irked her, too. As did her husband's use of the ridiculous nickname she couldn't shake. She grabbed a corn muffin out of the basket and pitched it at the video cam. Josh ducked.

The soft biscuit bounced off the door and rolled to a crumbly stop a foot from Josh's loafers. He picked it up and took a bite. ''Mmm, good, but it'll be better with honey. Won't it, honey?''

Grinning, he sauntered across the room. He set the camera on the counter then pulled Jenny into an embrace. He nuzzled the sensitive spot on her neck until her knees grew weak and she had to laugh. ''Stop it, you goofball. Everything's ready.''

''I'm ready,'' he said, making his fair eyebrows dance up and down. ''Oh, yeah, baby. Any time. Any place.''

Amid the laughter and kisses, it struck her. Finally, after all the tests, thermometers and frustration, they were going to have a baby. Did it matter in the long run where the sperm came from? Not if they loved their baby as much as they loved each other. The child now growing in her womb would be *their* child—hers and Josh's.

''You are completely nuts,'' she said, cupping his cheek with her free hand. ''But I love you.''

Josh tossed his half-eaten muffin in the sink then pulled her tight against him. He lowered his head and kissed her. Jenny felt herself blush, even though her family had seen them kiss before—many times. But for some reason, she felt weird this time. She tried to focus on the pleasure of Josh's touch but couldn't relax.

Apparently sensing something was wrong, Josh lifted his head and said, "Okay, everyone, dinner's up to you. Me and my woman are heading upstairs for a little quality time in one of the bedrooms."

"Maybe Andi's ghost will show up," Kristin joked.

"Ghost?" Josh righted them so quickly Jenny's vision blurred. "What ghost?"

Andi repeated her suggestion with obvious reluctance, probably because she knew the only way the marketing scheme would become a reality was if she returned to Gold Creek to implement it.

"Have you ever seen this ghost?" Josh asked seriously.

Jenny punched him. "No, but you've got to admit, a *haunted* bordello carries a certain appeal. Remember that restaurant we ate at on Jackson Square in New Orleans? Muriel's? It's supposed to be haunted. Just because we didn't see a ghost didn't detract from its charm."

Andi walked to the cupboard for a serving platter. "We'd just be embroidering on a story Auntie used to tell us about a young prostitute who lived here. She died when two men fought over her and a gun went off. Right, Jen?"

Before Jenny had a chance to answer, a diminutive elderly woman entered the room. "What's the holdup here?" she asked. "My dinner guests are waiting. Joshua, are you making trouble again?"

Ida Jane Montgomery, dressed in a purple and green silk jogging suit that would have put a peacock to shame, looked around, a mock frown on her deeply lined face.

"M-me?" Josh sputtered. "It's the girls' fault. They were holding a séance to get the bordello's ghost to join us for dinner."

"A ghost? What ghost?" Ida Jane exclaimed. "If there's a ghost, I want to know about it."

Sam approached Jenny's great-aunt and bowed with dignity. "Miss Ida, these wayward youngsters are holding up dinner with their tomfoolery, but I'd be delighted to escort you to the table. Maybe if we set a good example they'll take the hint."

Ida Jane, her cap of stiff blue curls sticking out at odd angles, lifted her chin regally. "Lord knows I've tried to raise them right, but those girls were a handful from the day they came home from the hospital." Her sigh fooled no one. Everyone knew Ida Jane loved her grandnieces more than anything, even the dilapidated old bordello that served as both antique store and home.

"Did I tell you about the time one of 'em filled the wringer washer with baby ducks?" she asked, taking Sam's arm. "I believe it was Andrea."

Together they made such a charming picture that Jenny's heart constricted, and her eyes filled with tears. Another memory to paint.

"Me?" Andi howled. "Why is it always me? I hated ducks. Still do. It was Kristin." She picked up the platter of turkey in one hand and the muffin basket in the other then followed after her aunt.

Kris gave Jenny a mischievous wink before wrapping an arm around the salad bowl. She also managed to carry the crock of mashed potatoes as she hurried after the others, loudly proclaiming her innocence. "It wasn't me, Auntie. I don't remember any ducks. Are you sure it wasn't Jenny? Just because she never got in any trouble doesn't mean..."

Before Jenny could follow, Josh pulled her into his arms. His Paul Newman–blue eyes were unusually serious. ''Have I told you today how wonderful you are?'' He kissed her lightly. ''I love you more than giblet gravy.''

Jenny relaxed into his safe, loving embrace. She'd been far too uptight lately. She had to try to be more like her husband, who could dash away the slightest worry with a wave of his hand. That same devil-may-care attitude was what had attracted her to him when she was sixteen.

''I love you, too,'' she returned. She didn't know what she'd do without his beaming smile, his spontaneous laugh. If even a fraction of his personality somehow found its way to their child, Jenny knew the agonizing choice would have been worth it. Setting her worries aside, she kissed him back.

A muffled chant, ''Gra...vy, Gra...vy,'' filtered through the wall.

Josh grinned. ''Duty calls, my sweet, but we're going to sneak away later. I promise. Is there really a ghost?''

Jenny shook her head. ''Of course not. It's a marketing gimmick that might attract customers to the antique store. Ida Jane's been very closemouthed about it, but I think her business is in trouble. I'm trying to talk Andi into moving home when her enlistment is up. She has a lot of good ideas and she knows computers. Maybe we can gently nudge Ida Jane into the twenty-first century.''

Using two oven mitts, Josh pulled a bake dish of marshmallow yams and another of pecan stuffing out of the oven while Jenny filled the gravy boat with the golden, aromatic sauce. She grabbed a serving dish of green beans on her way through, and together they joined the others in the dining room.

''Make room for the good stuff,'' Josh said, leaning forward to deposit the dishes on waiting trivets.

The yellowish glow from the candles in the centerpiece cast an odd shadow across Josh's face. A shiver raced up Jenny's spine.

She hastily deposited her two bowls on the table and sat down. *Get a grip,* she silently chastised herself. *Must be all those extra hormones I've been taking.*

''This is wonderful,'' Ida Jane said, clapping her hands with glee. ''The Sullivan girls are back together. Plus Sam and Josh and my dearest friends are here, too. What a joyous day!''

Four elderly women, as familiar to Jenny and her sisters as blood relatives, cheered with approval. The dignified Lillian Carswell, a retired librarian, sat beside Kristin. Directly across from her was Beulah Jensen, who lived around the corner and had left three May baskets on the porch of the old bordello every May Day until the triplets moved away from home. To Ida Jane's left was Mary Needham, whose poor hearing was probably a result of thirty years of driving a school bus. To Sam's right sat recently widowed Linda McCloskey, one of the nurses who had been at the hospital the night the triplets were born. Linda's only son, Bart, was celebrating the holiday with his wife's family in Santa Rosa.

Josh took his place at the head of the table opposite Ida Jane then reached out to take Jenny's hand. With his left, he made a ''gimme'' motion until Andi complied. She in turn connected with Kristin, who linked with Lillian and so on. Jenny and Sam completed the circle.

When everyone was holding hands, Josh spoke, his voice uncharacteristically serious. ''Thank you, Father, for the gifts we are about to share. Thank you, too, for giving us each other, and never let us forget that we're connected through time and space, spirit and heart. We are family."

He squeezed Jenny's hand; she did likewise to Sam, who held her hand in his big rough paw. Glancing sideways, she saw his lips compress slightly. Instinctively, she knew what he was thinking. They were connected all right. In a way, hopefully, no one else would ever know.

Josh lifted his head and slowly looked around the table. "And speaking of family," he said, pausing dramatically, "Jenny's pregnant."

After a round of cheers and congratulations, Andi said, "As long as you don't have triplets, right, Auntie?"

Ida Jane's gaze settled on Jenny. She lifted her wineglass in a toast. "To new life. The number's not important, it's the love that counts." Her gray eyes clouded a moment then she went on. "You girls never had a chance to know your parents, but I can tell you, they loved you from the instant you were conceived."

Jenny felt a flush creep up her neck. Her grip on her glass of cranberry juice tightened.

"To families," Sam said quietly, his deep voice making a big impact. "Thank you, Miss Ida, for always making me feel a part of yours."

A chorus of "Hear! Hear!" echoed around the table.

After each glass touched, the feast began, every bit as festive and noisy as any Jenny could remember. She went through all the motions. She smiled and chewed and answered questions when asked, but a part of her was out of sync.

"A little faith, please," Sam said softly, their shoulders almost touching.

Jenny startled. "I beg your pardon?"

"A little turkey," he repeated. One thin, sable eyebrow quirked in question. "Are you feeling okay? You look pale."

Jenny swallowed the lump in her throat. She reached for the platter and in the process dragged the sleeve of her blouse across the mound of untouched mashed potatoes on her plate.

Sam made a harsh sound between his teeth, and rose. He pulled out her chair and said to the others, "Gravy stain. This calls for quick action."

Jenny rose without thinking and followed him into the kitchen. He led her to the sink and carefully rinsed the brown smear from the ivory material. "Jenny," he said softly, "what's wrong?"

Distracted by his roughened fingers working the delicate material with exquisite care, Jenny didn't answer. Her emotions were too jumbled, too close to the surface. She couldn't put her anguish into words.

Wrapping a towel around her wrist, Sam squeezed firmly. "What is it? Tell me."

"This is so *not* my style, Sam. You know me. I'm a born-again flower child. If nature had intended for Josh and me to have a baby, it would have happened. I can't help thinking something bad is going to happen because we were greedy. We wanted more than we were supposed to have."

The last came out as a blubbering cry. Sam cursed softly then reacted as any compassionate person would. He pulled her into his strong safe arms and soothed her with quiet, calming words of encouragement.

"Jenny, you took advantage of a medical miracle. What's wrong with that? Nature's changed the game, sweetheart."

The endearment wasn't anything she hadn't heard him

say a hundred times, but it made her throat close. "You've seen my breeding operation at the ranch," he went on. "Not to be crude, but *I'm* Mother Nature in my part of the world, and nothing terrible has happened. The Rocking M has the healthiest, strongest stock around."

Jenny made herself take a deep breath. His scent was different from Josh's but comforting, fortifying. She pulled back enough to look up at him.

"You haven't done anything wrong, Jenny. If it weren't for Josh's cancer, he'd have enough sperm to get you both in a lot of trouble. It's not his fault, and he shouldn't have to pay. Neither of you should."

"Your mother blames herself for Josh's cancer," Jenny said. "She said she didn't get his vaccinations on schedule and somehow that made him prone to testicular cancer."

Sam's expression turned sour. His less-than-congenial feelings for his mother were well known, but even after all these years she'd never discovered the reason behind them.

"That's just Diane being Diane, but none of that matters. What's important is that you and my brother have a chance to start a family. I'm just hoping this doesn't ruin our friendship."

Jenny knew she had to try to get past her qualms. Josh loved his brother almost as much as he loved Jenny. It would tear him apart if the two people he loved most couldn't be comfortable around each other.

"You're right, Sam. It'll all work out."

He touched his knuckle to her chin—a gesture he'd employed since Josh introduced them when she was sixteen. "Can I finish my dinner now?"

Smiling, Jenny tossed the towel on the counter and

looped her arm through his. ''Just save room for pie. I bought them from the new bakery in town.''

Sam's low chuckle reassured her even more. ''That is not going to be a problem, believe me.''

SAM WATCHED JOSH WALK the last of the dinner guests—Lillian Carswell—to the door of her neat-as-a-pin mobile home. The old gal was a veritable font of knowledge about Gold Creek's history.

The subject on the drive to her mobile home in Restful Trails Senior Park had been the triplets. She had stories galore. ''Ida Jane was forever trying to dress them alike,'' she'd said with a chortle. ''I'll never forget the Easter when the girls turned six. Marge Grover—she passed away a few years ago—sewed these darling little pinafore-type dresses, and Betsey Simms, at McAffey's department store, donated white anklets trimmed with tiny daisies and the cutest little bonnets you've ever seen. But the triplets had other plans.''

She'd leaned forward to pat Josh's shoulder. ''Not Jenny, of course. She was a perfect angel, like usual. But Andrea claimed the shoes hurt her feet. She preferred to wear sneakers without socks. She wouldn't even consider wearing the hat. Kristin wore the hat but insisted on sticking a bunch of flowers from Ida's garden in it. By the time she got to church, the lilacs were drooping like clusters of grapes.''

Sam found the tale reassuring. The triplets were unique individuals, even at age six.

Once Josh was seated, Sam put the car in gear. He drove slowly to negotiate the park's many speed bumps. ''Your wife has some concerns about this arrangement, Josh,'' he said. ''We probably should have waited, maybe talked it through a little more.''

"There wasn't time, Sam," Josh said. "You had the China trip scheduled."

"So? We could have put it off a few months."

Josh, who'd been diagnosed as borderline hyperactive as a child, went atypically still. "We've waited long enough, Sam. It was now or never."

An icy chill down his spine made Sam lean forward to click up the heat.

Josh turned in the seat to face him. "Jenny's happy about it. I know she is. She's just had a lot on her mind."

Sam could believe that. Getting her sisters to the same table after all these years was quite a feat. And talking Andi into returning to Gold Creek next spring seemed very unlikely. "Well, I hope you're right. Jenny's a good lady, and I don't want this to come back to haunt us."

"Haunt," Josh repeated. "Ida Jane really liked Andi's idea of a resident ghost, didn't she?" Josh was a master at changing subjects, but his laugh—chipper, familiar and reassuring—eased Sam's odd feeling of trepidation.

"Don't worry, bro," he said, lightly punching Sam's shoulder. "Everything is working out just the way it's supposed to."

Sam hoped so. For all their sakes.

CHAPTER TWO

March 2001
St. Patrick's Day

SINCE THE DECK off the master bedroom afforded the best view of the courtyard, Sam headed there to take stock. He threw open the balcony doors off his bedroom and stepped to the railing to scan the crowd below.

Thanks to Josh's insistent nagging and organizational skills, the Rocking M sponsored a benefit barbecue each year on St. Patrick's Day weekend when the surrounding hills were their greenest and the California buckeyes were swathed in shiny new leaves. Members of the Gold Creek Garden Club—Ida Jane's pet group—handled the kitchen; the volunteer fire department cooked the chicken. Sam made sure he stayed in the background, while Josh played host.

Sam spotted Andi Sullivan sitting on the top rung of the corral chatting with Lars Gunderson, a cantankerous old miner who made Sam's solitary habits look downright social. Andi had only been back in town a week, but according to Josh, the changes she had in mind for the Old Bordello Antique Shop weren't sitting well with the store's owner.

His gaze circled the crowd of familiar faces until he spotted what he was looking for—a kelly-green Stetson. He had no idea where his brother had managed to find such a thing, but there it was atop Josh's head, pushed back at a jaunty angle to accommodate the video camera that never seemed to leave his eye.

Sam let out a long sigh. At least Josh was sitting still for the moment. Sam was almost out of patience where his brother was concerned. The past three months had been stressful. Jenny's full trimester of morning sickness and fatigue had coincided with Josh's seemingly unconnected series of colds and flulike symptoms, which had finally been diagnosed as something far more serious.

Josh's cancer had returned, popping up as a difficult-to-spot mass behind his liver. The oncologist Josh saw last week in Stanford had recommended an aggressive protocol of radiation and chemotherapy.

It couldn't be aggressive enough as far as Sam was concerned. His main problem was Josh's attitude.

"I beat it before, I can do it again," Josh said repeatedly. "Will you two lighten up?"

He was referring to Jenny and Sam. Sam hadn't spent a lot of time in his sister-in-law's company the past few months—he knew she still felt awkward around him. In hindsight, especially given Josh's condition, the timing of the pregnancy was all wrong, but there was little anyone could do about it at this point.

"He's going to wear himself out, isn't he?" a voice said from the doorway behind him.

Sam glanced over his shoulder, but he recognized the voice without looking. Jenny. Beautiful, glowing, very pregnant Jenny. "Not if I have anything to say about it," Sam replied, his voice gruff.

She sighed as she joined him at the railing. "You're not your brother's keeper, you know. But I do appreciate everything you've done to help."

Sam inched over to put more space between them.

Lately she seemed to possess an ethereal glow that made him yearn to touch her. Which, he reminded himself, was not a good thing. He knew this confounding attraction had to be based on the fact she was carrying his babies—her first sonogram had alerted them that she was carrying twins. His connection to her was purely biological, he told himself.

"Josh is lucky they finally diagnosed this," Sam said, staring at a group of people standing beside a patrol car. His buddy, Donnie Grimaldo, a local deputy, leaned against the front fender while his boss, Sheriff Magnus Brown, held court. The older man was a blowhard who'd never been one of Sam's favorite people.

"What do you mean?" Jenny asked.

Sam didn't turn his head but sensed she was studying his face. He regretted his candor but said, "I hate to admit it, but I was beginning to think Josh was turning into a hypochondriac, like our mother."

Jenny chuckled under her breath. "That summer in college when your mother stayed with us she practically lived at the clinic. She was on a first-name basis with all the pharmacists at Long's."

Sam turned slightly and said, "Good thing her new husband is a retired doctor. He's got just what she needs—money and a prescription pad. Maybe she'll keep this one."

Jenny frowned. "You really don't like her, do you?"

"I just don't like talking about her." His feelings were a mixture of anger and disgust, far too convoluted for casual conversation and best kept locked in the darkest recesses of his mind. He shrugged and looked away from Jenny's all-too-sympathetic eyes.

"Josh doesn't seem to hold as much bitterness toward

her as you do, but I guess you two have more history together, right?''

History. *I guess you could call a stab in the back that cost me my wife and unborn child ''history.''* ''Is that a polite way of saying I'm old?'' he teased.

She smiled wryly. ''Eleven years seemed like a big deal when I was seventeen and you were pushing thirty, but now that I'm almost thirty…''

Sam let his skepticism show. ''Twenty-eight is still wet behind the ears.''

''Oh, no. Not the old-age talk,'' a cheerful voice said, taking them by surprise.

Both Sam and Jenny spun around. For some reason Sam felt guilty, but fortunately, his brother didn't seem to notice. Josh strolled forward and looped his arm across his wife's shoulders. ''I was filming the festivities and happened to scan upward and what do I see but Romeo and Juliet on the balcony.''

His teasing brought a shot of heat to Sam's face, making him grateful for the setting sun. ''Yep, that's why I built this place. So I could spout poetry to my sister-in-law,'' Sam said, hoping his joke didn't sound as lame to Jenny and Josh as it did to him.

Jenny's lovely cheeks seemed to hold some extra color, too, but Sam attributed that to the afternoon's activities. She'd been in charge of the egg race.

''I guess it's about time to sound the gong for dinner,'' Sam said, starting to leave.

''It can wait. I, um, wanted to talk to you a minute,'' Josh said, his tone uncharacteristically serious.

Sam pulled over the folding chair he kept on the deck. ''Have a seat. I'll get you a chair, Jenny.''

She shook her head. In the mellow sunset, her wind-tossed locks looked bloodred. ''I'm fine.''

Josh squeezed her shoulders then whisked his silly green hat from his head and placed it on Jenny's. "She's a trooper, isn't she, Sam? Do you know anyone better than Jenny Perfect?" he asked, sitting down.

Jenny's lip curled up in a snarl, and Sam looked away to hide his smile. He knew she hated the nickname—even if it did fit.

"What do you want to talk about, Josh?"

"The big C. The ugly little growth in here." He pulled up his T-shirt, exposing his belly. The bluish-white scar that dissected his pale skin from sternum to navel was a product of the last go-around. When he was twelve, doctors removed a large mass near his liver along with the diseased testicle where the cancer had begun.

Sam shrugged, faking nonchalance. "What's to talk about? You fight it and beat it—just like last time."

Jenny nodded. Sam thought she looked close to tears.

Josh lowered his shirt. He closed his eyes and let out a long sigh. "I know that. But, I want to be up front about what's happening. I'm not going to give up living while I get these treatments.

"Jenny wants me to quit work. Being a park ranger has been my dream ever since I watched my first Yogi and Boo-Boo cartoon," he said, with a chuckle.

"Sam, you want to do your big-brother thing, which I appreciate all to hell, but the bottom line is—it's my life, my cancer, and I have to deal with it my way."

Something about Josh's tone, something too fatalistic for Sam's taste, made him blow up. "You mean laid-back? Take it as it comes? I don't think so, little brother. This isn't a game. It's war. We're fighting for your life, and I'm damn well going to be in the trenches with you."

Jenny put her hand on Josh's shoulder. "Listen to Sam, Josh. He remembers what it was like the first time. He—"

"You think I don't?" Josh exclaimed, jumping to his feet. "I was the one puking my guts out, not Sam. I'm the one who got razzed about my bald head. Been there, done that, Jen. And I'm not wild about doing it again."

Sam felt as breathless as he had when a horse had fallen on him, breaking three ribs.

Jenny threw herself against Josh and cried, "You don't have a choice, Josh. We have to think about the babies."

Josh's arms came up slowly, but finally he wrapped them around his wife and soothed her sobs. But over her shoulder, his gaze found Sam. There was something sad and very tired in his brother's eyes. Something that made Sam want to sit down and weep.

Three months later

"I'LL BE BACK in a minute. I'm going to put away some of this stuff," Jenny called, closing the door to the spare bedroom behind her.

Once the latch clicked, she leaned against it and slowly sank to the floor. Her belly made her feel graceless and top-heavy; her swollen ankles looked like gross stumps connected to her Birkenstock-clad feet. Her sleeveless denim maternity jumper was wrinkled and stained with Kool-Aid handprints from the end-of-school party. Happy tears, sweaty hugs and another year was over.

Then, before she had time to catch her breath, her colleagues had converged on her room to give her a baby shower. She'd survived both ordeals without breaking down, but her emotions were very close to the surface. When Sam's big white pickup pulled up to her classroom door and her husband gingerly lowered himself to the ground, she'd had to fight not racing to help him. But Josh, despite the weight loss and bald head, was still proud and independent. He tried to carry on as if the horrible disease wasn't getting the better of him. But everyone knew otherwise. Everyone except Sam, who refused to see the obvious.

She took a deep breath, readjusting her position to give a child's foot or elbow more room beneath her rib cage. As she eyed the booty piled on the daybed—a complete layette, bath provisions, stuffed animals and a vast assortment of tiny clothes—her gaze was drawn to the brilliantly painted rocking horse sitting on the floor in front of her easel. A gift from Sam.

"Your husband picked it out," he'd said, amid the oohs and aahs of her fellow teachers. "The last time we were in Stanford."

A month earlier. When there'd still been hope. When a miracle seemed possible, and Josh seemed to be responding to the high doses of chemotherapy pumped into his body.

Sam had taken charge of Josh's treatment schedule. It had made sense since Jenny couldn't take the time from work, nor was her body up to the long drives, but there was a tiny part of her that resented him. Sam had those hours on the drive to and from the clinic. He had the opportunity to talk to the oncologist and the nurses. He was the one Josh turned to with questions or concerns.

But her logical mind knew that way of thinking was petty. Sam was doing everything in his power to help Josh beat this disease. More, she feared, than Josh himself, who each day seemed less involved in his body's war.

A light knock on the hollow door echoed through her chest. "Jen?"

Andi. Lifesaver. Frustrated entrepreneur.

After several months of arm-twisting—combined with the kind of guilt trips sisters can lay on each other—Andi had agreed to come home. She'd moved in with Ida Jane in March and had immediately begun to implement her haunted bordello campaign. Unfortunately, Ida Jane had lost interest in the idea, and the two seemed to lock horns daily.

Jenny still worried about her great-aunt's health, but Ida's doctor blamed the memory slips and emotional swings on age. Jenny wasn't convinced, but she simply didn't have the energy to investigate further.

Struggling to her knees, she slowly rose and opened the door. "Sorry, I got sidetracked."

Andi, who was dressed in shorts and a tank top, shrugged. "No problem. I just wanted to tell you I'm taking Ida home. That punch went right to her head. You wouldn't believe the things I overheard her say. We really need to keep her off the booze."

"There was no alcohol in the punch."

"Really?" She looked puzzled. "I just assumed...well, I'm taking her home anyway. Sam just left, and I think Josh is ready to crash. He looked good today, though."

True. Josh had been his laughing, charming self, but Jenny knew he'd pay for the effort with a long, restless night of pain.

Andi seemed to understand. Her smile was tinged with sadness as she glanced at the gifts. "Nice haul. Do you need any help?"

Jenny shook her head. ''It can wait until tomorrow.''

''First day of vacation. Maybe you can find some time to work on your book, huh?''

Jenny looked at her easel and frowned. She finally had her wish—a summer off. But how could she paint the carefree, whimsical illustrations of a children's book, when terrifying questions assaulted her—questions like ''How am I going to live without Josh?''

Two and a half months later

''JOSH, SNAP OUT OF IT,'' Sam barked.

He hated using that tone on his brother. Lately, though, it was the only thing that penetrated the foggy blur of morphine-induced haze. Josh's eyes opened. Glazed with pain and painkillers, the blue eyes that usually danced with humor were dull and out of focus.

Sam put his face two inches from his brother's. ''Josh, concentrate. Your wife is on the phone. Do you hear me, Josh? Jenny wants to tell you about the birth.''

The babies. Andi had already given Sam the news. A boy and a girl. But he wasn't about to deprive Jenny of the right to share the news with her husband, even if there was only a slim chance that he'd understand what she said. In the past three days, even Sam had lost contact with Josh, who was slowly distancing himself from his body in preparation for death.

At least that was the hogwash the hospice nurses tried to sell. All Sam knew for sure was he was losing the baby brother he'd practically raised on his own, and Sam wanted to throttle someone—preferably the person in charge of fate. Never had he felt this helpless. Well…once, when he was nineteen.

A voice came on the line. ''Josh? Can you hear me?''

Sam recognized his sister-in-law's tear-ravaged voice. He held the phone to Josh's ear. Being careful not to disturb the tubes leading from Josh's body to the bags dangling from the portable hospital bed's metal sides, Sam rested his elbows on the railing and looked beyond the bed to the scene outside the picture window. The view wasn't as spectacular as what you'd get at the Rocking M, but this little house on one of Gold Creek's quiet side streets is where his brother had wanted to be.

"Promise me you'll let me die at home, Sam," Josh had asked shortly after they learned that the months of chemotherapy had been unable to stop the disease. "No more hospitals. I'm done with doctors."

While Sam hadn't been ready to concede defeat at the time—after all, Josh had beaten this enemy before—he'd agreed to honor Josh's request. "This is the place I've been the happiest. Other than the ranch, this was my first true home. I don't want to die in a hospital, Sam. You have to promise me."

Sam had given his word, but at the same time had extracted a promise from his brother that Josh would continue to fight the cancer with all his strength and will. "Miracles happen if you want them badly enough. You're going to beat this thing, Josh. You have to."

But none of the alternative treatments had contained a cure. Sam had even flown to Mexico to check out a facility that claimed to have a seventy percent cure rate. But Josh had deteriorated dramatically by the time Sam returned and had been too weak to travel.

Jenny spoke loudly, and Sam tried not to listen to what might well be the young couple's last exchange, but her words were unmistakable, as was her furor.

"You *cannot* die, dammit. Do you hear me, Joshua

Peter O'Neal? Not today. Not on the day your babies were born.''

Josh's eyes widened a tiny bit, and Sam's heart contracted. She was getting through in a way he hadn't been able to. Silently, he urged his brother to speak, to answer this woman who'd just spent twelve hours in labor, refusing drugs so she'd be alert enough to call her husband.

''I mean it, Josh,'' she said, her tone stern. Sam knew *he'd* pay attention if Jenny talked to him that way.

Josh's mouth opened slightly but no words came out.

Jenny let out a low cry of frustration. ''Oh, honey, I know you're trying, but you have to try harder. You have to hold on. For the babies' sakes.''

Josh's eyes closed.

Sam jostled his brother's bone-thin shoulder. ''Josh, stay with us, buddy. Hang in there.''

Apparently hearing Sam's low murmur of encouragement, Jenny made a high keening sound. ''No, Josh, no. You can't die. I don't care if the twins are Sam's biologically—you're their dad. Your name is on that birth certificate, and you can't die on the day they were born. Believe me, that's something a child never gets over. I won't let you do that to them.''

Josh's eyes opened again. For an instant, the briefest of seconds, his gaze met Sam's. Against all reason, Sam knew his brother would hold on.

He took back the phone. ''Come as soon as you can, Jen. He's hanging in. For you. And the babies.''

He hung up the receiver then reached out and took his brother's hand. Tears clouded his vision. He hadn't let himself cry. Not once in the past five months had Sam allowed himself to feel the loss that was coming.

He was losing the best thing in his life. His brother. The boy who had—in a way—saved Sam's life.

At twelve, Sam had been floundering. He'd just lost the only stepfather who ever meant a thing to him, and his mother was pregnant. "Never mind who the father is," she'd told him. "He's made it clear he won't be in the picture."

Sam wasn't surprised. Men passed through Diane O'Neal's fingers faster than money.

His mother had been hired as a makeup artist at Paramount a few months earlier. Sam was street smart; he knew about adult liaisons and the sexual dynamics involved in the entertainment industry. Rumor had it Josh's father was a popular television actor who wasn't divorced from his older, very rich wife.

Diane lost her job because the "star" didn't want a public relations risk, but miraculously came into some money. "An inheritance," she called it. She bought a small, cozy house in Culver City. After Josh was born, she went to work for a travel agency, and Sam became a makeshift daddy. Fortunately, the facility for troubled kids where he went to school offered enough flexibility for him to manage.

When Diane married Frank, the owner of the travel agency—and a man Sam detested—Sam left home. He dropped out of school to become a stunt double. The following spring, he got a break and landed a speaking role in a movie.

Eight months after that, everything went to hell. He lost his job, his bride, his unborn child and his dream of being a movie star. Worse than all of that was his mother's betrayal. Dangerously angry, Sam followed a friend's advice and joined the rodeo circuit. His career as a cowboy lasted until his mother tracked him down.

She'd divorced Frank and needed help taking care of Josh. Sam went home.

He stayed with Diane and Josh on and off throughout Josh's childhood, moving out whenever he couldn't get along with the current man in his mother's life.

It was never difficult to be with Josh—a child as cute and loving as a puppy. Josh was Sam's touchstone. The only time Sam didn't feel alone was when he was caring for Josh.

Walking to the kitchen for a glass of water, Sam looked around the living room. Josh had spent much of the past few months on the couch, until the night he'd fallen and been unable to get up. Jenny had called Sam in a panic. Sam had rushed into town—he made the half-hour trip in fifteen minutes—desperately afraid that Josh would be gone before he reached him.

Together, Sam and Jenny decided it was time to contact Hospice, the health-care professionals dedicated to helping terminally ill patients die with dignity. A hospital bed was set up in the living room to make it easier for the visiting nurses to tend to Josh's bathing, bedsores and bodily needs.

Soon after that, Sam moved his camper into town and parked it in his sister-in-law's driveway. "I need to be here," he'd explained to Jenny. "Josh needs me, and I think you could use a hand, too. You've been doing a great job, but it's going to get rough. I know. I went through this with Clancy."

Clancy Royson was the only one of Diane's husbands Sam had ever called Dad. A grizzly bear of a man, Clancy had given Sam the guidance and love he'd needed. Sam had been at his side when Clancy died of lung cancer. After his death, Sam's mother had sold Clancy's beautiful Pasadena ranch, and the proceeds were put in a trust for Sam until he turned twenty-five. Sam had used the money to buy the Rocking M, and not a day went by that Sam didn't wish Clancy were alive to see it.

Jenny hadn't put up a fuss about the travel trailer. Exhausted from worry and her pregnancy, she barely seemed to notice him. Since the St. Patrick's Day party in mid-March, Sam had watched his sister-in-law put every spare bit of energy into saving her husband. Fortunately, Andi and Ida Jane were nearby to help, and the women of the Gold Creek Garden Club stocked the kitchen with casseroles and baked goods. Even Gloria Hughes at the *Ledger* had written a tribute to Josh, suggesting the creation of a Josh O'Neal scholarship fund.

Josh made a soft groaning sound, and Sam checked his watch. He'd administered a shot of morphine just an hour and a half earlier. Hurrying to his brother's side, Sam took Josh's hand and squeezed it gently. ‘‘Hang tight, kiddo, Jenny's coming. I'll give you another shot after she gets here, but you don't want to be sleeping when she comes, right?''

Josh's eyelids fluttered and his lips moved but no sound came from his throat. Using a special sponge, Sam swabbed Josh's dry lips and tongue with water. Sam's chest felt tight and his hand shook. ‘‘Hang on, Josh. You can do it. You're Josh the Magnificent. Remember?''

Sam pictured his brother shortly after Diane divorced husband number four—a real loser who'd taken his frustrations out on Josh. Josh had been in his daredevil phase and he'd rigged up a body kite that he hoped would allow him to fly. Although he'd planned to test it on a bluff by the ocean, he'd opted for a practice flight from the top of the garage.

The words Josh the Magnificent were scrawled in blue

Magic Marker across the wings. Josh had suffered a broken arm in the fall, but his spirit had remained undaunted.

The sound of a car pulled Sam back to the present. He recognized the headlights. "Your wife's here, Josh. Jenny's here."

JOSH WAS GONE. That's the word they used. Not "dead." *Gone.* "When did he *slip away?*" one of the nurses had asked upon arriving at the door, minutes after Josh had taken his final, tortured breath.

Jenny had almost yelled at the woman, "He didn't *slip away.* He left. Josh left me."

But she didn't say anything. As the first light of dawn changed to pinkish-gold, she sat beside the cold stiff body of the man she loved more than life and blocked out everything, even the panic roiling beneath her skin.

"Sam, would you take Jenny outside? The nurses need a little space to finish up." Andi talked past Jenny as though she were mentally challenged.

Perhaps she was. Perhaps her brain had stopped functioning the minute Josh had stopped breathing.

"Jenny," Sam said softly. He put his hands on her shoulders and guided her to her feet. "Let go."

He broke the lock she had on Josh's hand—his oddly artificial-looking hand that felt too heavy, too cold to be real. Maybe they were right. Maybe he had slipped away when she wasn't looking, but when was that? She hadn't closed her eyes all night, even though she was so tired she felt as though she could sleep for a week.

"Would you like to lie down?" Sam asked, steering her toward the hallway. Toward her bedroom. The room she'd shared with Josh.

"No," she cried, turning so suddenly Sam's hands fell

from her arms. She rushed past him, not able to look at the scene by the window. At the hospital bed where two nurses were unplugging things that had been plugged into Josh's body.

She hurried through the kitchen and stumbled out the rear door, almost slipping on the dew-slick steps. She ran to the middle of the yard and bent over, trying to force air into her lungs when the pain made it almost impossible to breathe.

Her emotions were too jumbled to know what to do—scream, cry, rant and rave, shake her fist at a God who would rob her of the best part of herself? She squeezed her eyes shut tight to keep her tears locked inside. To cry would be to admit it was over. And it couldn't be over. Josh couldn't leave her. He wouldn't.

"Can I do anything to help?"

She recognized Sam's voice. "What can anybody do?" she said, her words passing through clenched teeth. "It's over. Everything good is gone. Just like that."

Sam didn't try to contradict her. Maybe he agreed with her. He simply stood beside her, waiting and saying nothing.

She looked back at the house. The sun had barely cleared the treetops. A beautiful summer morning. Josh had died at six twenty-two. He'd given her the time she'd begged for last night, but not the time he'd promised when he married her.

"We'll grow old together and die within a month of each other," he'd predicted. "You first, of course. And I'll be right behind you because I know your ghost would haunt me if I hung around here without you."

Anger bubbled up in her throat. "I'm never going to forgive him for this. Never."

Sam moved to a spot across from her, his bare toes

almost touching hers. Jenny straightened; her entire body ached from sitting in one position for too long. Her gaze met Sam's. His forehead was lined with deep grooves. The white around his hazel eyes was noticeably bloodshot. *When's the last time he slept?*

"Jenny," he said, his tone humming with feeling, "I know you're hurting. You have every right, but we have to be clear about something."

A lump formed in her throat. She pressed her hand to the saggy flesh at her middle—flesh that just hours earlier had been stretched to the breaking point to house the two children within her womb. Her babies…Sam's babies.

"I loved my brother more than anything in the world," Sam said, his voice raw with emotion. "I'd have traded places with him in a heartbeat if I could have met the devil to make the deal."

Jenny believed him too, so great was the suffering in his eyes.

"The Hospice people laid out all that stuff about the steps of grief, and I know that anger is part of the process, but don't take your suffering out on Josh. He suffered enough at the end. His pain—" Sam's voice cracked. He looked down, as if ashamed to let her see his weakness.

Somehow, without seeming to move, she was swallowed up by his arms. His low, rasping cry opened a floodgate of tears—tears that broke through her anger, her fear, to the grief below. They held each other like strangers who'd survived some mind-numbing catastrophe.

A single thought penetrated Jenny's fog of pain and grief. She recalled something Josh had told her right after his cancer had been confirmed. She hadn't been pay-ing too much attention because she'd known without a doubt Josh would be okay.

"I'll beat this, Jen, I always do, but if anything happens to me, at least you'll have Sam. He's always adored you and he'll never let anything bad happen to you and the babies."

Was that what Josh had said? She strained to remember. Or had he said *his* babies?

CHAPTER THREE

SAM SLOUCHED BACK on the couch and kicked his feet onto the now-empty coffee table. Someone had cleared it of the nursing clutter—the pink plastic spit bowl, the stack of towels, the box of tiny glass vials of morphine and the syringe that had pushed the stuff directly into the "butterfly," as the nurses called the portal on Josh's belly.

Gone, too, were the packages of swabs, the bottle of alcohol and the baby monitor device, which had allowed Sam to hear Josh from the travel trailer. The bed was still in front of the window but it had been stripped. Someone from the rental place would be by tomorrow to pick it up. Just as someone from the mortuary had been by this afternoon to pick up Josh's body.

Sam glanced at his watch. Had it only been sixteen hours since Josh stopped breathing?

Ridiculous details had filled the void he'd left behind. Questions to answer. Plans to finalize. Friends and family members to call. Thankfully, Ida Jane and Andi had taken charge of those tasks.

To Sam's surprise, Jenny hadn't fallen apart. Maybe she couldn't believe it was finally over. Josh had labored so hard all night to breathe, but he'd made it past the deadline she'd given him. "You can't die on the day your babies were born," she'd screamed on the phone, and somehow Josh had found the strength to comply with her request. Each breath had been such a struggle that from midnight on, Sam had started telling Josh it was okay to let go.

"You've done all you can, buddy. This one got the best of you, but you gave it a good fight," Sam had whispered. "Let go, Josh. Go find your peace."

At some point—Sam didn't know when—Jenny had added her consent. "I love you more than life, Josh O'Neal, but your body just can't fight this anymore. Take my love with you, sweetheart. It'll help you find your way to heaven."

Tears had streaked her face, but she'd remained strong right up to the end. Sam's respect for his sister-in-law had increased a hundredfold. She'd come from an entire night in labor and delivery directly to a deathwatch.

Sam leaned forward and looked down the hallway at the closed door of the master bedroom. Andi and Kristin had finally managed to get Jenny to bed after they returned from a quick trip to the hospital where she'd nursed the babies. The twins were strong and healthy, but they would have to stay in the hospital until they reached five pounds.

That was just as well, Sam thought. The next few days were going to be hell for everyone. A funeral was no way to welcome home two new babies.

Rocking back, he picked up the remote control and turned on the television set. He pushed the play button on the VCR, then quickly lowered the volume.

The scene on the screen was the white-white background of a hospital delivery room. The camera moved in the jerky rhythm of someone walking. The lens panned down, and Jenny's face came into focus.

"So tell us, Jenny Perfect, when was it you decided

this wasn't a mutant watermelon-seed debacle after all?'' Andi's voice asked.

Intently focused on blowing out a long breath of air, Jenny growled something indistinguishable and turned her chin toward the wall. The camera lifted, zooming in on Kristin, who stood beside the gurney. Her serious expression looked uncompromising and protective.

''Sam's right about filming this. It's what Josh would have done if he were here, but if you get in Jenny's face with any sort of nonsense, I'll boot your ass right out of the delivery room.''

''You and how many nurses?'' Andi returned.

''Girls,'' Jenny groaned. ''This is a happy time, remember?'' The last came out as a hiss, as if she was expelling pure pain. Sam's gut clenched.

The pandemonium that followed was somehow brilliantly orchestrated—nature blending with modern medicine in a way that left Sam gape-mouthed in awe. Jenny was the star of the show, focused and intent, concentrating on each breath. He saw her forehead tense and her jaw stiffen with each command to push.

For someone who'd helped deliver hundreds of calves and foals, Sam could honestly say he'd never seen a more magical birth. When a shout of glee went up as Lara slipped into the doctor's hands, Jenny leaned back for three short breaths then lifted her head and said, ''Don't forget. There's another one in there.''

Sam sat forward, his fingers linked. He brought his knuckles to his lips. Andi had told him Tucker's birth was the more difficult of the two. ''Jenny was tired from the first. It was like finishing a marathon then being told you had to run another ten miles,'' she'd said on the phone.

His gaze followed the camera, which panned back and

forth between Jenny and the baby, who was being attended by two nurses in masks. Lara Suzanne and Tucker William. Jenny and Josh had decided on the names after a sonogram revealed the sex of the twins.

Very red and most unhappy, Lara kicked her skinny legs like a bug on its back. The chatter in the room seemed elated and full of hope.

Sam couldn't help but marvel at that since he knew everyone involved had to have been aware of what was happening back here. Two lives entered the world as another prepared to leave it.

The camera returned to Jenny, who was obviously exhausted. She seemed to be breathing almost as hard as Josh had at the end. But she somehow remained upbeat, even joking with Andi about running out of tape if the second delivery took too long.

Sam was so completely engrossed in the drama before him he didn't sense another presence until a movement in the doorway caught his eye. Jenny. Like a little boy caught watching a dirty movie, he fumbled for the remote and hit the pause button.

''No. Leave it on,'' she said, walking toward him. ''I'd forgotten she'd filmed it.''

She was wearing a shapeless, faded pink robe that Josh had given her one Christmas. Sam knew that because she'd made a point of reminding Josh of its origins right before his downward spiral. ''I was looking for something sexy and you bought me this grandma robe,'' she'd complained, her voice thick with love and humor.

''Warm,'' Josh had whispered. Speech seemed to drain his energy. ''Pra…''

''Practical,'' Sam had supplied, immediately wishing he'd kept his mouth shut. When Jenny had looked his way, Sam had gathered up an armload of bedding and headed for the laundry room to give the couple some privacy.

Jenny moved stiffly and sat down gingerly. The robe gaped, exposing a nightshirt of fine white muslin with a lace insert that buttoned to the waist. Feminine, pretty—a gift from Ida's friends. Part of the bonanza she'd acquired at a recent baby shower—her only afternoon away from her husband's side until she'd gone into labor.

Sam fluffed up an olive-green couch pillow and put it behind her back. "Did you sleep?" he asked, noting something different in her smell. *Green apples?* Then he remembered the basket of toiletries and candles Beulah Jensen and her daughter had delivered that afternoon.

Aromatherapy, he'd thought with despair. Like anything's going to help.

But to Sam's surprise, the displaced reminder of spring eased his tension. He took a deep breath. Josh had loved spring.

"Kris gave me a pill," she said. "Something herbal. She said it wouldn't interfere with my nursing. She seems to know a lot about babies. I guess from living with our cousin, Moira, when she was pregnant."

"Whatever works. You're going to need your strength to get through the next few days."

She didn't acknowledge his words. Sam could have kicked himself. *Who am I to lecture her on strength? I've never seen this kind of courage in my life.*

"Is this the second one?" she asked, her tone the most expressionless he'd ever heard.

He nodded. "Andi told me it was more difficult."

One corner of her mouth twitched. "You could say that. Tucker was sideways. The doctor wanted to do an emergency C-section, but—'' She waved to the television. ''Turn it on. You'll see.''

Sam watched, both mesmerized and appalled. Kristin took her place at Jenny's side and intently massaged her sister's still-rounded stomach. Jenny's face contorted in pain as waves of contractions passed over her, but the doctor, who was working with his hand inside her kept telling her to pant. Finally, after what seemed like hours—but in truth was only ten minutes—she was given the command to push. Tucker put in an appearance just five hard pushes later. He immediately urinated all over the doctor.

Jenny snickered softly. ''His father's son, right from the start.''

The innocent words fell between them like a live snake.

Sam jumped to his feet and walked to the VCR and hit rewind. If Josh were alive, there'd be no question of the twins' parentage. But Josh wasn't here. The twins no longer had a father. Or did they?

''What's going to happen, Sam?'' Jenny asked softly.

Squatting on his haunches, he faced her. ''There's going to be a funeral, Jen. Saturday morning in the park—outdoors, just the way Josh wanted it. Let's concentrate on one thing at a time—just like you did when you were in that delivery room.''

She closed her eyes. ''I wanted it to be a joyous moment. Josh would have had balloons or kazoos or something crazy up his sleeve. I couldn't do that, but I could make the experience positive. Happy. Did you feel that? When you were watching it?''

The earnest tone in her question touched him. ''Absolutely. I don't know how you managed to laugh through some of that, but you did. And your sisters were great.''

She nodded. ''I know. You were great, too.''

''Me? I wasn't there.''

She swallowed. ''You were where I needed you to be. You kept Josh focused. I know you did. You probably gave him a play-by-play as if you were watching. Right?''

Sam turned slightly to remove the tape. He spotted a pen on the coffee table and used it to print Tucker and Lara's Birth and the date on the label. ''I blathered on.'' He gave a dry chuckle. ''It probably sounded more like a mare giving birth, but I don't know how much he heard.'' He added softly, ''The drugs really kicked in at the end.''

''Thank God,'' she whispered.

Sam silently seconded that. Josh had been in excruciating pain for the past week. The doctor said the tumor had wrapped itself around his spinal column; every nerve ending was probably on fire.

''What else has to be done before the funeral?'' she asked. ''I haven't been much help today.''

Sam rose and walked the short distance to the kitchen to make her some tea. He put the kettle on to boil. Ida Jane had left a box of tea bags for lactating mothers. He took a bottle of beer from the refrigerator and twisted off the cap. After a long guzzle, he sighed.

''I've taken care of most of the arrangements,'' he said, knowing she could hear him. For some reason, he didn't want to face her. They'd shared an intimacy—the death of a loved one—and Sam was feeling strangely vulnerable.

''Tell me,'' she said.

"Just a second," he said, stalling. He took another pull on the beer.

When the teapot whistled, he poured the water into a cup and added a tea bag and a dollop of honey then carried it to her. "The wake is Friday at the Slowpoke Saloon. My foreman, Hank Willits, is handling it. Lars is coming down from the mine to help.

"The funeral will be in the park Saturday morning at ten. Ida Jane has asked her minister to say a few words, and Donnie will read the stuff Josh wrote out."

In early May—a time when the results of Josh's chemo and radiation still looked promising, Josh had checked out a bunch of books from the library dealing with the rituals of death. Although neither Sam nor Jenny had wanted to talk about it—the idea smacked of giving up the fight—Josh had composed a list of things he wanted at his funeral.

"I want it festive, Sam," he'd said one day on the trip to the treatment center. "No black armbands or dirges. This is a part of life whether we like it or not."

Jenny held the mug between her hands and blew on the steam. "What did you decide about the doves?" she asked.

Sam couldn't help but smile. Both he and Jenny had argued about the impracticality of releasing doves in the Merced River canyon where Josh had requested his ashes be strewn.

"I'm working on that." He started to sit down but walked to the hall table and picked up a sheaf of papers, instead.

Sam was still embarrassed about the scene he'd caused that morning. He'd ranted like a madman when the poor undertaker told him it might take a week to get Josh's ashes back. "A week?" he'd shouted. "Are you telling me we have to go through this a second time? That my poor grieving sister-in-law is going to have to do this after her two little babies come home from the hospital?''

In the end, the man had agreed to rush delivery. But Sam felt like a jerk.

''I filled out most of the info on the obituary, but I'd like you to look it over if you're up to it.''

She took a sip of tea. ''Tomorrow?''

''Whenever.'' He dropped the papers back in place then walked to the door and looked out the narrow side window. Dusk had fallen and long shadows filled the yard.

''You're not leaving, are you?'' she asked suddenly. ''I mean, you probably want to get back to the ranch. To your life. To—''

Sam pivoted. He was barefoot, and his heel made a squeaking sound on the parquet flooring. The muscles in his lower back felt as if he'd just ridden cross-country on a mule. He set his beer bottle on the counter and walked to the couch. Instead of sitting beside her, he chose the coffee table in front of her.

''Jenny, I promised Josh I'd be here for you, and I meant it. I won't leave until you kick me out. Understood?''

She kept her gaze on the liquid in her cup. For all her strength, she seemed very fragile at the moment. Vulnerable. Helping females in need was Josh's forte, not Sam's. Josh was the sensitive one, the proverbial shoulder-to-cry-on. Sam never knew what to do. Touching her shoulder seemed wrong. Holding her hand wouldn't work when she was using both hands to hold her cup.

He reached for the phone. ''Andi told me to call if you need her tonight. I overheard her tell Ida Jane that a number of ladies had volunteered to stay with you once the babies come home from the hospital—like they did with Ida Jane after you and your sisters were born. Should I call her?''

Jenny shook her head. ''No. I'm too tired to talk to anybody, but I would like to thank Kristin. Is she here?''

Sam took that as a hint and stood. ''Sorry. She already left, but she said she'd be back in time to help with the funeral.''

Jenny took another sip then said, ''Poor Kris. Gold Creek is the last place she wants to be, but I couldn't have made it through that delivery without her. She has a healing touch. Too bad I can't talk her into moving home.''

''What's keeping her away?''

Jenny shrugged. ''Bad memories. Disappointments. I don't know exactly. I get the impression something is holding her in Oregon—a guy, probably.''

Sam liked Kris, but her living arrangements weren't his problem. He had enough problems of his own—like what to do with his mother when she finally showed up.

''Tomorrow morning, I have to run out to the ranch to take care of a little business, but I'll be back by noon,'' he told Jenny. ''Maybe Andi could drive you to the hospital to feed the babies.''

''Have you seen them yet?'' she asked.

Sam felt his cheeks color. He couldn't explain the crazy emotions that had hit him the instant he'd set eyes on the two tiny bundles in the covered isolettes. He'd been forced to duck into the men's room to give himself time to recover.

''Yup, I sure did,'' he said, his tone sounding artificially chipper. ''I ran over while you were sleeping. They're beautiful, Jenny. Absolutely perfect.''

She looked past him. Sam knew she was seeing the hospital bed, not the view beyond. ''The whole time I was giving birth, I kept thinking that this is what life is all about,'' she said, her voice barely louder than the tick of the mantel clock. ''Birth and death.

''Yes, it seems more dramatic when the two happen right on top of each other, but reality doesn't use a calendar. No matter our personal drama, life goes on.''

She lifted her chin, her eyes not really seeing him, as if she was talking more to herself. ''When we stopped at the store, I saw a flyer about the music festival in Strawberry. We went every year. Josh loved bluegrass. And all the people.'' She sighed. ''It's this weekend, Sam. Labor Day weekend. Don't you feel like you've been living in a vacuum?''

Sam knew exactly what she meant. When he'd called the Rocking M to discuss the wake, Hank mentioned they'd lost two calves to a mountain lion the night before. Normally, a loss of that nature would have disturbed Sam, who took his role as caretaker of his animals very seriously, but Sam had merely grunted, ''You'll have to handle it,'' and hung up. He didn't have it in him to care.

The Rocking M was his life, his escape from the unreality of Hollywood and all the bad memories it held. The only thing he'd brought with him from L.A. was Josh—a rebellious teenager with long hair and plenty of attitude.

The ranch and Josh were the two positives in Sam's life. Now he was down to one.

''Everyone says we need time. That eventually things will get back to normal,'' he said, parroting words he'd heard repeated all day.

''I seriously doubt that,'' Jenny said, her tone bleak.

"You're forgetting one thing. Two, actually. Tucker and Lara."

Sam swallowed. He wasn't a coward, but he knew he wasn't up to talking about that subject tonight.

"Can we hold off on that awhile, Jen? We just have to trust each other to do the right thing."

"Do you have any idea what that is?"

He sat back and stretched the aching muscles in his shoulders and back. "Nope. But we'll figure it out." He rose and put out his hand to help her stand. "You should get back to bed. It's still early but I plan to take the phone off the hook and crash."

She stood a moment then crossed her arms. "I wonder if my milk is coming in. Maybe I should try pumping my breasts. Do you know where Andi put that box of nursing pads?"

Sam didn't have a clue, but he jogged to the bathroom, ostensibly to look around. Mostly, he needed to get away. For some reason, such frank talk struck Sam as too intimate for what they were to each other. Brother-in-law. Sister-in-law. *Parents.*

"I found them, Sam," she called out.

Sam looked at his reflection in the mirror. He might be a father, but he wasn't a husband. Jenny's husband was dead, and nobody was ever going to take Josh's place—not in her heart, anyway.

MOST OF THE MOURNERS began to disappear within minutes after the close of the service, Jenny noted with relief. She didn't blame them—the heat in the river canyon was hellish.

She felt a little light-headed and giddy, but she wasn't sure that could be blamed on the heat. More than likely it was her mind coming to grips with the surreal nature of watching her husband's ashes drift in the air.

As an old friend from high school played taps on the trumpet, Jenny—with Sam at her side—had stood at the midway point of the Briceburg Bridge and somehow managed to empty the polished metal box of its gray ash. For the space of a heartbeat the ash had floated—a visible reminder of all that would never be—then melted into the water and disappeared.

Despite the glare of the sun, Jenny continued to stare at the river from her vantage point near the edge of the parking lot. At Sam's gentle prodding, she'd handed him the empty box before returning to the gathering place for handshakes and hugs that she was too numb to feel.

Why the river, Josh? she longed to ask. *Why couldn't you at least have left me a burial plot that I could visit with the children on your birthday or holidays?*

But there was no answer. Only Josh's four-page script. A final itinerary that had included a memorial service in Gold Creek's park then a motorcade following Donnie Grimaldo's patrol car to the Bureau of Land Management recreation area on the Merced River.

Behind her, Jenny sensed the exodus of cars. People were heading back to Ida Jane's for food and refreshments. *Maybe no one will notice if I don't show up.*

Fat chance, she heard a voice in her head answer. Josh's voice—Josh, who would have loved this send-off. Hundreds of friends, business associates and townspeople had put their Labor Day plans on hold to say goodbye.

She recalled their argument over the band. ''People love music,'' Josh had insisted. ''If you put up a tent in the parking lot, you could get the Lone Strangers to play,'' he'd suggested, naming a popular local band.

When Jenny had protested that the idea was "too upbeat," Josh had appealed to Sam. And so far, Sam had carried out Josh's wishes to the letter, even managing to find twenty-seven white doves to be released as Jenny started sprinkling the ashes.

"Jen?"

Jenny heard her sister but didn't answer. She had a feeling if she opened her mouth a terrible cry would spew out. As long as she nodded and smiled, like one of those toy dogs in the back window of a car, she'd be fine.

"I've got to get Ida Jane out of this heat, sis," Kristin said. "Andi went back with the Garden Club ladies to set out the food. You'll come with Sam, okay?"

Jenny nodded. *Maybe.*

She glanced over her shoulder to watch her sister walk away. Jenny would have been lost without her sisters, Ida Jane and the citizens of Gold Creek, but that didn't keep her from wishing they'd all just disappear.

"Jenny," a low voice said beside her, "you need to get out of the sun before you melt."

Sam.

He gently took her elbow and started leading her toward his pickup truck. In his other hand, he carried the empty mortuary box.

"No," she said, yanking free. "Just…no."

The word came out like the long, eerie screech of an owl hunting in the night. He stepped back, dropping the box in surprise.

"Okay," he said levelly. "I'll wait for you in the truck. Come whenever you're ready."

"Ready?" she cried, tearing off the woven straw hat Kristin had insisted she wear. A gust of hot dry wind snatched it from her numb fingers and sent it end-over-brim into the prickly branches of a nearby buckbrush. The same breeze pressed the gauzy material of her pale yellow sundress against her sweaty body. Instead of offering any kind of relief, the blast felt like the breath of a dragon trying to sear her skin.

"Ready for what?" she repeated hoarsely. "What's the plan, Sam? Did Josh mention what I'm supposed to do? Say, for the next twenty years or so? He didn't dictate that to you, did he?"

Sam ducked his head as if wounded by her anger.

"This isn't the way we had it planned, Sam," she said, her voice squeaky from the tightness of unshed tears. "We were going to die in our eighties, with our children and grandchildren nearby. We wanted to be buried side by side in the old cemetery, near the war veterans." She hauled in a ragged breath of scorching air. "Why'd he change the plan, Sam? Why?"

Despite the kilnlike temperature, Sam wore black. Black jeans, black boots, black shirt. And a green cowboy hat—Josh's hat.

See me sweet hat, Jenny luv? Josh had teased in his deplorable Irish brogue last St. Patrick's Day. *'Tis the luck of the Irish that belongs to the man wearin' this hat.* That had been in March—right before all hell had broken loose.

"The only plan I care about at the moment is getting you out of the sun and back to Ida's. Your family's there. Your friends. By the looks of all the food I spotted before we left, the whole town's there for you."

The town. Her town. Josh's adopted hometown. *Leave Gold Creek, Jenny? Are you crazy?* he'd once admonished her when she suggested moving. *This is a dream come true. The place where everybody knows your name. I finally feel at peace here. Why would I want to leave?*

For *me?* she'd been tempted to cry, but, of course, she hadn't. While no one would have believed it of affable, easygoing Josh, the fact was, he turned pure mule once his mind was made up.

"Can we go now?" Sam asked.

She looked down. Her feet and ankles were swollen—probably a by-product of labor. Her breasts were three times their normal size, her stomach flabby and the incision the doctor had made to keep her from tearing itched.

And she was burning up. The sun was melting her hair into her scalp. If she could just cool off, even for a minute, maybe she'd be able to think straight.

She spun on one heel and took off. Zingers of pain shot up her legs as she scrabbled clumsily across the stony embankment to the water's edge.

The Merced's high-water days of spring and summer were long gone, leaving behind a wide ledge of polished gravel and throw-pillow-size boulders, but the river's main channel still churned with the last remnants of melted snow from the Sierras.

Jenny's slick-bottomed sandals made the trek treacherous, and she was forced to keep her gaze on her feet instead of picking out a safe wading spot. Even this time of year, the river held danger—less of drowning than of being pummeled against exposed rocks.

She had her left foot in the water, sandal and all, when a firm hand grabbed her shoulder. "No," Sam growled. "No. I won't let you go, dammit."

The anguish in her brother-in-law's voice pierced Jenny's red haze. She understood instantly what he thought she'd intended to do, but before she could explain otherwise, her foot slipped on a moss-covered rock and she fell to one knee. Her ankle twisted awkwardly, and she lurched forward, scraping her palms on the abrasive rocks. Frigid water soaked the hem of her dress.

"Jenny," Sam cried.

One minute she was on her knees in the river, the next she wasn't. Jenny had never known the sensation of being lifted off her feet. Her vision swam, and she thought she might pass out, whether from the heat, the pain in her extremities or Sam's death grip, she wasn't sure.

"Sam, I didn't...I'm not...put me down."

He ignored her. Or maybe he couldn't hear her, since her voice seemed to come from the end of a long, hollow tube. Jenny closed her eyes and took a deep breath. Perspiration and fabric softener filled her senses. Not my brand of fabric softener, she thought for no reason at all. Where has he been doing his laundry?

Sam's broad chest was heaving from exertion by the time they reached the sparse shade of the dusty oak trees that ringed the parking lot. He set her down on a large boulder. Her soggy sandals made a squishing sound when they hit the ground. She looked down, but Sam grabbed her chin and made her look at him. "What the hell are you thinking? You can't...you just couldn't. You're a mother, Jenny. Doesn't that mean anything to you?"

Although his tone was harsh, bitter even, his hazel eyes expressed pure anguish. Jenny covered her face, ignoring the grit that was still attached to her bloody palms. "I didn't mean to scare you, Sam. I wasn't jumping in. I was just so hot..." Her excuse sounded lame. Maybe it wasn't even true. Didn't a part of her wish she'd died, too?

"What's going on in your head, Jenny? This isn't like

you. Maybe you need to join that grief group Linda McCloskey mentioned. She said it had helped her.''

Am I grieving? Yes, she thought, but not for the reasons everyone thinks. Mine are selfish reasons. I'm a coward. I'm afraid to be alone. I don't know how to be a mother. I can't do this without Josh, she silently cried.

That isn't the kind of truth you confessed to a group of people—especially in a small town.

''I'm okay,'' she said, starting to scoot forward to hop off the rock. ''I'll be fine.''

Sam removed his hat and tossed it onto a nearby table. He let out a deep sigh and said, ''I suppose we might as well get this out in the open and deal with it, but first we've got to cool down.''

Jenny knew what he was going to say and she didn't want to discuss it. Not now. Not yet. Her heart started hammering the instant he grabbed her hand and pulled her to her feet.

''Come on.''

To her surprise, he led her in the opposite direction of the truck. His grip tightened as they rounded a dense cluster of scrub oaks. The water had undercut the embankment, creating a tiny cove shaded by the pines and oaks on the steep mountainside.

He let go of her hand to bend over and take off his boots. His thin white cotton socks were next, and then he rolled up his jeans. ''Coming?'' he asked before gingerly wading into the calm water.

Jenny kicked off her sandals. The pebbles in this area had been worn smooth but she moved with care, since her ankle still throbbed. The chilly water brought instant relief. Just an arm's length away from Sam, she bent over and splashed scoop after scoop of water across her face and over her neck. The chilly water dribbled down her dress's neckline, soaking into the heavy-duty nursing bra she was wearing. For a girl who almost never wore a bra, this lactating physique took some getting used to.

Josh would have loved this, she thought, glancing down at her bustline.

Sighing, she cupped some water in her hands and studied it. Sunlight made the suspended particles of grit glitter like flecks of gold.

"Are you thinking you'll see Josh there?" Sam asked.

The question unnerved her. Given their relationship, she wasn't sure she liked the idea of Sam being able to read her thoughts. "Maybe," Jenny answered.

Sam didn't say anything, which, for some reason, irked her. "What do you think happens when you die, Sam? Heaven or hell?"

He looked at her a moment, as if hearing something she hadn't intended to share. "I don't know, Jenny. But I do know Josh didn't do this on purpose."

"I didn't say he did," she said, facing him.

"No, but you're angry. I can tell. And I'm assuming you're mad at him for going off and leaving you with two babies and...me. I'm a complication that doesn't help."

His empathy unnerved her, and it suddenly struck her that she wasn't the only one Josh had deserted. Sam was here, too. In limbo. As were Lara and Tucker.

"What are we going to do, Sam?"

"Do we have to decide today? Can't we just carry on like we have been?" He looked toward the bridge. Beads of water glistened in his dark-brown hair. Jenny could see the imprint left by Josh's hat. His squint made the lines around his eyes seem more pronounced. This has aged him, she thought.

He turned and caught her staring. ''Can we at least wait until after Diane leaves?''

Jenny had received a call this morning. Diane and Gordon, Sam's mother and stepfather, had been held up by engine trouble with their RV but would arrive later today. Sam had disappeared into his trailer shortly after hearing the news, not reemerging until it was time to leave for the park.

To Jenny, Diane's visit was just one more weight pressing down on her. She'd always gotten along with her mother-in-law as long as Josh was present, but who knew what would happen without him?

''Are you going to stick around while she's here or hightail it back to the ranch?'' She hadn't meant to sound quite so much like a nagging wife.

''I'm not going anywhere.''

Despite the flat, resigned tone in his voice, Sam's answer made her feel better.

He turned and walked back to shore. He sat down on a low rock, legs sprawled, while he used his socks to dry his feet. There was something very youthful in his pose. Sam never looked like a little boy, Jenny thought. That was Josh's department. For some reason, the thought irked her. Josh was gone—it was just her and Sam, now. Parents.

A shiver passed through her. ''What are you going to tell your mother if she asks? Do you think she knew about Josh's condition?''

He looked up sharply. ''Why would she? Josh and Diane weren't that close. Besides, she's not into babies. She'll show up, cry a little then leave. That's how she operates.''

His bitterness made her shiver. It reminded her once again how different Sam was from Josh. Josh had often joked about his mother's unorthodox methods of parenting. ''Mom believed in the free-range school of child rearing,'' he'd once told a group of friends. ''If you survived childhood, you had it made.''

''You can tell your sisters and Ida Jane, if you want. They might wonder why I'm hanging around so much, but it's up to you,'' Sam said. ''Are you ready? We should be going.''

Hanging around. What exactly did that mean? she wondered. She started to ask, but stopped. Did it matter? Did anything matter?

She limped to the water's edge.

''We'll stop at the hospital,'' Sam said. ''You can get your ankle checked and feed the babies.''

''I can try,'' Jenny said, picturing the trouble she'd had that morning. ''Lara isn't taking to the breast well. I thought I was doing something wrong, but Tucker's not having any problems. He's positively voracious.''

Sam's smile was sad and slightly wistful. Before she could ask why, he broke away to fetch first his hat then hers. Finally, he stooped to pick up the metal box that had held Josh's ashes.

Neither spoke as he helped her climb into the truck. He flicked the air-conditioning to high, and Jenny sank back into the upholstery and closed her eyes, trying hard to forget about the urn lying on the bed of the truck. But the image haunted her. It was, she decided, a perfect metaphor for her life—a pretty façade but empty inside.

''SAM, RUN ALONG to the party. You're the host, after all. I'll bring Jenny after she feeds the twins.''

Like so much of what his mother had said to him over the years, Diane's words held a barely veiled put-down. *You're the host, after all.* As if he'd made some gaffe by not greeting the mourners at his brother's funeral personally.

He and Jenny had been sitting in the lobby of the hospital, waiting to see an emergency-room doctor when Diane found them. In her wake trailed Gordon, a likable fellow who'd retired from active practice last year. Gordon had examined Jenny's ankle and pronounced it, "Tweaked, not sprained."

"I'll wait," Sam said, relishing the small delight he drew from doing the exact opposite of whatever his mother wanted. He knew it was childish, but Diane had that effect on him.

Diane gave him a look he'd seen a hundred times—one of pure exasperation. "I would think this is the least you could do for your brother, since you weren't able to do anything about the cancer."

Jenny leaped to her feet—sore ankle and all. "Diane," she said sharply. "Sam did everything in his power to save Josh. We all did. If you want to blame someone for Josh's death, blame Josh. He's the one who kept insisting he had a cold or allergies or the flu. He put off going to the doctor until it was too late."

His mother's carefully made-up face crumbled and she walked away. Gordon rushed to her side, providing the necessary comfort. Jenny looked stricken.

Sam wasn't sure what exactly just happened, but he blamed his mother. "Why don't you head upstairs to the nursery?" he said to Jenny.

"I'm sorry," she whispered.

"What you said was true. Now, go. The babies need you."

Sam walked her to the elevator, then returned to where his mother was standing, repairing her makeup with the help of a small compact and a tissue. Sam didn't know if women used compacts like that any longer, but it was a sight and smell he'd forever associate with his mother.

''Diane, let's get something straight. Jenny is very fragile at the moment. I know Josh was the light in your life and you're hurting, too, but you will watch what you say around Jenny or you won't be staying.''

Diane lifted her chin regally. ''Who died and made you king?''

''Josh.''

Her bottom lip trembled. ''That's a rotten thing to say—even for you.''

''I know, but it's true. Josh didn't plan to die. The cancer had metastasized by the time we started treatment. He was battling it on too many fronts—kidney, liver, stomach, lungs. There were things he wanted to do to help prepare his family and make sure they were taken care of, but he was just too sick, too fast. He asked me to look after Jenny and the kids, and that's what I plan to do.''

''You're the executor of the will?'' Gordon asked.

Sam nodded.

''Are you the twins' godfather, too?''

Godfather?

''Jenny can decide that. I don't need a title to know where my duty lies.''

Gordon gave Sam an encouraging nod. Diane, however, looked unconvinced. ''How much help can you be when you live on the ranch and Jenny and the babies live in town? You'd be better off putting your money where your mouth is and hiring a nanny.''

''I'll hire a nanny if that's what Jenny wants. First, we have to get the twins home, then we can worry about fine-tuning.''

She made an indignant sound and stuffed her compact

into her shoulder bag. ''At least you didn't suggest taking Jenny and the babies to the ranch. You may be content to play hermit, but no woman would want that lifestyle. Obviously.''

Usually Diane's jabs bounced off Sam like hot grease on Teflon. For some reason, this one penetrated. *Jenny and the babies at the ranch?* It might be the perfect solution, if he could get her to agree.

Not for long, of course, he told himself. Just long enough to bond with his children.

''Are you coming or not?'' his mother asked contentiously. ''I want to see my grandbabies.''

Sam shook his head. Not yet. He wasn't ready for his mother to see the depth of his feelings. Or Jenny, either. He didn't want to frighten her. He would never do anything to jeopardize Jenny's bond with her children—he just wanted to be a part of it, too.

JENNY WAITED until the last of the kind souls who'd stayed to help clean up the old bordello left. She was exhausted. Numb in a way that kept tears at bay. A part of her brain knew this was unhealthy, but she had one more thing to do.

Josh had lied to her. He'd promised a life with love, children and happiness. She was done with lies.

''Sit down, you two,'' she said to her sisters. ''I need to tell you something.''

Andi and Kristin trudged toward the table. ''Can't it wait?'' Andi asked. ''I'm dead.''

A second later she realized what she'd said and bent over, groaning. ''Oh, crap, Jen, I'm sorry.''

To Jenny's surprise, Kristin walked over and gently rubbed Andi's back. ''We know what you meant.''

Jenny motioned them to join her at the table. ''I'm

going to drop in a minute. But this is important, and there won't be time in the morning before Kris leaves.''

Andi and Ida had both implored Kris to stay for the weekend, but she'd insisted she had ''commitments.'' Jenny didn't blame her; there wasn't much she could accomplish here while the twins were still in the hospital.

Andi hopped up to the counter across from them. Kristin sat opposite Jenny. ''So?''

''I do appreciate everything both of you have done. You know that, right?''

Kris pushed a covered bowl of potato chips aside to squeeze Jenny's hand. ''We know.''

Jenny tried to take a breath but her chest felt constricted. *How do I say this? How do I tell them about Sam?* ''I have something I need to tell you. It's probably going to sound like something out of daytime TV, but when we discovered that Josh couldn't...''

A deep cough made all three jump. ''Sorry,'' Sam said from the doorway of the screened porch. ''Didn't mean to startle you, but I just got back from the ranch. You weren't at your house, Jen. I was worried.''

Jenny had planned to do this alone. It seemed befitting, but now that the moment had arrived, she was profoundly glad to see Sam. She motioned him forward. ''Come in. I was just going to tell them about the babies.''

He crossed the room, stopping a few feet away. Outwardly, he displayed none of the fatigue that showed on her and her sisters' faces, but Jenny knew that was a ruse.

''Like I told you,'' he said. ''It's your call.''

Andi, who'd never been easy to live with when she was tired, said crossly, ''Tell us what?''

Jenny opened her mouth, but nothing came out.

"Josh was sterile," Sam said. "An unfortunate side effect of prepubescent testicular cancer. He asked me to donate sperm so Jenny could conceive. I did."

Kristin gasped. It took Andi a second longer to get it. "And Jenny went along with this?" she croaked.

Jenny felt her face flood with color. "Josh wanted it so badly," she said lamely.

Kris jumped to her feet. "Thank God he did. Where would we be right now without those two perfect babies to look forward to?" Tears filled her eyes. "And this way, they'll have a father, too." She surged toward Sam and gave him a hug. "Oh, Sam, you'll be a wonderful daddy."

Jenny read the bewildered look on his face. It wasn't what he was expecting.

Andi leaned back, thrusting her tanned, toned legs into the room. "That's well and good, but what about the logistics that comes with that kind of arrangement? Do you share the kids? You each take one? What?"

Sam lurched back as if struck. Jenny saw the look of horror in his eyes.

"No," they cried in unison.

"Jenny is their mother. Babies need their mother," he said, as if that was the last word on the issue. He turned and walked to the door. "I'll be at the house if you need me, Jenny. I assume you're spending the night here."

Jenny nodded; she wasn't ready to face her empty bed.

A minute later the low roar of the diesel filled the air. She wondered how she'd missed his arrival.

No one said anything. "I know this looks bad, but at the time Josh was healthy. Who knew this would happen?"

Andi made a gruff sound. ''I'm sorry, Jen. That was a stupid thing to say. I'm used to dealing with jerks who think with their dicks, pardon my French. Sam's a good man. You can trust him.''

Jenny felt a tiny glimmer of hope. Maybe there was a chance she could pull this off. ''I love you guys. Thanks.''

They started to leave the room, but Andi stopped suddenly. ''Are you going to tell Ida Jane?''

Jenny sighed. ''Not now. Maybe someday, but Josh's death has been hard on her. I don't think she can handle much more.''

Andi stepped back to squeeze Jenny's shoulder. ''I think that goes for all of us.''

CHAPTER FOUR

"DON'T USE POWDER. Powder is bad for babies' lungs."

"Oh, phooey. We always used powder on your behind. Your lungs are fine, aren't they?"

"Andrea's right, Ida. My granddaughter told me that, too. She was picky about everything—even the kind of water she mixed with little Tory's formula. Water was water in my day."

Jenny tuned out the voices coming from the nursery. Her house was small, and the busy hum of people—her sister, her aunt, Beulah Jensen and the other volunteers—added to her exhaustion. She couldn't seem to find the strength to get up and care for her month-old babies.

Tears filled her eyes; sorrow twisted in her gut like a living, breathing monster. How was she supposed to be a mother to two tiny babies when her soul had been ripped from her body—right through the hole in her heart?

She curled into a fetal position. Her breasts were swollen—primed for feeding time; her cotton nightshirt felt damp against her knees.

She continued to nurse her babies, but each feed was a struggle. Lara fought the breast as if she were suffocating every time Jenny tried to put the nipple in her mouth. Tucker, on the other hand, latched on and suckled like a vampire then cried for more. And there just wasn't any more to give, which added to Jenny's sense of failure.

Staring at the glimmer of light filtering through the cracks in the miniblinds, she tried to make her mind go blank.

The door to her room—the room she used to share with Josh—opened a sliver. "Oh good, you're awake," Ida Jane said, peeking inside. "Sam didn't want to disturb you, but Tucker just will *not* take the bottle. He wants his mama."

Jenny longed to treasure each minute with her beautiful babies, but grief was robbing her of the ability. She didn't know what she'd have done without Ida Jane, her sisters and Sam.

"Go ahead and bring him in," she said. "I'm awake."

Ida disappeared. Jenny carefully scooted backward. She plumped a pillow against the plated-brass headboard. The bed—a wedding gift from Ida—was an antique that had been in the bordello when Ida's father bought the place. It took a double mattress, small by today's standards. When Jenny once suggested trading it in for a queen-size bed, Josh had argued against the idea.

"This our marriage bed, Jen," he'd said. "I can't walk by it without picturing your hands gripping those dowels…the look of passion on your face."

At the time, his words had embarrassed her. Now she'd give anything to hear his voice.

Blinking back tears, she tenderly ran her fingers over the metal.

"He's a bit cranky," a deep whisper said.

Startled, Jenny turned toward the door. Sam walked

to her, a tiny bundle in his arms. He carried the baby as if born to the role.

"Lara's happy as a little pig with the bottle," he said. "Beulah's feeding her now, but Tucker here won't have a thing to do with it. He says it's Mommy or nothing."

Jenny moved over to make room for Sam to sit down beside her. It made the transfer of the baby easier, she'd found. Plus, she liked Sam's unflappable calm. She'd always known he was rock-solid and dependable, but she'd never seen his leadership abilities put to the test. This little exercise in small-town helpfulness would have tested the patience of a saint.

During the eleven days that the twins were in the hospital, Sam had regulated visitations and food donations, shielding Jenny from the well-meaning but at times overwhelming support she'd received from the citizens of Gold Creek. When the pediatrician finally gave them permission to bring Tucker and Lara home, Sam had politely but firmly set restrictions on the number of volunteers who could help.

Although Diane regularly hinted that Sam should move back to the ranch so she and Gordon could park their RV in his spot, Sam seemed to ignore her. Jenny was glad. She liked her mother-in-law, but the woman was almost cruel in her criticism of her son.

For the most part, Jenny tuned everything out. One small part of her felt guilty about leaving Sam alone to deal with his mother—he was grieving, too. But ultimately, she just couldn't muster the energy.

His weight made the mattress sag. "Let me get you a pillow for your arm," he said, passing Tucker to her. Wrapped in a lightweight blue cotton receiving blanket and a yellow skullcap, Tucker was all face—a red, angry face. Sam disappeared before she could tell him not to bother.

Jenny took a deep breath and looked down. "Hello, son," she said softly. Jenny was ashamed of the fact that she'd spent as little time as possible with her children since they came home from the hospital. But her friends and family—including Sam—assured her that she would be her old self after she had time to mourn.

"Time," she murmured, unbuttoning her top with her right hand. "When will I even care about time?"

She was just reaching for the flap of her nursing bra, when Sam returned.

"Oops, sorry. Here. I'll be quick." He lifted her left arm—the one cradling the baby—and slid the pillow underneath.

"Let me fill your water glass, then I'll get out of your way. Somebody's hungry."

Tucker, as if sensing that mother's milk was near, let out a series of short, sharp cries. "Hang on, Buddy, Mom's coming. Just let Uncle Sam get this for her."

He paused midstep. A ghost of a smile flickered across his lips. "You know, Josh started calling me that when you first found out you were pregnant," he mused. "But he stopped a good month before he saw the oncologist. I wonder if he knew something was wrong even then."

"He knew," Jenny said flatly. *But did he know* before *I got pregnant?* The question plagued her.

"Call me when he's done, and I'll come get him."

With that, Sam walked away.

Jenny opened her bra and helped guide her son's lips to her engorged breast. She studied the baby's smooth pink cheek in the light from the lamp beside the bed. He'd changed so much in a month. Red wrinkles were gone, replaced by full cheeks and new hair—dark brown. Lara's was reddish blond—more Sullivan than O'Neal—but everyone insisted Lara favored her father. "I think Lara has Josh's nose," someone said just yesterday.

Jenny heard that kind of thing almost daily from the concerned friends and volunteers who stopped by. Everyone was eager to point out a resemblance as if that link might keep Josh's memory alive. Unfortunately, all it did was make Jenny feel guilty. She could have handled the duplicity with aplomb if Josh were at her side. But what was she supposed to do now?

Why aren't you here, Josh?

As her milk started to flow so did her tears. Tucker hung on while her diaphragm heaved. She used the sheet to staunch the deluge.

"Jenny? Are you okay?" Sam asked from the doorway.

She let a low cry of anguish. The door flew open. "To hell with modesty," he muttered, clearing the distance in three strides. "What's wrong, Jen? What can I do?"

"Nothing. Go away," she sobbed. She didn't understand how she could have a single tear left inside her body.

"I can't do that," he said, sitting beside her. "I'll do anything you ask—except that. You need me here. The babies need me."

He ran a hand through his uncombed hair. For the umpteenth time, Jenny noticed the pallor around his lips, the deep lines bracketing his eyes.

"Please don't ask me to leave, Jen," he said finally. "If I were alone at the ranch, I'd go crazy with worry." He looked at her, and in his eyes Jenny read the same anguish she saw in the mirror every morning. "Diane spends half her time at the golf course with Gordon. Ida can't handle a set of twins by herself, even with the Garden Club ladies helping out. And thanks to that advertising campaign, Andi's swamped at the store."

Jenny knew he was right, but she wanted the world to disappear and leave her to her memories, her very private pain. Tucker's lips stopped their fishlike motion. Without thinking, she switched him to the other breast.

Looking up, she caught the expression on Sam's face—wonder and awe were the only words to describe it. Is that how Josh would have reacted? she wondered. *No, he'd have curled up beside me and tickled me until I laughed.*

She tilted her head back and closed her eyes. "When, Sam? When will it stop hurting? I can barely breathe without feeling as though someone has scooped out my insides."

He touched her knee. Even through her baggy sweatpants Jenny felt the warmth of his hand, his support. Sam was kind. He was wonderful...he just wasn't Josh.

"It wasn't supposed to be this way, Sam. I can't do this without him. It's just not fair."

"I agree," he said, surprising her. "It's not fair to any of us—Josh included. But it's not like he could help it. The cancer spread too fast."

She'd heard others say the same thing, but she didn't buy it. "I think he knew it even before we did the in vitro," she said, her bitterness obvious. "He sensed it and that's why he pushed for you to be the one. He manipulated us, Sam. And I hate him."

Sam didn't say anything for a minute. His profile could have been carved from granite, but then he blinked rapidly, as if suppressing his emotions. Suddenly, his handsome face contorted in anguish, and Jenny was filled with remorse.

"I'm sorry. I shouldn't have said that."

"You don't mean it," he said, his voice gruff.

Maybe I do, maybe I don't, but Sam isn't the person to burden with my anger.

"How are things at the ranch? Don't they need you?"

He heaved a sigh. "Does it matter? This is where I am."

She felt Tucker's lips disengage from her breast. Sitting forward, she quickly closed the gap in her gown. The baby lay on her lap, eyes closed, satiated. A smile tried to find its way to her lips.

"That should help," she said, feeling a tiny glimmer of satisfaction. She pushed back a lank lock of hair. "Would you take him for me? I need a shower."

Sam leaned forward to pick up Tucker. The movement brought him within an inch of Jenny. The intimacy of the moment struck her hard. This should have been Josh, she thought, swamped by bitterness again.

"Well, there you go, little man," Sam said, rising. He placed Tucker against his shoulder and efficiently burped him. "Good job. Just like your daddy. I used to burp him, too, you know."

Sam nestled Tucker in the crook of his arm and walked to the window. He turned the little plastic wand and sunlight flooded the room. Jenny could tell by the angle of light coming through the long silvery needles of the bull pine that it was still early.

"Diane's in the kitchen, by the way," he said flatly. "She wanted to fix us all a big breakfast to thank Ida for letting them park the travel trailer in the lot behind the bordello."

"Your mother can cook?" Jenny had been surreptitiously fastening her bra and just happened to catch Sam's smile. The oddity of the question suddenly struck her, too.

"I've never thought of Diane as the domestic type," she added. To her surprise, talking with Sam seemed to help perk her up a little. "Josh used to tell the most bizarre stories about her."

"Did he mention the time she left him in the car at the 7-Eleven because the beer-delivery guy offered to take her out to dinner?"

Jenny immediately regretted bringing up the topic. Sam's expression went sour, and he paced to the far side of the room and back. His broad shoulders seemed bunched with tension, but he continued to cradle Tucker with utmost care.

"Usually, when something like that happened, Josh would dig around for change and call me if he got scared or too bored. I used to lie awake at night worrying about what might happen if I missed his call."

"You never did, did you?"

"Not that I know of. He used to say he lived a charmed life." The irony in Sam's tone was tinged with anguish.

Again, Jenny felt guilty for dumping so much on his shoulders. She slowly rose and walked toward him.

"He lived a good life, Sam. Too damn short, but Josh packed a heck of a lot of living into his twenty-seven years."

Sam leaned one shoulder against the wall. He stared out the window, but his gaze seemed fixed on something well beyond her small backyard. "I think he knew his time was limited, Jen. I don't mean specifically last fall. I mean years ago. Josh once told me he felt as though he'd cheated death, and every minute from that point was borrowed.''

Jenny returned to the bed and sat down. She looked at her bare toes. ''Did you know he used to paint my toenails? He'd buy the wildest shades of magenta or green or lavender nail polish then make me sit still so he could apply it.''

She wiggled her toes. The nails were dull and needed clipping.

''You have nice feet,'' Sam said.

Jenny smiled, remembering the first time she and Josh met. ''You must be that Jenny Perfect girl I've been hearing about,'' he'd said, catching her outside the Frosty Freeze, where she was sweeping up cigarette butts.

''What makes you think so?'' she'd returned.

''Because you have perfect feet.''

She'd been wearing sandals because a tub of ice cream had fallen off a shelf and broken her baby toe the day before.

That was the summer Josh and Sam moved to the Rocking M. Josh had been in town registering for school.

''I've decided not to go back to work after my maternity leave is up,'' she said suddenly.

Sam pushed off from the wall and walked to her. He stood a foot away. ''Good. You have a full-time job with the twins. The school will hire you back when the kids are older,'' he said equitably.

His tone irked her. She didn't want equitable. She wanted to lash out at someone. She wanted things to be different. ''That's easy for you to say. You have an income.''

He tilted his head as if hearing something she hadn't meant to say. ''Hold on,'' he said. ''I'll be right back.''

When he was gone, Jenny walked into the adjoining bathroom. She glanced in the mirror, but quickly averted her gaze. Her hair was a rat's nest; there were bags under her eyes and her skin looked like freckled construction paper. She splashed water on her face and brushed her teeth then returned to where Sam was waiting with a tall glass of orange juice.

''Gordon says nursing mothers often forget that their body is feeding two—in your case three,'' he said.

Jenny accepted the glass and took a long drink.

''I'm worried about you, Jen. You don't eat enough.''

She shrugged. ''I'm not hungry.''

''I know, but you need to make yourself eat—or at the very least, you need someone around to nag you to eat.''

Jenny smiled then. Josh would have sat on her until she ate every bite.

''That's one of the reasons why I want you and the babies to move home with me.''

Sam's tone was so nonchalant it took Jenny a minute to comprehend the meaning of his statement. ''To the ranch?''

Sam nodded. ''Think about it. I have plenty of space plus a housekeeper who could help with the twins. If you rent this place, you'll have a steady income. And you might even find time to work on your books.''

Jenny swallowed. ''And what do you get out of this?''

When he looked at her, his eyes—for once—were surprisingly easy to read. ''I get to be a father.''

MOVE TO THE RANCH? Was he crazy?

Jenny pushed her sunglasses back up on her nose and

returned her gaze to the road. Sam had been called to an emergency at the ranch before she could ask her questions. She'd waited as long as she could for him to return. Finally, she'd loaded up the twins for a drive to the Rocking M. The babies hadn't made a peep since the car pulled out of the driveway, but it bothered her that she couldn't see them. As per the directions, their infant seats were in the back seat of her Honda Accord, facing away from her.

"They're fine," Diane said, reaching over to pat Jenny's arm.

Ida had volunteered to accompany Jenny to the ranch, but Diane wouldn't hear of it. "I'll go," she'd insisted. "It's been ages since I've been there. I wouldn't mind seeing what Sam's done with the place. I'm sure it could use a woman's touch, but what woman would be content to live in the middle of nowhere?"

Jenny could name one. She'd always loved the Rocking M. Whenever Sam was away on business, or on those rare occasions he joined a few old friends on a fishing trip, Jenny and Josh would volunteer to ranch-sit. They'd take long trail rides, relax in the Jacuzzi tub, grill thick steaks on the patio and dine under the redwood gazebo. It was an idyllic retreat they both enjoyed, but Jenny had never imagined living there. Her mind churned. *Was this a ploy to gain custody of the twins? Does he think I'm unfit to raise them alone? What if he's right?*

"I used to despair that Sam would never marry, now I'm more afraid he might," Diane said as they passed under the Rocking M arch. "I can just see some woman imagining a life of peace and quiet on a beautiful ranch then hitting the reality of being stuck in the boondocks with a man who spends every spare minute reading cattle magazines and studying the pedigrees of longhorns.''

Diane's negative attitude baffled Jenny. It always had. But Josh had been philosophical about his mother's relationship with his brother. ''Sam and Mom don't get along, Jen. It's their problem, not ours. Maybe someday they'll mend their fences, but I have a feeling I'll be long dead before it happens.''

The memory made her shiver.

Diane glanced at her. ''Are you cold? Must be from not eating. No one could be cold in this heat. How do you stand it? Maybe you should consider moving to Santa Barbara. Gordon and I could help you find a place close to us. It's so beautiful there.''

The offhand suggestion was so *Diane.* ''Mom loves to make plans. You just can't count on them,'' Josh used to say. Like the oft-promised trip to Alaska, Jenny thought. Josh's dream trip. Finally, Sam had taken Josh camping in Denali National Park and fishing in the Gulf of Alaska for Josh's twenty-fifth birthday; Jenny had stayed home to let the two brothers spend time together.

''I'm sure Santa Barbara is lovely, but I couldn't move that far away from Ida Jane,'' Jenny said. *Or Sam.* Somehow she knew Sam wouldn't like the idea of Jenny and the babies moving out of the area.

''Maybe you and your sisters should look into getting Ida situated in one of those assisted-care facilities. She isn't getting any younger,'' Diane said, her tone slightly bored. ''She's amazing for her age. But it's obvious this ordeal has taken a toll on her. And that nonsense about the ghost isn't helping, either, if you ask me.''

Jenny kept her mouth closed and tried to absorb the peaceful setting. She never made the thirty-mile drive to the ranch without being filled with a sense of wonder.

At this time of year, the hills were a burnished gold, the sprawling oak trees scattered incrementally like pieces on a chessboard. As the road climbed, she began to see more live oaks, bull pines and manzanita bushes.

"I should have known Sam would buy another ranch. He always loved Clancy's place," Diane said.

Diane's perfume—something terribly expensive, no doubt—was making Jenny slightly nauseous. She rolled down her window a bit farther. "Clancy was Sam's stepfather?"

When Sam and Josh first moved to Gold Creek, there'd been a lot of talk about the rich southern Californian who'd dropped a bundle to buy the Rocking M, but Josh had been quick to tell people that his brother's wealth was a one-shot thing courtesy of his stepfather's estate.

"Yep, one of the best mistakes of my life," Diane said, her tone surprisingly wistful. "I was a single mother with a six-year-old kid. I'd moved West with a guy who turned out to be a real jerk. I was tending bar in a little dive and along came Clancy Royson. My cowboy. Too old for me, but damn, he was a good man. He made living on a ranch sound like a dream come true, so I married him."

Jenny had to slow down to turn onto the winding gravel road that led to the ranch house. "Was this in Pasadena?"

Diane nodded. "He raised prime cattle, thoroughbred horses, oranges and avocados. I gained twelve pounds the first year I lived there." Her tone was surprisingly light. "Sam fell in love with the place. And with Clancy. They bonded." She looked out the side window. "I knew right away the country life wasn't my cup of tea, but I stuck it out three years for Sam's sake."

Three whole years, huh? Jenny thought dryly.

''Actually, Clancy and I never divorced, but I moved back to town and went to beauty school. I had a dream of working in the movie industry as a makeup artist.''

''Sam stayed with Clancy?'' Jenny asked. She knew the answer. Josh had often talked about Clancy wistfully—not because Clancy left Sam an inheritance, but because Sam had had a true father figure in his life while Josh hadn't.

''Yes. Right up to the day he died.'' Her lips, shiny from a fresh application of berry-pink lipstick, pursed petulantly. ''I'll never forgive Sam for not calling me sooner. He said Clancy wanted to die in peace and asked Sam not to call me, but I don't believe him. I should have been here when Josh died, too, but Sam didn't call me until it was over. So I missed my own son's funeral.''

Jenny bit down on her tongue to keep from saying, ''Sam was carrying out Josh's wishes.'' With a sigh of relief, she turned into the circular driveway leading to the two-story cedar-log home. The barn and corrals were some distance away.

''Over there,'' Diane said, pointing toward a cluster of men standing beside an empty corral.

She parked in the shade of a sprawling oak tree and got out. Her mother-in-law did the same, and both women simultaneously opened the rear doors to retrieve a baby. Three dappled cow dogs raced toward the car, barking a greeting.

Jenny picked up the tiny bundle wrapped in a blue-and-white-checkered cotton blanket. Her insides contracted painfully with a jolt of love. Lifting Tucker, she inhaled that wonderfully heady scent of baby lotion and spit-up.

''Well, this is a surprise,'' a familiar voice hailed.

Sam didn't sound overly pleased to see them. Jenny hoped that was because of his mother's presence.

"What have we here?" Sam's foreman of many years asked. "A couple of new cowhands? We sure can use 'em."

Jenny noticed a cowboy tossing gear haphazardly into the back of a battered pickup truck. Several other men stood together talking.

"You took off so fast, I was afraid something bad had happened," Jenny said. Diane joined her, Lara in her arms.

Sam looked uncharacteristically edgy. Jenny wasn't sure why. Was he regretting his impulsive offer? Perhaps he sensed that she planned to turn him down. There was no way she could move in with him, even if their relationship was entirely platonic. Gloria Hughes would have a field day with the gossip. It wouldn't be fair to Tucker and Lara, and, it might have an adverse effect on her career. Jenny knew she would return to teaching eventually—she'd need to make a living to support herself and her children.

They're Sam's children, too, a little voice said.

Jenny was going to have to do something about that voice.

SAM HAD THOUGHT he was imagining things when the little brown Accord turned into his driveway. Normally, he would have been delighted to see Jenny up and about—everyone was concerned about her depression, but Sam had a feeling she was here to talk about his proposal. The one he hadn't intended to blurt out the way he had. He'd planned to wait until his mother was gone, before sitting down and discussing the matter rationally.

''We had a little ruckus,'' he said, kicking a rock with the toe of his boot.

''Yep, two bullheaded horny toads who tried to kill each other,'' Hank muttered.

''Just hormones and old grievances,'' Sam said, trying to downplay the disturbance. He didn't want Jenny to think his staying in town was affecting his business—even if that were true.

By the time he'd arrived, the two men had been separated and disarmed. He'd talked to each man individually and had learned that a woman was at the core of the dispute. He'd fired them both for brandishing weapons on his property, but at the same time, he understood what fueled their tempers. Love could make a man act in ways he normally wouldn't.

''Bad blood and thick heads,'' Hank added, ignoring the look Sam gave him. ''And now we're shorthanded.''

Suddenly, the trio of Queenslands resting in the shade erupted into a frenzy and took off toward the gate.

A thin trail of dust on the road explained why. ''Looks like Donnie,'' Hank said as Sam caught sight of the sheriff logo on the door of the car. ''Greta musta called him.''

Sam couldn't stifle his groan. ''I wish she hadn't.''

Hank stiffened at the hint of criticism of his wife. ''Greta don't abide guns.''

Sam saw his mother scowl. He knew Diane's opinion of the ranch and the roughnecks who worked for him. The last thing Sam needed was Diane influencing Jenny's decision—assuming she'd even consider his offer.

''Guns?'' Jenny asked, her eyes going wide.

''Typical cowboy mentality. Settle things with a draw,'' Diane said snidely.

"Nobody shot anyone," Sam said firmly.

Before he could explain further, Donnie Grimaldo joined them. A big man, nearly Sam's equal in height, Donnie had the look of a guy who'd played football in high school and college. Sam had come to know—and like—the deputy through Josh's association with the man.

"Hi, Donnie," Sam said, shaking his hand. "What brings you out here?"

"Heard you had a little disturbance. Just wanted to make sure everyone was okay."

"Just two hotheads blowing off steam. They both got their walking papers," Sam said, nodding toward the man who'd just finished loading his truck. "Hank, will you take care of cutting Tim a check? Rory asked me to send his to his mom."

After Hank left, Sam invited his guests to the house. "I think Greta made fresh lemonade."

Donnie walked between Jenny and Diane, cooing over the twins. Sam followed a few paces back. It was a pleasure to see Jenny outside; the breeze played with her hair and she moved with natural, lissome grace. He could picture her at the Rocking M permanently. Too bad he had a feeling she was here to turn down his offer.

A few minutes later, they were seated at Sam's massive pine table in his country kitchen.

"What's new, Donnie?" Sam asked after he'd poured everyone a drink. "I haven't seen you since the funeral."

The man glanced briefly at Jenny and Diane but seemed to shrug off any need for secrecy. "You may not have heard, but there's been a rash of wildfires in the area. Nothing big. A couple of hundred acres in

Hunter Valley was the worst, but the state guys think they've been set on purpose.''

Sam didn't like the sound of that. The dry spring had left the area more vulnerable than usual.

''I just wanted you to be on the lookout for anything suspicious,'' Donnie said.

Diane sniffed loudly. ''How can Sam do that when he's living in town?''

Before Sam could reply, Jenny pushed back her chair. The wooden legs made a screeching sound against the Mexican tile. The blue bundle in her arms let out a thin wail. Jiggling Tucker, she said, ''Feeding time. Can I use your office, Sam?''

Sam shook his head. ''It's a mess. Better to take one of the bedrooms upstairs. Do you need my help?''

''That's my job,'' his mother said firmly. She rose and followed Jenny from the room.

Sam and Donnie spent the next ten minutes discussing the possibility of initiating a public-awareness campaign to alert people to the danger. ''Wildfires hurt everybody,'' Sam said. ''Not just ranchers and people who live in the country.''

''That's for damn sure, but most people are oblivious unless it happens in their backyard. Just stay on your toes, Sam. I know you've been trying to help Jenny and the babies, but if this was my place, I'd move home ASAP. You don't want to make the Rocking M an easy target.''

Both men stood, and Sam led his guest to the front door. ''You know how I felt about your brother. He was a good man.''

Sam nodded. ''He was quite a guy.''

After shaking hands, Donnie left, and Sam closed the

door. He leaned back and closed his eyes, feeling more exhausted than he could ever remember.

"If it's such a burden, you could always sell the place and move back to L.A.," a voice said from the top of the stairs.

Sam reluctantly opened his eyes. He'd never understood his mother's antipathy for the ranch—unless it reminded her of Clancy. Guilt, he supposed, from the knowledge she'd left her husband to die with a twelve-year-old boy at his side.

He didn't reply to his mother's suggestion but watched her descend. Even through jaded eyes, Sam had to admit Diane was an attractive woman. Now nearly sixty, she looked ten years younger. Her artfully frosted hair was styled in loose waves around her face. She wore lilac slacks with a print top; the color complemented her fair skin.

"Where's Lara?"

Diane turned at the foot of the stairs and glanced upward. "Sleeping on the bed while Tucker is having a snack. I'd like to use the phone to call Gordon, if you don't mind. I forgot to tell him I was leaving. He's probably worried."

Sam doubted that. Gordon didn't seem capable of worry so long as you put a golf club in his hand and pointed him in the direction of a course. "There's a phone in the kitchen. And Greta left some cake, too. I'm going to check on Jenny."

He strode past her, but she stopped him with a firm hand on his forearm. "She's still Josh's wife, you know."

The pointed remark stung like a poisoned barb—which was probably his mother's intent. "Thank God you reminded me, Mother. Who knows what lecherous thing I might have done if you hadn't told me?''

Her lips compressed in a way Sam remembered all too well from growing up. ''Don't be snide. I simply meant—''

''I know what you meant, Mother, and you can save it. Jenny and I have business to discuss. I want to help her. You're the one who suggested a nanny. Are you saying I shouldn't offer to hire one?'' He'd already decided his suggestion this morning was a bad idea. A selfish idea.

She gave a sigh of frustration and turned on one heel to walk away. ''Oh, do what you want. You always have.''

Not always, Mother. Not where Carley was concerned. Stifling the old, familiar ache that came from thinking of that time in his life, Sam took the stairs two at a time. He paused at the top of the landing trying to decide which way to turn—his suite was on the left, the two guest rooms and connected bath to the right. Knowing Jenny, he turned right.

Sure enough, he found her in a padded rocking chair in the alcove that overlooked the rear of the ranch. This was one of Sam's favorite spots. He often would sit in that chair and read on a Sunday afternoon when the last of his paperwork was done.

He approached slowly, not wanting to disturb Jenny's peace. As if drawn by a magnet, he detoured to the antique sleigh bed he'd bought from Ida Jane shortly after he and Josh had moved in. This had been Josh's room. Sam knelt beside the bed and lowered his chin to the down-filled comforter. Tilting his cheek to one side he had a perfect view of Lara's face.

Her soft cheeks had filled out nicely on a combination

of mother's milk and formula. Tiny heart-shaped lips puckered ever so slightly. Her lilac-hued eyelids were fringed with reddish-toned lashes. The fine down covering her head was a few shades lighter than her mother's auburn color. ''You are going to be a beauty someday, princess,'' he whispered.

Jenny made a small sound, as if just becoming aware of his presence. Sam pushed back and turned around, letting his butt sink into the plush carpet; his back rested against the bed rail. ''I didn't mean to disturb you,'' he said softly.

She stroked her son's cheek with the pad of her thumb and said, ''You didn't disturb us. Tucker's just about done.'' Glancing up, she said, ''Is everything okay? You look wiped out.''

Sam felt wiped out. He couldn't remember the last time he'd gotten a full night's sleep. There was so much to take care of; two houses, a fleet of vehicles, the animals, the people, the funeral and Josh's affairs, and now the threat to his ranch. He knew where he needed to be, but the thought of leaving Gold Creek without Jenny and the babies made him feel ill.

But knowing the kind of gossip her moving in with him might generate was equally as unpalatable.

''Are you here to talk about what I asked you?''

Her rocking sped up a notch. ''Yes.''

''Before you say no, can I suggest something?''

She nodded. ''Of course.''

''Talk to Ida Jane before you make up your mind. Maybe she could move here, too.'' Jenny's mouth dropped open, but she didn't say anything, so he went on. ''As I was driving out to the ranch, it occurred to me that Ida might benefit from a change of scenery. Josh's death has been hard on her. I think it brought back the memory of your parents' accident and her sister's death.'' Sam didn't know Ida Jane well, but he'd always regarded her as one sharp old gal. Something had changed these past few weeks.

''I saw something on TV the other night about depression in the elderly,'' he added. ''The death of a loved one can trigger it. So could the changes Andi's been making.''

Jenny didn't say anything for a moment, but her expression was pensive. He held his breath.

''I'd planned to tell you flat out no way, but maybe I should discuss the idea with Ida and my sisters first.''

Sam nodded. ''I want to help you and I want to spend time with the twins, but I can't be two places at one time.''

He slowly rose and walked to the rocking chair. He averted his eyes while Jenny moved Tucker, but peripherally he was struck anew by the beauty of seeing his child suckle from his mother's breast. It touched something deep inside Sam's chest, loosening a dam of emotion that had been held in check for almost twenty years. *My kid would have turned twenty-one this year. If he—or she—had been allowed to live.*

Pushing the thought from his head, he took Tucker from Jenny when she offered and walked away. Some things hurt too much to think about. Some gifts were too wonderful to resist. This ready-made family was the latter.

''WHAT'S GOING ON HERE?'' Diane asked as Jenny made the turn into the paved lot beside the old bordello.

''I don't know. Is that a flashing light?'' Jenny craned her neck to see past the truck in front of her.

"Looks like an ambulance," Diane said, her voice rising in pitch.

Jenny took the first empty parking place and jumped out. She reached in to grab Tucker. "Hurry," she urged Diane as she picked her way through the bystanders to the rear stairs that led to the veranda that wrapped around the front of the building.

"Your aunt fell," Lillian Carswell told her as she reached the door. "We'd just brought her home from Garden Club a few minutes earlier. Beulah and Mary and I were standing here talking when Andi called for help."

"Looks like her hip," Mary Needham said, shaking her head morosely. "Hips are bad."

"As long as it wasn't a stroke," Beulah said ominously.

Jenny's mind was reeling by the time she made it to the parlor where Andi stood beside a gurney containing a very vocal Ida Jane Montgomery.

"Auntie, what happened? How bad is it?"

Ida's right arm was strapped down with a drip line attached to it, but she managed to reach out with her left and clasp Jenny's hand. "Hello, dear, I banged up my hip. Don't know how. One minute I was fine, then boom." She closed her eyes and added under her breath, "Maybe Andrea's ghost pushed me." Her white eyebrows drew together.

Something about the way she said it made Jenny's heart turn inside out. *No. Not Ida, too. I can't lose Ida, too.*

One of the paramedics shouldered past Jenny, breaking her contact with her aunt. Apologizing, he told her they needed to transport the patient to Merced, where an orthopedic surgeon was waiting.

"We'll be right behind you, Auntie," Andi said, opening the door for the emergency crew.

Gordon materialized and offered to take Tucker from Jenny. After checking to see that Diane had the diaper bag and two bottles of frozen breast milk, Jenny followed Andi to Rosemarie, their aunt's big pink Caddie.

"Tell me what happened," Jenny asked a few miles later.

Andi's shoulders tensed. "I don't really know. One minute she was fine, the next she was on the floor."

"Maybe it's her blood pressure medicine. Or something she ate. She wasn't drinking, was she?"

"Who knows what they do at Garden Club?"

Jenny wasn't sure which idea bothered her more—Ida hitting the bottle or Ida thinking an imaginary ghost had pushed her. Neither sounded like the Ida Jane she knew and loved. Maybe what Sam had said was right. Ida Jane was emotionally fragile.

Aren't we all? All except for Sam, who seemed as centered and in control as ever. There'd been those two fleeting moments when he seemed close to tears, but he'd gotten himself back in check almost instantly. Maybe that was why Jenny suddenly felt inclined to take him up on his offer.

"Sam suggested I move to the ranch," Jenny said, keeping her gaze straight ahead.

Andi didn't respond right away. Finally, she asked, "Are you thinking about it?"

"I wasn't, but now I'm wondering if it might not be the best thing for Ida Jane. If she has a broken hip, she'll need weeks of physical therapy. That will mean trips back and forth to Merced. You can't take her and run the shop. I can't drag two babies everywhere. Sam's housekeeper would help."

"We could hire a baby-sitter or leave the twins in day care. Or get the Garden Club ladies to help."

Jenny considered the suggestions. They made sense, but they didn't solve her underlying problem. She wanted to escape to the ranch, to hide from the world. It might be a foolish, emotionally risky decision, but she needed to leave behind the image she had of Josh dying in the living room of their home.

"But when Ida comes home, we'll have to build ramps or put in an elevator or something at the bordello unless she stays with me. And my house is too small. Plus, there are ghosts there, too," she added under her breath.

Andi drove in silence for a few minutes then said, "We can't afford to build ramps, Jen. I haven't wanted to say anything because you have so much on your plate, but Ida Jane is just about broke. If I can find the money to hire a carpenter, it'll be to fix the stairs before someone falls and sues us. And then there's the roof. It leaks."

"So maybe moving to the ranch would be a solution. Sam suggested it. He said Ida Jane seemed depressed lately. She would have the guest suite on the main floor. The twins and I would be upstairs."

As they pulled into the parking lot of the hospital, Andi said, "This is going to sound selfish, but I'd like you to go. And take Ida Jane, too. I can't move a display case without getting in an argument with her. I know it's her business, and she's old and set in her ways, but she's driving me crazy."

"People will talk if I move in with Sam."

Andi sighed. "This is Gold Creek. Gossip is a fact of life. You have to decide how much other people's opinions matter. Are you Jenny Perfect? Or do you put family before your reputation?''

Jenny started to protest, but something stopped her. Was it that simple? Because if it was, then her decision was made. As far she was concerned, family came first. Always.

CHAPTER FIVE

AS JENNY PULLED her car into a parking spot in front of the Anberry Rehabilitation Hospital in Atwater, she marveled at the difference a mere three weeks had made in her mental and physical health. She could take a deep breath without breaking into tears. Some days she went an hour or more without thinking about Josh. Of course, a whiff of his cologne could reduce her to sobs, but she knew she was healing.

So were those around her. Sam commuted to the ranch most days but continued to spend his nights in the travel trailer in her driveway. He used the baby monitor he'd once used for Josh to listen for the twins and was often at their crib before she could stumble to the nursery, a room the twins shared with Jenny's artwork and computer.

Jenny and Josh had planned to convert the guest bedroom into a nursery, but Diane had commandeered that room when Gordon left to check on things at the couple's Santa Barbara home two weeks earlier. He was due to return today to pick up Diane so they could continue their travels.

Jenny had tried to discourage Diane from staying, but neither subtle hints nor Sam's "Mother, the babies will be fine without you," worked. Perhaps she was worried about protecting Jenny's reputation—an issue that would become moot once Ida was released from the rehab center. Everyone had been apprised of the plan. Ida Jane, Jenny and the twins were moving to the Rocking M for the duration of Ida's recuperation…and possibly longer.

It was the *and possibly longer* that made Jenny nervous, but she was determined to do this for her family. Sam and his crew had revamped all of the entrances to accommodate Ida's wheelchair. The decks were now accessible, and Ida would even have a small private patio. The ranch house offered more mobility than the cramped quarters at the old bordello could possibly give, and the promise of Sam's housekeeper's help was a bonus.

"Greta is dying to get her hands on the twins," Sam had told Jenny. "Her grandchildren live in Alaska, so Greta and Hank don't get to see them often. And Greta was a nurse's aide before she married Hank and moved here, so she'll be a big help with Ida Jane, too."

Jenny felt a little guilty about unloading her problems on a stranger, but as Kristin said, "How would that be any different from letting Sam hire a nanny to help out?" The nanny had been Diane's idea, and she'd even gone so far as to put an ad in the paper, but no suitable applicants had shown up.

Grabbing her purse—she felt almost naked without a diaper bag—Jenny opened the Honda's door and got out. The air was warm and dry, but she detected a hint of autumn in the breeze. October was usually one of her favorite months. School was well under way but it was still too early for the holiday frenzy. Her class would have celebrated Columbus Day and the discovery of America by now and would be starting to make art projects for Halloween.

She missed teaching, but, except at odd moments like this, rarely had the luxury of thinking about it. She barely had time to eat, let alone pine for her old life.

Between visits to the pediatrician, the orthopedist and the obstetrician, every minute of Jenny's life was spoken for.

Thankfully, Ida Jane was healing with remarkable speed, given her age. The doctor said she could go home as early as Friday, just two days from now. The movers were coming tomorrow. And Jenny wanted some last-minute reassurance that she was doing the right thing for everyone.

"Hello," Jenny called out as she entered her aunt's room. "Aunt Ida?"

Ida Jane's bed—the one closest to the window—was empty and her roommate, a talkative woman who'd had knee surgery, had been released yesterday. Jenny knew where to look: the aviary—her aunt's favorite spot.

"Ida Jane?"

"Over here," came a loud whisper.

A responding flutter of wings and cooing filled the air. The air temperature was at least ten degrees cooler beneath the covered arbor. Jenny's heart tightened when she spotted her aunt in a wheelchair a few feet away. A white sweater enveloped her hunched shoulders, making her look sunken and withered; a knitted throw covered her legs.

"The doves spook easy," Ida Jane said, her voice croaking. "They're kinda simple."

Jenny smiled at her aunt's kindhearted appraisal of the dim-witted birds. She sat down on the park bench beside her aunt and took Ida's hand.

"Hello, dear heart," Ida said, squeezing her hand with remarkable strength.

Her smile was surprisingly bright and perky, and Jenny decided it was the wheelchair that made her look old and sick. *We'll get her up and walking when we get to the ranch.*

''Who did your hair?'' Jenny exclaimed, reaching out to feather back a lock of silver. ''I love it.''

The simple cut was shorter than usual, but there was enough natural curl to keep it from looking austere.

''A gal comes in twice a week. I decided I needed something new because I get to go home soon,'' Ida said emphatically, as if daring Jenny to dispute the fact.

''I know. The day after tomorrow the doctor said. That's what I came to talk to you about. I want to be a hundred percent sure you're comfortable moving to the ranch. You won't be able to see your friends as often, you know.''

Ida waved off the suggestion. ''They know where to find me if they want to visit.''

Jenny fought down a grin—very few of the old gals still drove. Ida Jane had stubbornly kept driving, despite her great-nieces' concerns. Whether or not she'd ever be able to get behind the wheel again was still up to debate.

''I just don't want you to get lonely,'' Jenny said.

Ida smiled. ''I'll have you and the twins. And Sam.''

Sam. Jenny wondered if she should explain to Ida Jane about the twins' paternity, but decided against it. There would be time once they were settled.

''And Greta—Sam's housekeeper,'' Jenny added. ''I think she's really looking forward to having some female company. She said it's been too quiet with Sam staying in town.''

Ida's smile took on a wistful edge. ''Suzy never liked living on the ranch. After she got married, she always found some excuse to go to town. But the Rocking M still feels like home to me.''

Jenny looked down at the withered hand still holding

hers. Despite Ida's enthusiasm, Jenny had reservations. For one thing, it felt as if she was running away.

"You don't think this is the coward's way out?" she asked in a small voice. "That I'm dumping my problems in Sam's lap?"

Ida made a huffing sound. "That sounds like something Diane would say. You had lunch with your friends last Saturday. What did they tell you?"

She'd met five of her teacher friends at the Golden Corral for a "girls'" lunch. The school talk had made Jenny slightly blue, but she'd also walked away feeling better about her decision to stay home with the babies.

"You'll never regret giving yourself this time with the twins, Jen," Martha Rhodes had told her. "And if Sam's housekeeper is willing to help, I say go for it. My sister hired a nanny with her two—they were eighteen months apart, and it really saved her sanity."

"The change will do you good, Jenny," another friend had stated supportively. "Being away from the house will give you a break from the memories."

Jenny sincerely doubted that. Josh was everywhere, and he was very much a part of the ranch, but at least the well-meaning citizens who popped in and out of her kitchen ten times a day wouldn't be making the drive to the ranch.

"They were very supportive and didn't see anything wrong about taking help when it's needed and when it's offered," she said to Ida now. "And they understood when too much help is no help at all."

Jenny felt guilty about her feelings, but the plain truth was that the Good Samaritans of Gold Creek were driving her mad. She was tired of parenting by committee—arguing over how to feed, burp, diaper, comfort, bathe and dress the babies.

Ida Jane chuckled. "What now?"

This morning's debate had centered on whether or not Lara was fussy because she didn't stay on the breast long enough. "Breast-feeding," Jenny answered. "Lillian Carswell thinks Lara might be colicky because she stops nursing too soon and doesn't get enough of the hind-milk."

Lillian, the retired librarian, was sixty-nine and unmarried, but she read a lot and was deeply concerned with the twins' welfare.

"Lillian's an old maid with too much time on her hands," Ida said, shaking her head. "She wouldn't know a teat from a hole in the ground."

Jenny sighed. "She showed me the article in a baby magazine. It had something to do with the amount of lactose intake from the foremilk and not getting enough hindmilk to digest the lactose."

Jenny had wanted to scream. She didn't question the article or Lillian's worry, but a part of her—a part she seldom had a chance to listen to—thought her daughter's problem might be something else.

"Could it be that Lara is just a little fussier by nature?" she'd asked.

"Heavens, no," Beulah Jensen had exclaimed.

"Absolutely not," Diane had chimed in.

"Lara is an angel," was Lillian's verdict.

An angel who had everybody wrapped around her tiny finger. Jenny loved her daughter, but she had a feeling the child was going to grow up to be a diva if they didn't get away from this opinionated crowd of do-gooders.

That was the Rocking M's most attractive lure. Solitude. Jenny wanted to be alone with her babies, her memories, her thoughts. No Garden Clubbers, no church ladies, no big-hearted friends, no mother-in-law.

"Am I being selfish by moving?" Jenny blurted out. "Diane thinks this is a huge mistake. She says I'm moving away from my support base. You know, the whole 'It takes a village to raise a child' thing."

Ida Jane made a sweeping motion with her hand, which startled the doves. A white feather drifted to the ground, settling at Jenny's feet. "Diane isn't exactly a font of maternal wisdom," Ida Jane said.

Jenny fought back a smile. "Aren't you being a little hard on her? Diane was a single mother most of the time the boys were little." An unpleasant thought struck her. "Like me. I'm a single mom. What if twenty-seven years from now Tucker's wife has this same conversation with her aunt?"

Jenny's temporary panic evaporated at Ida's merry giggle.

"Silly girl. You love others more than you love yourself. That's always been your problem. Diane, on the other hand, loves herself first. When she criticizes you about going to the ranch, it's probably because she knows she's never been invited there, nor is she likely to be."

Jenny sighed. "I've never understood Sam's antipathy toward his mother. Whenever I asked Josh why they didn't get along, he'd just say, 'Ask Sam. It's his business.'"

"Have you?"

"Asked him? No. Not exactly."

"Then do it."

"Now?"

"Why not?"

Jenny was caught off guard by Ida's succinct responses. The Ida Jane of Jenny's youth never used one word when fifteen would do.

"Are you tired?" Jenny asked.

"A little. They made me walk on a machine today. Sam doesn't have one of those machines at his house, does he?" Ida asked. "Because if he does, I'm not going."

Jenny smiled. "Do you mean a treadmill? No, he doesn't have a home gym, but he offered to buy anything we need. Stairstepper, treadmill, stationary bike."

Ida shuddered with mock severity. "Torture devices. That's what they are."

Jenny pictured Sam's response when she'd asked why he didn't have workout equipment. "If I need exercise, I go to the barn and lift bales," he'd said simply. And Jenny hadn't been able to keep from looking at his broad, well-muscled shoulders. She didn't know any man as fit as Sam.

Ida pushed back slightly with her toes so the wheelchair rolled an inch. "It's time for my nap. If you're worried about Sam and his mother, you should go ask him. No sense putting it off if it's stuck in your craw."

"You know, Auntie, that's a good idea. Maybe I will."

Jenny rose and took hold of the wheelchair handles. The apparatus was lightweight and agile, but Jenny felt more awkward than she did pushing the double stroller.

"Will you do me a favor when you're at the ranch?" Ida asked as they entered her room.

"Of course."

"Make sure my bed is under the window. That's what I hate about this place. I can't breathe at night if my bed isn't under the window."

Jenny hadn't been to the Rocking M for over a week. Ida Jane's room had been empty. "Okay. I'm sure that won't be a problem."

"Good. Do you know where my room is? It's on the first floor—just past the kitchen. Suzy's is upstairs beside Mama and Daddy's room, but it's my job to get the fire in the stove going in the morning so the downstairs is warm and toasty. I'm a good fire maker."

Jenny felt herself blanch. The original farmhouse that Ida and her parents had occupied before her father lost the ranch in a poker game had burnt down many years earlier, killing Suzy's husband, the triplets' grandfather. Some blamed the tragedy for pushing their grandmother over the edge.

Jenny cleared her throat. "Um, Auntie, you do know the old place is gone, right? We're going to be living in Sam's log home. He built it a few years ago. Remember?"

Ida blinked, owl-like, then frowned. "I know that. I just want my bed by the window if that's not too much to ask."

Her testy tone made Jenny blush with chagrin. "I'll check on that first thing." Jenny tried to make allowances for Ida Jane's mercurial temperament of late—no one liked being in a hospital. But Ida had changed radically since her fall, and Jenny couldn't wait to get them moved so she could keep an eye on her aunt.

SAM HAD JUST FINISHED the last screw on the mounting bracket, when he heard Jenny's voice.

"Sam?" she called.

"In the nursery."

He held his breath as her footsteps neared. She hadn't visited the ranch in nearly a week, preferring to let him handle the changes as he saw fit. He attributed her reluctance to take an active role on his mother.

Diane had made it abundantly clear what she thought of Jenny's decision to move.

"You're not doing that girl any favor, Sam. Jenny needs time to get over her loss. Imprudent change will just postpone the grieving process," his mother had said the evening before last.

"I'm grieving, too," he'd pointed out.

She'd made a scoffing sound. "Men don't know the meaning of grief."

Sam would have argued the point—some days it took every ounce of willpower he possessed to get out of bed. He was pretty sure he'd still be holed up in his room with a bottle if it weren't for two things: Tucker and Lara.

"Oh, my heavens!" Jenny exclaimed, stepping into the east-facing room. "Look at this place. Wow. Sam, who did this?"

A jolt of pure happiness—a feeling so rare it took him a second to identify it—made him grin. "I did."

She spun in a circle, head tilted back to take in the ceiling. "It's like walking in the sky. Look at that cloud formation—it's two horses rearing up, isn't it?"

Sam forced himself to remain composed. "It's whatever you see. The view changes when you step over this way."

She walked toward him, her chin lifted. "Now it's a camel on a biplane."

Sam hooted. "You've got some imagination, Jenny Perfect!"

Her eyes narrowed and she pointed to another spot. "Do you see that?"

Thinking he'd missed something, Sam stepped closer and followed the line of her finger upward. Squinting, he frowned. "What?"

"That tiny dot. It's a black hole where my ridiculous nickname is going to magically disappear."

Sam chuckled and moved away. Her scent was too appealing, too real. It made him want to loop his arm around her shoulder and— He cut off the thought. Leaning close to the newly painted wall, he took a deep breath. *Fresh paint.* Now, that was a safe smell.

"I had no idea you were such a gifted artist, Sam," she said, walking to the matching oak cribs.

FedEx had delivered the bedding earlier that morning. The design they'd chosen had black-and-white pandas peeking through bamboo stalks. The bright-orange accents added a cheery touch.

"It's just paint, Jen. Two colors. Couldn't get much simpler. I did the same thing in Josh's nursery when he was a baby."

"You were just a kid when Josh was born, and you painted a mural like this?" She picked up a stuffed panda and hugged it to her chest. The movement might have meant her milk was letting down, or she might have been trying to block his view of her ample bustline. Instead, it drew his attention to her outfit—khaki capri pants and a stretchy black top. He felt a very unwelcome flicker of desire.

"Maybe not quite as complex—it was a tiny house, but I tried." He turned back to finish snapping the blinds into their metal brackets. He'd vacillated between sunny yellow and plain white, which would have been more practical, given the possibility the twins might only be here for a few months. That was an issue he and their mother had yet to resolve. "Unfortunately, Diane made us move about six weeks later, so Josh never really got to enjoy it."

Sam pressed the hinged guides closed and then lowered the shades. ''How do they look? I was going for that warm-sunshine look.''

He glanced over his shoulder and saw her frown. ''Wrong color?''

She shook her head. ''No. It's perfect. The room is wonderful. The cribs, the layette...'' She put down the bear and absently brushed her hand across her breasts. She was such a wonderful mother, just as Josh said she would be.

''Sam, why do you and your mother dislike each other?''

Sam almost dropped his power screwdriver. He started to deny her accusation but changed his mind. She had a right to know the truth.

He put the Makita back in its turquoise metal box then swept the shrink-wrap packaging from the blinds into a plastic bag. ''How much time do you have?'' he asked, facing her.

She stuffed her hands in the pockets of her pants. ''If you don't want to talk about it, just say so. You don't have to be facetious. That was Josh's way of dealing with things he wanted to avoid.''

Sam paused, befuddled, then he understood. ''No. I meant, how soon do you have to leave? I can give you the long version or the short one.''

She blushed and looked down to consult her watch—a slim gold bracelet–type that Josh and Sam had shopped for together in San Francisco the Christmas before last. Sam had advocated practical—''She works with fourth-graders.'' Josh had held out for sexy. Now Sam could see why—Jenny had delicate, very feminine wrists.

''I suppose I should head back in an hour or so. I stopped at the house on my way back from seeing Ida Jane. I left two bottles with Diane. We're mixing breast milk with formula, so the twins should be fine. Beulah was there, too.''

''Good. I don't suppose you packed your boots, did you?''

She shook her head, obviously puzzled.

He picked up his tools and clamped the trash bag under his arm. As he walked past her, he said, ''I was going to suggest a horseback ride, but it's only been seven weeks. You probably shouldn't be on a horse yet.''

''Where are you taking me?''

''Josh's favorite spot. Come on. We'll take the quad-runner.''

Sam wasn't looking forward to the topic of conversation but he'd put it off long enough. It was time to tell Jenny about the past.

SAM WASN'T WEARING his hat. Sitting behind him and enjoying the ride on the padded seat of a vehicle that resembled a cross between a motorcycle and a tank, Jenny could see a few silver hairs glistening in the sunlight. They blended so nicely with his thick, wavy brown hair, she'd never noticed them before. Of course, she wasn't usually this close to him, either.

''We're not going too far, are we?'' she asked.

''No. Just to the top of the ridge.'' He patted the cell phone in his pocket. ''Don't worry, we can check in at any time.''

Sam parked beside an area of lichen-covered slabs that she and Josh had named Stonehedge Unhinged. The long flat boulders resembled the mysterious circle laid flat, like dominoes.

She dismounted gingerly, acknowledging the reminder that she hadn't used certain muscles since the delivery. Nothing hurt, thank goodness, but she still moved with care as she followed him to a spot not far from an established fire pit. He dropped with careless grace to an armchair-shaped hunk of granite.

"When was the last time you were here?" Jenny asked, stretching to feel the cool breeze the altitude afforded.

Sam took a deep breath. "Josh and I camped here last May, remember?" he asked. "We came up right after he finished the second round of chemo. He was sicker than a dog." He cleared his throat. "You weren't real pleased, if I remember correctly."

Instead of sitting, Jenny leaned her hip against a waist-high formation and crossed her arms. "I was pissed as hell, actually. Josh was so weak. I thought he'd fall off the horse and break his neck."

"Maybe that's what he was hoping for," Sam said.

A flicker of pain wound through her ribs. "If I'd known how bad it was going to be for him, I wouldn't have minded. Truly."

His lips flickered sympathetically then he sat forward, hands linked together in front of him.

"I'll tell you what happened between me and my mother," he said, looking up at her, "but I need your promise you won't bring the subject up again. You can get Diane's side of the story if you want, but whatever excuses she gives you are of no interest to me. Deal?"

His serious tone made her hesitate. Not because she couldn't keep a secret but because this sounded like the kind of revelation that bonded people. Did she want to be the keeper of Sam's secret? Did she have a choice? Like it or not, they were already bonded.

"Deal," she said softly.

CHAPTER SIX

JUST START TALKING, Sam told himself. Should be simple enough. But the second he opened his mouth, his brain refused to cooperate.

He jumped to his feet and paced to the brink of the lookout. Below was the Rocking M. He gazed at the rolling pastures where his cattle grazed, the top-notch fences and the irrigated fields. The forest-green metal roofs that topped both his home and barn were easy to spot in the afternoon sun. He caught glimpses of vehicles moving, employees at work. He was proud of the fine working ranch he'd created. But none of it quite filled the void in his heart, left by a bitter betrayal.

He couldn't help wondering where he'd have wound up if things had worked out differently with Carley. No doubt he'd have stayed in Hollywood. Perhaps he'd now be rich and famous. There was no way to know. He probably wouldn't have grown as close to Josh. At least there was one saving grace to this saga, he thought.

He let out a long sigh. "I don't like to talk about what happened. It's old news, and Josh's death has taught me that bad things just happen. You can't dwell on them."

He swallowed against the tightness in his throat. "I fell in love when I was nineteen. I'd just gotten my first speaking role in a film and thought I was on my way. She was the director's daughter. Eighteen. Gorgeous. Dangerous as hell, but I was cocky and full of myself."

Sam closed his eyes to recall the pleasure of their first kiss. His palms had been so wet he hadn't dared touch her anyplace but on the lips. But within days, they'd moved beyond simple kisses to wild, sinful tangles of arms and bare skin and hot need. In empty dressing rooms, abandoned sets, the back seat of his car and on the sprawling private beach below her parents' million-dollar Malibu home.

''First love is unique, I guess. You feel like you invented something that could cure cancer or save humanity.''

Jenny smiled at his wry tone and nodded. Sam was sure she and Josh had felt the same way. In fact, he'd been forced to listen to months of gushing details about ''Jenny this, Jenny that'' when he and Josh first moved to Gold Creek.

''Anyway, we talked about getting married, but she was sure her parents wouldn't approve since they wanted her to go away to college. I wasn't too concerned about what Diane would say. I'd moved out when she married a jerk named Frank and hadn't seen much of either her or Josh for a few months. I wasn't crazy about the idea of eloping—until Carley told me she was pregnant.''

Sam rolled his shoulders against the tightness. He didn't look back often because the what-ifs always did a number on him. *What if I hadn't called Diane first?*

''Carley told her folks she was spending the weekend with friends in San Diego. I, unfortunately, told Diane the truth. Josh was just a little tyke, and I was afraid she'd pull some typical Diane stunt and I wouldn't be there to take care of him.''

Jenny looked grave, her lips pursed. She was a good listener, Sam thought, momentarily distracted from his story.

"Did something happen?" she prompted.

Sam blinked. "Yes, but not to Josh." He put a little more distance between them. "Carley and I got married in some sleazy little chapel in Vegas. We stayed in the honeymoon suite—" he snickered to let her know it had been anything but glamorous "—of some joint on the Strip."

He looked at her and sighed. "That was twenty years ago. Vegas has spruced up a lot, but back then, the Golden Fleece was the best I could afford." He couldn't help but smile—the irony of the little joint's name never ceased to amuse him. He'd been fleeced all right—of his innocence.

He shook his head. "You get the picture. It wasn't what I wanted, but...we said our vows, paid the guy twenty bucks then stocked up on beer and fast food and hopped in bed." He caught Jenny's blush and bit down on a smile. "Wasn't quite the honeymoon you and Josh took, was it?"

There was a sad look in her eyes when she said, "I never understood why you were so adamant about us going away for our honeymoon. When you gave us tickets to Maui and a week in a hotel for a wedding present, my first thought was we could have used that money as a down payment on a house if you'd have given us a choice." She frowned. "Now I feel like an ungrateful brat."

"Don't. I should have asked you, but I was afraid something would happen to jinx things."

"Like with you and Carley?" she asked.

The memories rushed back. The chatter of a silly game show in the background. Carley's risqué parody: *I'll take door number one, Sam. Oh, Mr. O'Neal, what a lovely package—it's so much bigger than I expected.*

Slick bodies because the window air conditioner couldn't keep up. Naked giggles. Kissing Carley's flat, Malibu-tanned belly and trying to imagine what it would be like to hold his child in his arms. They'd teased each other with preposterous names: Lulu Blue, Xerce Cayenne, Rowdy Merriweather, O. Neal O'Neal.

Sam brushed away the wave of emotion that gripped him. "The morning of the second day, there was a knock on the door and three guys showed up demanding that Carley return with them to L.A. They said they worked for her father."

Sam's pacing picked up a notch. He couldn't contain the agitation this memory brought. Three hulking goons. Carley in pink baby-doll pajamas. Sam in jockey shorts. Two of the men pinned his arms while the third punched him senseless. He could still hear Carley's screams and the crowd of curious tourists pressing in the doorway to see what was going on. Sam fought back, but it was three against one. In the end, the lead guy landed a solid kick to Sam's kidney that knocked him out. When he came to, he was on gurney on his way to the hospital with a police escort. His wife was gone.

Suddenly, a soft hand touched his closed fist. "What happened? Can you tell me?" Jenny asked.

Sam jumped back. He needed space to tell his story. He didn't want its ugliness to touch her. "Sit down."

He hadn't meant to sound so gruff but her expression looked slightly wounded. She did as he asked. Instead of apologizing, he told her, "There was a fight. I landed in the hospital with a Vegas cop outside my door ready to haul my ass off to jail for a long list of charges including statutory rape."

Jenny gasped.

Sam looked away. He didn't need her sympathy or

outrage. Not now. Back then, he'd have given anything for a helping hand, a shoulder to cry on, some adult guidance, but the only person available was his mother—the one who'd betrayed him.

"When I got to L.A., after I'd used every penny I had on hiring a lawyer to talk the police into dropping the bogus charges against me, I found out Carley's parents had taken her to France."

He took a deep breath. "To make a long story short, Carley's dad managed to get our marriage annulled, me fired and my name on a studio blacklist. I was broke and out of work. A buddy of mine was heading out on the rodeo circuit, and I thought, Why not? Nothing like a two-thousand-pound bull stomping on you to give you a little perspective."

Jenny shook her head from side to side. "What about Carley? She just left? Without even talking to you?"

She would pick up on that first. Jenny—whose sense of honor would never allow her to act so callously. "I've never seen her since that morning. I heard she married a Frenchman a few years later. Probably still lives in France."

Jenny was silent a moment then asked the question he'd hoped might escape her notice. "What about the baby?"

"Aborted," he said simply.

Her gasp sounded like a wounded bird's cry. He tried to cover his own emotion. "It was a long time ago, Jenny."

"She did it without your consent?"

He made a dry, harsh sound in his throat. "Her father was rich and powerful. I was a nobody." He shook his head. "Save your sympathy. I probably would have given my permission if anybody'd asked." *Liar.* "I was madder than hell at the time, and there's no way I would have wanted any kid of mine to be raised in that kind of life.''

She rose and walked a few steps in the opposite direction. Sam understood completely; it was the way he felt about this story, too. He kept her in his peripheral vision. Her lips were compressed in a thoughtful frown. When she looked up and caught him staring, he turned away.

He heard her approach, and was grateful she didn't do something foolish like touch him. Even after all this time, these memories left him feeling splintered. One touch and he might crumple like a pane of broken safety glass.

''It's a tragic story, Sam. I'm sorry. You deserved better. But how does your mother figure into it?''

Sam closed his eyes and sighed. He'd almost forgotten about this part of the saga. ''Diane sold me out.''

''I beg your pardon?''

He faced her squarely and made eye contact so she would understand the significance of what he was telling her. ''Carley was flighty and headstrong but she also had every intention of marrying me. I know she did. She knew her parents would try to stop her, so she didn't tell anyone—even her best friend—where we were going. The only person I told was Diane.''

The look of comprehension on Jenny's face made Sam swallow thickly. This wasn't something he'd shared with anyone else, even Josh.

''She accidentally let it slip?'' Jenny asked in a small, hopeful voice.

Sam shook his head. ''She went to Carley's parents and told them. She admitted it.'' He closed his eyes, trying not to remember the horrible argument that had followed his mother's revelation.

He wasn't proud of the way he'd acted, but he'd been crazy with anger, frustration and disappointment, not to mention the pain of three broken ribs and a bruised kidney. He'd truly loved Carley and his unborn child, and as far as he could see, the only one to blame for this situation was his mother.

"A few days later, Diane took off with Josh for Mexico with enough money to spend the next couple of years there," he said, leaving Jenny to draw the same conclusion Sam had twenty years earlier.

"Oh, Sam, that's awful. There must have been some reason. Did she tell you why?"

Sam turned to look at the view. Usually, he could escape to this vista to find peace, but today its serenity was lost on him. "She said Carley's father had planned to have me arrested as soon as we returned. She claimed Carley had lied and was only seventeen. Even if that were true, they would have had to prove that our association was forced, which it wasn't. But Diane said she didn't know that. She did what she thought was best—for me."

How simple and logical the words sounded, given the cushion of time, but Sam hadn't believed them then and he didn't believe them now. He had no idea which side Jenny would take.

She was silent for several minutes. "I feel terrible for both of you," she said. "But the person I'd really like to get my hands on is Carley's father. What a bastard!"

Sam smiled. She seldom swore—another reason Josh called her by her unwanted nickname. "He did what he thought was best for his daughter. Maybe I'd make a similar choice if Lara's future was at stake."

He'd spoken candidly, realizing too late what his words implied. Fatherhood. His connection to Jenny's child.

"We should go back," he said, not ready to get into another heavy subject. That could wait until he had his paperwork assembled.

JENNY WAS PUTTERING in the kitchen, just finishing up the last of the dishes when the thought hit her. *No wonder Diane is so mean to Sam—he's her guilty conscience.*

"Hey," Kristin said, flopping onto the padded stool at the counter across from Jenny. She'd driven down from Oregon for a quick visit and to help Ida Jane move. "That Lara makes it so darn hard to put her down. She's such a lovebug."

Jenny smiled. Lara liked to cuddle; Tucker was a miniature action figure. When he was in your arms, he wanted to see everything; Lara was content to be the center of your attention. "Is she asleep?"

"Yup. But Tucker's a bit restless."

Jenny poured the last of the coffee into a cup for her sister and put it in the microwave then turned on the gas under the teapot. She missed coffee but was still watching what she ate and drank. She hadn't eaten anything with peanuts in it because Sam mentioned reading something about the peanut enzyme causing future allergy problems in nursing babies. His fascination with the birth process made more sense to her now.

"Ida told me you went to the ranch today," Kris said conversationally. "I stopped to see her on my way here."

Jenny removed the coffee cup from the microwave and put it in front of her sister. "Wait till you see what

Sam's done with the nursery. It's amazing. I didn't realize he was that...creative.'' The significance of the word took on new meaning when she saw Kristin's impish grin.

Jenny let out a low growl. ''You know what I mean.''

She turned around to fill her cup with boiling water then added a chamomile tea bag. The aroma riding on the billow of steam eased her tension. This was a crazy time, some might say she'd made a crazy decision, but in many ways, Jenny felt more relaxed than she had in months.

''Let's sit in the living room,'' Jenny said, carrying her mug to the recliner. She still avoided the couch, which had been returned to its usual position under the window. To her, that couch would forever be associated with Josh's dying. It was on her list of things to give away once the house was rented. But there were a number of minor repairs that would need to be done before that could happen. A window Josh broke the summer before last. The screen door that didn't latch. New vinyl flooring in the bathroom.

Sam had told her to make a list, but she hadn't gotten around to it yet.

Kristin sat across from her. ''What did you think of Diane's offer to rent this place? I noticed you nearly choked on your egg roll, but I thought you recovered quite nicely.'' She spoke softly, her voice a near whisper.

''Why are you whispering?''

Kris blushed. ''I don't know. Diane has a way of popping in when you least expect it. Are you thinking about her offer?''

Jenny sighed. ''Like I told her, there's a bunch of work to be done before the house is ready to rent, but I suppose I could rent it to her. She seemed sincere about wanting to be close to the twins, and I know Sam wouldn't want her staying at the ranch.''

Jenny's mind was still caught up in the sad story of his mother's betrayal. It had taken every bit of willpower to be nice to Diane during dinner. Jenny kept telling herself there were two sides to every story, but her instinct was to take Sam's side unequivocally.

Thankfully, Diane and Gordon would be heading off on their travels in the morning. Canada, Gordon said. Maybe even Alaska.

''I probably shouldn't say this, but I'm glad she's leaving,'' Kristin said. ''I know she's been trying to help, but it really irks me the way she treats Sam.''

''I know. Sometimes I want to shake her. She's lost one son, and she seems to have no feelings for the one she has left. Why can't she see what an incredible person he is.''

Kristin looked at her. ''You like him, don't you? I don't blame you. He's damn attractive. But, Jen, things could get even more complicated if you two—''

Jenny took a gulp of too-hot tea. ''There's never been anything inappropriate between us,'' she snapped.

''Of course not. We don't call you Jenny Perfect for nothing,'' Kris said lightly. ''However, we both know he adores you. He thinks you're better than perfect. But he's far too much of a gentleman to overstep his bounds, especially now with the babies.''

Jenny felt a funny warmth in her belly; she chose to blame it on the hot tea. ''What does that mean?''

Kris gave her a don't-be-dense look. ''Jen, this arrangement is going to take a lot of finesse. Sex would only complicate things. You're both grieving. You both loved Josh. You share two babies. Living together might work out nicely or the whole thing might blow up in your faces. I think Sam's smart enough to know that—which is why he's not here tonight.''

Jenny had been puzzling over Sam's earlier call but now understood. She'd thought he was embarrassed about having shared his secret. Now, she realized he was giving her a chance to rethink her decision.

''Am I making a mistake, Kris?''

Kristin shook her head, her fair curls dancing. ''No. I told you what I think—this has Josh's fingerprints all over it.'' Kris had been the first to say she thought Josh would not only approve of the move but probably had it in mind all along.

In the back of her mind, Jenny agreed. Josh liked to see people happy. He once drove a young couple all the way to Tuolumne Meadows to watch the sunset because that had been their honeymoon dream, but they'd run out of funds and couldn't afford another night in Yosemite.

Jenny looked around. ''You know, sis, what I'd really like is for you to move in here.''

Kristin sat back stiffly. ''I already have a house. In Ashland.''

''I know that, but we need you closer. Even if Ida recovers to the point that she can walk, it's doubtful she'll ever drive again. With Andi running the shop and me at the ranch, we could really use your help.'' Andi had been the one to suggest this, but since she and Kristin still had some issues between them, she hadn't wanted to put it to Kris.

''Is there any reason you can't hang up your shingle—or whatever they call a massage therapist license—here in Gold Creek?''

''Yes.''

"Why?"

It was Kristin's turn to sigh. "I have a life in Oregon, Jen. I make good money. Besides, I'm a pariah in Gold Creek. The girl most likely to screw up. How much business would I get from locals?"

Jenny scowled. She didn't understand why her sister insisted on thinking of herself in such negative terms. "That's ancient history, Kris. Nobody cares about some stupid fight between a bunch of kids."

"I do. And I know other people—Gloria Hughes, for example—who feel the same way. I feel their looks, Jen. They tolerate me when I'm here to help you, but that's because you're their golden girl. You can do no wrong. Even moving to your bachelor brother-in-law's house is okay because you're Jenny Perfect."

Kristin rose abruptly and walked to the kitchen. Jenny admired her sister's slim build and graceful movement. Kris was the prettiest and most feminine of the sisters, yet she seemed to have the least amount of self-confidence. Jenny had never figured out why. Nor did she understand why Kris seemed fixated on something that had happened in high school.

Unfortunately, Jenny just didn't have the energy to make another soul-searching trip down memory lane. Sam's tortured past was quite enough for one day.

"Well, you don't have to decide right away, Kris. Diane and Gordon will be gone for a couple of months."

Kristin nodded. "I'll think about it, but I can't promise anything. There are…other considerations." She walked to the back door. "I'm kinda wound up from the drive. I think I'll go for a walk."

Secretive, as usual, Jenny thought as the door closed behind her sister. She'd given up trying to second-guess

Kristin's motivation. But Kris had been there for Jenny in the delivery room, and Jenny would never forget that.

A couple of minutes later a car pulled into the driveway. It wasn't the rumble of a diesel engine, so Jenny knew it wasn't Sam. Disappointment washed over her, but she didn't have time to examine her reaction before her mother-in-law opened the door and walked purposefully to the couch. She sat down facing Jenny.

"We need to talk."

Before Jenny could reply, there was a faint cry from the bedroom and she jumped to her feet. "I'll be right back."

Diane followed her to the nursery. The twins shared a crib—an arrangement that worked out just fine except when one woke the other. Jenny swooped in and grabbed Tucker before he could work up a howl. His tiny face scrunched up angrily, and his fists were tightly locked.

"Shh...hush, little man," Jenny soothed. "Mommy's here."

She carried him to the changing table and quickly unsnapped his terry-cloth sleeper. His feet kicked when the cooler air touched his skin, but he kept quiet. Diaper changing still left her feeling as graceless as a fourth-grader handling papier-mâché, but she was getting better. Sam was much more efficient.

"Practice makes perfect," he'd claimed. "Even as a baby, Josh was full of you-know-what."

"I think you're making a mistake," Diane whispered.

Jenny glanced at the baby wipe she'd just pulled from the plastic container. "What?"

"Don't move to the ranch," Diane said bluntly.

Jenny looked around at the crowded conditions—desk, easel, bookshelves crammed with art books, children's books and baby paraphernalia, then pictured the cloud-adorned walls and ceiling that Sam had prepared for his children. "I want to move."

"Aren't you concerned about what this will do to your reputation? I know things were different in my day, but this is a small town. People will talk."

Her day? Josh had told Jenny all about the men his mother had lived with without benefit of marriage. Still, what Diane said touched the very core of Jenny's self-image.

She swallowed. The move made sense at so many levels. And as long as there was nothing between her and Sam—other than the twins—where was the harm?

"I'm sorry you feel that way, Diane, but I'm moving. Sam has the space. Greta is anxious to help with Ida Jane *and* the twins. It may sound selfish, but I need some time to get back on my feet, both financially and emotionally. If people can't accept that, then..." Her throat closed.

She pressed the sticky diaper tabs round Tucker's pudgy belly then slipped his feet back into the fitted sleeper. She picked him up. He fit so perfectly against her chest, his head right beneath her chin. A tidal wave of love welled up from her toes and swept through every particle of her being. She'd never expected to feel anything this powerful.

"Your dad would have loved this," she whispered against Tucker's temple. "He would have loved you, sweet boy."

Diane made a low keening sound and rushed from the room.

Jenny started to put Tucker back in his bed, but he seemed too wide-awake. "You're just like your father—he couldn't stand to miss a thing," she whispered, catching her mistake after she said it. With a sigh, she went in search of her mother-in-law.

Diane was standing in front of the grouping of framed photos on the wall near Jenny's bedroom door. ''We all miss him, you know,'' Jenny said, joining her. ''We always will.''

''I know,'' Diane said, her voice tearful. She lifted her chin and pointed to a photo of Sam and Josh. Jenny had taken it while she and Josh were in college. Sam had visited them in Fresno, and they'd gone to the fair one afternoon. The brothers were standing, arms linked, in front of a display proclaiming Hybrid Bull Semen.

''Josh worshiped Sam,'' Diane said. ''From the minute he was old enough to walk, he followed Sam everywhere.''

Jenny nodded. ''And Sam loved Josh just as much.''

''Then he shouldn't try to take over Josh's family the minute his back is turned,'' Diane said.

Jenny fought down a strangled laugh. ''Diane, dead is a little more serious than *turning your back*. Josh left me alone with two babies and no set of instructions on what to do next. I'm doing the best I can here.''

Diane nodded. In the harsh yellow light of the hall fixture, her features showed her age. Black mascara was blotted under her eyes. ''I know you are, Jenny. This isn't your fault. It's Sam's.''

Jenny started to defend Sam, but Diane walked away. She motioned for Jenny to follow. Jenny lifted Tucker up so she could whisper in his ear, ''I don't want you to pay any attention to what's said here, okay?''

He opened his mouth in a big yawn.

Once seated opposite each other, Diane took the lead. ''It's easy at this age, you know,'' she said, nodding to the baby in Jenny's arms. ''You can't go wrong. All you have to do is love them, and they love you back. Only when they get older do things get tricky.''

Jenny didn't argue. She knew that raising a child wasn't easy—especially for a single parent.

''It's when you make a mistake and they can't forgive you, that everything really starts to go to hell in a handbasket.'' Diane's ominous tone made Jenny clasp Tucker a little tighter.

''I was young when Sam was born—too young, I suppose, but try telling that to a girl in love.'' She smiled fleetingly. ''I tried to be a good mother. The thing about Sam is—he was born serious.'' She made a nervous gesture. ''Sam never cooed and smiled like other babies. It was like he was judging me right from the very beginning. And I was never good enough. Never.''

Jenny looked down at Tucker who blinked twice and opened his mouth. Would he judge her harshly for what she did...what she was about to do?

''Josh, on the other hand, was Mr. Sunshine from the minute he was born. That's what I called him when he was little. Mr. Sunshine.''

Tears suddenly materialized in Jenny's eyes. The name fit. He'd been the sunshine of her life, and now he was gone. Forever.

Diane seemed too wrapped up in her own memories to notice Jenny's distress. ''Anyway,'' she went on, ''I did my best to raise those boys. There were men in my life off and on. A few—like Clancy—stuck around longer than others, but mostly it was just me and my boys.'' She looked at Jenny imploringly. ''Until I did something that drove Sam away.''

Jenny gulped. Sam had told her she could get Diane's side of the story, but Jenny wasn't sure she wanted it. Still, something made her ask, ''What did you do?''

"I saved his life—not that he ever saw it that way."

Jenny waited for Diane to go on.

"When he was nineteen, Sam got involved with a spoiled little brat who set her sights on him." Diane gave Jenny a knowing look. "You'd have fallen for him, too, if you could have seen him then. So handsome. Those eyes. And shoulders out to here."

She held up her hands to about the width that Sam's shoulders were today. Jenny ignored the funny little hum in her belly. "Sexy, huh?"

"Tom Cruise and Daniel Day-Lewis rolled into one. The girls flocked to him, but he was very picky—until this little rich girl came along. She was beautiful and willful and she managed to get pregnant so Sam would marry her."

Jenny didn't point out that Sam must have taken an active role in that matter. "I did my student teaching in a high school in the Valley and I saw that happen all too often. Usually, the girl gets stuck being a single parent."

Diane looked at her sharply. "Sam's an honorable man. He offered to marry her. But the little twit was only seventeen. She lied to Sam—told him she was eighteen. She begged him to elope with her to Las Vegas. Sam stopped by my house on his way to pick her up. He told me what he was doing and where he'd be. He didn't ask for my advice—or my blessing." Her tone was surprisingly hurt. "So, when her father called, threatening to have Sam arrested, I decided to cooperate—for Sam's sake."

Jenny looked at Tucker. As much as she didn't want to sympathize with Diane, she couldn't help wondering how she'd react if Tucker's whole future was in jeopardy.

"I take it Sam didn't appreciate what you did?"

Diane threw up her hands and let out a cry of exasperation. Tucker, who was starting to doze off, startled as if pinched. Jenny hugged him close and murmured softly in his ear. "It's okay, sweetie. Go back to sleep."

"Appreciate," Diane muttered ruefully. "God, no. He came home madder than heck. Only stayed long enough to tell me off. He didn't want to hear my side of the story. When I mentioned that I was leaving, he stormed off. Josh and I caught a bus to Mexico a few hours later."

Using the payoff money. Jenny's heart started to harden, but suddenly Diane burst into tears. "That's where we were living when Josh got sick. I didn't even know he'd missed those booster shots until we were back in the States," Diane cried. "Immunizations weren't that big a deal back then. How was I supposed to know he might get cancer from the infection in his gonads?"

"Why'd you go to Mexico, Diane?"

She took a deep breath and clasped her hands together in her lap. "To get away from Frank, the man I was married to at the time. He claimed I'd embezzled a bunch of money from the travel agency he owned." She shook her head and said softly, "I took some money, but it was only a fraction of what it should have been."

Jenny thought she heard her add, "After what he did," but she couldn't be sure. Diane stood and walked to the door.

"Do what you want, Jenny, but never forget that Sam has his own agenda. He's an unforgiving, humorless man with ice water in his veins, but if you choose to live under his roof, there's nothing I can do about it. Gordon and I are leaving in the morning."

After she was gone, Jenny continued to rock the warm, now-sleeping bundle in her arms. ''Cold and humorless?'' she repeated. ''Sam?''

She kissed her little son's forehead. Jenny might not know much about mothering, but she knew Sam O'Neal—a whole lot better than his mother did, apparently.

No man who painted white clouds on a blue-sky ceiling could have ice water in his veins.

CHAPTER SEVEN

THE NEXT MORNING, Sam handed out assignments like an army general. ''Hank, I need you and Bill to move Jenny's things into the spare room. Kristin will meet you at the house to show you what goes and what stays. Jenny and I will bring the baby stuff with us. Andi's bringing Ida Jane's things after work.''

Jenny and the twins were moving in today. Ida Jane would join them tomorrow—provided her doctor signed the release papers. Jenny had told him on the phone a few minutes earlier that Ida was trying to strong-arm her doctor into letting her go a day ahead of schedule. ''She really wants to be with us when the twins and I move in,'' she'd said.

Sam understood and respected that, but there were a few things he and Jenny needed to iron out before anyone moved anywhere. Sam regretted leaving this until the last minute but his lawyer had been out of town until Monday. His office hadn't called to say the documents were ready until after Jenny had left the ranch yesterday. He'd thought about taking the papers to her last night, but with his mother still there, he'd opted to wait until today.

Shifting gears, he looked at his housekeeper. ''Greta, if you need any help inside grab one of the cowboys.''

She blushed as if he'd suggested something dirty. ''I

can handle everything that needs to get done in here. You just worry about your own problems.''

Sam chuckled at her tone. Greta could be quite bossy—after all, she'd been the woman of his house for nearly nine years—but they'd had a long talk the night before, and she'd seemed optimistic about having Jenny and Ida move in.

''We could use some new life in this place,'' she'd said. ''And I'm sure your brother would like the idea of Jenny and the twins being here. He always loved the ranch.''

That was true. Sam was positive his brother would have approved of the move, but he wasn't sure how Josh would feel about what Sam was about to propose.

Hank walked up and laid a hand on Sam's shoulder. In his late fifties, Hank retained the lean, beanpole body of many professional cowboys. Lanky legs and extra-long arms that could pitch both a rope and horseshoes with surgical accuracy. ''You 'bout ready, boss? We can follow you with the trailer.''

Sam took a deep, calming breath. He'd been up since four making East Coast calls and returning e-mail. His business had picked up just at the wrong time. The next two weeks were going to be jam-packed with sales, breeding schedules and prior commitments he couldn't change.

''Go ahead and take off. I need a couple of things from my office.'' He turned to leave and caught the look that passed between his housekeeper and her husband. Sam knew Hank had reservations about this move.

But unlike Jenny, who cared what people thought, Sam had long ago learned it was impossible to please everyone, so he'd given up trying. As long as he felt right about what he was doing, then to hell with what other people—including his foreman and his lawyer—said.

He retrieved his briefcase from his office then fished in his pocket for the key to the new minivan he'd purchased the day before. Smiling, he walked around to the driver's side and climbed in. Despite the leather seats and new-car smell, something didn't feel right. He glanced in the rearview mirror and saw his cowboy hat atop his head.

Chuckling, he took it off and sent it sailing toward the back. It bounced against the window and dropped into the rear storage compartment. A part of him—the cowboy, he guessed—never pictured himself behind the wheel of anything that didn't have four-wheel drive and a gun rack. But Jenny and the babies needed reliable transportation and more room than her little compact afforded.

Ignoring the howls of mirth from three cowboys mending fence, Sam reached over to engage the CD player. The salesman who'd delivered the car yesterday had included six of his favorite CDs in the package. As Diamond Rio started to play, Sam relaxed. The vehicle might be a bit lower to the ground than a sporty SUV, but it would be more practical for Ida Jane and two infant seats. He wondered what Jenny was going to say when he handed her the keys.

How she'd react to the van worried him almost as much as how she'd react to the papers in his briefcase. He'd had weeks to think about this, but hadn't actually sat down and faced the reality of their situation until he'd met with his lawyer.

''Are you sure this is what you want to do?'' Dave Dunningham had asked.

They'd been friends for years; business associates

even longer. Dave's uncle, Jasper Lancaster, was the Realtor who sold Sam the Rocking M.

Sam hadn't hesitated when he outlined his plan to Dave, but now his stomach was in a knot. He had to sell it to Jenny, and although he was pretty sure she'd understand the rationale behind the arrangement, he knew better than to second-guess what another person would do.

I'll find out soon enough, he thought, turning his focus to the music.

The melody was beautiful, the harmony soothing, but the words made his throat tighten. The song was about love that ended too soon, the wish for more time to spend together. Another sunset, another chance to say, "I love you."

Sam saw a turnoff and took it. The minivan gave a little shudder as it pulled to a stop on the dusty shoulder. Sam reached into the molded console between the seats and picked up the plastic CD cover: One More Day, it read. The title of the song that was playing. *What would Jenny give for one more day with Josh?*

He closed his eyes and let the music wash over him. The words brought back the pain of the goodbyes in his life—the one with his brother, the one he never had a chance to share with Carley. He told himself he wasn't expecting a miracle with Jenny. He didn't expect her to fall in love with him or give up her future to make him happy. He was only postponing the inevitable. Sam knew that. He just couldn't handle another loss in his life at this moment. Not yet. Maybe with time.

When the music ended, Sam pushed the eject button and tucked the disc into the case. He dropped it into the allotted space, then turned on his blinker. He'd have an answer to his grand plan soon enough.

"YOU'RE CRAZY, aren't you?" Jenny shouted, pointing first at him, then at the shiny new vehicle. Her animation brought a smile to his lips. It was good to see her as vibrant and engaged as she'd been when Josh had been alive. Sam had wondered if that feistiness had died with his brother.

"A new minivan? What were you thinking?"

Sam was certain she didn't want to know that. "Josh called *me* a spendthrift? The kid who had to have every new gizmo and gadget ever made? He'd have had you in bankruptcy court if you hadn't cracked down on him. I know, he told me so."

The diversion worked. Jenny stopped staring at the desert-sand-colored van long enough to roll her eyes skyward. "So, it's genetic, huh? Does that mean I'm going to have to break your check-writing fingers, too?"

The teasing tone let Sam relax some. Maybe buying the car had been an uncharacteristically impulsive move on his part, but it stemmed from seeing Jenny squeezed between two infant seats in the back of the Honda when she and her sisters had taken the babies to visit Ida Jane.

"I really did it for Miss Ida," he said, using what he hoped would be the deciding argument. "She's going to be needing the wheelchair at first and a walker for another month or so after that. How are you going to carry a wheelchair in your little car? And why subject her to that kind of indignity?"

Sam's heart made a funny wiggle when he saw her face soften. Jenny loved her aunt and would do anything to make life easier for the older woman. She looked at him a moment then shook her finger like a teacher. "You are as sneaky and manipulative as your brother. But just because it makes sense doesn't mean I'm going to let you pay for it." Her forehead crinkled. "I'll get a loan just as soon as I have all the hospital bills figured out.''

Sam stifled a sigh. Money was only one small part of what they had to talk about. ''Are you ready to go?'' he asked.

She turned on one heel and dashed back into the house without answering him. With her hair in a ponytail and her black jeans and white, man's-style shirt with the tails hanging out, she looked about sixteen. He clamped down on his gut reaction—which was also reminiscent of age sixteen—and followed. *Business. Think business. Jenny's going to be your new partner in the business of bringing up the twins.*

He ignored the other voice that snidely said, *Right.*

To Sam's surprise, Gordon and Diane were in the living room, each holding a baby. He'd been under the impression they were leaving at sunrise to beat the traffic in Sacramento. In the corner by the telephone stand were two plump diaper bags and an assortment of boxes labeled Twins.

''Hi there, Sam,'' Gordon called out cheerfully.

Sam smiled. ''Hello, Gordon. How's the golfing?''

''Shot a two under yesterday. Couldn't believe it,'' he said, shaking his head. ''They wanted me back today to prove it wasn't a fluke, but your mother has her heart set to leave.''

Diane passed the baby in her arms to Jenny. ''You take good care of this little boy, you hear me?'' she said with mock ferocity.

''I will,'' Jenny said gravely. Then she looked at Sam and added pointedly, ''We will.''

Sam's heart nearly fell out of his chest. He sucked in a breath and didn't let it out. What did that mean? Had she told Diane about the babies' paternity?

Diane looked at him a moment, her lips pursed. ''Josh would have expected nothing less.''

Well, that answers that. He let out the breath he'd been holding then took a step closer to Gordon.

''Here's your little angel,'' Gordon said innocently. ''I'm going to miss these punkins more than I would a hole in one.''

Sam knew the feeling. He wanted to spend as much time as possible with his children, which was why he'd made his lawyer spell out the terms of his relationship in the documents in his briefcase. Now, all he had to do was get Jenny's signature on the dotted line.

JENNY RAN HER HAND across the plush leather upholstery one more time. She still couldn't quite believe that Sam had purchased this beautiful new car for her. Now they were on their way to Atwater to see Ida Jane, after which they would return to the ranch to begin… *What? Playing house?*

''Um…Sam. The car's wonderful. Really. You've done so much. I'm really grateful, but…'' She swallowed, trying to find the right words.

''Jenny, I'd planned to bring this up at the house, but I didn't want to start anything with Diane and Gordon there. Do me a favor and open my briefcase.'' He nodded toward the floor. ''That antique by your feet.''

Jenny reached down and picked up an amber-colored leather satchel, so old it had that soft feel of a well-traveled suitcase. She set it on her lap, inhaling the almost-smoky quality of it.

''It was Clancy's. He gave it to me before he died. Still smells like cigar smoke, doesn't it?'' The fondness in his tone made Jenny run her hand across the embossed initials on the flap. S.S.O.

"I don't know your middle name," she said, oddly disturbed by the fact. Sam was her brother-in-law. She should know that about him. Why had she never bothered to ask? What was wrong with her?

Sam chuckled. "Probably because I never use it. Sam Stuart O'Neal—sounds too much like a distress call."

"Stuart?" The name was familiar to her.

"It's Diane's maiden name."

"Oh. That's right." Jenny felt her tension abate... until a few seconds later when Sam said, "Open it. I had my lawyer draw up a couple of things for us—just to be safe."

Safe? Oh, God, here it comes.

As if reading her panic, Sam turned the van sharply to the right, pulling into a fruit stand that Jenny had never stopped at before. He drove to the far corner of the parking lot and turned off the engine. With his hands on the steering wheel, he said, "It's not what you think."

"How do you know what I'm thinking?"

His lips flickered. *Has he always had such compelling lips? Josh's lips weren't like that. Were they?* She couldn't remember. She couldn't bring her dead husband's face to mind and the fact made her start breathing too fast, too shallowly.

She pushed Sam's heavy leather satchel off her lap and clawed around blindly for her purse, which had fallen to the back. She sensed Sam watching her with growing alarm, but she had to see Josh's face. Right this instant. Finally, her fingers connected with the strap of her shoulder bag. She dug inside for her billfold.

She caught the look of confusion on Sam's face. She whipped open her wallet and flipped past the driver's license and insurance cards to the photo section. *There,* she thought with instant relief. *There he is. Happy eyes. Smiling lips. Not Sam's lips—Josh's lips. The lips I kissed good-night for ten years.*

Heaving an unintentionally loud sigh, she sank back in the soft seat and closed her eyes. "Sorry about that."

Her heartbeat was almost back to normal when Sam said, "What happened?"

"I don't know. I just couldn't remember what Josh looked like for a second, and it scared me."

"Oh. I said 'papers' and you got that deer-in-headlights look. But you don't have to be afraid, Jenny. Not of me. This isn't a custody issue," Sam said, leaning over to pick up the papers that had spilled to the floor. "It's for your protection, in case anything happened to me."

Jenny swallowed the restrictive lump in her throat. "I see."

He shook his head. "No, you don't. You can't. Not until you read the documents."

His tone was sharp, but Jenny thought she understood why. Sam had had to deal with the many loose ends after Josh's death, and he'd said several times that he planned to do things differently with his estate.

She took the papers from his hand and tried to focus on the legalese. Sam leaned between the seats to check on the twins, who seemed to associate automobile travel with sleep. His shoulders barely fit between the opening. His bulk made it hard for her to concentrate. His smell—something clean and fresh with a hint of outdoors—made her want to lean up against him and inhale deeply.

She tugged on her seat-belt strap and put her right shoulder against the window. The sunlight highlighted her reading material, making it impossible to miss the words *beneficiaries of his estates.* She gasped. ''Oh my God, Sam. This is your will.''

He pulled back sharply, facing her. ''It's a codicil to my will.''

''You've put my name on everything. The ranch, your patents, your life insurance. Everything. Why?''

He sat back, his shoulders against the door. ''You're the mother of my children, Jenny,'' he said simply. ''I know you didn't plan to be. And it seems like some cosmic farce that you wound up with me—a man eleven years your senior—instead of the love of your life. But, we don't have any control over that, Jen. We do have control over how we proceed, and if you read a little further, you'll see that all of those material things come with a price.''

Jenny's heart sped up, a low roar hummed in her ears. She didn't dare look down at the papers in her lap; her hands were shaking too badly. ''What is it?''

He swallowed first then said, ''Five years.''

Jenny squinted. Maybe the hum had blocked her ability to hear. ''What?''

''I want you to give me the next five years. Live with me, at the ranch—basically, until the twins start school.''

''Five? Why five?''

''To be honest, I really want eighteen, but that wouldn't be fair to you. You're young and beautiful and at some point you'll want a real life—dating, a new husband, more kids. I understand that. And I can live with it, if I can have the early years with Tucker and Lara.''

There was something so sad about what he was saying Jenny wanted to cry, but he was acting very businesslike and she tried to do the same. ''That's all?''

He shook his head. ''I also want to be named as their father, legally. We don't need to broadcast it, but it's the smart thing in case anything happens to you. I will always be their father, but I only expect you to stay with me five years.''

''What happens after that?''

''I'll give you child support, and you can move back to Gold Creek. Maybe by then your writing will have taken off, but if not, you could probably teach again.''

''What about you?''

He showed his first sign of vulnerability. ''I go back to the way my life was before this happened, except that I will have established a bond with my children. They'll know me. And I won't have missed out on the early years.''

Like I did with Josh. And with my own child that was never born. Jenny heard the unspoken words, and her heart melted. She knew this man better than he thought. His businesslike facade hid a very fragile heart.

''I think I can do this,'' she said. ''Although I'd like to think about the arrangement for a while before I sign anything. But even if I do it, you don't have to make me heir to your ranch. Put the twins' names on the deed.''

He smiled for the first time. ''I trust you to pass my estate on to them when I'm gone. You're not like my mother.''

''What does that mean?''

''When Clancy was dying, he instructed his lawyer to sell the ranch and put the money in a trust for me until my twenty-fifth birthday—he said I'd be smart enough by then. He knew if he left it to Diane, the whole thing would have been gone by the time I was old enough to vote. You, I trust.''

Jenny was honored, but saddened, too. ''You know,

Sam, I talked to your mother. She told me her version of what happened.''

He swung about sharply and reached for the key. ''Good. Now you know both sides of the story, but I don't want to discuss it.''

He started the car. ''One more thing. I think we should tell Ida Jane today. About the babies.''

Jenny closed her mouth and sat back, arms crossed. At times, Sam could be even more bullheaded than his brother had been, but he was right about one thing—Ida Jane needed to know the truth.

''YOU AND SAM DID IT in a laboratory? That doesn't sound very romantic.''

Ida Jane's response to Jenny's revelation almost made Sam burst out laughing. Jenny's mouth dropped open but no words came out, so Sam said, ''What's worse is neither of us was even in the room at the time. But look what we have to show for it.'' He held Lara up like a blue ribbon won at a fair.

Ida looked from Lara to Jenny, who was nursing Tucker in the armchair across the room, and grinned. ''And you got two for the price of one.''

The elderly woman was sitting in her wheelchair, looking quite regal in her purple jogging suit and bright-white sneakers. Sam wasn't certain Ida Jane understood the mechanics of what they'd just told her, but she didn't seem particularly scandalized. However, she had yet to give her opinion of Sam's five-year plan.

''So, what do you think about Jenny staying with me for five years?'' he asked. ''Is that unrealistic?''

Ida Jane took a breath. ''If I were you, I'd just marry her and get it over with, but you young people have a different way of looking at things, I guess.''

Sam's stomach did a little flip-flop. He'd purposely avoided using the M word in his contract. He would have offered to marry her in a heartbeat, but Jenny was still in love with Josh. You didn't just turn that off when the person you loved died.

"That's right," Sam said, forcing a lightheartedness he didn't feel. "We like to keep our options open. Jenny is free to do anything she wants, as long as she lives at the ranch so I can spend time with the twins."

Ida Jane frowned. "For five years. But what happens then? Won't it break your heart to give them up?"

Sam looked down at the child in his arms and couldn't keep from flinching. "It won't be easy," he admitted, trying to keep his pain from showing in his voice. "But I want to do what's right for Jenny and the twins. I suppose it'll be like a divorce, but, at least, Jenny and I will be able to handle it amicably since we don't… I mean…we won't have a lot of baggage to throw at each other, like some people. We're doing this for the good of the children."

Ida gave him a look that called him a liar, but she didn't say the word out loud.

Sam was grateful, because they both knew he was one. His fancy legal contract was a sham—in every way that counted. He might have agreed to five years on paper, but in his heart he wanted much more. Ida Jane was a sharp old gal. She'd no doubt guessed Sam's ultimate goal was to get Jenny to fall in love with him, or, at the very least, to marry him and provide their children with a stable, loving home.

Sam was no fool. He accepted that Jenny would never love him the way she did his brother. First love was too special, too perfect to compete with. Sam knew he could never take Josh's place.

Lara made a cooing sound, startling Sam. The babies seemed to change every time he looked. She waved her tiny fist and he gave her his finger to grab. Her grip amazed him, as did the way her gaze seemed focused on his lips when he spoke her name.

"Hello, Lara, love. Are you ready for lunch?"

He pressed a kiss on her knuckles. She blinked twice as if surprised by the movement. "Do you want Ida to give her a bottle, Jen? Or does she get the other side?"

He'd gotten over his embarrassment about helping with breast-feeding. Once Jenny and Lara had worked out the kinks in their nursing relationship, the little girl seemed to enjoy the time and nourishment her mother gave her as much as her brother did.

"There's a bottle in the bag," Jenny said. "She won't mind if Ida Jane feeds her."

After placing the baby on Ida's lap, Sam found the plastic bottle and handed it to the older woman. He watched his daughter suckle in bliss, her hand gripping the slick fabric of Ida's jogging suit.

"Well, since everyone is busy here, I'll go find that doctor and see if he plans to sign your get-out-of-jail-free card." He draped a receiving blanket over the arm of Ida's wheelchair then left.

His gaze met Jenny's as he walked past. Her smile seemed slightly troubled, but he hoped a private chat with her great-aunt would help ease her mind. At least Ida hadn't accused him of trying to steal his brother's family—the way his mother would have if she'd been privy to the agreement.

Thankfully, Diane would be gone for two months. Her parting words to Jenny had been, "We'll be back in time for Christmas…maybe even Thanksgiving. Take good care of those babies."

Sam paused in the hallway, trying to remember which way to turn. He hated the sounds and smells of hospitals. He hated seeing people confined to beds. An image of Josh wheezing for each breath made his knees wobble and he touched the wall until the moment passed.

The Hospice nurses had warned him to expect a full year of mourning. They were wrong. Sam would mourn his brother for the rest of his life, but Sam also knew that he couldn't live in the past. He had to move on. For Tucker and Lara who needed a father. And for Jenny, too.

Even if his grand scheme didn't work out, Sam planned to make the next five years as happy as possible for Jenny. She deserved nothing less.

TUCKER HAD FINISHED nursing a full minute before Sam left the room, but Jenny had waited to move until he was gone. It was difficult listening to him talk so dispassionately about their living arrangements. True, theirs was a passion-free relationship, but there was something so one-sided about his proposal, it made her want to cry. He was doing all the giving, she, the taking. It was almost as though he didn't think he deserved anyone to love him.

He was offering her his life, but only long enough to bond with his children. The whole concept boggled her mind. And there were so many questions she needed to ask. *Will we be roommates, relatives or what?* And what would happen once Ida Jane was back on her feet? If Ida returned to town to live, wouldn't that make Sam and Jenny's living arrangement look suspicious—even if they were just friends? They were friends, weren't they?

"What do you think, Auntie? Am I crazy to say yes? Or would it be more crazy to say no?"

Jenny rebuttoned her blouse, stood and walked to her aunt's bed to change Tucker's diaper. He liked nothing better than to fill up on one end and discharge on the other. She laid him down then fished in the bag for a disposable diaper. He'd just moved into a bigger size; Lara still had a couple of pounds to go.

As she worked the snaps on the crotch of his sleeper, she looked at her aunt. "I'm serious, Auntie, I need your advice. Should I sign Sam's papers?"

Ida Jane seemed intent on feeding Lara, who was happily batting the bottle with her fist. She liked to slug Jenny, too, when she was nursing. "Sam's taking me home today."

Jenny's heart made a funny, fluttering sensation. There was something odd in Ida's singsong tone, as if her mind was somewhere else. "By *home* you mean the Rocking M, right?" Jenny asked, trying to keep her alarm from showing.

Ida nodded as if hearing something Jenny hadn't intended. "I used to live there, you know. Before Daddy lost it in a poker game. Gambling is a terrible vice."

Jenny braced herself for the "horrors of gambling" lecture. She'd heard it a million times.

Instead, Ida sighed and said, "But what in life isn't a gamble? Sometimes, you just have to do what feels right, regardless of the risk."

Jenny watched her gently brush one gnarled finger against Lara's plump cheek. "If you hadn't taken a chance, we wouldn't have this little gal, would we?"

Jenny couldn't argue with that logic. She wouldn't trade Lara and Tucker for anything. Even another fifty years with Josh? a voice in her head asked. The answer that flitted through her mind left her a little shaken.

"Life has a strange way of working out the way it's

supposed to,'' Ida Jane said. ''Did I ever tell you about the night you and your sisters were born?''

''Your friends still talk about it like it happened yesterday,'' Jenny said.

''It was a big deal to this little town. A terrible tragedy—two lovely young people killed in a senseless car wreck, and at the same time, three precious little miracles were born. You spent twelve days in the hospital, then you and Andi came to live with me. Poor little Kristin didn't join us for nearly a month. We almost lost her, but the doctors and nurses never gave up.''

Jenny smiled. Kris had always loved that part of the story.

''I became a mother at age fifty-four,'' Ida said, her tone bemused. ''An unmarried spinster. A dried-up shell of a woman, and I suddenly got my dream come true, three times over.''

She shook her head, obviously musing over fate's little trick. ''Some gifts are too wonderful to question, Jenny girl. But you know deep in your heart, they come with a price.'' Her eyes filled with tears. ''My poor Lori. She and Mick should have been the ones to raise you. That's the natural order of things. But it was probably best they went together. They were so much in love.''

Jenny heard the sadness in her aunt's voice and hastily finished diapering Tucker, who fussed a little because he much preferred being naked.

''I'm so glad you're coming to the ranch with me.''

Ida looked confused. ''To my daddy's ranch?''

Tears welled up in Jenny's eyes. She didn't understand Ida's sudden slips in clarity and it scared her.

''The Rocking M was your family's ranch, but it belongs to Sam now. Some of Sam's workers are moving your things out there today, remember?''

Ida looked unperturbed. She lifted Lara to her shoulder and burped her with efficiency. "Sam's a good man, and he'll be a good father to these little tykes. Josh knew that."

Jenny knew it too, but she was still nervous about signing Sam's papers. *Why?*

She didn't get a chance to raise the question aloud because Sam entered a minute later with a nurse in tow.

"All set, Ida Jane. Just need your John Hancock on the bottom line and we're out of here."

"Good," Ida said, motioning him to her. She signed the three sheets of paper, then the nurse left.

"I'll pull the van around to the front. What do you want me to carry out, Jen?" Sam asked.

For some reason, his voice sounded very much like Josh's. Either that or Josh's voice was fading from Jenny's memory. The possibility robbed her of her ability to speak.

"My suitcase is right by the door," Ida Jane said. "We'll be ready as soon as Jenny finishes changing the baby."

Jenny felt Sam's gaze on her, but she didn't look up. She couldn't. Not when Josh was out of touch.

Once Sam was gone, Jenny glanced at Ida. Her great-aunt smiled. "Don't fret, child. The people we love are obliged to stay around as long as we need them, but they have a journey to make, too, you know."

"They do?"

Ida Jane nodded. "We all do." She sighed. "I'll be getting on with mine, too, pretty soon. But not before I see each of you happily settled."

Jenny smiled. She'd heard that line before. "No wonder our lives are a mess. We want you to live forever."

Ida shook her finger at Jenny threateningly. "Don't

say such a thing. We all have to go sometime. Besides, you girls are making progress.''

''We are?''

Ida nodded. She turned her head to gaze out the window. ''You're leading the way, Jenny. Just like always. All you need is a little time.''

Time. Jenny wished it were that simple. *If time's all it takes, then I'm in luck. I'm about to sign up for five years. Maybe by then, I'll have a clue.*

CHAPTER EIGHT

JENNY WASN'T SURE if she'd actually heard Tucker's cry or just anticipated it. In the two and a half weeks that she'd been living at the ranch, she and Sam had discussed the merit of letting him cry himself back to sleep as a way to eliminate the middle-of-the-night feeding, but in all honesty, neither of them could do it. Jenny really cherished the peaceful interlude with her son.

She was out of bed at the first muted whimper. She shrugged on her heavy robe—November had brought with it a couple of light showers and even some frost. Shoving her feet into her alpaca slippers, she dashed through the bathroom to the nursery. Two strategically placed night-lights guided her way.

In the shadows, the white clouds of Sam's painted-sky ceiling looked like friendly angels smiling down on her. After picking up Tucker—who blinked at her and smiled with such Joshlike charm her eyes misted—Jenny peeked into the hallway. It surprised her that Sam wasn't on the scene. He often beat her to the punch, sometimes delivering Tucker to her in bed so she didn't have to get up.

Sam was hands down a gracious host. If Jenny still felt a little tentative about their relationship, she could place none of the fault on Sam's shoulders. He was a perfect gentleman every evening and spent most daylight hours either in the fields or in his office.

That first Sunday after she'd moved in, he'd invited Jenny's sisters to a barbecue, which he'd prepared. During dessert, he explained, line by line, his five-year plan, as Jenny had come to think of it.

After what Jenny thought amounted to very little discussion, Kristin and Andi had endorsed Sam's plan. Ida Jane gave her blessing by nodding off in the lawn chaise.

The following morning Sam had escorted Jenny to his lawyer's office to sign the papers. They then stopped by the bank to add her signature card to Sam's checking and savings accounts.

"You'll need to buy things for the house, for the kids, for whatever," he'd told her. "Think of this as a job, if you like."

A job with very long hours, Jenny thought, smiling at her little son. *But one I wouldn't change for anything.* She yawned, then after waiting a minute to see if Sam would appear, she strolled to her room and sat down in the padded rocking chair in the alcove. She kept the curtains open at all times to enjoy the panoramic view.

Tucker fussed impatiently.

"I know. I know. Mommy's slow tonight." She fumbled with her robe and the buttons of her gown. "It's because your daddy's still asleep, and I'm not quite awake."

Somewhere along the way, Sam had become the twins' daddy. Jenny wasn't conscious of making the switch in her mind; it had just happened. And although still a bit conflicted, Jenny accepted it. There would be time to tell the twins about Josh's role in their lives.

And he was never far from her mind. Or Sam's, either, it would seem. Just that morning, Sam had strolled into the breakfast nook where Jenny and Greta were experimenting with the twins' first taste of solid foods—mashed ripe banana.

Sam had pulled up a chair and watched with rapt attention, applauding when Lara successfully swallowed a tiny dollop, but Jenny had sensed he was distracted. A few minutes later, after each baby was finishing off the meal with a bottle, Jenny asked what was on his mind.

"The school called yesterday and asked if I could put together something outlining the goals and requirements for the Josh O'Neal scholarship. I prepared a rough draft and I'd like your feedback."

Sam's rough draft would have put most finished products to shame. He'd scanned a photo of Josh standing at Glacier Point with Half Dome in the background and had incorporated it into text that summed up Josh's philosophy of life: "Respect nature as the gift it is and work toward lessening man's impact on the environment." In addition, Sam had attached a list of the donations that had been received to date, including a ten-thousand-dollar gift from the Rocking M Ranch.

"By next spring when they start passing out scholarships, the Joshua O'Neal Scholarship Fund will be able to award two each year to students—one male, one female—interested in studying forestry, earth sciences or conservation," he said. The quiet pride she heard in his voice had touched Jenny, and she'd had to blink back tears.

Fortunately, Ida Jane had chosen that moment to enter the room pushing the high-tech walker, which she'd graduated to earlier that week.

Tucker's warm little body wriggled against her. Blinking, she sat up a little straighter to get settled and was just about to put the baby to her breast when an odd flickering light in the distance caught her attention. The glow—whatever it was—was too far to see distinctly but close enough to be on Rocking M land.

"What's that? Taillights? A police car?" Rising, she walked to the window. Putting her nose to the glass, she squinted into the blackness.

Red. Yellow. White. Dancing. The answer hit her like a slap across the cheek. "Fire."

Tucking the startled baby under her arm like a football, Jenny raced out of the room and down the hall. Sam's door was partly open; she stiff-armed it, making it explode against the wall.

"Sam," she cried. "Come quick. Fire."

He sat up. "Where?"

"Outside. Toward the road."

He was out of bed by the time she reached the light switch. He dashed into the adjoining bathroom, but not before Jenny got an eyeful. A lean back tanned to the waist. Rock-hard buttocks, pale white. Wide, powerful thighs adorned with sparse dark hair.

"How far away?" he asked, emerging a second later wrapped in a white terry-cloth robe that reached to his calves.

His tone was all business, but Jenny stuttered, trying to get her brain to cooperate. "I don't know." She pointed in the direction of her room. "I could see it from my window."

He grabbed the portable phone from its cradle beside his bed and hurried past her. Jenny sagged against the wall, pressing Tucker to her chest like a shield.

He returned a few seconds later, handing her the phone. "Call Donnie. It looks pretty close to the hay barn. Hank's rounding up the men."

Without giving her a second glance, he dropped his robe and opened a drawer in the built-in wardrobe. Jenny flattened her back to the wall, juggling both child and phone. In the reflection of the French doors opposite them, she had a clear view of Sam dressing. Jeans, no time for underwear. Socks and boots followed. He grabbed a gray-and-green plaid flannel shirt as he turned around.

"Hurry."

His voice was low and calm, but Jenny's fingers wouldn't cooperate. Tucker, undoubtedly picking up on his mother's agitation, started to cry. Finally, she punched in 911.

Sam disappeared into the bathroom. He returned just as she gave the information to the dispatcher. Her voice sounded strained and brittle. "And can you patch me through to Donnie Grimaldo? Please."

Sam paused for a millisecond then brushed his knuckle against her chin before dashing off. A blur of plaid flannel and denim, he took the stairs three at a time. "Be careful," she called from the top of the staircase. She didn't know if he heard because the front door slammed but a heartbeat later.

"Oh, Tucker, I don't like this," she whispered, feeling her baby son's tears on her cheek. Or were they hers?

"Jenny?" a thin, reedy voice called from the first floor.

Ida Jane. Always a light sleeper, her great-aunt would want to know what was going on. Soothing Tucker's sobs as she went, Jenny trotted down the staircase.

"There's a fire out in the field, Auntie. Sam and the men are headed there now. I think I heard him say something about a hay barn, so it could be bad," she added hoarsely.

Ida Jane was already out of bed by the time Jenny reached the first-floor bedroom. She angled her walker past Jenny and started toward the kitchen. ''They'll need coffee when they get back. Come along.''

''Let me get Tucker fed and in bed, then I'll be right down.''

Half an hour later, Jenny returned to the brightly lit country kitchen to find Ida Jane and Greta working side by side making biscuits. The smell of coffee made Jenny's stomach growl.

''Emergencies build appetites. Might as well be prepared to feed 'em,'' Greta said, glancing over her shoulder. Her thinning brown hair stood up in back; and over her jeans she wore a shirt that had to belong to Hank.

''Let me do that for you, Auntie,'' Jenny said, rushing to help. ''You should sit down and rest your hip.''

Ida put up a small fuss, but Jenny could tell she was grateful to sit in the padded armchair Sam had moved into the kitchen just for her. Jenny knelt down and pulled the ottoman over so Ida could elevate her feet. ''How's that?''

''Just fine,'' Ida said a trifle breathlessly. ''All this commotion reminds me of the first fire out here.''

''When was that, Miss Ida?'' Greta asked.

Ida let out a sigh. ''The actual date escapes me, but it wasn't long after your mother was born, Jenny. I remember thinking it was a good thing Suzy and Lorena were in town at the time. I was living in Oakland, working for the telephone company, when I heard about the fire.''

Jenny finished placing the last of the dough cutouts on the cookie sheet Greta had prepared. The sprinkling of cornmeal made her fingers slick. She inhaled deeply, enjoying the comforting smell of flour, salt and water.

''What was the old house like?'' Jenny asked. ''I don't think I've ever seen a picture of it.''

"You wouldn't have," Ida said. "Daddy destroyed every picture there was of it. I truly thought it would kill him when Suzy married Bill Scott, the man he claimed cheated him out of his family's homestead."

Jenny knew the story well. Suzy, Ida's younger sister, was a beauty who could have had any man in the county. For reasons no one seemed to understand, she chose to marry Bill Scott, her father's archenemy. A man sixteen years her senior.

"Suzy was in town, visiting Mama when it happened. She only visited when she knew Daddy was going to be away. The night of the fire, Daddy was at his lodge. Those were the war years and things were rationed, but Bill was quite well off, and Suzy always had gas coupons. She would have returned to the Rocking M before Daddy got home, but the sheriff came and told her the ranch house had caught fire with Bill in it."

Even though Jenny had heard this story a hundred times or more, tonight she had a sudden image of Sam caught in an inferno, blazing timbers crashing about him. Her hands started to tremble and she almost dropped the cookie sheet. She quickly deposited the pan in the prewarmed oven and walked to the window. She heard the sound of the dogs' frenzied barking. Cupping her hands to the glass, she looked into the distance.

"Headlights," she said, her heartbeat speeding up. "Someone's coming."

She beat Greta to the door and hurried out to the porch, clasping her arms about her against the cold. She'd changed into sweatpants and a bulky sweatshirt, but the night had turned bitter.

The yard lights helped illuminate the arrival of a patrol car. Donnie Grimaldo leaped from the driver's seat and rushed around to the passenger door. His obvious haste heightened Jenny's fear. Her fingers closed around the fabric at her throat as she watched him bend to help someone stand. *Sam.*

Jenny grabbed a post for support. Her knees suddenly had less substance than the dough she'd just handled.

As Sam and Donnie neared the porch, she spotted burn marks and a long rip on the sleeve of Sam's jacket. "Oh my God," she cried. "Is he okay? Should I call an ambulance?"

At the sound of her voice, Sam lifted his chin. His eyes were watery, his face blackened and streaked. He pushed away from Donnie. "I can manage," he said, his voice an unrecognizable growl that was followed by a gut-wrenching cough.

He wavered on wobbly legs before Donnie grabbed his arm. "Shut up and hang on."

Together they stumbled up the ramp that Sam had recently built for Ida Jane.

"Smoke inhalation," Donnie barked, brushing through the door she held open. "Damn fool won't let me call the paramedics."

"I'm fine," Sam muttered, his voice three tones deeper than usual.

Donnie helped Sam to the armchair at the head of the table—his usual spot. In the bright light of the kitchen, Jenny could take stock of the damage. His hair was plastered to his head with sweat. Soot streaked his face and hands. His canvas jacket was charred and looked like a rag. A red gash dissected the top of his hand, but it was hard to see how deep the wound was because Sam kept tucking it out of sight. Other bloody spots had already crusted over—a cut on his neck, another at the top of his ear.

''What the hell happened?'' Jenny demanded to know.

Sam looked at Donnie, not her. Something in their silent exchange told her that Sam knew how close he'd come to adding to her problems. She was hit by a melange of emotions so powerful she almost collapsed to the floor.

Luckily, Greta took charge. ''Jenny, run out front and break off a few stems of rosemary for me. I'll get a pot of water boiling. We need to make a steam bath for his lungs.''

Jenny glanced at Donnie for one brief second. The deputy's grim expression revealed more than she wanted to know. It had been close, too close.

SAM USED the tented towel above a pan of steaming water as an escape. If he breathed deeply enough and closed his eyes tight enough, he could almost block out the look of fear he'd seen in Jenny's eyes. Only a fool would take the kind of risk he'd taken tonight. An idiot. A moron. He wanted to kick himself but couldn't work up the energy.

''How's the water, Sam?'' Ida Jane asked. ''Hot enough?''

Not as hot as it's going to get when Jenny learns the truth, he thought. He nodded and pulled the towel a little tighter. He could sense Jenny hovering behind him, as if afraid he might keel over.

You risked everything for a cat. What the hell kind of fool are you?

Sam tried to reconstruct the series of events that led to his impulsive act. He'd raced off to the fire in his truck while Hank and the rest of the crew loaded another truck with shovels, a generator and hoses.

By the time he got there, the fire was less than a hundred feet from the shed that housed his well pump and secondary-holding tank. The dried grass snapped and crackled as the flames snaked forward.

Sam had grabbed a shovel and started to create a firebreak between the shed and the hay barn, which if it ignited, would create an inferno of horrific proportions.

The men were making progress—and they could hear the sound of the California Department of Forestry fire trucks in the distance. Sam had been in the process of hooking up a portable generator to a pump, when a pile of straw and windblown leaves that had collected against the wall of the pump house caught fire.

Shovel in hand, he raced toward it, knowing instinctively it was too late. The wind was fanning the flames. No thin stream of water from a garden hose was going to put that out.

From the corner of his eye, he saw a silver streak enter the hay barn. A barn cat. One of several that lived in this compound. Periodically, Sam visited the SPCA to purchase mousers to rid his barns of pesky critters. This particular tabby was a shy sort that spurned human contact.

For reasons Sam couldn't explain, the thought of that cat being burned in his hay barn was not acceptable. He left Hank to work on the pump and raced to the spot he'd seen her enter the building. A thin meow was his only guide. He scaled the ten-foot wall of bales. A layer of smoke, which had become trapped under the metal roof, blinded him. His lungs burned. He was about to give up, when he spotted her in the far corner.

He reached for her and was rewarded with a stiletto-like gash on his hand. He caught her by the scruff of the neck and stuffed her under one arm while he tried to figure out an escape route. His heavy canvas jacket took a beating but gradually she quieted.

Through the building's lone window, Sam saw that the flames had branched. Time was running out. Unfortunately, the wind had shifted and smoke was pouring in behind him, forcing him to crawl arm over arm, without squishing the cat, to the far side of the building. He couldn't rappel down the face of the bales with a cat in one hand, so he shimmied between the stack and the wall with his back against the building's metal skin.

A small secondary grass fire on the north side of the building scorched his jacket through the metal siding. Sweat blinded him, and his foot slipped. In a desperate attempt to fling the cat to safety, he twisted sideways and his head collided with a steel beam.

Sam didn't recall losing consciousness, but the next thing he remembered was Donnie calling for help. "Over here. Get him to my car."

Sneaking his hand under the towel, Sam eyed the four-inch red streak on the top of his hand. There's going to be hell to pay when Jenny hears about this, he thought.

Ida Jane's voice brought him back to the present. "Is the steam helping?"

Sam inhaled slowly, deeply. He had to fight to keep from coughing, but managed to keep the breath inside for almost a second. "Yes," he said, exhaling. "It's worked magic. I'm gonna go clean up."

"Wait," Jenny cried, placing her hand on his shoulder. The touch held a charge that tingled all the way to his arches. "Aren't you going to tell us what happened? We barely got two words out of Donnie before he left."

"We lost a couple of outbuildings, but Hank and the boys saved the barn."

A burning sensation at the base of his throat made him cough. Jenny passed him a mug of something hot; Sam thought he tasted lemon and honey. It soothed the seared lining of his throat. ''Thanks,'' he muttered, not making eye contact.

Jenny gently touched the red stripe on his hand. ''How'd you get cut?''

Sam was prepared to lie in order to postpone the inevitable, but Ida Jane rescued him. ''Tall tales are best left till morning,'' she said firmly. ''Jenny, help the poor man to bed—although I'd suggest a shower first. He smells like the main course at a pig roast.''

JENNY HURRIED to do her aunt's bidding. ''Let me help you,'' she said, putting out her hand.

She didn't like the way it trembled, but Sam didn't appear to notice. He grabbed the edge of the table and hauled himself to his feet. He seemed just as tall and in control as usual—until he stumbled against a chair.

Jenny looked at his face, which was still streaked with soot. ''You can lean on me,'' she said softly.

''I can make it by myself,'' he replied gruffly.

''Quit being cantankerous. It doesn't become you,'' she said, sliding under his arm so it was looped over her shoulder. ''I'm going upstairs anyway. You might as well let me help.''

He made a grunting sound but didn't pull away.

''Your sharp eyes saved the ranch,'' he said when they were about halfway up the stairs. ''Jenny Perfect to the rescue.''

His tone was dripping with sarcasm, which momentarily threw her, until she figured out that it was his way of keeping her at her arm's length.

When they reached the landing, he started to push her

away, but Jenny dug her fingers into the softer flesh at his waist. Sam wasn't reed thin like Josh, but he wasn't fat either—just substantial. "Let me get your shower started."

He let out a sigh, but didn't object. Jenny knew why. She'd felt the slight tremor that passed through his body and knew he was reaching a state of exhaustion. She guided him to the master bathroom, decorated in Santa Fe tile and turquoise accents. The shower was the size of Jenny's walk-in closet in her old house. There wasn't a shower door.

After closing the lid on the toilet so Sam could sit down, she pushed up the sleeve of her sweatshirt and leaned into the stall to turn on the water. The gush of warm water was almost instantaneous. She fiddled with the adjustment, getting a bit damp in the process. Water beaded up on her arm.

Pulling back, she used the end of the towel that was still draped around Sam's neck to wipe off her arm.

"Do you need help getting undressed?"

He shook his head from side to side. He was hunched forward, his elbows on his knees, fingers linked.

Jenny squatted in front of him. "Sam, I've been a wife. I'm not a prude. I can hel—"

Whatever platitude Jenny had been about to spout was ripped from her mind the second Sam lifted his head to look at her. The bright light of the bathroom revealed what had been hidden before. Sam's eyebrows were nothing more than tiny shriveled wisps, his lashes appeared to have melted and the soot on his cheeks and forehead cloaked red welts that looked like burns.

She grabbed his right hand—the one with the red sliver of blood across it. The hair on the back of his hand was gone.

"Oh my God," she cried, rocking back so suddenly her feet gave out and she landed on her butt on the cold tile floor. "You...you're hurt. Burned. You could have been killed."

He closed his eyes and sighed but didn't try to refute her charge.

Panic made her lash out. She kicked her heels against the slick floor trying to scoot backward. One slipper popped off. "You put yourself in jeopardy for a few lousy bales of hay?" she cried. "You selfish bastard."

Sam heard her fury; he understood her fear. He wanted to comfort her, console her, even refute the argument, but he couldn't. His brain felt full of smoke. His nostril hair was singed; all he could smell was smoke. He sure as hell didn't need Jenny yelling at him to know he was a screwup. He'd heard that all his life from Diane.

Desperate for some relief, he put his hands on his knees and pushed himself up. Through a blur of watery haze, he turned toward the sound of running water. Barefoot—he'd managed to get his socks off while Jenny was turning on the faucet—he stumbled toward the big open cavern.

He didn't bother undressing. The water offered a refuge. The clean mist was warm and healing.

"Dammit, Sam, I'm not done talking to you," she said, following on his heels.

"Fine."

He turned just enough to grab her arm. With one quick tug, she stumbled after him, propelling him deeper into the shower stall. His foot slipped and she wound up plastered to his chest, her chin brushing his shoulder.

Water cascaded over his head. It ran into her face when she looked up at him, her mouth open. She spit out a mouthful of water like a swimmer surfacing, then arched back as if to scold him more.

The last thing Sam wanted to hear was a lecture. He wanted someone to hold him and tell him things were going to be okay, but he'd settle for a pair of lips on his. Jenny's lips.

Ducking his head beneath the cascade, he kissed her.

She struggled against him for the space of a heartbeat then her fists went flat. Her eyes closed—against the emotion she was feeling or the water he didn't know. Or care. Separated by a sopping sweatshirt and saggy flannel—two of the least sexy materials known to man—Sam's body reacted as if Jenny were modeling the latest fashions from Victoria's Secret. The steam finally loosened the knot in his chest, but now another knot built—lower.

A voice of reason tried to push past the greedy, life-affirming rejoicing in his mind. But she felt so good in his arms, so right, he couldn't quit.

And somewhere in the middle of his pheromone-saturated brain, a truth solidified. Jenny was kissing him back. Her lips parted to give him freer access. A tiny sigh passed between them, and he swallowed it like a balm to his parched soul.

She tasted of mint toothpaste and herbal tea. Her tongue started out shy but quickly dived into a passionate exchange that made Sam think about where he might have stashed his condoms. It had been so long since he'd needed them, he couldn't remember.

That tiny foray into reality sucked Sam into a big white room with a warning beacon flashing: *What the hell are you doing, O'Neal? Think.*

Reality hit like a bucket of ice water. *Too much. Too soon.* He wasn't a hormone-driven kid the way he'd been with Carley; this wasn't any ordinary lustful urge. This was Jenny, the woman he loved. And if he didn't stop now, he might never get a second chance to prove how much he loved her.

CHAPTER NINE

JENNY WASN'T PREPARED for the sensation to stop. For one heart-stopping moment—the second Sam's lips touched hers—she'd been transported to a safe place, a place where the loneliness of the past months was replaced by heat and need. A place where she wasn't just a mother or a niece or a sister or a widow. Where she was Jenny. A woman. Desirable. Alive.

Her response may have been fueled by months of deprivation—Josh had been in too much pain those last few months to tolerate touch of any kind—but all Jenny knew was that whatever Sam was offering, she wanted more of it. She needed the reassurance that Sam was alive. And so was she.

"No," Sam said, breaking the lock she had around his neck.

Jenny blinked away the moisture beaded on her lashes. The mist that enveloped them was steamy and smelled of smoke and Sam. Her fingers clung to the scruff of his soaking-wet collar. Although he'd pulled away with his upper body, she was still pressed against him from the chest down. His hardness, his desire, was muted only by the layers of wet clothing between them.

"Please," she whispered. The neediness in her voice resonated in the tiled stall.

"No. This isn't right."

She knew that, but it didn't stop her from reaching up

to cup the line of his jaw. His beard was rough, and she wanted to feel its abrasive quality against her skin.

Sam shifted them sideways so the water slanted between them like a silver diagonal from shoulder to hip. A fine mist clung to his melted eyelashes. Jenny noticed for the first time a small scar that would normally have been hidden by his eyebrow. She put her index finger on it and asked the question with her eyes.

His upper lip pulled back in a look Josh called Sam's run-for-cover smile. ''A tribute from my ex-wife's father,'' Sam said, adding an extra couple of inches to the space between them.

Despite the warm water and the steam, Jenny shivered.

Sam dropped his arms, accidentally knocking Jenny's hand away. ''Go to bed, Jenny. It's been a long day, and tomorrow's going to be worse.''

''Why?'' she asked, folding her arms across her chest. The emotional charge between them had triggered a release of her milk, which reminded her all too vividly who she was—Tucker and Lara's mother. Sam's dead brother's wife.

''Why what?'' Sam asked, coughing. He turned into the steamy water and let it wash over his upturned face. He continued to cough, a loud rattle that echoed acoustically.

The smart thing would be to leave, but she couldn't get her legs to move. ''Why will tomorrow be bad?'' she asked.

He leaned one shoulder against the wall and started to unbutton his flannel shirt. The rush of water combined with fatigue made him fumble like a drunk.

Jenny brushed aside his hands. ''Let me do that. Then I'll go. Why is tomorrow going to be so tough?''

He let his head loll back. ''Because you're going to find out what really happened out there, and you'll pack your bags and leave.''

Jenny's heart knocked erratically. ''What do you mean?''

''About the cat,'' he swore, turning away just as she finished the last button. ''Go, Jenny. I...''

He turned his back to her and slowly took off the shirt. Jenny stepped away, needing the space to keep from touching him. His broad tanned back was corded with muscles; faint whorls of hair were flattened by the torrent of water cascading over his shoulders. Red welts—scrape marks, she'd guess—marred the sleek perfection.

When he started to unbutton the waistband of his jeans, she retreated, recalling all too vividly the lack of underwear beneath those pants.

She grabbed a big thick towel from the bar opposite the shower and fled. Heedless of the wet footprints she left behind or the trail of water dripping from the hem of her sweatpants, she ran down the hallway to the safety of her room.

She dashed into her bathroom and quietly closed the door to the nursery. After stripping off her wet clothes, she toweled dry as briskly as her skin could tolerate.

Fool. Idiot. She turned on the overhead light and looked at herself in the unflattering brightness. Her wet hair hung in scraggly lengths—it really needed a cut. Her eyes were red from the water, her skin blotchy. Her breasts were large and unfamiliar and her belly sagged in unattractive folds.

If Josh were alive he'd have teased her out of her funk. He'd have reassured her that she was beautiful, desirable. But he wasn't here and she was so pathetically needy she'd turned to the only man around for comfort.

She leaned across the counter, careful not to disturb the baby paraphernalia. ''You are a miserable excuse for a human being,'' she told her reflection. ''Sam has enough problems without you throwing yourself at him for reassurance that you're not just a pair of mammary glands with feet.''

A chuckle made her turn sharply. Andi stood in the doorway that connected to Jenny's bedroom. ''Naked and talking to yourself. Not a good sign,'' she said, grinning.

Jenny let out a low groan and reached for her terry-cloth robe hanging beside the bathtub. ''What are you doing here?''

''Ida called to tell me about the fire. I came out to see if I could help. Wanna tell me what all that muttering was about?''

Snugging up the fabric belt, Jenny reached for the hair dryer—anything to postpone the inevitable. As she feathered her damp tresses with her fingers, she looked at her sister's reflection in the mirror. Jenny and Andi hadn't talked about anything besides Ida Jane and business for so long, she didn't know where to begin. Would this sister understand? Jenny had a feeling Kristin would, but she was in Oregon and wasn't scheduled to visit for another couple of weeks.

''It's nothing. I was upset with Sam. He put himself in danger and...'' Jenny turned off the dryer. *And what? He kissed me? Or I kissed him? Which was it?*

''Yeah, sure. Like I believe that. Come on. I'm sleeping with you, and you're going to tell me everything. I learned how to interrogate people in the marines. You'll be putty in my hands.''

Andi's teasing laugh made a shiver course down Jenny's spine. She'd been just that and more in Sam's hands. Sam's wonderful hands. Even now, that one thought was all it took to make her hungry for more.

You're in bad shape, girl. Bad, bad shape.

Minutes later, the two sisters were snuggled together in the down mattress of Jenny's double bed. A yellowish glow from the night-light in her bathroom cast long shadows across the walls and ceiling.

"So?" Andi asked. "What's gives with you and Sam?"

Jenny shook her head. "It was no big deal."

Andi pinched the fleshy part of Jenny's upper arm. "Ouch!" she hissed, batting Andi's hand away.

"I told you. I know torture."

The silliness of the comment made Jenny giggle and within seconds she was consumed with laughter that quickly segued to tears. Andi watched, her obvious mirth turning to concern. Jenny grabbed a tissue from the box beside the bed and blew her nose. "Sorry."

Andi turned on her side, placing head on hand to look at Jenny. "Okay, then, the truth this time. I heard that anguished plea in the bathroom mirror so don't even think about lying."

Jenny stared at the ceiling. The semidarkness made it a little easier to confess. "I was helping Sam into the shower and I sort of stumbled and wound up in the shower with him—fully dressed, of course—and we kissed. I'm sure it was just a close-brush-with-death kind of thing for him." She didn't add, *But I liked it. It felt wonderful.*

Andi ran her free hand back and forth in front of Jenny's eyes. "Are you smoking crack?"

Jenny turned her head. "What?"

"Drugs of some sort? I've met a few delusional drug

addicts over the years. They're good at building elaborate fantasies…like that one.''

Jenny frowned. ''It was just a kiss.''

Andi made an impatient snort. ''I know Sam O'Neal, Jen. If he kissed you, it was because he wanted to, not because you were handy.'' She snickered. ''I know because I've given him ample opportunities over the years to kiss me and he never did. Not once. Well, *once*. On the forehead. When I was particularly persistent, but that was it.''

Jenny pulled the covers over her head. ''I kissed him back,'' she mumbled. ''It was really good.''

Andi's chuckle made the mattress jiggle. ''Way cool. Can I tell Kris?''

''No.''

She shrugged. ''She'll find out. You'll blab sooner or later. You always do. Jenny Perfect has to confess, otherwise she's not perfect.''

Jenny sat up sharply. ''Dammit, would you quit with that name? Would someone so perfect be attracted to her own brother-in-law when her husband has only been dead two and a half months?''

The words, once spilled, seemed to take on a life of their own, echoing in the big room like a yodel.

''Wow,'' Andi whispered in hushed awe. ''This is serious? You've actually got the hots for Sam?''

Jenny sank back down. She felt sick to her stomach admitting it, but there was no use lying. Andi was right—Jenny always blabbed. ''Maybe. I don't know. I don't think I want to know.''

Andi snuggled close and patted Jenny's cheek. ''It's okay, kiddo. You're young, you're alive. Sam's a sexy guy.''

Jenny closed her eyes and sighed. Those sounded like

weak excuses for what was surely immoral behavior. Jenny owed Josh more loyalty than two and a half months of mourning. She owed it to herself, too.

"That kiss was an aberration, Andi. It's not going to happen again. I'll talk to Sam in the morning and make it clear that we can't be attracted to each other. Period."

Andi flopped back. "Yeah, that'll work."

Jenny ignored the sarcasm. It *would* work. It had to.

SAM PAUSED beside Jenny's door. At first, he thought he heard her crying, but the instant his hand touched the doorknob he knew the sound was laughter. And a second voice was evident. *Andi.*

He relaxed. His apology could wait.

He had no excuse for his behavior. He just hoped it wouldn't ruin the fragile balance they'd created the past couple of weeks. He'd planned on slowly courting Jenny over the course of the next year or two. Instead, he'd lost his mind and attacked her in the shower.

Turning, he headed downstairs to get a drink. Maybe whiskey would help, he thought. The scrape marks on his back hurt and his right shoulder ached, but that was nothing compared to the knot of dread in his belly.

Sighing, he trotted down the stairs in stocking feet. His exhaustion had vaporized the instant they'd kissed. Unfortunately, the encounter had left him recharged in more ways than one.

After struggling out of wet jeans that had stuck to him like melted plastic, he'd lathered and scrubbed until his skin hurt, but no amount of mental gymnastics could minimize his body's longings. Finally, a blast of cold water had done the trick.

With teeth chattering, he'd dried off and dug through his drawer for his lone pair of flannel pajamas, last year's

Christmas gift from Ida Jane. Normally, Sam was such a light sleeper he'd never had to worry about being awakened accidentally while sleeping in the buff. But he should have known better with guests in the house.

He went to the liquor cabinet beside the fireplace. The orange glow of the fire burning in the hearth filled the room with a warm, pleasant homey quality—a far cry from the raging blaze he'd encountered a few hours earlier. After downing a shot of single malt, he poured a second then wandered toward the east-facing glass doors at the far end of the room.

"Are you here to watch the sunrise, too?"

Sam jumped a full foot to the right before his brain registered the voice. Ida Jane. Patting his chest until his heartbeat returned to normal, he faced his guest, who was sitting in the recliner, a woolen throw gathered across her legs. "Miss Ida, you almost gave me a heart attack. What are you doing up?"

He sat down on the matching mahogany leather sofa across from her. He'd picked the furniture because it fit the decor, but he seldom sat here, preferring instead the solitude of his office or the coziness of the reading nook in Jenny's bedroom. Jenny and Ida Jane had made more use of the great room in the past weeks than he had in twelve years. The addition of two baby swings and a playpen made it look like a real home.

"I like to watch the sunrise. I'm a bit early, but when you get to my age, you don't take anything for granted."

Sam smiled. He liked this old woman more than he could say. He'd never known a grandmother, only having met his mother's mother once when he was seven or eight. He vaguely remembered the experience as a tedious bus ride winding up in a busy town with rows and rows of brick houses so close together they almost touched. They didn't stay long at the skinny building with the planter box outside the window.

Sam couldn't picture his grandmother, but he vividly recalled the flowers in the box—purple and white with round faces that looked like little men with black mustaches and bushy eyebrows. On the bus home, Sam had asked about the flowers, but Diane had cuffed him, saying, "I don't want to talk about it. Or her. Ever again."

And they hadn't. That was Diane's way. When Josh was old enough to ask about his heritage, Sam had said, "All dead. Don't bother asking."

"Quite the adventurous night, wouldn't you say, Sam?"

To put it mildly. "Definitely."

"It got me thinking about our old home. It burnt down, you know."

Sam knew. The people who'd owned the ranch before Sam had lived in the mobile home Hank and Greta now occupied. When Sam had expressed an interest in placing his house on the flat area across from the barn, they'd told Sam the story of the original homestead.

"You lived here growing up, didn't you, Miss Ida?"

She nodded. Her hair looked a bit wild in the dim light. Her face seemed amazingly alert. "Up until I was sixteen. That's when Daddy lost the place in a poker game."

Sam blinked in surprise. He'd always pictured her as a child, not a young woman, when her family moved into town.

"Suzy was eleven at the time. It almost broke my heart, but I think Suzy preferred living in town. She was the social one." Ida made a swishing motion with her hand. "She loved action. I was content with the animals and the quiet. She was bored to tears."

Sam pondered that point a few seconds. ''And yet, she wound up marrying the man who won the place from your father, right?'' he asked, trying to recall all the pieces of the story he'd heard over the years.

''That's true,'' Ida Jane said. ''Of course she sold the place after Bill died. Said it held bad memories for her.''

Sam sipped his drink, savoring the slow burn that eased the harsh tightness in his throat.

''Bill was her husband? The man who was killed in the fire that destroyed the farmhouse?'' Sam asked. He felt a little strange asking—after the close call he'd experienced, but he couldn't deny his curiosity.

''Poor Bill,'' Ida Jane said sadly. ''He and Suzy had only been married a short time when he died. Less than two years, I believe. From what my mother told me, it was a difficult period for him. He loved Suzy and adored Lorena, but Suzy was a bit high-strung, she could exhaust a person. Especially someone as quiet and laid-back as Bill.''

''Did you know him well?'' Sam was curious about the man—Jenny's grandfather.

''Heavens, yes. He was our neighbor the whole time I was growing up. The Rocking M was much smaller than it is now. After Bill got this property, he deeded the two parcels together.'' She chuckled. ''He kept the Rocking M name and brand instead of his own. Daddy always said Bill did it just to annoy him.''

''I take it your father was something of a poor loser?''

Ida Jane sighed. ''Truth is, Daddy liked gambling a whole lot more than he liked ranching. Bill was a good rancher, Daddy wasn't.

''The ranch had belonged to my mother's family. She inherited it when her parents and brother passed away in an influenza epidemic. Daddy tried to keep it up, but his heart wasn't in ranching. The only reason he risked the deed in that poker game was because the back taxes had come due and he couldn't pay them. He'd have lost the place one way or the other, but he'd never admit that.''

Sam smiled. He'd always been charmed by Ida Jane's ability to tell a story. ''So how'd your family end up with the old bordello?''

She gave a small laugh. ''When we moved to town, Daddy started working in real estate. He made good money—the man could sell fleas to a dog, and Mama put her foot down about the gambling. We were living in a nice little place not far from Jenny and Josh's house when the old bordello went on the market. It had been used as a boarding house for a number of years and was in pretty bad shape. Daddy snapped it up. He planned to turn it into a hotel and was in the process of fixing it up when Mama got sick. Cancer.''

''That's too bad.''

Ida nodded. She seemed caught up in the past and went on as though he hadn't spoken. ''Suzy was working at the diner, and Mama was worried about her, but there wasn't anything she could do. I was in my last year of college in Missouri. I came home for Suzy's graduation, then the next thing I know she's run off to Reno and married Bill Scott.

''Daddy didn't take it well. Suzy had always been his little princess, and Bill was quite a bit older than her. Daddy went on a bender and threatened to kill Bill.''

Ida sighed. ''The trouble with old grudges is they make you a prime suspect when the person you hate dies under mysterious circumstances.''

Sam sat forward, resting his elbows on his knees. ''The fire wasn't an accident?''

Ida Jane made a who-knows motion. "I was living in Oakland at the time. But there was a lot of talk. You know how small towns are."

"Did the sheriff name your father as a suspect?"

She shook her head. "I don't think so. There wasn't any proof. But there was gossip. Some speculated Daddy did it out of revenge, others said Suzy did it for the money."

"People thought your sister killed him?"

Ida frowned. "You have to understand. Suzy was a bright shiny penny in a bowlful of nickels. She didn't have a lot of friends. The other girls didn't trust her with their boyfriends. She had a bit of a reputation."

She paused in thought. "Bill wasn't the most handsome fellow around, but he was one of the richest. Mama told me he'd come into town almost every day to eat lunch at the diner where Suzy worked. Leave big tips. Treat her nice. I think my sister was looking for a way out of Gold Creek and she thought Bill would give it to her."

Sam didn't like the uncomfortable feeling in his midsection. *Must be the booze.* "Why do you think she married him?"

Ida Jane sighed. "Suzy and I were never real close. When I came back for her graduation, I brought along my beau—the man I thought was going to ask my father for my hand in marriage."

Sam heard a tangible sadness in her tone.

"But he took one look at my sister and fell out of love with me and in love with her. I was pretty bitter at the time. I blamed Suzy, but the fact is, she couldn't help being pretty any more than Kristin can."

She sighed. "We didn't speak for years. I dropped out of school and took a job in Oakland. Daddy chased off my beau, threatening to have him shot. And a few months later, Suzy ran away with Bill.''

''What happened to your boyfriend?'' Sam asked, caught up in the story. ''Did you ever hear from him?''

''Yes, I did. He joined the army after he left here. He wrote me from Fort Benning, Georgia, right before he was shipped out. He apologized for breaking my heart and hoped we could still be friends. A month or so later, I got a telegram from his mother telling me he'd been killed in action.''

Sam reached out and took her hand. Her paper-thin skin was cold, and he chaffed it between his palms. ''That's a sad story, Miss Ida. I'm sorry I brought it up.''

''It was a long time ago. Every one of them is dead. My mother passed away right before Lori's third birthday. Daddy lived another six years, but he'd failed a lot by then. Suzy died the year Lori graduated from high school.''

Neither spoke for a minute, then Sam asked, ''Do you think Suzy cared for Bill when she married him? Or was he just a means to an end?'' He hated the tentative tone of his question. What did any of this matter to him?

Ida thought a moment. ''Well, there was a lot of talk in town about *why* she married Bill. Particularly when Lori was born two months prematurely. The gossips had a field day. Snickering behind Suzy's back. They didn't make it easy for her.

''But I think they felt badly about the way they treated her when she and Lori came back here to live. You could tell Suzy wasn't right in the head. And Lori was the sweetest little girl that ever lived—all sunshine and sugar. That could be why people tried so hard to help when the triplets were born.''

Sam had heard a number of tales about the night of

the triplets' birth and the heroic efforts that had gone into trying to rescue Lorena and Michael Sullivan when their Volkswagen bus slid off the road in a snowstorm and crashed down a steep embankment.

"But to answer your question—I get a little sidetracked sometimes—I do think Suzy cared for Bill. He was a bit of a hermit and set in his ways, but he was kind to her, and generous to a fault. He bought her a new car for a wedding present—one of the first convertibles in the county. It was a thing of beauty."

"But they never determined how the fire started?"

Ida shook her head. "Some thought Bill might have been drinking and fallen. Perhaps hitting his head on something and somehow the log fire sparked the blaze."

Sam made a steeple with his fingers and stared at the flames dancing behind the protective screen.

"I never believed the gossip about Suzy," Ida Jane said softly. "People said it was suspicious that Suzy had Lori with her when the fire broke out. They wondered why a mother would take a toddler out on a cold winter's night instead of leaving her home with Bill."

"Did you ask her why?"

Ida looked away. "No. I never did. But I had a hunch it was because Bill was drinking. Suzy never said so, but that's what I think."

"And you're not sure Bill was the baby's father, are you?" Sam was just speculating, but by the look on Ida Jane's face he knew he'd guessed correctly. "I'm sorry, Ida Jane. I shouldn't have said that."

Ida lifted her hand wanly. "Looking back at the past is like turning over a rock. All the dark critters scatter, and you see things you don't really want to know exist."

Sam lifted her hand and kissed the back of it. "Especially late at night."

Her fingers closed around his, her grip surprisingly strong. "What you should know is that Lori—the triplets' mother—was lightness and love. She and Suzy showed up on my doorstep when Lori was about ten. They moved in with me, and I knew right away that Suzy was sick. She'd spend weeks at a time in bed. The doctors couldn't find anything wrong and labeled her a hypochondriac. After a while, she refused to leave the house. Eventually, she stopped talking. I was afraid she might hurt herself. Or Lori. So I had her committed.

"But Lorena would ride her bike to the Pine Glen Rest Home every week to visit her mother. She never complained, never whined about how unfortunate she was. She was a sweet girl, and everyone in town loved her. That's why it hurt so badly when she died."

Like my brother. Sam squeezed her hand supportively. "But she left behind three wonderful gifts."

Ida Jane nodded, tears spilling over her eyes. "They were my blessings. A reward I never deserved. Oh, Sam, if you only knew—"

"I do know, Ida Jane," he said. "You're an amazing woman and you did a fabulous job raising those girls. Look at how incredible Jenny is. What a terrific mother she is to the twins."

"And you're a good father, too, Sam. I hate to say it, but you're probably a better father than your brother would have been."

When Sam started to protest, she looked at him sternly. "I don't mean to speak poorly of Josh. I loved that boy to pieces, but he reminded me of Suzy in some ways. Like the world revolved around him. You're just the opposite. You put others first. Even cats."

Sam blanched. "You heard about that, huh?"

She nodded, a wry smile on her lips.

"Well, believe me, I'll never do that again," he said, rubbing the scratch on his hand.

Ida Jane snickered. "Yes, you will. That's just the kind of man you are. And, Sam, two words of advice—don't apologize."

He blinked. "I beg your pardon."

"Don't let anyone—even my niece—make you feel badly about doing the right thing. You saved that poor creature's life. You deserve a reward."

The whiskey in Sam's belly somersaulted. He felt his cheeks burn. "Thanks, Ida. I'll…ah…tell Jenny you said so." *Right after I apologize.*

"You do that. Now, help me up. I'm plumb tuckered out. Would you hand me my walker?"

Sam did as she asked and accompanied her to her door. "Get some sleep, Sam. The babies will be awake soon, and both you and Jenny will be crying the blues."

Sam nodded. The twins were never far from his thoughts. They were the reason he had to cool his ardor. Gossip was destructive, as Ida Jane had just reminded him, and he refused to do anything that might compromise Jenny and the twins' futures.

Sam started away, but paused. "Miss Ida, do you think Jenny and I…never mind."

Ida's chuckle eased the knot that seemed permanently lodged in his chest. "Jenny is a lot like her mother, Sam. She loves easily and is easy to love. Things will work out the way they're supposed to whether we worry about them or not."

Sam blew her a kiss then walked upstairs. Ida was a wise old woman. Worrying wasn't going to change a thing. Sam could only hope things would work out the way he wanted them to.

CHAPTER TEN

"AND THEN OUT FLIES this bag of bones with fur. Butt over ears, hissing like an old tire with a pinhole in it. Scared the devil out of me."

Sam caught just enough of Hank's impassioned speech to know he was never going to live down the story of his encounter with the barn cat. Bracing himself for the worst, he squared his shoulders and entered the sunny kitchen.

He'd overslept and wasn't moving too friskily thanks to the ache in his lower back, but he'd figured his tardiness might work to his advantage—obviously, he'd been wrong.

"'Morning, everyone," he said from the doorway. He nodded at the group sitting around his table then made a beeline for the coffeepot.

Greta had a cup poured for him by the time he got there. "The least I can do for a hero," she said, grinning.

With her hair pulled back in its standard bun, Greta looked all business—except for the twinkle in her blue eyes. Sam vaguely remembered seeing her last night—well past midnight. Was he the only one who felt as though he'd been trampled by a fire-breathing dragon?

He focused on the window ledge just past her shoulder. Something new caught his eye. A series of mismatched jars with cuttings from plants in them. Tender white roots were spinning tangled webs. *Jenny's touch.*

Her house in town was filled with plants. Sam had helped with the rigorous watering schedule toward the end of her pregnancy. It suddenly occurred to him that she hadn't brought any plants with her.

Sam took a sip of the scalding liquid then looked at his foreman. "Have you been telling lies again, Hank?"

The man chuckled and shook his nearly bald pate. "Just expounding on what I saw. Not everybody would put his life on the line for a mangy barn cat. Might be some cat-lover society that would give you a medal or something. Ain't that right, Miss Jenny?"

The coffee lodged in Sam's throat, making his eyes water. Without waiting for Jenny's answer, he turned to Greta and asked, "What's for breakfast?"

"Griddle cakes and eggs." She stepped to the stove and fiddled with the burner. "I was getting worried—you're usually such an early riser, but Jenny said to let you sleep in."

Jenny. Sam stared at the black abyss in his cup. Jenny was as much to blame for his sleepless night as the fire. He'd replayed the incident in the shower a hundred times and couldn't forget the moment she linked her arms around his neck and sighed against his lips. That was more than capitulation—it was exaltation. Sam knew because he'd felt the same way.

He took another sip of the hot, powerful brew before turning to face the group at the big pine table. Ida Jane was sitting in Sam's usual place. Andi and Jenny flanked her; each was holding a twin. Ida Jane had her hands folded in her lap and was looking around like a spectator at a hockey game. Hank lounged near the hat rack, his long, lanky frame as relaxed as a human could be without falling over.

When they made eye contact, Hank nodded ruefully

and raised his mug in acknowledgment. That was when Sam spotted a white bandage on Hank's hand. "Is that a burn?"

"Naw. Got a scratch moving that darned generator. Thought the fire truck was gonna run over it."

"Have you had a tetanus shot recently?"

Hank gave Greta an inquiring look.

"Year before last," she said, cracking three eggs into the pan. "When he tangled with that rusty fence."

Sam smiled. He knew Hank hated to be reminded of the ignoble landing he'd made into a pile of old barbed wire.

Hank scowled. "What about you, boss? Had your rabies shot yet?"

Sam glanced at the mark on his hand. Before he could say anything, Jenny said, "Good point, Hank. Maybe we should find the cat and get her tested. The only other choice is for Sam to have those shots. I've heard that's pretty painful."

Sam didn't like the way that possibility brought a smile to her lips. *Her lips. I kissed those lips last night.* "The cat's fine," he said shortly. "She had all her shots when I got her. I get all my cats from the SPCA and I make sure they're vaccinated and fixed."

He couldn't read the look Jenny exchanged with her sister, but whatever the coded message, it made Andi grin. Had Jenny told her sister about their encounter in the shower? Sam wondered.

Andi looked at him just then and winked.

I'll take that as a yes, he thought, stifling a moan. He turned away, ostensibly to retrieve some silverware from the drawer, but mainly to hide his embarrassment.

"Here you go. Sit down and eat while it's hot," Greta ordered.

Sam took the empty chair directly across from Ida Jane. As he smoothed his napkin in his lap, he glanced from one sister to the other. Even though he'd known them both for almost twelve years, he'd never really realized how different they were. Andi was an attractive woman—a live wire, Josh called her. But not his type. *Not the way Jenny is.*

He knew better than to focus on that thought. He dropped his chin and tried to concentrate on the perfectly cooked eggs on his plate. Using his fork, he hacked into the first yolk and mopped it up with a hunk of griddle cake. The tacky texture of the egg mingled with the sweet flavor of maple syrup. "Mmm, good, Greta," he mumbled, his mouth not quite empty.

Jenny leaned forward and pushed a glass of milk his way.

"Were you able to save the hay?" Ida asked.

Sam had talked with Hank on the phone before turning in last night and he knew the answer, but he gave his foreman a nod to fill them in.

"Yes, ma'am. The pump house is a goner, but the hay is safe and nobody got hurt outside a few scratches."

"You and the boys did real good last night, Hank," Sam told his foreman. "We'll talk later about some bonuses."

Hank pushed off from the door and carried his cup to the sink. "Still a mess of mopping up to do," he said, giving Sam a nod. After shrugging on his western-style jacket, he walked to the door. "See y'all later."

Before Hank could make his exit, a visitor arrived—Donnie Grimaldo. In uniform. Greta offered him coffee, which he accepted. After he sat down, he looked at Sam and said, "You got lucky last night, my friend. Real lucky."

Sam's appetite disappeared. He knew how close it had been. He'd awakened periodically with the smell of fire in his nose and the sensation of heat pressing against his back. The metal siding of the wing walls had felt like a frying pan against his skin.

"Do you know what caused the fire?" Jenny asked. "Hank said he thought it might have been set off by an electrical spark in the pump."

Donnie planted his elbows on the table. "The arson team from Sacramento is on its way down. I'm not an expert in this field, but even I know a setup when I see it." He paused and looked at each person sitting around the table.

Sam grabbed the glass of milk to help dislodge his last bite of egg that had become stuck in his throat.

"How can you tell?" Andi asked.

Sam looked at Jenny. He recognized the whiteness around her lips. Fear. He'd seen it often those final few weeks before Josh died. Now he'd inadvertently brought it back into her life.

You invited her to live with you so you could take care of her, not put her life in jeopardy, he thought.

"...buckets," Donnie was saying.

Sam coughed. "What about buckets?"

Five-gallon buckets weren't an uncommon feature on a farm. Everything from motor oil to disinfectant came in them. Sam discouraged his employees from leaving them lying around, since any vessel that caught moisture could become a breeding ground for mosquitoes, but he didn't remember seeing any near the barn.

"We found some half-melted buckets near the site where the fire began. There appeared to be traces of kerosene in them. We won't know for sure until we get the lab tests, but that's a working guess.''

The four women gave a collective gasp. Sam pushed his plate away and took a sip of coffee. ''Let me get this straight. You're saying someone came on to my property with the express purpose of setting it on fire?'' Sam shook his head. ''Nope. Couldn't happen. The dogs—''

''Whoever set it knows your dogs don't range that far,'' Donnie argued. ''He or she stayed at the boundary of your land. The person started the fire then banked on the wind pushing it to your barn before you could react.''

Sam's sick feeling intensified. He rose. ''Let's talk about this in my office.''

Jenny jumped in. ''I don't think so. We all need to hear what's going on. Donnie, even if someone dumped those buckets of kerosene, what makes you think the barn was the target. Maybe they were just stupid. Or careless.''

The look Donnie gave Sam said he didn't believe that scenario. And neither did Sam.

''Sam, I hate to say this, but somebody tried to burn you out. Or, at the very least, hurt you financially. This wasn't a sophisticated setup, so I'm guessing that it was a spur-of-the-moment thing. Someone trying to get back at you for something.''

Jenny let out a small squeak.

Sam wished they were alone so he could put his arm around her shoulders and reassure her that everything was going to be okay.

He gave Donnie a look he hoped conveyed his displeasure at the fact that Donnie had brought this up in front of Jenny. ''I'll have to see some evidence before I believe it. I don't have any enemies.''

Donnie shrugged his broad shoulders. ''It was arson, Sam. The who, how and why are up to the investigators to determine. But my gut feeling is this was someone with a grudge and a match. If a pro had set it, believe me, the hay would have been a complete loss.''

Sam repressed a shudder. The hay was a valuable item, but it was secondary to the sense of violation he felt. Fire fighting was dangerous business. Someone had deliberately put the California Department of Forestry crew and the men working for Sam in danger. Sam knew they were damn lucky nobody had been seriously hurt.

''But who would do such a thing?'' Jenny asked the question that was on the tip of Sam's tongue. ''Everyone knows how dangerous and unpredictable a range fire can be. If the wind had shifted, it might have doubled back on the town.''

Or headed toward the house, Sam thought, his stomach heaving.

''I don't know, Jen, but we're investigating. And we will find the person who did this,'' Donnie said.

Jenny sat forward, lifting Lara to her shoulder. The baby was starting to fret—no doubt picking up her mother's agitation. Sam started to suggest Jenny take the babies upstairs, when Jenny looked at Donnie and said, ''This doesn't make any sense. Sam can't be a target. He's a great guy. He helps sponsor youth rodeo teams and he opens up the Rocking M for the fund-raiser every year. It just isn't possible.''

Her support warmed Sam from the inside out.

Donnie shrugged. ''Everybody pisses off someone at some time or another. Even Sam,'' he said with a congenial wink. ''Anybody from your past that might want to give you a hard time, Sam?''

''The only person who regularly tells people I'm a

jerk is my mother—and this doesn't seem like Diane's style,'' he said, trying to inject a little humor into the group.

Andi laughed, but Jenny frowned. ''What about those two guys who were fighting the day Ida Jane fell and broke her hip?'' she said, patting Lara's back vigorously. ''The one I saw didn't look very happy about getting fired.''

Donnie pulled a wire notepad from his breast pocket. ''That was Tim Collier, right?''

''Yes.'' Sam frowned. He hated to believe that any of the men who worked here could be that vengeful. ''I suppose it's possible that Tim could be responsible, but it doesn't seem likely. Cowboys come and go all the time. A job is just one of those things you do till you get your stake together for your next go-around. It's not like I blackballed either one of them.''

''He's got a reputation for being a hothead,'' Donnie said. ''Maybe he's vindictive, too.''

Sam sighed. It was possible. Tim was a troubled young man with an arrest or two on his record. Sam had never let something like that stop him from giving a man a chance, but now he couldn't help wondering if Tim was a danger.

''I'll bring him in for questioning,'' Donnie said. ''Until we get some answers, you should be extra careful.''

Sam planned to be. He'd start by making sure his family was safe. ''You're right. That means, Jen, you, Ida and the twins need to move back to town.''

''What?'' Jenny asked.

Donnie rose. ''Guess I'll be going.'' He looked at Andi. ''Andi, do you want to walk me out? I wanted to talk to you about the last town council meeting. There's something going on you aren't going to like. Someone has reintroduced the idea of a by-pass around town.''

''I thought that got shot down years ago,'' Andi responded.

Donnie shrugged. ''Maybe it was only wounded.''

Sam cleared his throat. ''Actually, Donnie, if you don't mind seeing yourself out, Andi could help Jenny pack.'' A residual scratchiness made it that much harder to say what he had to say. He looked at Jenny. ''Just the stuff you need to get by. I'll move the rest later on.''

Her expression went from bemused to incredulous. She looked at Ida first, then her sister. Sam might have smiled at the disbelief he read in her eyes, but he was serious. There was no way he could allow Jenny and the children to live here while the Rocking M was the target of an arsonist.

''Move?'' she repeated slowly, as if the word had more than one syllable.

''Yeah. Back into town where you'll be safe.'' He looked at Ida Jane for support. The older woman's eyes sparkled as if he'd just won a prize.

Momentarily confused by Ida's impish grin, he added, ''Your aunt told me last night your grandfather died in a fire in this very spot.''

''Did I say that?'' Ida asked.

''So what?'' Jenny shrugged.

Sam pushed back his chair and rose. ''So, I'm not about to risk your life or the twins' lives. And we can make arrangements at one of the lodges or a motel for Ida Jane until we can get ramps built at the old bordello.''

His speech done, he picked up his plate and walked to the sink. He noticed Greta slipping out the door just when he could have used some moral support. He was about to call her back, when he felt a tap on his shoulder. He turned to find Jenny a foot away. Her hands were on her hips, and her eyes were blazing. She was obviously pissed off.

"If you want to give me grief about the damn cat," he said, "it'll have to wait. We've gotta get you moved first."

He glanced over Jenny's shoulder to see Ida holding Lara. Andi was bouncing Tucker on her lap; his chubby legs wobbled like a newborn calf's. Sam's heart twisted. He couldn't believe how much the twins had grown in just ten weeks. God, he'd miss not having them here.

"May I speak with you a moment?" Jenny asked, her tone formal and tight. "In your office, perhaps?"

Sam didn't recognize the look in her eye, but it made him feel like a student in her class—a student who'd been caught cheating. "All right. But I really think you should be packing. If we hurry, we might be able to get Donnie to escort you into town."

Jenny turned and looked at Andi, her eyes rolling in obvious disbelief. "Give me a break, Sam. This isn't an old western with bad guys perched on bluffs with rifles. Jeez."

Sam's face heated up. Maybe he was overreacting a little, but that didn't mean Jenny shouldn't return to town. That was nonnegotiable. Period.

He stepped aside to let her lead the way to his office. He'd have given anything to be able to span her trim hips with his hands and spin her around to face him. If things were different, they could sneak a little necking in the hallway. *Wake up, Sam. You're a responsible adult—act like one.*

Jenny opened the door, walked in then closed the door

behind him. She didn't give him time to put the desk between them.

"Let's get one thing straight," she said. "Either I'm a houseguest or I live here. Which is it?"

He blinked, totally unprepared for either her response or her attitude. Without waiting for him to reply, she continued. "What is it with you O'Neal men? Are you throwbacks to some other age? Maybe it's Diane's influence. She was always looking for a man to take care of her, right? So you think all women are like that. Well, here's a tip, Sam. That doesn't work for me. I can take care of myself."

Sam took a step back defensively, but she closed the gap. "We made a deal, Sam. Five years. Now, at the first sign of trouble you're trying to get rid of me."

Temper darkened her eyes to a rusty brown. The sunlight streaming in through the windows highlighted little gold flecks that hinted at passion. "No. Yes," he stammered. "It's for your own good, and the babies'."

She jabbed her finger right below the button at the center of his chest. "Let me tell you what's not good for babies, Sam. Being carted back and forth like so much baggage is not good for babies. We're just getting settled into a routine. Tucker didn't even wake up for a second feeding last night. In another week or two, he'll be off the midnight feeding all together. Do you want to ruin that?"

I like that feeding best, he thought, but shook his head. "No, of course not. But we're a long way from town, Jen. We were lucky last night. What if—"

She interrupted him. "No. *You* were lucky. I heard the whole cat story from Ida Jane, and frankly, I'd send you to detention for a week if you were one of my students. That was a totally unacceptable risk, Sam, but I'm willing to cut you some slack because you're not used to thinking like a married…like a father,'' she amended.

Was she going to say *married man?*

Sam didn't have time to consider her slip. Jenny paced to the far side of the room and stared out the window. The midmorning light added such vibrancy to her hair he ached to touch it.

She'd been in his dreams again—dreams that had moved to a new level of intimacy given their encounter in the shower. That memory made her attitude all the more baffling. Why wasn't she grabbing at the chance to leave? Surely she knew things were bound to come to a head between them if she stayed.

''I don't understand,'' he admitted, walking around his desk to his high-backed chair. He dropped into it and rested his elbows on the desk. ''Why the hell aren't you hightailing it back home? I just don't get it.''

Jenny didn't reply immediately. She knew that Sam meant well. She even sympathized with him to a point, but she was sick and tired of O'Neal men making decisions for her. Josh had picked their town, their friends, when Jenny should get pregnant, who the father would be. True, she'd agreed to everything, but often her capitulation came after relentless lobbying on Josh's part.

The decision to move to the Rocking M had been at Sam's suggestion, but it was Jenny's choice. This was her home—for the next five years, at least, and she wasn't letting some punk with a pack of matches scare her away. The sooner Sam understood that, the better off he'd be.

She left her spot by the window and marched to Sam's desk. He looked so powerful and in charge. His western-style shirt, open at the throat, showed the white edge of an undershirt. Such a cowboy thing, Jenny thought. And why is that the least bit sexy? She couldn't explain why, but it was.

"Jenny," Sam said, his tone patient. "Think about it. That fire was virtually in our backyard." *Our.* He said, *Our.* "If the wind had been stronger, there's no telling where it would have wound up. I'm not willing to take that risk. Not where you and the twins are concerned."

She placed her hands on the desk and leaned on them. She watched as his gaze was drawn to her breasts. His reaction gave her a small, womanly thrill that she couldn't deny. And she liked the feeling, even if it scared her a little. "Well, I am."

He gave his head a shake. "Why? I'm not saying this is forever. Once they catch whoever did it, you can come back."

Could she? Maybe this was Sam's way of getting rid of her. Last night had obviously affected him, too. Sam was a loner, a guy who didn't need a woman in his life. He was probably just as shaken up over the shower incident as she was. She had a feeling that was the real reason he wanted her to leave.

Her heart picked up speed as if she were about to take a leap across a vast abyss. "Listen, Sam, I'm not a coward." She looked him squarely in the eye. "But you are."

He blinked as if she'd hit him on the nose. "What?"

She took a deep breath. "You're having second thoughts about me being here. I can understand that...especially after what happened between us last night."

She hated the way her skin tone always betrayed her feelings. To hide what had to be a flame-red face, she walked to the window again. In the three weeks that she'd been living at the Rocking M, she'd grown to love its solitude, serenity and beauty. She wanted all that it had to offer, including, quite possibly, the man behind the desk.

She wasn't blind to the attraction percolating between them. Maybe fear and loneliness had triggered some of what she was feeling. Maybe it was something more. But that didn't mean she was ready to act on her feelings.

''Jenny, I apologize for last night. It was crazy—*I* was crazy. I felt like I'd cheated death and—''

She turned, suddenly furious. ''Don't say that. Josh always talked like that—as if life was a game and he had an extra ace up his sleeve. But it's not, and he didn't.''

Sam sat back. ''I'm sorry.''

''Are you sorry you kissed me?''

He looked like a man with two choices—neither appealing. ''I would never deliberately do anything to hurt you, Jenny. You're grieving, and I don't want to screw that up. Maybe I was being selfish when I asked you to move here. Maybe I should have given you more time.''

Jenny let out a low squeal of frustration. ''Time,'' she spit. ''Don't talk to me about time, Sam. Josh promised me time—it was the only thing we ever argued about. Every May, he'd tell me, 'This is your summer, Jen. Three months to devote to your writing.' But something would always come up.''

She swallowed against the bitterness in her throat. *If you'd teach summer school, we could pay off the car, Jen, but I promise next summer is all yours,* Josh had said.

''That's how you got me to agree to this move, Sam. You promised me time to mourn, to write. Remember?''

He nodded, his expression grim. "Well, I've used it for both."

She looked at the floor. It wasn't easy to admit that she'd finally put words to paper. Twice that week she'd found herself with a few free minutes on her hands and she'd escaped to the gazebo to enjoy the solitude. And to her surprise, words and thoughts had pressed against her mind until she'd jotted them down.

"Just free verse," she admitted, feeling her blush intensify. "Nothing wonderful, but thoughts. Images. Memories."

She'd come to the conclusion that before she could write a children's book, she needed to write Josh's story—the legacy he'd left behind for the children he would never know. But she couldn't do that if she left this place. Josh was linked to the Rocking M, and somehow, her creativity was centered here, too.

"I need to be here, Sam. You're right about one thing, though. I wasn't ready—emotionally—for what happened in the shower. It's too soon...I owe Josh...I can't...."

She didn't know how to ask for the emotional distance she needed without giving up the routine and peace she craved.

The look on his face told her he took her plea seriously. His singed eyebrows were knitted, his lips pressed together. Andi was right—Sam was a very sexy guy. To distract herself she turned sideways and sat on the desk.

"I suppose we could beef up security," he said gruffly.

Jenny's heart gave a little leap. "I'll volunteer for the night shift," she said, smiling. "I'm up half the night anyway."

His chuckle rumbled in his chest—and echoed in

Jenny's. "I didn't mean you. You have enough to do—Ida, the babies...your book."

Jenny felt her cheeks ignite again. "I've got a long way to go with that."

Sam rose. He leaned forward and put his hands flat on the desk. "You have to start someplace. Might as well be here."

Jenny was close enough to smell his just-showered scent. His damaged eyebrows made her yearn to touch them, but she controlled herself. She'd never tell Sam, but his heroic efforts on behalf of the barn cat touched her deeply. However, since she was the one setting the limits, she had to make sure they both lived up to them.

"Does that mean we can stay?" she asked, hopping off the desk.

"Against my better judgment." He shook his head. "Maybe that talk about your grandfather's death got me spooked."

Suddenly anxious to put this behind them, Jenny walked to the door. "It was a long time ago, Sam. And Ida always told us it was an accident."

She waited for him to join her in the hallway. Shoulder to shoulder they walked toward the rear entrance of the house. The cedar logs still gave an inviting smell of permanence that made her feel safe, just like Sam did.

He had his hand on the doorknob, when he paused. He tilted his head in a way that was pure Sam and asked, "Did you give Josh this much trouble when you were married?"

Jenny bit down on a grin. She liked this man, more than she dared admit. His rare flashes of humor made them all the more precious. "Of course not. I'm a very acquiescent wife." Then she grinned. "Too bad we're just living together."

She batted her eyelashes coquettishly.

Sam's soft hoot made her think of Josh. She missed his playfulness. Suddenly blue, she walked into the kitchen and kept on going, right past her sister, her aunt and her babies.

She stopped when she reached a safe spot around the corner of the living room. Hauling in a deep breath, she fought the pain that suddenly engulfed her. Sam. Josh. Josh. Sam. If anyone had told her she'd be facing this kind of emotional dilemma so soon after Josh's death, she'd have been furious. She loved Josh, she still cried for the future they would never share. But she genuinely liked Sam. And at some level she desired him.

Maybe I should have taken the out he gave me, she thought. *Played it safe.*

Oh, Jenny Perfect, there's no such thing as safe, she heard Josh say. *You know that.*

She closed her eyes against the tears that clustered. Sweet tears for a man who'd played hard and played well but had never played it safe.

ONCE SAM DISCLOSED the verdict to Andi and Ida Jane—she won't budge—he returned to his office to think. Jenny had leveled with him, and he appreciated that. She hadn't said how she felt about him, but she liked what he had to offer. His home. A routine. Time.

It was a start.

As he pictured her finger poking him in the chest, his lips twitched. Damn, he liked her.

Don't kid yourself, buddy, you love her.

Sam heard the words as clearly as if Josh had spoken them aloud. He closed his eyes and tried to feel his brother's spirit, but it was gone—a wisp of his imagination. Somehow he knew Josh wouldn't object to Sam loving Jenny, but at the same time, Sam was certain that he was on the verge of blowing it. Jenny needed more time. If she was determined to stay, he'd let her, but there'd be no repeat of last night's performance.

He stood up abruptly. He needed to talk to Donnie about the investigation. The more he thought about someone deliberately starting that fire, the madder he got. He'd been an active member of the Gold Creek volunteer fire department for years. He knew firsthand what a huge toll range fires extracted on the land and on the firefighters who battled them.

The first thing on his agenda was to find the guy who'd done this. Then he planned to make sure people knew about the dangers of grassland fires. Maybe a public service campaign—a sort of ''Wild Fires Cost You'' kind of thing.

A meaningful challenge was just what he needed. Something to keep him from thinking about Jenny. Or more specifically, about being in love with his grieving sister-in-law.

CHAPTER ELEVEN

JENNY PAUSED beside the open nursery door. She closed her eyes a moment and listened to the sound of Sam chatting with the twins, who, at four months, loved to talk. Both babies were making cooing sounds and smiling, even laughing when tickled. She loved every single moment with them and could barely keep up with the changes, which seemed to happen hourly.

She smiled as she caught bits and pieces of Sam's one-sided monologue. "…traffic was abominable… maybe they'll have flying cars by the time you two learn how to drive…saw the Washington Monument…take you there someday…breathe history so you don't have to study it…"

He'd returned home a few hours earlier after a meeting in Washington, D.C., with the National Park Service. Since starting his wildfire awareness efforts six weeks earlier, Sam had traveled to Wyoming, Colorado and, now, the capital. He'd also met with a nonprofit group about sponsoring a publicity campaign before next year's fire season.

Jenny was proud of how much Sam had accomplished, but she was glad to have him home. Although he was seldom gone more than two or three days at a time, Jenny missed him.

He'd returned from D.C. a day ahead of schedule at her behest. She'd wanted him to attend Andi's Christmas

Open House at the Old Bordello Antique Shop and Coffee Parlor this evening. The coffee idea was yet another attempt to save their great-aunt's business. Since attention from the ''haunted bordello'' brouhaha had died down, Andi hoped she might increase traffic and profits by selling fancy coffees in the building's front parlor.

''This town needs a place where you can get a good latte,'' she'd explained to Ida Jane, Jenny and Sam at their very quiet Thanksgiving dinner. How she'd pulled off the conversion so fast was pure, ex-marine determination, and something called a grandfather clause. Apparently Ida's father had operated a diner in the front parlor years ago, which allowed Andi to expedite the application with certain upgrades to meet new health codes.

Jenny looked down at her floor-length black velvet skirt and ivory satin blouse. Not exactly sexy, but elegant, she thought. Andi had been critical of Jenny's choice. ''How are you going to entice Sam with an old-lady outfit like that?'' she'd asked.

An hour later, Kristin had phoned to suggest something less ''teacherish.'' ''How about a short skirt with your red boots and that sparkly sweater?'' *Josh's favorite.*

''This isn't a date,'' Jenny had argued. ''Sam's just being supportive of Andi.''

''Oh, right. He flew across the continent for a cup of Andi's espresso. That's it. I'm sure it's not because he misses you and is waiting patiently for you to admit that you're interested in him, too.''

I'm not! she'd wanted to yell. But it would have been a lie, so she took the high road.

''He also came back because his mother is in town,

and he needs to prepare himself for Christmas with the whole family.''

''Uh-huh.''

Jenny had ignored her sister's sarcasm. Sam was an astute man. He'd sensed that Jenny needed time alone with her grief, her confusion, her guilt. He'd given her that by taking on an ambitious project that kept him so busy their paths barely crossed—except when the twins were involved. He was at her side when Lara spiked a fever—a result of an ear infection. He'd accompanied the three of them to the pediatrician for immunizations.

And although Jenny missed having other times with him, she'd kept busy, too. She had something she couldn't wait to show him. She switched the manila folder from her right hand to the left and walked into the room.

''Hi, there. You must have slipped in while I was helping Ida dress. I'm glad to see you're home safely.''

Sam stood upright from the table where he was changing Tucker's diaper. Keeping one hand on the wiggly baby's tummy, he looked over his shoulder.

Jenny felt the look he gave her clear down to her toes.

''You look very beautiful,'' he said. His gaze went to her hair, which she'd arranged in an upsweep. She'd liked the old-fashioned style, but her neck felt exposed, especially when his gaze settled on the antique choker Josh had given her the Christmas before last.

Sam picked up Tucker, whose red flannel sleeper resembled long johns. Sam held the baby's chubby fist to his lips and pretended to give a wolf whistle.

''Are you teaching him sexist behavior?'' she teased.

''You're never too young to appreciate beauty,'' Sam said, his gaze following Jenny as she walked toward him.

Swallowing the sudden moisture in her mouth, she lifted her chin. ''You look pretty good yourself. How'd you manage a shower so fast?''

''I tried to get back in time for a haircut, but Mel's Barbershop was closed when I got to town,'' Sam said, lifting Tucker overhead in a way that made the little boy squeal with delight.

Jenny's heart constricted at the sound. She loved to watch Sam interact with the children. He was a natural parent, and the twins loved him. He needed to be around more; maybe it was time to talk about what was between them.

After the holidays. After Diane leaves.

''Beulah Jensen called Ida Jane and told her Mel had emergency gallbladder surgery,'' she said. ''He was giving Ron Campbell a crew cut and suddenly collapsed in pain. You know Ron. Music teacher at the high school, choir director at the Methodist church. A nice guy, but no muscle man by any means. Still, according to Beulah, he carried Mel—who's a good two hundred eighty pounds—to his car and drove him to the hospital.''

Sam looked impressed. ''That's what I love about this town. People aren't afraid to get involved. You wouldn't believe the apathy I've encountered since I started this campaign. It's disheartening.''

He walked to the crib where Lara was attempting to push herself up on her elbows, her bottom bouncing up and down. Sam scooped up his little daughter with his free hand. ''Do we have time for a story?''

Jenny's fingers clutched the folder behind her back so tightly she was sure there'd be imprints on the paper inside. ''We have half an hour. Ida would like to see the twins before we go, then Greta's going to put them to bed.''

He gave her a puzzled look. ''What's wrong?''

''Nothing.''

''Jenny.''

She took a deep breath and produced the folder. ''I have this...um, it's nothing important. You can look at it tomorrow.''

''Why don't I look at it right now?''

Her heart started to race. ''No. That's okay. Tomorrow will be fine.''

His chin dropped, and he gave her a look that told her he didn't believe her. She wished now she'd left the damn pages in her notebook where they belonged. She should have waited, but the story had been done for days, and it was killing her not to share it with someone. *All right, with Sam.*

He nodded toward the rocking chair in the alcove. ''You rock. I'll read.''

With a little maneuvering, the kind that involved arms brushing breasts and shoulders touching chests, they exchanged twins for folder. Jenny was practically breathless after the encounter, but Sam seemed to handle it with ease. Tucker immediately reached for the beads on her necklace and tried to pull himself close enough to taste them.

''Read fast,'' Jenny said in a strangled voice.

Smiling, Sam handed his son a purple frog rattle that Tucker waved, delighting in the sound it made.

Sitting on the nearby window seat, Sam opened the folder. ''What is it? Tax stuff?''

Jenny shook her head. Her heart was beating so quickly she felt a little light-headed. ''It's for a children's book. The sketches are really rough. The text is probably too adult.'' Her voice rose and picked up speed; she forced herself to take a breath. ''I'm sure there's no market for this kind of thing, but we can always give it to the twins. Someday.''

''This is your work? You wrote this?'' His tone was hushed with awe. ''And you're letting *me* read it?''

''You really don't need to read it now. It can wait till we get back,'' she said, stalling. What if he hated it?

Sam sat forward, cradling the open manila folder between his hands like a hymnal. Two sheets of heavy white watercolor paper were exposed. In the overhead light, the sketches looked stark and crude, the block printing childish. Jenny fought the urge to snatch it back.

''*The Green Cowboy Hat* by Jennifer Sullivan O'Neal,'' he read aloud.

Jenny's face filled with heat. ''It's sort of free verse mixed with prose. A cross between Robert Frost and Dr. Seuss,'' she said, forcing a laugh.

''Two of my favorites.'' His earnest smile made the butterflies in her stomach stop flitting about. ''Shall I read it aloud?''

''God, no!'' she exclaimed so loudly Tucker dropped his rattle and started to cry. ''Oops. Sorry, sweetie,'' she said.

Lara, picking up on her brother's woes, joined in, her wails escalating in volume.

Sam closed the folder and rose. He set the folder on the cushion then took Lara from Jenny. He made soothing sounds that distracted the baby from her impassioned sobs.

''Is someone hurting my little angels?'' Greta asked, standing in the doorway.

''Just sympathy cries,'' Sam said, brushing away his daughter's tears with his thumb. ''I think these two are tired.''

He looked at Jenny. ''Why don't we take them downstairs for good-night kisses then let Greta give them their bottles.''

Jenny nodded and rose. This wasn't exactly the way she'd planned his return, but having children required flexible scheduling.

Ten minutes later, he helped her into her wool coat, then handed her the keys to the van. ''Can you walk Ida Jane out? I forgot something.''

He charged upstairs, his western-style raincoat flapping against his calves. She watched for a second, struck by how handsome and fit he was. When she felt Ida Jane's gaze on her, she blushed and took her aunt's arm. ''Are you ready? This will be the first time you've been to the bordello since your accident, isn't it? I hope you're prepared for a few changes. Andi's been a busy little beaver.''

Andi had tried to keep Ida informed, but Jenny wasn't sure how much her aunt had taken in. Despite the weekly visits from her Garden Club friends, Ida seemed disinterested in what was happening in Gold Creek or the changes Andi was making to her beloved bordello.

''Yes. Yes. I know. The ice-cream parlor. Won't that be tasty,'' she said, wrapping both hands around Jenny's forearm.

Jenny fought a grimace. ''She's selling espresso and cappuccino, Auntie. Those are kinds of coffee. Andi looked into selling iced drinks, but she's decided to hold off until after the holidays.''

''Oh, yes, I forgot.''

They slowly walked down the well-lit ramp to the van. Jenny had already stowed Ida's cane and their purses in the back of the vehicle. Today was the winter solstice, the first day of winter and the shortest day of the year. The chilly temperature reflected the light smattering of snow they'd received last night.

Sam caught up with them just as Jenny opened the sliding door to the back seat. "Let me help," he said. His closeness, the wonderful woodsy smell of his cologne, made her almost drop the keys. "Miss Ida, would you mind riding in front with Jenny? I have something important I'd like to read on the way in."

"Sam," Jenny hissed. She hadn't mentioned her story to either her aunt or her sisters. "Can't it wait?"

"Nope. I don't think so." His face was shadowed, but his tone was dead serious.

The trip to town was the longest of her life, Jenny decided as the lights of Gold Creek, decorated for the holidays, came into view.

"Doesn't it look pretty?" Ida Jane exclaimed. "I just love this town at Christmas. Did somebody put up my lights? I meant to do it, but I can't remember if I did."

The panic in her voice made Jenny reach out and squeeze her hand. "Andi hung them, dear. The old bordello looks like a fairy palace."

Ida Jane let out a long sigh. "Oh, good. I don't want people to think we lack holiday spirit."

Jenny glanced into the rearview mirror. Were those tears on Sam's cheeks or a trick of the van's lighting?

Ida Jane suddenly yanked on the steering wheel. "Jenny girl, I'd just as soon get there in one piece, if you don't mind."

Stricken with chagrin, Jenny gripped the wheel with sweaty palms and focused on her driving. As she turned into the parking lot, she barely noticed the multitudes of tiny white lights that encircled the turret, outlined every gable end and wrapped around the porch. The pine in the front yard was gaily festooned with colored bulbs and ornaments crafted from old pie tins.

"Oh, my, it's just lovely," Ida Jane exclaimed.

Jenny pulled to a stop in front of a sign marked Ida Jane Montgomery ONLY. She looked behind her and saw Sam sitting motionless, his face turned toward the window. Jenny exchanged a look with Ida then got out and hurried around to help her aunt.

"Is he okay?" Ida asked when they were standing.

Jenny closed the door. "I think so. Probably just tired."

Jenny quickly fetched Ida's cane from the rear compartment then walked her to the steps. Impatient to hear Sam's impression of her story, Jenny hurried her aunt along.

"What was he reading?" Ida asked.

Jenny gulped. "Something I wrote. About Josh."

Ida moved along the uneven concrete with exaggerated care. "Sam's opinion matters to you, doesn't it?"

"Of course. He's Josh's brother."

Ida stopped at the foot of the steps. Her mink coat, an antique with three or four bald spots where Jenny and her sisters had gotten carried away grooming it when they'd played dress-up, smelled of cedar and White Shoulders perfume. "He's also...Sam," she said to her niece.

Before Jenny could reply, a threesome—Linda McCloskey and her son, Bart, a local roofing contractor, and his wife—joined them. After a few seconds of pleasantries, Bart gallantly offered Ida Jane his elbow, and the four ascended the steps and disappeared inside.

Inviting smells of coffee and pine lingered in the air, and the faint sound of Christmas carols and laughter beckoned, but Jenny turned on the heel of her sensible black pumps and dashed to the van.

She yanked open the sliding door and hopped inside, closing the door against the chilly night air. She tugged the lapels of her wool coat together; her fingers felt numb, but she barely noticed the discomfort.

Sam was sitting with his back against the window, legs stretched on the rear bench seat.

"Well?" she asked, sitting sideways in the middle seat.

He looked at her. His expression somber. "You said not to read this aloud, but you were wrong. It deserves to be read aloud. It's wonderful."

Tears rushed to her eyes. "Really?"

He shifted position, sitting forward so Jenny could see the page as he read.

"*'Josh was not a cowboy, but he loved his big brother, Sam, who was one. Every spring Josh would ride with the other cowboys to round up the cattle. He couldn't ride as well as the others, and sometimes he'd fall behind and get lost, so Sam bought him a special hat—a green cowboy hat. This made Josh easier to spot.*

Josh loved his hat even though it was a little tight.

He wore it to bed.

His wife was not amused.

This was not a good thing, but it wasn't bad, either.' "

Sam smiled and turned to the second page.

"*'One day, Josh got sick. Real sick. The doctors told him he had cancer. He'd had the same thing once before when he was a little boy, and he thought he would get well with medicine. He took the medicine, but it made him too weak to chase cows. He still wore the green hat, though, when he sat on the fence and watched Sam and the other cowboys round up the herd.*

The medicine made Josh's hair fall out.

His hat fit better.

This was a good thing, but it wasn't perfect.'"

Sam took a deep breath. Jenny knew he was remembering all the chemo and radiation treatments. All the questions. The fear of not knowing what would happen next. Would Josh rally? Would the next round of chemo send him into remission? Would herbs help keep food in his stomach? Would he live long enough to see the twins?

Sam turned the page. Jenny saw him tilt his head to study her drawings. His lips flickered, and she knew which image he was looking at—Josh playing poker with four aces stuck in the band of his green hat.

Sam cleared his throat then started again.

"'*As sometimes happens, the medicine didn't work. The doctors couldn't think of anything else to do to help Josh's body fight the disease. And Josh was getting very tired of fighting, anyway. He wanted to rest and laugh and remember all the good times in his life. His friends dropped by to play cards, and he always won. His family came to see him. Sam brought Josh's favorite horse to the house. Some nice nurses made Josh very comfortable in a special bed where he could watch the birds and hear the sound of the wind in the trees.*

Josh died early one morning when the dew was on the grass, so you could see his soul's footprints as he left.

His family cried. Sam cried. The other cowboys cried, too.

But Josh wasn't in pain anymore.

That was a good thing, but it was hard to say goodbye.'"

When he lifted his chin, Jenny saw tears. He blinked

them away before they could fall, but she saw them. After a moment, he turned the page.

"*'Time passed, as time does. The green hat sat in a closet, getting dusty. But one day, a little boy named Tucker found it. He put it on and it fit just right. Like it had been made for him. He ran to his cowboy daddy and said, "Look what I found. Can I have it?" Sam smiled and told him, "It belonged to a special person. He was the best cowboy of all. He wore this green hat so everyone could see him doing his job. His name was Josh, and he was my brother."*

Tucker wore the hat with pride.

He wore it to bed.

His mother was not amused.

But Josh's spirit looked down from above and smiled.

This was a good thing. A very good thing.'"

Sam passed his hand across his face, then closed the folder. "I don't have the right words, Jenny," he said gruffly. "It's Josh. His spirit. The love he had for us. Thank you."

Jenny couldn't swallow. She felt slightly faint. "Do you really think so? Really?"

He nodded. "I'd never lie to you, Jen. About anything. Especially something as important as this."

His empathy gave her the courage to say, "It came to me right after you left for D.C. As you were driving away, I had this image of Josh last year at the St. Patrick's Day party. Sitting on the fence wearing that silly green hat. You were mad at him, remember?"

"I thought he was going to wear himself out. I wanted to cancel the party, and he wouldn't let me."

Jenny reached across the distance to touch his shoulder. "That wasn't Josh's style. He loved life, Sam. That's what I wanted to show in this story."

She'd never forget the feeling that had come to her after writing these words. She'd wept. Not out of grief, but from a sense that finally everything was going to be okay.

"I'm glad you liked it."

He looked as though he had something say, but before he could speak, there was a knock, then the door slid open. "Jenny? Are you okay?"

Diane.

Sam let out a harsh sigh and lunged to his feet, hunched slightly to exit the car. "I'll be inside. I'm suddenly dying for a cup of coffee." Once he was standing, he adjusted his coat then said, "Hello, Diane. Merry Christmas." Then he turned and walked away.

Jenny glanced furtively toward where he'd been sitting, hoping he hadn't left the folder behind. She wasn't ready to share her story with the world—especially not with Josh's mother. The seat was empty.

"Hi, Diane. Sam and I were catching up. He just got back and there hasn't been time to fill him in on all the holiday plans."

Diane and Gordon had arrived three days earlier for a two-week stay. They'd missed Thanksgiving because of engine trouble with their motor home, which they'd finally sold. Since Jenny had been too busy to do anything about renting her house, she'd gladly handed the key to Gordon and Diane for their visit.

"Did you tell him we'll be at the ranch on Christmas morning?"

"Of course. Everyone wants to be there for the twins' first Christmas."

Diane moved aside to let Jenny out. "I would have preferred you to come to Santa Barbara. The weather's so much nicer, but I know traveling is hard on Ida Jane.

She looks marvelous, by the way. She's inside flirting with my husband.''

Jenny laughed. ''Then we'd better go rescue him.''

''Or her. Ever since we got here, Gordon has become fixated on the old bordello's history. He and Andi have been poring over the old photos. They're both talking about historical preservation.'' She made a clucking sound. ''As if the town needs to celebrate *that* aspect of its past.''

Jenny hid her smile. She knew that some of the town matrons had from time to time begged Ida Jane to change the name of her antique shop, but Ida had flatly refused.

''Well, it *was* a house of ill-repute at one time, Diane. That's public record. The red light above the old bordello sign used to hang beside the door. I think it makes us unique.''

''Perhaps,'' Diane said, following Jenny up the steps. They entered the hall together. The low hum of voices filtered through the door leading to the store. Jenny felt a twinge of sadness as she looked toward the kitchen.

''So,'' Diane said, hanging her coat on the old-fashioned hall tree, ''when are you coming to Santa Barbara? I'm dying to show off those babies to all my friends.''

''Possibly Easter. We can't do it before then because we have the St. Paddy's Day party to plan.''

Diane's forehead creased. Her lips pursed in a flat line. ''You're doing that? Without Josh?''

''Diane, everything I do is without Josh.'' Jenny didn't mean to be hurtful, but she was losing patience with her mother-in-law's effort to thrust Josh into the center of every conversation.

''Besides,'' she quickly added, ''Josh would want us to do it. He loved to party.''

Jenny took off her coat and hung it on top of Sam's. She happened to see a corner of the folder sticking out of his sleeve and made sure her coat covered it.

''Well, you knew him best,'' Diane said, studying her image in the ornate beveled mirror hanging opposite the door.

Jenny touched up her lipstick, then put the tube in her pocket. Lately, she'd been wondering just how well she had known Josh. They'd come of age together, but there were questions Jenny didn't have answers to. Like what Josh would think about her feelings for Sam.

She touched the necklace at her throat, then opened the etched glass door that separated the family quarters from the store. ''We should go inside. My sisters are going to wonder what happened to me.''

Suddenly, she wished Andi had decided to open a bar instead of a coffee parlor. She could really use a drink.

SAM OBSERVED the action from a secluded spot behind a potted palm. The dusty fronds were adorned with tiny twinkle lights like the ones on every pinnacle and cornice of the bordello's roofline. He liked the festive quality it gave the place.

He knew that some townsfolk resented the idea of celebrating the bordello's sinful past, but they were in the minority. Unfortunately, the vocal contingent was headed by Gloria Harrison Hughes, author of ''Glory's World.'' Gloria considered herself the moral adjutant of Gold Creek. Fortunately, most people considered her a narrow-minded gossip.

''Gloria's had it in for the triplets ever since—according to Gloria—Kristin led her son astray in high school,'' Josh had confided last summer when Sam had read him something spiteful from the amazingly biased column. ''Don't you remember the girls' eighteenth birthday party? Donnie and Tyler Harrison got in a big fight. Ty left town a short while later and didn't graduate with his class.''

Sam vaguely recalled the incident.

''Ever since then, 'Glory's World' has been very snippy toward Ida and the girls,'' Josh had said indignantly. ''If I felt stronger, I'd give that old witch a piece of my mind.''

Unfortunately, by then, Josh barely had enough energy to walk to the bathroom.

Sam shook off the troubling memory when he spotted Jenny enter the room with his mother following. The two looked somber, but Jenny's pensive frown changed to a smile the moment she made eye contact with him. Sam's heart turned over in his chest.

She was so beautiful. And talented. He'd never guessed she was such a sensitive, gifted writer. Her words had touched him deeply.

''Nice party, isn't it?'' a voice asked beside him.

Sam glanced down and saw Ida Jane smiling up at him. Thanks to Jenny's gentle prodding to do her daily exercises, Ida was showing amazing improvement. ''Has anyone told you how lovely you look tonight, Miss Ida?''

Ida batted his arm with the paper menu Andi was passing out. ''Save all that sweet talk for Jenny. She's the one who's been pining for you.'' Her words made Sam's heart jump—particularly when she added, '''Bout time you got home.''

''D.C. was my last stop. The rest is up to the people.''

Ida looked at him shrewdly. ''It always was, Sam.

You can't legislate against human perversity. There will always be that careless fellow who tosses a cigarette out the window. But, at least Donnie caught the fellow who set your field on fire.''

Sam nodded. Tim Collier had been arrested in Reno. He'd admitted starting the blaze, but claimed he was drunk at the time. Drunk and mad at Sam for firing him. Sam wished Tim's arrest had been enough to ease his fears but he still worried every time he was away from home overnight. No one had been apprehended in the other cases.

''May I get you a refill?'' he asked, lifting his cup.

Ida Jane shook her head. ''No, thank you. I've had enough caffeine to keep me awake till Christmas.''

The word reminded Sam that in three days he'd be entertaining his mother and Gordon and Jenny's family at his home for the first time since he'd bought the place. He was scared spitless.

''Are you looking forward to the festivities?'' she asked, as if reading his mind.

''I'm anxious to see how the twins react to all the hoopla,'' he told her truthfully. ''I've bought them way too much junk. Jenny's going to shoot me.''

She chuckled. ''You can't help it. You're a generous man. Always have been.''

Something about the twinkle in her eye made him wonder what she was getting at. ''Not really. I just made the mistake of going into FAO Schwarz when I was in San Francisco.''

She gave him a look. ''I was referring to the bonus you gave Hank. Greta told me about it. Quite magnanimous. They're planning a cruise to Alaska next summer.''

Sam took a sip of the powerfully fragrant coffee. ''I

learned a long time ago you pay for what you get—one way or another.'' Because that came off sounding a bit harsh, he added, ''They've earned every dime. Hank helped tremendously with the fire and he's practically had to run the place single-handedly with me gone so much, and Greta is a huge help with the twins.''

Ida nodded. ''Some men would make Jenny hire a sitter when she's doing her writing. Your brother would have.''

Sam frowned. ''I beg your pardon?''

Ida shrugged. ''Don't get me wrong. I loved Josh as much as anyone, but he wasn't terribly supportive of Jenny's dreams. In fact, he was a little jealous of them.''

Her words bothered Sam, but she went on before he could say anything. ''You may not believe me, but it's true. Ask Jenny. Why do you think she's never written anything before now—when she's so busy with a crippled old aunt and two babies.''

Sam didn't know the answer to that, but he was curious to find out. ''Maybe she just didn't have the right space.''

Ida smiled. ''You mean like your office?''

''Excuse me?'' *Jenny works in my office?*

''It's her favorite spot,'' Ida said offhandedly. ''I see her go past my room after the twins are asleep. She uses that walkie-talkie thing of yours to listen for them.''

The baby monitor. But it didn't answer the question why Jenny would choose to work in such functional surroundings. ''Why my office?'' he wondered out loud. ''Oh, to use the computer, I bet.''

Ida made a scoffing sound. ''To be close to you.''

Sam choked on his coffee and doubled over coughing. Ida shook her head. ''Men. You can't help but love 'em, but, Lord, I've known dogs that had a better understanding of the human heart.''

Sam straightened and scanned the room. This wasn't a conversation he wanted his mother to overhear. He knew how she would react if she found out about Sam's feelings for Jenny. He spotted Diane standing with Jenny talking to a group of women.

''Jenny looks good, doesn't she?'' Ida Jane said, apparently drawing her own conclusion about the object of his focus. ''Your mother certainly missed the mark this time.''

Sam turned his chin. ''What do you mean?''

''Diane visited me when I was getting my hip fixed. She wanted me to talk Jenny out of moving to the ranch. Told me Jenny wouldn't last a month in that kind of isolation. I told her, 'Hogwash.' My sister wasn't made for ranch life. And Josh wouldn't have been happy there for long, either, but Jenny's more like me. We don't need whole bunches of people to be happy. Just the few we really care about.''

Her broad hint was almost enough to make Sam blush. ''Miss Ida, are you trying to play matchmaker?''

''Somebody should,'' she muttered.

Sam leaned down and kissed her cheek. She startled, then batted him with her menu again. ''Save that for my niece. She's the one who needs kissing.''

Sam wished that were true, but he knew better—especially after reading the story she'd written about Josh. Jenny was a long way from over Josh. Despite Ida Jane's attempt to play Cupid, Sam needed to keep his distance from Jenny. Especially with his eagle-eyed mother in the room.

AFTER A QUICK CALL to check on the twins, Jenny wandered through the house that had been her home for so many years. It smelled of furniture polish, mildew, coffee and Christmas potpourri. She'd missed the place, but it was no longer home. Neither was the house she'd shared with Josh.

She'd stopped by earlier in the week to make sure the furnace was running, and she'd been struck by how empty it felt even though Gordon and Diane were staying there. In truth, Jenny felt closer to Josh when she was sitting in Sam's office than she did wandering through the rooms of their old home.

Maybe, she thought, *he moved with us. He'll always be a part of our lives, no matter where we live.*

In no hurry to return to the party, Jenny decided to check out the changes Andi had completed on the second floor. To her left were the two large rooms that faced the street. She and her sisters had shared one room as a bedroom; the other was for studying, talking on the phone and painting their nails. Ida had called it their playroom when they were little. It was where Jenny had lost her virginity to Josh—on a bed of beanbag chairs, with a Sting song playing on the radio.

Jenny poked her head inside. Empty except for some boxes. Andi had been lobbying Kristin to move home and set up shop there, but Kris refused to consider it.

''Oh, sure, just what one needs to achieve a peaceful, therapeutic environment—the threat of a ghost popping up during the massage,'' she'd argued the last time she'd visited.

Jenny didn't understand why her sister was so resistant to moving back to Gold Creek, but Kris insisted this wasn't the place for her. She tried to visit Ida Jane every couple of weeks but seldom stayed longer than a day—two at the most.

Jenny closed the door and backtracked down the long hallway that led to the six remaining bedrooms. Rooms that had at one time accommodated the ladies of the evening, then later housed railroad workers and miners.

Just last week, Jenny and Ida Jane had talked about Andi's advertising campaign. Sadly, interest in the ghost story had died out not long after it was introduced, but Andi hadn't given up on the idea. She was in the process of designing an old bordello Web site, which would include a "ghostly" apparition displaying the items up for sale.

Jenny hated to think what Gloria Hughes would make of it. If rumors were correct, the columnist was anxious to put the old bordello out of business so her hotshot builder son could buy the land.

"She wants the old bordello closed and the building torn down to make way for some civic center Tyler Harrison is promoting," Andi had explained just minutes earlier to Jenny and her teacher friends. Andi had started attending meetings of the Gold Creek Chamber of Commerce in their aunt's absence.

Jenny knew Gloria still harbored a grudge against the Sullivan sisters, but she couldn't believe the woman would go so far as to have the old place bulldozed. It was a historical landmark, for heaven's sake.

Sighing, Jenny wandered along, listening to the cheerful sounds coming from the first floor. The volume increased momentarily then faded. Someone had opened the door leading to the living quarters. She heard footsteps ascending the stairs.

Jenny put on her "public" face, as Josh called it. He alone knew that she played the role of gracious hostess under duress. He'd been the social one in the family; she'd gone along with it because she'd known it made him happy to entertain people, throw dinner parties and get together with friends. But secretly, she was happiest when they were alone.

Maybe that was one reason she felt so comfortable living at the ranch. Visitors were few and far between. The Rocking M's employee Christmas party would be her first attempt at entertaining since August, but the ever-efficient Greta seemed to have that under control.

She heard voices, male and female. Suddenly feeling guilty about avoiding the party, she hurried toward the stairs. Two people were almost at the top, apparently caught up in a serious conversation, because neither of them noticed Jenny.

Sam and Kristin.

Sam looked up as if sensing her presence. His smile almost robbed her of breath. "There you are. Kristin was leaving and wanted to tell you goodbye."

Jenny wasn't sure she believed that explanation, but before she could say anything, Kristin cleared the three steps between them and gave Jenny a hug.

"We haven't talked all evening, but I heard there's a storm coming and I don't want to get stuck in Redding and not be able to get over the pass."

"Why don't you stay? I still don't understand why you aren't going to be here for the twins' first Christmas. You were with us in the delivery room. You're a part of their lives."

Kristin's eyes filled with dismay and…guilt, but the emotions were replaced by stubbornness. "I have prior commitments, Jen. People who need me more than you do. I can't let them down."

Jenny looked at Sam for help but he moved his shoulders as if he didn't understand her reasoning, either. "I invited her to come to the ranch Christmas party. We have a new employee. Lars dropped him off last week. He's a good-looking guy. Probably single.''

Jenny and Kristin exchanged a look. ''*Probably?*''

''Lars said he found him wandering around up near the mine. Apparently the guy suffered a head injury in a motorcycle accident during the big storm that came through last month. Doesn't seem to remember much about his past. Lars named him Harley after the emblem on his jacket. He let him recuperate in his cabin at the Blue Lupine for a few weeks, but you know how suspicious Lars is.''

Jenny had visited Lars's old mine once years before with Josh. She knew the crusty old miner's reputation as a pot-smoking hermit. Sam was practically his only friend.

Kristin made an impatient gesture. ''Well, thanks for the attempted matchmaking, Sam, but you'll have to introduce him to Andi. Or Jenny, for that matter. I'm not in the market for a man.''

''Me neither,'' Jenny said.

Sam flinched—just barely, but Jenny noticed. She'd been referring to the new man. But she'd spoken the truth. *Hadn't she?* She wasn't in the market for *any* man. To hide her confusion, she stepped down to hug her sister goodbye. ''Drive safely. Especially if there's a storm coming.''

Kristin squeezed her fiercely. ''I will. Give Tucker and Lara a big kiss for me. 'Night, Sam. Merry Christmas, and remember what I told you.''

She turned and dashed down the stairs, slipping into the antique store a second later. Jenny took a breath, deliberating on what to do next. Go back to the party or stay here. With Sam. Alone.

''What did she tell you?''

Even in the dim light, she spotted the discomfort on his face. "I'd rather not say."

"Why? Was it about me?"

"In a way."

She stepped to stand directly in front of him, bringing them eye to eye. "I hate secrets. Tell me."

"She said you weren't going to need a year to mourn."

A blush heated her cheeks. "Really? Is that all?"

He shook his head, then took a breath before adding, "She said if I waited too long, you'd get scared and run away."

Her sister knew her well. She was probably right, but that didn't make Jenny any less furious. "I'm going to kill her."

"No, you're not. You love her," Sam said, touching her cheek with the back of his hand. "Like I love…Josh."

Had he meant to say *Jenny?* She didn't ask. Instead, she kissed him. And Sam responded as though he'd been kissing her all his life. He tilted his head and started to deepen the kiss, but she stopped him. "This is a very public hallway."

"And you're worried about what people will say."

Jenny was embarrassed to admit that she cared about public opinion, but she did.

"Would it make a difference if I told you we have a perfectly good excuse?" he asked, drawing her hand to his lips. His lips kissed her fingers.

"We do?"

"Look up. Your sister went crazy with mistletoe."

Jenny glanced up. Sure enough, hanging from the old-fashioned light fixture was a straggly clump of mistletoe adorned with a red ribbon. Laughter bubbled up from deep inside.

"You're as bad as Josh," she said, but the words seemed to come from a long way off. The light quivered and suddenly Josh's shimmering image superimposed itself over Sam's body.

"Jenny?" Sam said.

His voice sounded as if he were speaking through a block of ice. Which made sense, because the hallway had suddenly turned cold. Deathly cold.

Panic flooded her veins. A blinding fear possessed her. Without conscious thought, she struck out at the image that didn't belong there.

"No," she cried. "You're dead. Leave me alone."

One minute Sam was standing in front of her; the next he was gone. So was the vision of Josh. All that remained was an odd groaning sound.

Dizzy, Jenny grabbed the handrail until the vertigo passed. She looked down and spotted Sam sprawled at the base of the staircase. Jenny let out a terrified scream. "No. Sam." *What have I done?*

CHAPTER TWELVE

SAM DIDN'T MOVE for a good four or five seconds. *What the hell happened?* One minute he was kissing Jenny, the next he was cartwheeling down the stairs.

Jenny pushed me.

Thank God for years of stunt work, he thought. A fall like that could have broken something. Bad enough his pride was in pieces. At least nobody had seen it happen, he thought, opening his eyes.

The angles of the walls in the dim hallway shifted two or three times before finally coming into focus. He was about to move, when a piercing scream made him freeze. Almost simultaneously, the sound of footsteps snapped on the staircase beside his cheek. Rolling his eyes as far back as possible without lifting his chin, he saw Jenny flying down the stairs, her long skirt flowing.

A door opened somewhere behind him. ''Good heavens,'' a voice said from the opposite direction. ''What happened?''

Sam slowly turned his head. *Neck seems fine,* he silently gauged.

Warren Jones, Sam's tax accountant, stood frozen in the doorway leading to the antique shop.

''Sam, Sam, are you okay?'' Jenny cried, dropping to her knees beside him. Her hands skittered over him, sending shock waves in all directions. ''I'm so sorry. I didn't mean to...I don't know why... God, tell me you're all right.''

Her plea fell like sparkling drops of honey on Sam's ear. *She cares.*

''Call 911,'' she ordered Warren.

Sam pointed at the hapless man. ''Do and you'll regret it,'' Sam threatened. He started to sit up, but Jenny pressed both hands flat against his chest, rendering Sam immobile. ''Don't move. You could have a neck injury.''

''I'm fine, Jen.''

''You don't look fine.'' She ran the tips of her fingers down his torso then his legs as if checking for broken bones. His response was the kind that would have proved to anyone looking that he was healthy—and horny.

''Jennifer. Stop it. I'm fine.''

He rolled to his side. Twinges zinged him from hip to lower back. Apparently his grimace showed.

''Is it your back?'' She slid her fingers beneath his shirt at the small of his back and gently probed his spine. Her touch was agony, but not for the reason she assumed.

''Believe me. Nothing's broken,'' he muttered through clenched teeth. ''Can we go home now?''

Suddenly the door flew open, and a dozen people poured into the tiny anteroom.

''What happened?'' a familiar voice asked. ''Sam, you okay, bud?''

Donnie. Sam had never been as glad to see his old friend. ''Just peachy,'' Sam said, pushing into a sitting position. He gingerly rubbed a tender spot on his elbow. He must have clipped the banister on his way down. ''I lost my footing and fell.''

Jenny made a squeaky sound. ''He's lying. I pushed him.''

''No, she didn't. I slipped,'' Sam stressed.

Jenny's gaze met his, and through her tears he could read her confusion.

Before either of them could say anything more, the crowd parted to let Diane and Gordon past. Donnie backed away. ''I'll see if I can catch Kristin before she leaves.''

Sam wasn't sure he understood the reasoning behind that, but maybe a good masseuse could help.

''How'd this happen? Were you feeling dizzy before you fell?'' Gordon asked, his tone professional.

''He didn't—'' Jenny started.

Desperate to prevent a second impassioned confession, Sam said the first thing that came to mind. ''There's a board loose on the stairs. It made me lose my balance.''

The crowd gave a collective gasp and murmurs started to build. Sam caught a few words like ''liability insurance'' and ''litigation.'' He stifled a groan.

His elbow was starting to throb, and he could feel a painful area under the knee of his jeans that was probably bleeding. He needed a hot bath and a couple of aspirin. ''I'm okay, Gordon. Really.''

''I don't like that goose egg on your head,'' Gordon said, gently probing a spot Sam hadn't even been aware of until Gordon touched it.

''Ouch. Quit it.''

''Uh-oh,'' someone muttered. ''He'll probably sue.''

Sam almost laughed until someone else said, ''He won't sue. He's practically family.''

''Don't be stupid,'' Ida Jane said, pushing her way past a cluster of onlookers. ''He *is* family, you dolt.''

The *dolt* in question—Linda McCloskey puffed up indignantly. ''He's an in-law. I meant *real* family.''

A twinge in Sam's belly, totally unrelated to the fall, made him flinch. Ida Jane looked him straight in the eye and said, ''He's the twins' daddy. Does that make him family enough for you?''

Oh, Miss Ida, what have you done?

A hush fell over the crowd for several heartbeats. Sam was still looking at the old lady. He saw something that looked an awful lot like satisfaction in her eyes. He didn't understand it, but he knew without turning his head that her great-niece wasn't going to feel the same.

''Ida, you're mistaken,'' Diane said loudly. ''Josh is Tucker and Lara's father. Sam's their uncle.''

''Don't tell me what I know,'' Ida Jane said angrily. ''Sam's the daddy.''

Sam looked at Jenny. Stricken. Mortified.

A murmur of questions and speculation was building. Snippets like, ''They had an affair when Josh was dying? How could they!'' came through loud and clear.

Andi jumped atop an inverted bucket and whistled. ''Good grief, people,'' she shouted. ''What planet do you come from? Haven't you heard of science?''

She swept the crowd with her indignant glance then pointed at Sam. ''Yes, Sam is the twins' biological father. He helped his brother and Jenny conceive because Josh was sick. Remember? Dying. Remember?''

The group looked uncomfortable. One or two people gave Sam conciliatory smiles. He grabbed the railing and pulled himself to his feet. Unfortunately, he stood up too fast, and black spots flashed before his eyes. He swayed unsteadily.

Gordon grabbed one arm, Jenny the other.

"We're going to the hospital and get a couple of X rays," Gordon said.

"Andi, please call the ranch and tell them we might be late," Jenny ordered.

Kristin suddenly appeared; Donnie followed a few steps behind. "What happened? Donnie just caught me. How can I help?"

"Take Ida Jane home for me?" Jenny asked.

"Of course."

Sam tried to navigate under his own power, but neither Gordon nor Jenny would let go. Donnie parted the crowd with a single command.

Sam kept his head down and focused on not stepping on Jenny's toes, but something made him look up. His gaze met his mother's. Her eyes were filled with accusations.

He swallowed a sigh. *Oh, the joy of Christmas.*

"ARE YOU Mrs. O'Neal?" the desk clerk asked Jenny.

Sam had already disappeared down the hallway, Gordon at his side.

"Yes," Jenny said without hesitation.

"I need you to fill this out," the young woman said. "Insurance forms. Medical history."

Jenny absently reached for the paperwork. She was a pro at filling out forms—she'd done a million for Josh.

Sam had been understandably subdued on the trip to the hospital. No doubt his injury was only part of it; they also had to deal with the gossip that would be flying around. Diane would want answers.

Gordon hadn't said a word about Ida's revelation, but Jenny knew she wouldn't be that lucky where her mother-in-law was concerned.

She tried to focus on the lines of the form. *Heart*

disease? No. High blood pressure? No. Kidney problems? She scanned the list and suddenly felt swamped by fear. So many things could go wrong. There were so many ways she could lose him. Just like she'd lost Josh.

The antiseptic smells and the bright overhead lights of the hospital brought back memories of Josh on his downward slide. The fear and desperation. The unspoken prayer that a miracle was in the making, when deep in her heart she knew there was no hope.

Where's Sam? What if they found something wrong?

She jumped to her feet and started toward the door that said Authorized Personnel Only.

"Wait," the admittance clerk said.

"I can't. I have to make sure he's okay."

The girl—who couldn't be older than eighteen or nineteen—gave her an odd look. "You're Mrs. O'Neal," she said. "The teacher."

Jenny paused, torn between good manners and her need to see Sam. The girl walked toward her. "I'm Mandy Sogerson. You taught my little brother, Robbie. I was sorry to hear about your husband."

Jenny was still trying to pull an image of Robbie to mind, when she saw a light go on in Mandy's face. If Jenny's husband was dead, then Jenny wasn't the *right* Mrs. O'Neal.

"Thank you, Mandy. Your brother was quite a character! Tell him I said hello. Now, I have to see Sam."

"Um…but…you're not…I can't…"

Jenny sympathized with the young woman's dilemma but she was beyond caring what anyone thought.

"Listen, Mandy, I'm the person who lives in Sam's house, fixes his food, raises his children. If you want to see a marriage license, you'll have to get in line. I need to be with him."

The stalemate ended a second later when the door opened and Sam walked out, followed by Gordon. He looked at Jenny. ''Are you ready to go home?''

Jenny's knees felt weak, but she managed to clear the distance between them. ''Are you okay?''

He hugged her tight, as if to convince her that he was healthy and whole.

''He's going to be just fine,'' Gordon said, patting her shoulder. ''It helps to have a hard head.''

''I prefer to think it was my years as a stuntman that saved me,'' Sam said, his tone thick with humor. He pushed back a lock of hair that had come loose from Jenny's elaborate hairdo. ''No concussion. Hairline fracture of one rib, but I still think that's an old break.''

He and Gordon exchanged a look. ''Don't tell your mother, but I'm going to sneak a cigar before you take me back,'' Gordon said. He picked up his coat from the pile Jenny had been watching and walked through the pneumatic doors.

''He's a good man,'' Sam said, then he put his arm around Jenny's shoulders. ''Let's sit down and talk a minute.''

Jenny wasn't sure she could. Her emotions were all over the place: relief, residual panic, dismay at being the center of all the gossip once word hit the grapevine, and shock from the unnerving memory of Josh's image blocking her view of Sam. Maybe she was losing her mind. Her maternal grandmother had gone crazy. Maybe mental instability was an inherited trait.

''Can we go home instead?''

He steered her to an uncomfortable-looking chair in the far corner of the waiting room. ''Soon.'' He sat beside her, then leaned close enough to take both of her hands in his.

"Jenny, Gordon and I were talking. We can do some damage control. If you move back to town—"

She blinked. "What?"

"I was wrong. I should have known this would come out and that people would think the worst. They always do."

"You don't care what people think."

"No, but you do."

Jenny looked at the admittance desk. Just the top of Mandy's head was visible behind a magazine. "I read somewhere that most people's attention span is just slightly longer than the life span of a mayfly. I'm through living my life worrying about keeping the rest of the world—even the people of Gold Creek—happy." She stood. "Can we go home now?"

FACEDOWN ON KRISTIN'S massage table the next morning, Sam blinked the last vestiges of sleep from his eyes. By the time they'd dropped Gordon off, replayed the whole fiasco for Greta and checked on the twins, it was after midnight. Lack of sleep—plus the jet lag from his East Coast trip—left him feeling slightly hungover.

"You know, Jenny thinks she saw Josh's ghost, Sam," Kristin said as she dug her fingers into the tender muscles of his upper shoulder.

He gritted his teeth when she touched a particularly tender spot. "I beg your pardon?" he asked, his voice echoing from beneath the table.

Kristin had spent the night in Jenny's room at the ranch and had offered to give him a massage before she headed home to Oregon. Despite their little talk at the hospital, Sam and Jenny hadn't really discussed what happened the night before. He'd been wiped out on the ride home, so much so he let Jenny drive.

"I believe the human spirit never dies. And I'm sure Josh is still a part of our lives, but I don't think his ghost suddenly appeared on the stairway, blocking her view of you," Kris said.

Sam lifted his head. "Ghost?"

"Whatever she saw was probably a result of a combination of stress and grief," she went on as if he hadn't spoken. "Her first Christmas without Josh…all suddenly got to her. Unfortunately, now she thinks she's lost it."

"Lost what?"

"Her mind. Like Grandma Suzy."

Sam pushed his face into the cutout and cussed.

"There's been too damn much talk about ghosts," he muttered.

Kristin plied his lower back with her thumbs. "I agree, but I *did* feel a chill right before I left. Maybe the place *is* haunted."

Sam kept his groan to himself. He lifted himself up on one elbow. "Does it really matter? My fall was an accident. I'm fine. Jenny's fine. Isn't she?"

Kristin nodded. "She and Ida are feeding the twins breakfast. They're getting so big. I can't believe they're nearly four months old. Where does the time go?"

Sam plopped back down on his belly. Time wasn't on his side. He'd locked Jenny into a five-year plan that might be the worst thing for her. She was under great stress and now the gossip in Gold Creek was going to make it worse.

Kristin added more oil to her hands then attacked his upper back, probing the tense muscles in his shoulders. After a minute, she said, "You love her, don't you?"

Sam kept his head buried. "Where'd that come from?"

"I can tell. Andi said you did, but I wasn't sure before now."

Sam wasn't thrilled to know he was so transparent. He changed the subject. "My right calf still hurts. Can you work on it?"

She applied her strong hands to his leg muscles, and Sam let out a soft groan. Neither spoke for several minutes, then Kristin said, "Maybe Josh appeared because he knows Jenny loves you, too."

Sam rolled to his side and sat up, making sure the flannel sheet was tucked securely around his waist. "You know, Kris, I appreciate the massage, but this kind of talk isn't relaxing."

Her look of chagrin made him give her a light punch on the shoulder. "It's okay. I feel great, and you have a long drive ahead of you. Thanks. I mean it."

She smiled apologetically and started to leave the room but stopped by the door. "Maybe Josh came to say goodbye. He was your brother, Sam. He'd want you to be happy. He loved Jenny and he'd want her to be happy, too. If the two of you can make each other happy, then why wouldn't he be cool with that?"

Sam didn't answer. He didn't believe in ghosts. Josh was gone, and Sam had a big mess on his hands. Not the least of which was Diane, who would no doubt show up any minute with a slew of questions. Questions Sam didn't want to answer.

"SO, HOW BAD is the gossip?" Jenny asked.

Andi had arrived twenty minutes earlier toting a six-foot spruce that she said Sam had asked her to pick up.

"Not too bad," her sister answered. "I'd say only about sixty percent of the town has heard."

A naughty grin played across her lips. "Of course, the

other forty percent is away on vacation, but most people aren't checking their e-mail, so you're safe.''

Ida Jane snickered. Jenny wasn't sure Ida fully understood the ramifications of her disclosure last night. She'd tried bringing up the subject, but with Greta popping in and out of the kitchen to work on the preparations for tonight's feast, Jenny hadn't had much private time with her aunt.

She stuck her tongue out at her sister.

Andi laughed and gave Ida Jane a kiss on the top of her head. ''Lighten up, sis. Ida Jane and I did you a huge favor. Now, you and Sam can do the right thing and get married and everybody will understand why.''

''Married?'' Jenny croaked.

''Who's getting married? Jenny and Sam? When?'' Ida Jane asked, nearly dropping Tucker's bottle.

''The sooner the better in my book,'' Andi said, adding her helping hand to Ida's. ''But you'll have to ask them.''

Jenny's head throbbed so badly it felt as if she'd fallen down the stairs. She hadn't slept well. Kristin talked in her sleep. She kept saying the name Zach over and over.

When Jenny questioned her about it this morning, she'd huffily snapped, ''That's my business. Keep your nose out of it.''

Jenny had been too wiped out to fight. She still was. She could barely muster the energy to contemplate decorating a Christmas tree—something Josh always made a big production of. Eggnog, decorated cookies, carols on the stereo. One year he rented an electric fireplace to give their home that ''holiday ambience,'' he'd said.

''Can we not talk about this, Andi?'' Jenny said with a sigh. ''Poor Sam is probably—''

She didn't get her sentence out because the kitchen

door opened and Sam walked in, looking as fit as she'd ever seen him. "Good morning, everyone. Miss Ida, you look lovely. Nice sweater. Very festive." He smiled at the older woman before nodding at Andi. "Hi, Andi, thanks for picking up the tree. How much do I owe you?"

Andi made a swishing motion with her hand. "I figure we're even. Word got out about your fall and before the night was over, half the town had stopped by for a cup of coffee and to pick my brain."

Sam didn't look alarmed. "Did you get a sense of what people are thinking?"

Andi took Tucker from Ida Jane and kissed his plump belly. "Of course. Nobody is shy about speaking their mind in Gold Creek."

Sam poured himself a cup of coffee then casually leaned back against the counter. "Tell us."

"I tried telling Jenny but she got huffy."

Sam turned his gaze her way. Jenny's heart did a somersault. With the bright sunlight pouring in through the window behind him, he looked vital and alive. Suddenly she yearned for something she didn't dare acknowledge. Josh had only been dead four months. Jenny owed him more loyalty than that.

"We have a tree to decorate," she said. "And food to prepare for the employees' party. We don't have time for chitchat. If the people of Gold Creek want to think badly of us, then let them."

Chin high, she set Lara's bottle on the table and rose. "I'll be in the living room setting out the Christmas decorations."

She knew it was childish. She couldn't run from this, but she wasn't about to talk about the future until she'd had a chance to talk to Sam. Alone.

JENNY LOOKED AROUND the large spacious room. She'd set up her easel in one corner. The soft morning light and panoramic view inspired her in a way she'd never dreamed possible. Some mornings she flew out of bed charged with a sense of discovery and wonder. In many ways, she'd never been happier.

She wasn't going to let gossip or public opinion, or even Josh, run her out of this haven that felt so homelike.

Nor was she going to let anyone else dictate her morality. She knew what was going on between her and Sam. The attraction was undeniable, but they were adults. Friends. Parents. They could handle it. There wasn't going to be a hasty wedding just because the people who'd once changed her diaper thought there should be.

''Where do you want the tree?'' Sam asked, waltzing the ungainly tree through the doorway.

''Where do you usually put it?''

He looked at her blankly.

''You've never had a tree here before?''

He shrugged. ''Why bother? I was always invited to your holiday get-togethers at Ida Jane's. It never seemed worth the effort.''

He scowled at her. ''Stop looking at me like I'm some kind of Grinch. I put up lights outside. Most years. And I always take my crew to dinner at the Golden Corral. You're the one who suggested having the party here.''

''I know. I didn't say you were cheap.''

He manhandled the tree past the furniture, propping it up against the wall in the far corner of the room. ''Where's the stand?''

She kicked the cardboard box labeled Xmas Tree Stand in Josh's neat script.

Sam went on in his own defense. ''I give the guys

who live around here a big fat turkey to go with their bonuses. The bunkhouse brigade get bottles of Jack Daniel's and movie passes.''

''I know. Josh always said there were guys lined up to work at the Rocking M over the holidays. It's just that I can't imagine celebrating without a tree. Josh used to spend hours selecting the perfect one. Not too tall, not too fat, not too skimpy.''

''Just pick one,'' she'd cry in exasperation when her toes were ready to fall off from the cold.

Sam opened the box and extricated the stand, which could revolve, play music and make the lights flash. Josh had ordered it from a catalog the first year they were married.

Sam carried it to the center of the windows where the glass formed a triangle. ''Here or in the corner?''

Jenny's throat closed. ''There.''

She laid Lara, who was almost asleep on her shoulder, down in the fabric-sided playpen. Andi and Tucker were nowhere to be found. Probably in Ida Jane's room, plotting her and Sam's next public fiasco.

''Where are the ornaments?'' Sam said, rising to his feet after securing the tree in the stand.

Jenny looked at him. ''Are you serious?''

His eyes went wide in question. ''What? You don't have any ornaments?''

''Of course I have ornaments. Your brother was an ornament nut. He couldn't pass by a Christmas shop without buying something. I meant, we put the lights on first, then the ornaments. Isn't that how you do it?''

His face flushed, and he walked toward the kitchen. ''I'll get some water. It takes water. Right?''

His snippy tone made her flinch. What kind of teacher

made a student feel badly about not knowing an answer? she asked herself.

Feeling crummy, she eyed the six boxes sitting beside the leather couch. She picked the one that said Lights and Decor. She peeled back the tape and looked inside. Nice and neat. Josh not only put up the tree to exacting standards, he took it down just as precisely.

Jenny yanked out the carefully wrapped strands and pitched them toward the tree. The thick carpet would keep them from breaking. When the last had made its flight and was lying on the floor like a deflated balloon, she pulled out a box labeled Angel.

"Angel?" she questioned, examining the box. She lifted the lid and looked inside.

Her hands started to shake and she nearly dropped the box before she managed to sit down. She let it rest on her thighs as she stared at the finely crafted angel made of lace and beads with a porcelain head. She remembered all too clearly the first time she'd seen it.

Last year. The Sunday before the Christmas break. Jenny had been exhausted from her pregnancy and from rehearsing the play her fourth-grade class was performing. Josh had insisted on dragging her out of their nice warm house to attend the Gold Creek Garden Club's holiday gift bazaar.

"You don't feel well enough to bake, Jen, and we can't decorate the tree without Christmas cookies and eggnog," he'd said. She'd gone along even though the smell of baked goods had made her stomach heave.

It had taken him an hour to pick out his selection of goodies—mostly because he had to talk to everyone he met. Then, just as Jenny was ready to drop, he spotted the angel.

''Jenny, I found her,'' he'd exclaimed so loudly everyone in the Methodist Hall turned to look.

At seventy-five dollars, the angel decoration didn't impress Jenny. ''It's pretty, Josh, but what's wrong with the star we always use?''

He'd wheedled, cajoled, argued and begged, and like always, Jenny had been tempted to let him have his way, but maybe because she was tired and cranky, for once she'd put her foot down.

''No, Josh. We have a baby on the way. We can't afford it.'' They hadn't learned about the twins yet.

Unwilling to listen to any more of his arguments, she'd walked home. Josh had shown up fifteen minutes later full of apologies and sweet talk. He'd stashed his grocery bag full of goodies in the kitchen and put on Mannheim Steamroller—his favorite album—while they decorated the tree.

He'd hung the star without a word.

But, secretly, he'd bought the angel. Then packed it up until next year. No doubt hoping that Jenny would be too busy with their child to care about his extravagance.

Sam entered the room with a watering can. He stared at the haphazard display of lights scattered across the floor then looked at Jenny. ''I take it we use all of them?'' he asked with aplomb.

A funny little tickle wiggled through her chest. Sam didn't play games. He didn't plot and plan then disappear. He would never buy a seventy-five-dollar angel then hide it in a box for a year.

''Sam?'' Jenny said, watching him dig through the tree's thick branches to fill the reservoir.

''Uh-huh?''

''Sam,'' she repeated.

He set the watering can aside and looked up from his kneeling position. ''What?''

''I love you.''

CHAPTER THIRTEEN

SAM REGISTERED the words, but before he could think of a reply, Kristin appeared, carrying her massage table in its zippered canvas tote.

"I'm leaving," she announced.

Sam jumped to his feet and jogged across the room. He relieved her of the strap of the weighty bag and hefted it to his shoulder. "Let me carry that for you. It's the least I can do after a free massage. Where are your keys?"

She fished them from the pocket of her jeans. "Thanks. That'll give me time to tell Ida Jane and Andi goodbye."

As he walked toward the door, he saw the two sisters embrace then head for Ida Jane's room.

Kristin's Subaru wagon was parked to the right of the flagstone walk; Ida Jane's massive pink Caddie, sat cockeyed off to the left. Sam took his time loading the table then drove the wagon across the compound to the gas pump where he filled up her tank. He also checked her oil and cleaned her windshield.

The mundane tasks helped keep his mind—and his heart—from overreacting to Jenny's unexpected announcement. Love? What kind of love? Her comment was too out of the blue to be anything but gratitude. Or holiday turmoil. Right?

He parked Kris's car where he'd found it but left the

engine on and the heater running. The early-morning sunshine had given way to valley fog that had pushed its way up the hillsides. He shivered, wishing he'd grabbed a jacket.

As he started toward the house, the sound of hooves in a hurry stopped him. Hank, atop his old favorite, Jughead, pulled to an abrupt halt in front of the gate. The bay's huffing breath appeared dragonlike in the cold air.

"What's going on?" Sam asked, sensing the urgency in his usually unruffled foreman's manner.

"Blue's down."

The health of any animal in his care was always a concern, but the loss of Blue would prove a significant setback to his breeding program. The bull was one of the Rocking M's most important longhorns, and one of Sam's favorites. "Can we reach him by truck?"

Hank nodded. "He's not far off the road. Be faster if we cut the fence."

"Load up what you need, I'll call Rich." Richard Rumbolt had been the ranch veterinarian for years; he was both a dedicated professional and a friend.

Sam dashed to the house. The three sisters were just coming out, with Ida Jane between them. "Hi, ladies. Kris, your car is gassed up and ready to go. Jen, I'm sorry, but you'll have to start the decorating without me. We have an emergency in the field."

Jenny reached out to touch his arm. "Can I help?"

Her concern made him want to take her in his arms and kiss her, but, of course, he couldn't. There was still too much between them to take anything for granted. "I appreciate the offer, but we won't know how bad it is until Rich gets here."

He handed Kris her keys and gave her a friendly hug. "Have a happy holiday."

As he hurried past, he looked at Andi and said, "You're sure we can't talk you into joining us tonight. Got a few lonesome cowboys who'd think Christmas had come early if you so much as smiled at them."

Her cheeks took on a rosy hue; she gave him a pointed look. "Thanks, but I'll be pumping caffeine into the veins of Gold Creek's finest until eight o'clock, then I'm going to crash. I still have two more days of retail, but I'll be here Monday night. Your mother and Gordon offered to pick me up."

Christmas Eve. Sam's stomach made an unhappy sound.

"You missed breakfast this morning, boy," Ida Jane said, giving him a wink. "Better grab a handful of cookies before you run off to work. Greta and I decorated them."

He gave her a quick kiss on the forehead then hurried inside. He'd been looking forward to a relaxed "family" day, but it couldn't be helped. Besides, what did he know about tree trimming? Josh had been the Christmas guru, not Sam.

"HAVE YOURSELF a merry little Christmas..."

Vince Gill's CD provided the background music as Jenny stepped away to scrutinize her creation. She'd never had this much autonomy in tree trimming before. Josh had been a control freak when it came to "his" tree.

"What do you think?" she asked Ida Jane, who'd given up an hour earlier and was now supervising from the recliner.

"The tree's absolutely lovely," Ida Jane said.

Something in her voice made Jenny drop the strand

of gold beads in her hand back into the box. "Is something wrong, Auntie? You sound a little sad."

"I was thinking about my sister. Suzy loved pretty things. Looks were important to her. Some said that's why she married Bill—for all the things he could give her."

Jenny sat across from her on the sofa. "You mean she married Grandfather for his money? She didn't love him?"

Ida shrugged slightly. "She had her reasons for marrying Bill. He was a good man. Kind…and lonely. I think they cared for each other—even if he was older."

"How many years?"

Ida smiled, as if hearing something Jenny hadn't meant to impart. "Far more than you and Sam."

Jenny realized it was no use trying to hide her feelings for Sam from Ida Jane. "Ida, I think I'm in love with Sam. I know I shouldn't be. It's too soon. It's not fair to Josh—"

Before she could finish, Ida made a rude sound. "Life wasn't fair to Josh, but you can't make up for that, Jenny. You've got no say in who lives and who dies, and you don't have a lot of control over who you love. I know, honey, believe me."

Jenny found her aunt's words reassuring, but she sensed Ida was not talking about her niece and Sam.

"Are you referring to a man in your life, Auntie? Someone you loved?"

Ida nodded. She turned her head to stare at the fire. Her profile looked impossibly young. "Yes, dear. There was a man, but, like Josh, he was gone too soon."

"He died?"

"Killed in the war."

Jenny reached across the distance and took Ida's hand. "I'm sorry."

It broke her heart to think that Ida had loved this man so much that she'd never married or had children of her own. "How come you never told us about him? Does it still hurt to talk about him?"

Ida squeezed her hand. "No, dear, death is a part of life and, if you're brave—like you are—you accept that and move on. Sometimes in my dreams I still see him. He was a charmer. So handsome. But we would never have had a life together."

"Why?"

"Because he loved my sister."

Jenny took in a quick breath. "Oh no."

"Yes. It wasn't her fault. Or his. She was so very lovely—a butterfly men yearned to hold. At the time, I wasn't terribly gracious about what I considered my sister's defection, but Suzy was just being Suzy."

Jenny sighed. She'd seen firsthand what could happen to sisters when a man came between them. Andi and Kristin had tussled over Tyler Harrison, and the episode had triggered years of hard feelings. "At least you and Grandma Suzy made up before she died," Jenny said. "And you helped her when she came back to Gold Creek to live."

Ida looked at her strangely. "She came home, but only after she'd been on the lam for ten years."

Jenny blinked in confusion. "I beg your pardon?"

Ida sighed and closed her eyes. "Suzy blamed herself for what happened with Bill. Later on, after the money was gone and she'd lost her looks, her mind went, too. Guilt will do that to you."

A shiver passed through Jenny, and she inched closer to the fire. A gray mist had moved in, giving the sky an ominous feeling. ''Auntie, did our grandmother kill our grandfather?''

Ida's eyes snapped open. She blinked twice as if coming out of a trance. ''No. Of course not. What gave you that idea?''

''You said she felt guilty.''

Ida pushed the knitted throw off her lap and started to stand up. ''There are all kinds of guilt, Jenny girl. Sometimes we feel guilty about things that aren't even our fault—like the way you feel about Sam.''

Jenny helped the elderly woman to her feet and handed her the cane. ''I'm going to lie down a little while so I'll be fresh for the party tonight. I want to look my best for those studly young cowboys.''

Ida's use of the word *studly* made Jenny laugh. ''I'll come down later and help do your hair,'' she offered.

Ida Jane gave her a scornful look. ''You just worry about impressing Sam. I can take care of myself.''

''I don't know if I'm ready,'' Jenny confessed. ''It feels too soon to be talking about this.''

Ida gave her a hug. ''Life moves on, Jenny love. Whether you're ready or not. Just take what comes and try not to hurt too many people in the process.''

The last sentence seemed oddly introspective, but Jenny couldn't imagine what Ida Jane had to regret. She'd been a caregiver her whole life. She'd given up a career to help when her mother was dying of cancer and her father started to fail; she'd taken in her sister and niece when Suzy's mental health crumbled, then later raised her niece's three orphaned babies.

''Ida Jane, I don't tell you this often enough, but I love you. And I'm so glad you're here with me. I don't think I could have survived Josh's death and the birth of the twins without you.''

Her aunt smiled and patted her cheek. ''Of course you could have, dear. You have Sam.''

After Ida was gone, Jenny finished picking up the boxes and bits of paper strewn on the floor. She set the four ornaments she'd selected for Sam to hang on the end table. She didn't know why it mattered, but she wanted him to be a part of this ritual.

Although he'd celebrated every holiday for the past twelve years with Jenny and her family, this was different. The dynamics had changed, and Sam was now a part of her life in a way that meant they could never return to the old patterns. It was up to her to create new patterns. Even if it hurt.

She still had one ornament to put in place. The tree-topper. She'd left it till last because she couldn't decide whether to use the angel or the star. Swallowing against the knot in her throat, she gazed at the tree, hoping for an answer.

''Use the angel, Jenny penny. I bought it for you.''

She heard Josh's voice as clearly as if he were standing beside her. ''No,'' she said aloud. ''You bought it for yourself. Because you wanted it. Because you always got everything you wanted.''

''Not everything.''

His dry wit—so perfectly Josh—hit her like an avalanche. Tears filled her eyes; mucus closed off her breathing passages. A harsh cry clambered up her throat and escaped like the desperate wail of a drowning woman. She sank to her knees as if in prayer.

''Oh, Josh, I'm so sorry,'' she whispered, clasping her arms around her ribs trying to keep her sobs inside. ''I'm so very, very sorry.''

She wasn't certain what she regretted most—loving Sam or not missing Josh enough. Despite all that she and Josh had shared—the laughter and tears, the squabbles and disagreements—Jenny was finding it harder and harder to hold on to the past. Maybe the time had come to move on.

IT WAS DARK by the time Sam got back to the house. The day had stayed cold and dreary. The wet chill was the kind that worked its way into the bones, and he planned to detour to the living room to stand in front of the fire before dashing upstairs to shower.

His guests would be arriving in less than an hour, but he knew that everything was ready. Hank had talked to Greta several times, updating her on Blue's condition. After Rich's initial diagnosis—a respiratory infection—they'd transported the massive animal to the barn and pumped him full of antibiotics. There was little Sam or Hank could do, but they'd stayed close by on a kind of deathwatch that seemed all too familiar to Sam.

Then just fifteen minutes ago, the bull seemed to perk up, getting to his feet to take some water and feed. Sam had been so relieved he'd had to leave so no one would see how much he'd been affected.

Sam left his manure-covered boots on the deck and walked inside. Several scents hit him—candles burning in a yule log, cinnamon and pumpkin, prime rib and pine. The whole place seemed alive with color and warmth. He hung up his coat in the closet then walked to the great room.

At the far end, in front of the windows, the Christmas tree twinkled with tiny lights of every color. Awash with ornaments too plentiful and diverse to appreciate from a distance, Sam stood with his back to the fire and smiled.

''She did a good job, wouldn't you say?''

Sam turned to find Ida Jane standing in the doorway.

She looked elegant in a silver and black pantsuit. A sprig of holly adorned one lapel. Sam walked to her and kissed her cheek. "Hello, Miss Ida. You look lovely. And my house has never looked better. You and Jenny did a great job of decorating."

He turned and looked again. Crystal snowflakes were suspended in the windows by what he assumed was fishing line. The artful arrangement actually made them look like falling snow. Colorfully wrapped gifts of all sizes clustered around the base of the tree, which made a slow revolution to the music-box-sounding rendition of "We Three Kings."

Squinting, he noticed several ornaments lying on the end table closest to the couch. "She missed a couple," he said to Ida Jane.

"She left those for you to hang."

He glanced at her. "Why?"

"So you'd feel a part of the festivities. I put up my couple, and the twins did their part," she said with a grin. "Those are yours."

Sam's heart swelled at the thoughtful gesture. He walked over and picked up one. It was a metal cast of a San Francisco streetcar. For some reason it triggered a memory.

Jenny, Josh and Sam had been in the city two years ago to see a Giants game. They'd taken B.A.R.T. in early and were wandering around SoMa, the artsy area South of Market, when Josh spotted a little shop selling Christmas things. Sam and Jenny had groaned in unison, knowing what that meant to their agenda. But he'd emerged just minutes later. "Perfect," he'd declared. "Now, whenever we hang this, we'll remember the great day we had together."

Sam took a deep breath. Instead of the pain he expected to feel, there was a warm sense of nostalgia.

''Where should I put it?'' he asked.

''Wherever it belongs,'' a different voice said.

He spun around. Jenny.

His mouth dropped open. She was dressed in red. Her skirt was snug around the hips and stopped well above her knees. The sparkly sweater—also red—had a scoop neck that made the simple gold chain she wore look dazzling against her pale skin.

By sheer willpower he managed to say, ''How do you know where that is?''

She walked toward him. ''You'll know. Trust me.''

He glanced at Ida, who appeared to be watching them with interest. He set the little cable car back down and shoved his hands in his pockets. ''Later. I've got to grab a shower and sign the cards for my crew. I thought I'd have time this afternoon... If you ladies will excuse me, I'll be back shortly.''

He sidled past Jenny, being careful not to breathe in her fragrance. He'd already stood in a chilly rain most of the afternoon, he didn't want to do anything that would require another cold shower. He paused before leaving the room, though, and said, ''You both look wonderful, by the way. Really beautiful.''

Then he turned and took the stairs two at a time. His shower was quick. He didn't want to give himself time to think, to wonder, to read anything into Jenny's dress and the gesture of the ornaments. And he still hadn't figured out what she'd meant when she'd said she loved him. Brotherly love? Fatherly love? Husbandly love?

''Coward,'' he muttered as he dressed. He opened his closet to find a tie—the least he could do was dress properly since she looked so elegant, and his gaze was drawn to a hatbox on the shelf overhead. He knew without looking what it contained: Josh's green cowboy hat.

His fist closed around a Jerry Garcia tie—a gift from Jenny and Josh. He tied it quickly and left the room. Keeping his mind on business, he took the back passage to his office, opened the door and went straight to his safe, which was located in a cabinet under a lighted drawing table.

Greta had purchased a box of western greeting cards and left it on his desk. All Sam had to do was count out each employee's bonus then sign the card and label it. He withdrew an envelope of cash that he'd put aside for this purpose and walked to his desk. It didn't take long. He'd already decided on the dollar amounts weeks before. When the last one was finished, he was surprised to see four, hundred-dollar bills remaining.

Tim and Rory. He'd forgotten about the two men who'd gotten into a fight and been fired. Rory was living at home with his widowed mother. Tim was still in jail awaiting trial. He'd have to remember to send Rory a check next week. He was a good kid—just full of piss and vinegar. Much like Sam had been at that age.

He returned to the safe and knelt on one knee to work the combination. When he heard the click, he opened the door and placed the bills on top of some envelopes. He was about to close it, when something made him look a second time. *That's Josh's handwriting.*

He took out a slightly yellowed envelope and looked at the postmark: 1992. He opened it and found a greeting card with a cheesy image of two men in a fishing boat. The caption read, For My Brother on Father's Day.

Sam couldn't remember receiving it, but that had been a long time ago. When Josh and Jenny were in college, and Sam had been feeling more alone than he thought possible. He'd tried dating for a while but couldn't find the right person. Finally, he'd given up and devoted his time to his business.

He opened the card, expecting to see Josh's sloppy but effusive signature. Instead, there was a fairly neatly written message on the inside flap.

Sam,

Just a little note to say thanks. Jenny told me I don't do that enough. She's right. But it's not because I don't appreciate everything you've done for me. I do. I just get busy and forget to say the words.

Without getting too sappy—and because Jen's standing here waiting to mail this—thanks for giving me this way-cool life. College is a kick and we both know I wouldn't be here without you footing the bills. I love you, brother, and I promise someday I'll find a way to give back a little of what you've given me.

Your loving bro,
Josh

Sam's hand trembled. Was this a sign? He didn't believe in signs.

It's okay to love her, Sam. Jenny needs you, and you need her. It's the way it was meant to be. I did my part.

Sam heard the words as clearly as if Josh were talking on the baby monitor in the next room. He closed his eyes and rocked back on his heels. ''Oh, great, I'm losing my mind.''

''I hope not. We have fifteen people coming for dinner.''

He turned to look behind him and lost his balance, landing on his butt on the oak flooring. It wasn't far to fall but he winced. His hip was still sore from the previous night's tumble.

Jenny walked across the room, her sexy high heels snapping in a sultry manner. "Are you okay? It's not your head, is it?"

Could be. "I'm fine. I just… I'm fine."

She stopped a few feet from him and took a breath. "Yeah, me, too. Fine, but about this close to tears." She held her hand up with the finger and thumb almost touching. "Right?"

Sam nodded. He knew she wouldn't think less of him if he admitted how sad he'd been the past few months. "I found a card from him. A Father's Day card. I don't remember getting it, but you know how that goes. We always assume we'll have another holiday and another."

She walked a little closer and held out her hand to help him up. "I know. Every ornament I hung today had a memory attached to it."

He took her hand and rose. "That must have been hard. I'm sorry I wasn't here to help."

She shook her head. He liked her hair down instead of swept off her neck like last night. "It was probably better that you were gone. It gave me a chance to take my time and come to grips with what was happening."

"What do you mean?"

"I was saying goodbye." She looked at him, her eyes luminous with tears. "To Josh. To the way things were."

Sam wanted to take her in his arms and comfort her, but he didn't trust himself. He'd kissed her twice and both times he'd felt his heart would burst if he didn't tell her how much he loved her. This wasn't the time nor place.

He returned the card to the safe. ''In his note, he mentioned how much fun you were having in college.''

She made a little sniffing sound. ''It wouldn't have been quite as carefree without your help.''

''I didn't do—''

She shook her head in warning. ''Sam, Josh was very frank about his finances. He didn't see anything wrong with spending your money, since you offered. He said I didn't have a problem using the Gold Creek scholarship money the town had set up for me and my sisters, so why should he turn down what you offered?''

''He was right. I was glad to help. I didn't go to college until I was twenty-five, and then mostly night school. Believe me, it wasn't that much fun. Hearing about your parties and road trips was my chance to live that life vicariously.''

She didn't say anything, so he started toward the desk. ''Shall we go? Our guests will be arriving soon.''

Jenny reached out and touched his arm. ''I wanted to talk to you about what I said this morning.''

Sam's empty belly growled from the sudden shot of acid that hit. ''Could it wait? I know you planned to help Andi at the shop tomorrow, but we have all of Monday before Gordon and Diane show up, don't we?'' He'd made it clear that tonight's party was for employees and guests only—although he would have made an exception for her sisters. The family get-togethers were scheduled for Christmas Eve and Christmas morning.

She looked slightly crestfallen, and he couldn't stop himself from going to her. He pulled her into a light hug. ''Jen, I'm not fooling myself into thinking you meant anything serious. It's the holidays, emotions run high this time of year. Let's just try to get through the next couple of days without saying or doing something we'll regret later, okay?''

She looked ready to protest, but in the distance he heard the sound of the doorbell ringing. They looked at each other a moment, then she smiled. She reached between them to fiddle with his tie. ''This looks sharp. I've never seen you wear it. Josh insisted it was too flashy for you, but I told him it would bring out the green in your eyes.''

She lifted her chin and ran her tongue over her bottom lip. ''I was right.''

She's flirting with me. It took every ounce of willpower in his soul not to kiss her. He was going to make it through the holidays if it killed him—which at this rate was a distinct possibility.

CHAPTER FOURTEEN

SAM STOOD in the middle of the kitchen enjoying the rare moment of total quiet. The twins were down for their morning nap. Jenny and Ida had just left to deliver gifts to Ida Jane's friends in town and to pick up last-minute supplies for tonight's Christmas Eve gathering. Greta and Hank were on their way to her sister's in Bakersfield.

His housekeeper had outdone herself preparing the Rocking M feast that had left every one of his guests groaning in bliss. The party didn't break up until midnight, and by then Jenny and Sam were both ready to drop.

Sunday had been hectic with Jenny pitching in to help Andi at the bordello. Sam and Ida Jane had been in charge of the twins. Jenny had returned with sore feet and a raging headache, so Sam sent her to bed early. There hadn't been time to talk this morning, either, since Jenny was up at dawn to start cooking her cioppino. "I like to start the stock early so it can simmer all day, then we throw in the fish at the last minute," she explained when he stumbled downstairs following the aroma that had woken him.

The fog had disappeared and the day, while a chilly forty-five degrees with a crisp northerly wind, was sunny and clear. She'd looked so bright and full of life, he'd longed to pull her into his arms. A part of him wanted to beg her to marry him. Right here, right now. But he knew better than to spring the idea too soon. He would ask her when the time was right. And if she said yes, they could plan their wedding for autumn, waiting the respectful year.

If she says yes. He wandered to the stove and picked up the lid of the steaming cauldron. A heavenly aroma of fish stock, basil and stewing tomatoes filled the air. He closed his eyes and took a deep breath. *I could get used to this.* He hadn't realized just how lonely he'd been.

He stirred the mixture then replaced the lid and walked to the laundry room where Jenny had wrapped presents. He'd asked her to leave everything out because he had a couple of gifts to wrap. The majority of his purchases had been wrapped at the toy store, but these last two had been impulse buys.

The utility room sat just off the kitchen. Its large window faced the driveway. He left the door open so he could hear the phone, and he set the baby monitor on a shelf.

He still couldn't get over the fact that Jenny had entrusted him with baby-sitting. Alone. Her trust was the best gift of all.

The counter was littered with scissors, tape dispensers, ribbons of various widths and colors and bright rolls of wrapping paper. He eyed one with cartoon characters. "No." He considered a green metallic paper, but settled on an old-fashioned design in wine and cream.

"Perfect," he said, withdrawing a postcard-size jeweler's box from the chest pocket of his flannel shirt.

He opened the box; a heart-shaped locket on a gold chain rested on a bed of ivory satin. His work-roughened fingers looked ludicrous touching the delicate piece, but he pried open the catch and glanced inside. Tucker on the left, Lara on the right.

The photos were ones that he'd taken with his digital camera. The images captured each child's individual personality. Princess Lara, Court Jester Tucker.

Smiling, he closed the locket and started cutting the paper. Totally engrossed in his project, he jumped when he heard someone cough from the doorway behind him.

With a muffled curse he spun around to find his mother in the doorway. "Damn. You scared the..." He dropped the epithet. "Hello, Mother, you're a little early. Jenny and Ida Jane are in town. Dinner's not—"

"I know when dinner is, Sam. Gordon and I are picking up Andrea at six—right after she closes the shop. We'll be here at six-thirty as planned."

He hastily finished wrapping the package then pushed it aside. The second gift—which he wasn't even sure he was brave enough to give—would have to wait. The last thing he wanted was to show it to his mother. He knew what she'd say about his plans.

"So, why are you here?"

She gave him a droll look. "Why do you think? To talk to you."

Sam should have known he couldn't avoid this confrontation forever. "Okay. Let's take a cup of coffee into the living room. It's warmer by the fire."

As he grabbed the monitor, he spotted his mother's car parked in the driveway. How had he missed her arrival? Why hadn't the dogs barked? Or was he that oblivious? Shaking his head, he led the way to the kitchen.

"It smells good in here," Diane said.

Sam poured two cups of coffee and handed one to his mother. "Cioppino is Jenny's specialty. She makes it every Christmas Eve.'' As he followed Diane into the living room, he said, ''One year, she couldn't find any fresh crab locally, so Josh and I drove to the fish market in San Mateo to buy some. Two hours one way! God, we laughed about that, but it was the best we ever tasted.''

Diane paused at the entrance of the room to look around. She walked slowly to the tree. Sam still hadn't hung the ornaments Jenny had set aside for him. He'd been planning to do that this morning. Alone.

''It's lovely. The room looks so…lived in,'' she said, her surprise obvious.

''The place needed a family, and now it has one.''

''Your brother's family.''

Sam looked her in the eye and said, ''*My* family, Mother.''

She turned to gaze out the window. ''Ah, yes, the test tubes. Andi explained it to me after you and Jenny left for the hospital, but that doesn't entitle you to take over your brother's life, Sam.''

Sam set down his cup then walked to her side. He waited until she looked at him. ''Josh is dead, Mother. I would do anything in my power to change that, but I can't.''

''You're dishonoring his memory,'' she snapped, her eyes flashing with pain.

''How? By providing a home for the children he went to such great lengths to conceive? By loving the woman he loved? Josh would be the first to tell you that he had great taste. He'd expect nothing less. Jenny is a wonderful woman, and those babies upstairs are a part of the three of us—Jenny, Josh and me. By being a family, we honor Josh's memory. It's what he would have wanted.''

Her lips curled in a sneer, but the tremor in her voice was one of pain not anger. "How can you be sure?"

"I can't," Sam confessed. "Maybe I'm wrong. Maybe I'm looking for the answer I want to hear because my life was an empty shell before this." He made a gesture that encompassed the room, with its homey decorations, toys and baby swing, candles and snowflakes.

"Maybe you're right, Mother. I didn't have a life of my own so I've taken what Josh left behind," he said, the ache in his chest almost paralyzing.

To his surprise, his mother set down her cup and dropped her purse to the floor then closed the distance between them. "If Josh were here, he'd say that your life made it possible for him to live his life so well."

Her words echoed what Josh had written on that card Sam had found. She placed her hand on his upper arm. "Sam, there are things I've never told you about my life, about Josh's childhood."

Sam didn't want to hear it. She'd try to talk him out of loving Jenny, from asking her to marry him. "The past is over, Mother. Can't we just forget it?"

"Not when it has bearing on the future. Sam, please. Listen to what I have to say. Let that be your Christmas gift to me."

Her pleading tone made him give in. He nodded toward the grouping of chairs by the fireplace. "Let's sit."

She picked up her purse and led the way. Once seated, she opened her large leather satchel and withdrew a videotape. "I also came out here to give you this. Josh sent it to me a month or so before he died. His letter asked that I give this to you and Jenny when the time was right. I called him and asked how I'd know when that was and he said, 'You'll know, Mama.'"

Her eyes filled with tears. "He had such faith in people. I never understood why. I used to disappoint him all the time. I'd say we were going someplace then something would come up and I'd cancel, but he never lost his optimistic outlook on life. And he never stopped trusting the people he loved.''

Sam's chest tightened. ''I know. I once called him a cockeyed optimist, and he said, 'Beats the hell out of being a myopic pessimist.' I figured that was me.''

His mother's lips flickered in a near smile. ''Or me.''

A second later she handed him the tape.

''What's on it?''

''I have no idea. It's yours, not mine.''

That surprised him, and he studied her face to see if she was lying. She'd had this tape for over six months and hadn't peeked?

''I couldn't bear to view it, Sam. I loved that boy with all my heart and, frankly, I was hurt that he sent *you* a tape. I didn't want to know what he could say to you that he couldn't say to me.''

Sam understood. ''But now that you know about the twins' paternity, you figured whatever is on this video has to do with that.''

She didn't deny the charge. Instead, she asked, ''Why didn't you use Josh's sperm to make the babies? I went on the Internet and read about the advances they're making in fertilization. It doesn't take much sperm to work.''

Sam sighed. He honestly didn't want to discuss this, but perhaps it would be best to clear the air. ''In most cases of testicular cancer, once the diseased testicle is removed, the person still has some sperm available, but young boys who are treated with radiation and chemotherapy before puberty may be left sterile. That's what happened to Josh.''

The color drained from Diane's face. ''That was my

fault, too, wasn't it? He got cancer the first time because I didn't get his immunization shots when we were in Mexico. Then he got mumps, and that left him more vulnerable to cancer.''

Sam interrupted. ''Mother, nobody knows why some people get cancer and others don't. Josh never blamed you, and neither do I. It's just the way things worked out.''

He sighed. ''I think Josh set this particular ball in motion just to cover the worst-case scenario. I've talked to a lot of cancer survivors, and they told me there's always a niggling fear the cancer will return.''

She didn't say anything for a moment. ''Andi mentioned that Jenny wanted to use an anonymous donor's sperm, but Josh twisted her arm to use yours.''

Sam nodded. ''He was a master of elaborate plans. I know in my heart Josh didn't plan to die. He was just covering all the bases—looking out for Jenny's welfare. You know how much he loved Jenny.''

Tears welled up in Diane's eyes. ''And you, Sam. He loved his big brother, too.''

Sam reached across the distance and squeezed her hand. ''Josh had a big heart. He loved us all.''

She took a shaky breath and said, ''Even me.''

She broke into tears and clawed in her bag for a tissue. Sam felt helpless; Josh's was the sympathetic shoulder to cry on, not Sam's. ''Of course he loved you. You're his mother.''

''But if it wasn't for me, he'd still be alive.''

''Like I said, you didn't intentionally screw up Josh's immunizations. It couldn't have been easy living in Mexico with a small child. The only thing I never understood is why you went there in the first place.'' He took a breath then asked the question that had been plaguing him for years. ''Was it to get away from me? Because of the Carley thing?''

Diane shook her head. In the morning light, she looked older than he remembered. She looked vulnerable—not an adjective he could ever remember using to describe Diane O'Neal. ''I knew you'd be mad at me about Carley. But the truth is, Carley was a spoiled brat who would have drained you dry then left you for someone with more money. Believe me, son, it takes one to know one.''

Sam's mouth dropped open. Had he unintentionally married Carley because she reminded him of his mother? An odd shiver passed through him.

''I have friends who are still in show business, and they told me Carley's on husband number four at the moment,'' Diane said. ''Who does that remind you of?''

''Wouldn't Freud have had a heyday with that one?'' Sam asked, swallowing a chuckle.

Diane made an offhand gesture. ''Probably too conventional—they say every man wants to marry his mother and every daughter her father. I'm a slow learner. Three of my husbands were exact replicas of my father, who, unfortunately, was a horse's behind.''

Was my father one of the three?

''Your father and Clancy, bless his heart, were the two keepers—and Gordon, of course.''

''Why'd you divorce him?'' Sam asked.

''Who?''

''My father.''

She looked at him blankly, then shook her head. ''Oh, my heavens, I never told you about your father?''

Sam shifted uncomfortably. He wasn't sure he wanted to know. ''It doesn't matter. Clancy was as good a father as anybody could want.'' Clancy had given Sam both a sense of identity and a secure future.

Diane had a sad, slightly bemused look on her face. ''Pat O'Neal was just a kid. Like me. We were stupid and in love. I got pregnant and he married me. My father didn't give him any choice,'' she said with a chuckle. ''But it was what we both wanted.''

Sam frowned. ''If you loved him, why'd you split up?''

''He was killed in a car accident, Sam. Six months after you were born.''

''I don't remember ever hearing you talk about him,'' Sam said.

Diane sighed. ''His death hit me hard. I was alone with a baby. My mother was no help. My father—like I said—was a jerk. I packed us up and headed west. I ran, Sam. That's what I do when things get hairy.''

Her honest self-appraisal earned her a nod of acknowledgment. Sam understood. After what happened with Carley, he had run, too. Straight to the rodeo circuit.

''I didn't set out to interfere with you and Carley, Sam,'' Diane said, changing the subject. ''I was trying to protect you. You didn't tell me there was a baby. You just blew in that morning and said you were eloping to Vegas. You didn't even give me a chance to wish you good luck.''

Sam suddenly realized she was right. He hadn't been living at home at the time because he'd despised Frank, Diane's then husband. ''Why'd you tell Carley's parents where we were?''

''I wanted them to stop the wedding before you said your vows. I know you, Sam. I knew if you married that twit you'd have stuck by her to the bitter end. Her dad was Mr. Bigshot. I figured he could talk you out of it. I didn't expect him to hire a bunch of thugs to beat you up.''

Sam believed her. Diane may have been distant and flighty but she wasn't purposefully mean or vindictive.

''I knew you'd be angry—you were usually mad at me for something. But I thought we'd get past it. We always had. This just happened to be bad timing.''

Sam didn't understand what she meant. ''Timing?''

Her sigh seemed to carry the weight of the world. ''I was married to Frank, remember? You hated him. But he was good to me and he adored Josh. Sometimes, when I was working late, he'd pick up Josh from the baby-sitter just so they could have quality time together.''

Something about the way she said the words made gooseflesh race across Sam's neck and arms.

''On the day I went to see Carley's parents, I couldn't find a sitter, and Frank offered to stay with Josh. The visit didn't take as long as I thought it would. I got back, and when I walked into the bedroom I saw something…terrible. Something sick.'' Her eyes filled with tears and she looked away.

Sam shook his head. ''He abused Josh?''

She sank into the cushy depths of the chair and closed her eyes as if to block the image. ''Years later, I saw a therapist. All I could do was cry for days on end. I thought I was the worst mother ever born.''

''What did he say?'' Sam asked.

Diane opened her eyes. ''She. My therapist was a woman. She told me that sexual predators like Frank are very clever chameleons who outwardly play one role just to get close to children. She said I might have saved myself years of self-hatred if I'd turned him in to the police and pressed charges, but, instead, I ran away.''

His mother went on. ''For two days, Frank begged me not to call the police. He said he'd get help. I waited until I knew for sure he would be busy, then I cleaned out the accounts at the travel bureau and packed everything I could carry. I was just leaving when you showed up. You were so mad you didn't even ask me about our suitcases.''

Sam's only memory of the incident was his own fury.

''After you left, Josh and I hopped a bus to Mexico. I spent the next five years terrified that Frank would find us, but one day I called a friend in L.A. and she told me Frank had been killed in a ten-car pileup on the 405.''

Sam felt a knot the size of a T-bone steak in his gut. He would have given anything to be able to get his hands around that old sleazeball's scrawny neck. ''Did Josh remember any of it?'' he asked.

''I don't think so. I asked my therapist if I should bring it up, but she felt it was Josh's call. As long as his life seemed to be happy and well adjusted...'' She shrugged her shoulders, then let out a small cry. ''But what if it had been eating away at him. Underneath the surface all these years. What if *it* made the cancer come back?''

In the past, Sam might have let his mother blame herself, but not any longer. Life was too damn short to spend agonizing over old hurts.

''Mom, Josh loved you. And, frankly, it took a lot of guts to leave everyone and everything to try to protect your son. If anything, you saved Josh a lot of painful memories by leaving. Like you said, the timing sucked, but that isn't something any of us has control over.''

Diane lowered her head and started to weep. He cleared the short distance, dropping to one knee. He couldn't remember the last time he and his mother had hugged, but it wasn't as difficult as he expected it to be.

"Oh, Sam," she cried, throwing herself into his arms. "I'm so sorry. I tried to blame you because you weren't there when I needed you to be." Sniffling against his shirt, she said, "Isn't that pathetic? I was the parent. I should have been the one to take care of things all along, but you were always my rock—even when you were a little boy."

Sam took the praise to heart, and felt the rift between them begin to heal.

Before he could say anything, a sound crackled from the plastic rectangle at his waist. A baby's cry grew in volume. "Tucker," he said, recognizing his son's voice.

Sam pulled back and touched his mother's wet cheek. "Your grandson is calling. Want to help?"

The olive branch hovered between them. "Okay. I have to get back to town to finish up some gift wrapping, but I always have time for my grand—for your children."

Sam stood then held out his hand to help her rise. "Let's go. Tucker hates a wet bottom."

Diane chuckled. "You were the same way. Josh never complained about anything, but you knew what you wanted and wouldn't settle for less."

They were halfway up the staircase when Diane said, "Sam, whatever you and Jenny decide to do is fine with me. I just hope you'll let us—Gordon and me—be a part of your lives."

He took her hand. "Does that offer include babysitting if Jenny and I decide to take a honeymoon?"

She squeezed his hand with barely a second's hesitation. "Of course. What's a grandmother for?"

JENNY WALKED in the door of the ranch house at four o'clock. Their guests were due at seven. Andi would close up shop at six. After Diane and Gordon picked her up, they'd swing by Beulah Jensen's to get Ida Jane, who'd decided to "stay awhile and visit" when she and Jenny had stopped by to drop off a plate of Greta's famous rum cake.

Jenny knew she should be exhausted after all the socializing she'd done in the past few days, but she felt oddly wired—like a kid waiting for Santa to show up. She checked her cioppino base, smiling at the rich, mouthwatering aroma. The shellfish, shrimp and hunks of halibut would be added once their guests arrived. A green salad and French bread made this a simple but festive meal.

She arranged a selection of homemade goodies—gifts from Ida Jane's many friends—on a crystal plate, then carried it to the living room. "Hello," she called out, expecting to see Sam and the twins.

When no one answered, she set down the plate and walked to the Christmas tree. The ornaments she'd left for Sam to hang were no longer on the end table. Kneeling, she depressed the switch that made the base revolve.

By the second rotation, she'd spotted each of Sam's choices. "Nice job, Sam," she said softly. She was about to leave, when she noticed something else. Two ceramic panda bears, adorned with wreaths of holly, dangled side by side from a branch. When she looked closely, she noticed one bore the name Lara, the other, Tucker.

"Souvenirs from the National Zoo," she said to herself. "That's something Josh would have done."

Shaking her head, she went in search of her family.

She found all three on Sam's king-size bed. Sound asleep.

The twins were snuggled in the curve of Sam's body. Petite, ladylike Lara was closest to her daddy, one hand curled beneath her chin. Tucker was sprawled on his back, mouth open like a little bird. A large, brightly colored children's book rested on the pillow nearby.

Jenny paused in the doorway to soak up the beauty of the scene. The artist in her longed to record it for posterity. She didn't have time for paints, but Sam's digital camera sat by the television on the built-in stand across from the bed. The thick carpet muffled her footsteps as she crossed the room and picked up the compact camera.

He'd demonstrated how to use it months ago, and although Jenny hadn't used it often, she managed to click a few shots without disturbing her subjects. After turning off the power, she returned the unit to its spot.

As she did, she noticed a video sitting half out of the VCR. The label bore Josh's handwriting. The title said, For Jenny and Sam.

A funny little squiggle moved into her chest. Was this something Sam had had for a long time but never shared with her? She nudged it into the machine and took the remote with her to the foot of the bed. She pressed the mute button and stared at the blue screen.

''I was waiting for you to get home before I watched it,'' Sam said in a soft voice.

Jenny almost dropped the remote. ''Where'd you get it?''

He didn't answer. Instead, he slid off the bed, taking care not to disturb the children. A moment later, he sat beside her. Almost as if on cue, the screen filled with images of a party. Familiar faces, laughing and mugging for the camera.

''Last year's St. Patrick's Day party?'' Sam asked.

They watched a moment longer. ''Oh, yeah, there I am. Large with child,'' she said ruefully.

Sam's chuckle was like a pat on the back.

''I wondered what had happened to this tape,'' she said. ''When I was packing, I went through our videos and couldn't find it. I was afraid it might have gotten erased.''

They watched in silence. Every so often Josh would hold the camera at arm's length and give some kind of commentary. Jenny was tempted to turn up the volume, but wasn't sure she dared.

Josh made a goofy face—one she'd seen many times. ''What a nut,'' she said, her voice tight with emotion.

Sam took the remote from her hand and pressed pause. ''Jenny, we need to talk.''

She turned slightly to face him; their knees touched. ''Okay.''

''I'm not Josh. I'll never be him.'' He sighed deeply. ''He was a unique person who filled our lives with joy and silliness—'' He nodded toward the TV. ''I miss him too much to even try to take his place—not that I ever could.''

Jenny responded without thinking. ''Who's asking you to? I agree one hundred percent that you're not Josh. He was lightness and air. And, at times, he could be annoyingly shallow and petty. You're solid and substantial. Reliable. And I've never known you to act unjustly toward anyone.''

''He made you laugh.''

''And cry,'' she admitted. Remarkably, she felt no guilt at sharing this truth.

Sam studied her face. ''Are you saying you didn't love him as much as I think you do?''

Jenny looked down. *What am I saying?* ''No. Josh was everything to me, but in a way he kept me so distracted I never had time to be me. Some days I felt more like a press agent than a wife. Does that make sense?''

Jenny shivered. She'd never expressed those feelings before, even to herself.

''He was a bit like a celebrity,'' Sam said, an understanding smile on his face. ''He'd enter a room and all the attention would turn to him.''

Jenny nodded. ''Exactly.''

''Which worked great for me,'' Sam said starkly. ''He got me off the hook. As long as Josh was around, I could hang out in the background.''

Jenny felt a dawning of understanding. ''That's how I felt, too,'' she exclaimed softly. ''And I know why I craved that kind of anonymity. Until Josh moved to Gold Creek, my sisters and I were the town's pet project. Everybody had a say in our lives, but Josh distracted them. He was so charismatic and preposterous. Even Gloria Hughes was charmed. She never had anything bad to say about Josh in her column.''

Jenny pictured the piece of paper in her pocket. One of the younger members of the Gold Creek Garden Club had printed it off an Internet community loop. It included a copy of the ''Glory's World'' column that would appear in Thursday's edition of the *Ledger*.

Sam distracted her by running a hand through his dark hair, so different from Josh's golden waves. ''I used to think he came by it naturally,'' he said. ''Rumor had it Josh's father was an actor. I don't know if that's true. I never asked Diane, but Josh did have a natural affinity for people, which I certainly lack.''

"You're more alike than you think, Sam," she told him. "Look at the way you persuaded people to back your wildfire-awareness campaign. That was just like Josh."

Sam looked away—as if her words were a little too intense for him to handle. "You'd have thought he was Steven Spielberg the way he controlled that camera," Sam said, smiling.

He aimed the remote, adding volume to the action then handed it back to her. Josh's voice—loud enough to be heard over the crowd—made Jenny's heart speed up. A frame later the scene changed to the rocky summit where Sam had taken Jenny to talk after the twins were born. Josh was narrating a commentary about the glorious spring.

"Did you know he'd gone up there?" Jenny asked Sam.

Sam shook his head. "No. In fact, I told him flat out to stay off the four-wheeler and no horseback riding. Ridiculous as it sounds, I was afraid the jostling might spread the disease," he admitted, shaking his head. "I was pretty uptight. I'm not surprised he ducked out for a while."

Jenny sighed. She hadn't wanted the party, either, but for a more selfish reason. "I was mad at him, too. I told him I didn't want to share any of the time we had left with other people."

Josh's voice filled the silence between them. "Even if this turns out to be the last spring I ever experience, I refuse to be sad," he said. "Isn't this a glorious day? How can I be anything but thankful? None of us knows the time limits on our lives, but we put so many limits of other kinds on ourselves, we forget to enjoy what we have."

Jenny sighed. "He said that so often—even before he

got sick. But it always seemed kinda phony to me. Who doesn't worry about tomorrow?''

Sam leaned forward, resting his elbows on his knees. He was wearing a new flannel shirt. The dark heather color made his eyes look enigmatic. ''When Josh started chemo, I acted like a coach whose star player was goofing off. It must have driven him crazy.''

Jenny snickered softly. ''It did, but he loved you for it. Same with me. I was horribly bitchy at times. I accused him of not taking his illness seriously.'' Sam's look of empathy made her want to curl up in his arms.

She forced herself to look at the screen where Josh was interviewing Beulah Jensen's four-year-old great-granddaughter, Tory. Jenny turned up the volume. Josh's playful, singsong tone made her smile. He asked simple, innocuous questions that made the little girl giggle, then he said, '''Know what? My brother, Sam, is going to be a daddy soon.''

''Rewind that,'' Sam said sharply.

Jenny's hand shook so badly on the slim black device that Sam scooted over and took it from her fingers. The set made a whirring noise then replayed the clip. Sam cursed under his breath.

''He's going to be a terrific daddy,'' Josh continued. ''I know because he practically raised me, and look how wonderful I turned out!''

The little girl giggled. ''You are funny.''

The video camera nodded up and down. ''That's me. Life-of-the-party Josh. But the party will go on without me. That's the way life is. I know it, but I'm afraid Sam might not.''

Sam started to say something but paused when Josh added, ''That's what kids are for. They make you live whether you want to or not. They don't give you a choice. And Sam and Jenny are both going to need those babies if things don't work out for me,'' he finished in a serious tone.

The interview ended when Tory's attention span gave out. The viewfinder followed her running to where Jenny was organizing a sack race. ''Well, hello, beautiful,'' Josh said, his tone playfully lecherous. ''Look at the belly on that woman—isn't she gorgeous?''

Jenny laughed. Tears stung her eyes, but they weren't the painful tears she was used to.

''You were the most beautiful pregnant woman I've ever seen,'' Sam said softly. ''Josh used to talk about you every morning when I brought him his meds. 'Just wait, bro',' he'd say. 'She's going to be even more beautiful this morning.'''

In her peripheral vision Jenny saw that their shoulders were close but not touching. She craved human contact but didn't know how to ask. Shyness had never been a part of Josh's makeup.

''The last time we made love was a week after this was taped,'' she said. ''After he started chemo, everything pretty much came to a stop.''

Sam let out a sigh. ''He'd joke about it. You know, telling me to turn off the monitor because he was going to make mad, passionate love with his wife and he didn't want me turning into a voyeur. But I knew he was too sick. He'd wince when I'd help him roll over.''

Josh's coverage of the egg race continued, but Jenny tuned it out. ''I wasn't complaining, I just meant that it's been nine months since...you know.''

The fact that she couldn't say the words aloud brought a surge of heat to her face. What kind of wanton pervert thinks about sex when watching a video of her dead husband? She started to turn off the tape, but an image on the screen caught her eye. Sam. Standing on the balcony.

She reached across Sam and tapped the volume button. "There he is," Josh said. His tone was proud, boastful even. "The man of the hour. Not that Sam would ever think of himself in those terms, but that's what he is. My big brother. My hero."

Sam let out a short burst of air, as if he'd just been punched in the gut. Jenny spontaneously reached behind him and patted his back. "He loved you so much," she said, trying to ignore how good his heat felt against her palm.

"Sam has saved my life so many times he's lost track," Josh went on. "But I haven't. That's why I asked him to be a surrogate father—in case anything happened to me. Because as far as I'm concerned, he was the best father any kid could have."

Sam sighed again and cocked his head to rest against Jenny's. He brought up his left hand and put it on her knee. Josh continued to exude praise for Sam until, apparently, something caught his eye off screen. The camera panned sideways.

"'But, hark, what light on yonder balcony shines. 'Tis Jennifer, a rose by any name at all.'"

Jenny and Sam both chuckled at Josh's butchering of Shakespeare's prose.

In a softer voice, Josh added, "If you two are ever watching this, and I'm not around, I want you to know one thing. Love never dies. You both love me. I love both of you. And the greatest gift you could ever give me would be to love each other."

Suddenly, the screen went black. Jenny and Sam froze.

Sam muttered an expletive then jerked his hand from her knee and tucked it under his armpit.

"That was..." Jenny said. "Eerie."

Sam rose, turned off the TV. He took a deep breath

and slowly let it out. He felt as gut-twisted nervous as he did the first time he rode a bull.

Glancing toward his bed, he looked at Jenny. She seemed nervous, too, and he knew instinctively that they were sitting on the same fence. He returned to her side, sat down and looped his arm across her back. He squeezed her gently and nuzzled his face against the crown of her head.

"A part of me wants to throttle him. He never saw anything wrong with manipulating a situation if the outcome was the one he was looking for," Sam said, picturing his brother grinning like a well-fed cat. "But just because he wanted this doesn't mean—" He closed his eyes for a moment. "What we have to decide is whether or not we care enough for each other—"

"No," Jenny interrupted. "We need to decide if we *love* each other, Sam."

That word again.

Jenny lifted her chin and opened her mouth, but Sam kissed her before she could say anything. He engulfed her in his arms, crushing her to his chest as tightly as he dared. Her soft moan seemed more encouragement than distress. He deepened the kiss.

If it weren't for their children asleep behind them and Jenny's great-aunt puttering around downstairs, he would have pulled her into his bed and demonstrated just how much he loved her. And desired her. Instead, he pulled back.

She let out a soft groan. "You're not changing your mind, are you?"

He snickered softly. "Just the opposite." He looked around. This wasn't the most romantic setting… *Just say it, dufus,* he could almost hear his brother shout.

He scooted off the bed and sank to one knee in front of her. "Jenny, you're the mother of my children *and*" he stressed, ''the woman of my dreams. I love you more than one word could possibly convey. Will you marry me?''

He fished his second gift—one that he'd spotted in a jeweler's case in a trendy little shop near his hotel in D.C.—out of his pocket. He hadn't planned on giving it to her this soon, but his talk with Diane had changed things.

He blew a speck of lint off the fat little box before presenting it to her. ''It's an antique ruby. I thought it might look nice with a simple band.''

Jenny's mouth was open but no words were forthcoming. ''Sam,'' she finally cried, tears shimmering in her eyes. ''I...we...oh, my. Yes.'' She took the ring from the box and slipped it onto her finger.

Sam hadn't realized he was holding his breath until he heard the word. He kissed her hard—losing his head in the rush of emotions that surged between them. The possibilities. The future.

''Can we...should we tell people?'' she asked.

''That's up to you. You know this town better than I do.''

For some reason, his answer made her laugh. She removed a folded piece of paper from her hip pocket. ''Read this,'' she said.

Sam rocked back on his haunches. From the format and the long list of names in the header, he recognized it as an e-mail post. After a few sentences he realized it was an advance copy of Gloria Hughes's column for the upcoming edition of the *Ledger.*

In related news, it turns out Sullivan triplet Jenny isn't so ''perfect'' after all. Word has it she gave birth to her brother-in-law's twins last summer—

just hours before her husband passed away. Did she actually believe she could keep something like that a secret?

Blood racing with fury, he crumpled the offending missive. "That small-minded bitch," he growled. "We'll sue that cowardly excuse for a newspaper into oblivion."

Jenny's delighted laughter caught him off guard.

She cupped his jaw, which he'd clamped together in rage. "Don't you get it, Sam? The reason I tried so hard to *be* perfect is that I always felt like I owed it to the town of Gold Creek because its citizens did so much for me and my sisters when we were growing up."

Sam wasn't sure he understood her logic, but his anger disappeared at her touch.

"And later on, when Josh and I got together, he was adamant about staying here. He loved this town, and he wanted so badly to belong that I tried to be perfect for his sake."

Sam's gut twisted at the sadness he heard in her tone.

But suddenly she brightened. "However, you read what Gloria wrote. It's there in black and white, so it must true. I'm *not* perfect."

Sam pulled her into his arms. "You are to me."

She snickered softly. "Don't tell anybody, okay?"

Sam kissed the corners of her lips. "So, should we announce our engagement in the ridiculous *Gold Creek Ledger*?"

She hesitated. "I don't care about the town's opinion, but what will your mother say?"

Sam smiled. "Who do you think gave me the video?"

She pulled back in astonishment. "Really?"

"Josh sent it to her with instructions to give it to *us* when the time was right."

She thought a moment, her teeth worrying her bottom lip. ''What made her decide today was the day?''

Sam shook his head. ''I don't know. You can ask her when you see her.''

Jenny looked momentarily blank then glanced at her watch. ''Oh my God,'' she exclaimed. ''We've got to get ready. It's Christmas Eve. We have company coming.''

The twins, disturbed by their mother's outburst, moved restlessly. He caught her hand before she could go to them.

''Jenny love, just one thing. I know this is going to sound hopelessly old-fashioned, but I'd like to be able to tell our children that, as improbable as it seems, we waited until we were married before we had sex.''

She did a double take. ''I beg your pardon?''

He pulled her back into his arms and kissed her. ''I don't think Josh would expect us to wait a full year from the date of his death. In fact, after watching this video, it occurred to me that St. Patrick's Day might make a fine day for a wedding. We can wait till then, right?''

She relaxed in the circle of his arms. ''Well, I'll have to change my plan to seduce you tonight.'' She grinned at him. ''I think Josh would love it. What better day to become Jenny O'Neal O'Neal?''

Their mutual chuckles were muffled by their kisses.

A minute later, she tilted her head, as if silently doing the math. ''I guess I can wait that long. If you can.''

There was something challenging about her smile; Sam silently groaned. She wasn't going to make the next few months easy for him, but he had a feeling he was going to enjoy every sweet minute.

CHAPTER FIFTEEN

THE CIOPPINO HAD BEEN a great success, but everyone had been too full to do justice to the four pies his mother had brought, so Sam decided to deliver one to the bunkhouse, where his employees without family in the area were spending a quiet Christmas Eve.

The night had turned cold, but after the steamy warmth of the kitchen, Sam relished the brisk night air. He'd grabbed his lined denim jacket and the hat hanging on the peg beside the door then made his escape.

With one hand carrying the pie and the other a plastic container of whipped cream, he had to use the toe of his boot to make his presence known at the bunkhouse door.

The door opened and a head popped out. Harley. The mysterious stranger who'd been dropped off by Sam's miner pal, Lars. "Care package," Sam said.

"Great," the man said. He seemed an easygoing sort, eager to learn, though often baffled by the simplest of tasks. The disparity between Harley's obvious intelligence and his functional skills frustrated Hank, but Sam liked the guy. In some ways, Harley reminded him of Josh. Just as good-natured and affable but far less self-confident.

Sam passed the dishes through the gap in the door but didn't go inside. He had a lot on his mind and needed a few minutes alone before returning to the family gathering. "Merry Christmas," he called as he left.

"You, too. And tell the missus—I mean, Jenny, we said thanks," Harley returned.

Sam touched the brim of his hat in acknowledgment. Harley's mistake would be rectified in March. Jenny had made the announcement over dinner. She'd called Kristin with the news while Sam greeted their guests and served eggnog and mulled wine.

Sam had suggested that they hold off on the announcement until after the holidays, but Jenny said she couldn't wait to share the good news.

After Gordon's eloquent prayer, Jenny had risen and held out her glass in a toast. "This is a very special holiday for us all. We have so much to celebrate—" She'd smiled at the twins who were sitting in their bouncy chairs, having already been fed. "And yet, we can't help but miss Josh." She lifted her glass. "To Josh. Forever in our hearts."

After the ceremonial clinking, she'd reached to take Sam's hand. The table had grown instantly quiet, as if each guest knew what was coming. "Sam and I are getting married," she'd said without preamble.

To Sam's surprise, the reaction was unanimously positive. Andi had chortled with delight when she heard the proposed date for the nuptials. "Too cool. That means Kristin owes me twenty bucks. She said you wouldn't tie the knot until after that whole year-of-mourning thing. I told her she was full of…garlic bread. More bread, anyone?"

While consuming heaping bowls of fish stew, Ida Jane, Diane and Gordon had discussed the pros and cons of a St. Patrick's Day wedding. His mother volunteered to hire someone to play the bagpipes, but Jenny politely declined the offer. "We want to keep it simple but festive, don't we?" she'd asked Sam.

He'd nodded as if he had a clue, but in truth Sam felt overwhelmed. Life had changed—and was still changing—at Mach speed. *But is this the right trajectory?* he asked himself. After shoving his cold hands into the side pockets of his jacket, Sam walked blindly toward the corral instead of returning to the house.

Building this corral had been Josh's first job after they moved the travel trailer onto the property while the log house was being built. With the typical cockiness of a seventeen-year-old, Josh had promised to complete it in one day if Sam would purchase tickets to some rock concert Josh wanted to take his new girlfriend to see.

"You've only been in town two days and you already have a girlfriend?" Sam had exclaimed.

Josh had removed his glove to puff on his nails and polish them against his grimy shirt. "That's me. Josh, the Stud Muffin. Too bad you're only into cows, man. I could give you lessons on the art of love."

Sam chuckled at the memory. A sudden gust of wind lifted his hat—which he just then realized didn't feel quite right on his head—and sent it tumbling across the hard-packed ground. He chased it a few steps. When he picked it up, it dawned on him that the felt was too stiff to be his hat. Holding it up to the light of the half moon, he saw the color—green, not black.

"Damn," he cursed.

After dinner, Jenny had passed out copies of her poem/story. With Sam's permission, she'd retrieved Josh's green cowboy hat from his closet and had set it on the table while Andi read the story aloud.

Everyone had loved the piece. His mother had cried, of course. Ida Jane had insisted the story needed to be published, though Jenny was reluctant to submit even a query letter until the illustrations were complete.

"I plan to work on the drawings once the holidays are over," she'd explained. "From everything I've read, getting something published is no easy task, but I promised Sam I'd look into it."

Sam hung the hat on a nearby post. It tilted at a jaunty angle just the way Josh liked to wear it. A shiver—entirely unrelated to the freezing temperature—passed through his body. "Weird," he muttered under his breath.

Another rogue breeze made the hat rattle as if in answer.

Sam sighed. Just what he didn't need was for people to see him talking to a hat.

Since when do you care what people think?

Sam looked behind him, almost positive he'd heard the words spoken aloud. When he turned back, he saw the green hat sitting atop his brother's head. Josh was perched on the fence. As healthy and vibrant as Sam could remember.

Sam's automatic expletive made Josh laugh.

I'm here to say goodbye and that's the best I get?

The pressure on Sam's chest made it almost impossible to breathe. "No," he choked out. "Wait."

Josh gave the hat a nudge so it tilted back on his head. The starlight made Josh's form shimmer like magic. *I can't, Sam. This is my path. Yours is here. With Jenny. Make me proud, Sam. Live it well.*

He grinned, then disappeared.

Sam dropped to his knees the same instant the hat clattered to the hard ground. Deep, racking sobs echoed in the stillness.

"Sam?" Jenny called, rushing out of the darkness. "What's wrong? Are you okay?"

He struggled to his feet, wiping his cheeks with the sleeve of his jacket. His throat was too tight to speak.

Jenny flew to his side, wrapping her arms around him as if to protect him from whatever demons were attacking him.

"Josh," he managed to say through his hollow sobs.

She nodded, kissing his wet face. "I know, honey. It's hard to say goodbye. I went through this months ago, but you've kept it bottled up inside."

He wasn't sure how to make sense of what he'd seen—or didn't see. Maybe it was an illusion brought on by all that had happened—his and Jenny's decision to marry, viewing Josh's video, the talk with his mother.

"It isn't fair," he managed to croak. "I should have been the one to go. This is Josh's life, not mine."

Jenny grabbed him by both arms and gave him a stern shake. "Don't ever say that again, Sam O'Neal. We don't *own* our time on this planet. It's a gift. Josh's life was way too short, but it was beautiful. And he left us so much. Two babies. Each other. Our families, united and whole—except for Kristin, but I'm working on getting her to move home."

His pain began to subside. Her words were a balm to his soul.

"Sam, your mother and I were just talking. I told her that in my opinion the best way for us to honor Josh's memory is to live with passionate optimism." Her beautiful smile quelled his anguish. "Doesn't that sound like something Josh would say?"

Sam took a deep breath. The frigid air was healing and invigorating. He felt more alive than he had in months.

He gave her a quick but meaningful kiss. "You're

right, Jenny. Life goes on, and we're going live it with gusto—just the way Josh would have wanted.''

He grabbed her hand and pulled her toward the house, pausing only to pick up the hat. ''Your sister was whining about not getting to open a gift, so I think we should resurrect an O'Neal family tradition. We each open one gift on Christmas Eve, then the rest on Christmas morning.''

''I thought you didn't remember anything positive about your childhood?''

''We had our moments. Especially after Josh was born. He loved Christmas. I used to lift him to my shoulders so he could put the angel on the top of the tree.''

Jenny suddenly grabbed the railing that had been installed along with the ramp to accommodate Ida Jane's wheelchair.

''What's wrong?'' he asked.

''The angel,'' she said. ''I thought it was just Josh spending money.''

Sam shook his head. ''What are you talking about?''

''Come with me,'' she said. ''I have to fix something and I need your help.''

Jenny shed her coat in the entry without bothering to hang it up. She kicked off her shoes and was about to walk to the living room, when Ida Jane suddenly appeared. The older woman managed to get around quite well, but she insisted on using her cane—as if afraid to be without it.

She still had moments when she seemed depressed or lost in the past, but those had been noticeably fewer since moving to the ranch. Jenny credited Greta and the twins for the improvement.

''Oh, there you are, dear,'' Ida said cheerfully. ''I want to talk to you a minute.''

Jenny was in a hurry to fix her oversight. She knew what she needed to do. ''Can it wait, Auntie? I have to—''

Ida interrupted. ''I just wanted to tell you that I'll be leaving soon.''

Jenny halted so suddenly Sam bumped into her. ''W-what did you say?'' she sputtered.

Ida gave them both a knowing look. ''A young couple doesn't need an old lady around to cramp their style.''

Sam walked to Ida Jane's side and put his arm around her shoulders, much the way Josh would have done. ''Miss Ida, you can't leave. You're our chaperon. The town gossips—Gloria Hughes, in particular—would have a field day. She'll butcher us in her column then I'll have to sue. We'll spend a fortune in court and won't have anything to show for it. So, please say you'll stay.''

Ida Jane looked unconvinced until Jenny added, ''Please, Auntie. I have so much to do between now and March. I'll need your help more than ever.''

Those words seemed to be what Ida needed to hear. Jenny reminded herself how important it was to hold the ones you love close to your heart and never forget to tell them how much they mean to you. Josh's death had taught her that.

''Well…okay,'' Ida Jane said. She started to return to her room, but Jenny took her hand. ''Come with us, Auntie. We're starting a new tradition. One I think you'll like.''

Five minutes later, Sam gave Jenny a questioning look.

She nodded, after winking at her sister who was sitting on the couch with Ida Jane. Diane and Gordon—each holding a twin—stood nearby.

Sam bent down and picked her up, his strong arms

wrapped around her thighs. His face was level with her belly. Jenny remembered another time when he'd held her like this. Then, she'd been flustered, this time she felt she could stay in his arms forever.

With her left hand, she removed the crystal star and replaced it with Josh's angel.

Once she took away her hand, Sam stepped back and eased her down. But he didn't let go.

"Can we open our presents now?" Andi asked as petulantly as she had when the triplets were children.

Sam's lips—his wonderful lips—turned up in a smile. Some gifts were worth the wait. And Jenny knew that in two and a half months they'd share the best gift of all—a love that was meant to be.

* * * * *

Unexpected Babies

ANNA ADAMS

To Sarah Greengas, Sharon Lavoie,
Jennifer LaBrecque, Amy Lanz, Carmen Green,
Wendy Etherington, Jenni Grizzle, Karen Bishop,
Theresa Goldman and Michele Flinn –
Thank you for reading my unpolished pages.

And to Paula Eykelhof and Laura Shin.
Thank you for the chance and for all I've
already learned from you.

CHAPTER ONE

CATE TALBOT PALMER opened her car door and stepped into the sand-blown street that paralleled the beach. Above the small, stucco building in front of her a metal sign rattled like faint thunder in the wind off the ocean. The sign read Palmer Construction, Leith, Georgia.

Her husband, Alan, was inside at his desk. Nearly two hours late for the burned five-course dinner she'd abandoned on their dining room table.

Cate ran one hand across her stomach. The stench of dry, overcooked lamb mingled with ocean salt. She swallowed, her throat almost clenching she felt so nauseous. She'd suggested a special dinner tonight because she'd finally decided to tell Alan the secret she'd been keeping. Thank God she hadn't told him before.

She'd waited for him, staring at a bottle of sparkling grape juice she'd set on the table between their plates as a hint. She'd memorized that bottle while she'd opened her eyes to the facts. She and Alan had both kept secrets for the past sixteen weeks, only she'd been desperate enough to pretend she didn't see what Alan was doing.

Late nights at the office, fierce silences at home, see-through excuses for the cell phone he'd practically strapped to his hand. Most women would suspect an affair, but Alan Palmer had a different problem.

His mother had left him and his father when he was ten because his dad couldn't give her the material things she'd wanted. As a result of that long-ago abandonment and the way his father had used him as a confidant during the divorce, Alan tied his worth to his success with Palmer Construction.

He'd do anything to provide for Cate and Dan, their eighteen-year-old son, but he kept his emotional distance, afraid to risk the kind of pain he and his father had barely survived. His need to protect Cate had pushed her away, because she wanted a husband who would let her help him solve his problems, not pull away when troubles came.

She sprang from a long line of Talbots who'd failed at marriage or any relationship close to that kind of commitment. She and Alan had tried to create the family they'd both craved in their childhoods. Instead, they'd created an emotional divide.

She felt as if she'd already raised Dan on her own. She'd made up excuses for Alan's absences, for his distraction when he showed up late at one family gathering after another. She couldn't start that over again. This time, if she raised a child alone, it would be because she no longer lived with her baby's father.

A car passed her. She knew the driver. Another mom whose son was about to graduate from high school. Cate pasted a smile on her face. After today she wouldn't have to pretend everything was normal.

Wind from the car blew her hair across her face,

and Cate brushed the strands out of her eyes. She refused to wait for Alan to tell her what was wrong with the business. Hurting from the pain of another betrayal cost her more than knowing the truth. She'd make him tell her.

Squaring her shoulders, she marched across the street to the office. Her legs felt like jelly. She opened the frosted glass doors that were engraved with the company's name.

The moment she stepped inside, the temperature dropped. Even in mid-May, the South Georgia heat made air-conditioning a requirement. Cate swiped at perspiration on her forehead. Her hand trembled in front of her eyes.

She'd offer Alan a chance to explain because she still didn't want to leave him. When they were good, they were very, very good.

Alan's voice murmured from the office area. For a moment she hoped he had a late appointment with a client. Then she recognized a tone she always dreaded hearing. She couldn't understand what he was saying, but he was in trouble.

Her anger simmered as every excuse Alan had given her in the past few weeks repeated in her head. She wouldn't have kept her own secret if she'd trusted him.

Not that she could give him all the blame. She'd stayed. She hated feeling dependent, and her relationship with Alan made her feel dependent rather than stronger. When they were bad, they were unbearable.

Striding past models of the buildings and homes the company was contracted to build or renovate,

Cate tried to imagine why her husband had decided his success here meant more than their marriage.

She passed empty offices. Her twin sister, Caroline, who worked as an interior designer for the company, had already gone home.

Alan's office lay at the end of the hall. The air conditioning's whisper cushioned the sound of Cate's feet on the Berber carpet. Suddenly, John Mabry, Leith's chief of police, leaned into Cate's view, his bulk bending the frame of his chair as he crossed his arms behind his head.

"I know," he said on a hefty sigh. "A trained cop had no business losing Jim Cooper in the men's room, but I didn't train the cops who work the Newark airport. Just chill, Alan. We'll find him and your money before you have to shut your doors for good."

The carpet's warp seemed to rise up and trip Cate. Jim Cooper was their CPA, an oily man who always stood too close, tried to talk too intimately. She stumbled to a halt, flexing her fingers against the creamy, patterned wallpaper. The truth came as no surprise, but hearing it in plain words felt like a near fatal wound.

"What if we're already too late?" Alan asked. "I'm working my creditors now as if I were the criminal."

"What?" Mabry said in a sharp tone.

"With my banker's help." Alan placated the other man. "But I don't do business this way, and I don't like knowing my employees may be working on borrowed time."

The scream in Cate's head must have translated to some kind of sound. John Mabry turned to her, surprise widening his eyes. She pulled her hand off the wall. Nearly twenty years of pretending her marriage was healthy had honed her skills. She'd pretend nothing was wrong. Next best thing to acting as if Alan had talked to her about the problem.

"Hey, John."

"Evening, Cate."

Alan's chair squeaked. After a few muffled steps, he came around the door, tall, dark and clueless. "Is something wrong with Dan?"

Startled at his unexpected question, Cate searched tanned features that had thinned over the past weeks to an ascetic sharpness. His problems in this office had distracted him. He'd forgotten their meal and his promise to come home early. Naturally, he only expected her to show up if something was wrong with their son.

"Dan's fine."

A father's fear haunted his eyes. Alan loved the idea of family. He truly loved their son—as much as she did.

"I came because you're late," she said.

He turned a wary gaze on the police chief. "John..."

Mabry pried himself out of his chair. "I'll get back to you later, Alan."

Cate watched the other man leave. With each step he took toward the front of the building, she braced herself to face the reason for her husband's guilty expression.

"Cate." Taking her arm, Alan forced her to look at him before she was ready.

She shook him off. "Don't." All she wanted was

for him to tell her she was wrong. "Why was John here?"

"Please believe I wanted to tell you." He took her hands again. Heat throbbed from his callused palms.

She splayed her fingers over the undersides of his wrists, where his pulse tapped an alarm. A measure of calm came to her despite confusion that had become familiar. "Something's happened. Again."

He tightened his hands, but he couldn't seem to answer her. She studied his face, intent on every nerve, every shadow of guilt that flitted behind eyes that knew her both too well and not at all.

"This time was different, Cate."

"You always say it's different, but it never is." The future yawned in front of her like a hungry mouth. "You keep problems from me because you think I'll leave if the business goes sour."

Sweat beaded on his upper lip. He didn't look well, but she couldn't spare him any more of her empathy.

"I would have told you." He released one of her hands so he could wipe the drops of moisture off his mouth. "I had to make sure I knew how much trouble we're facing."

"I don't trust you." She flattened her free hand over her belly, tracing the mound she couldn't hide much longer. She wouldn't expose another child to a part-time father. "I can't go on the way we are, and you can't change. You never would have told me about Jim. You planned to clean up the mess by yourself."

"I haven't told anyone except Mabry and the bank. Jim Cooper embezzled from the business accounts. He stole from every company he worked for. We've all lost money, and we're trying to find Jim before he knows we're looking for him.''

She fought to control her anger, but reason hadn't worked with him in the past. ''First, you should tell the employees if they're in danger of losing their jobs. Second, I don't work for you, and I'm not a newspaper reporter. You have no right to keep me in the dark. I'm your wife, and I have an equal share in this business. I turned myself into a stay-at-home mom for Dan, not because I'm not intelligent enough to be part of this company.''

''I never said you weren't bright enough to understand the business, Cate.'' He frowned, deep lines leaving furrows between his nose and mouth. ''John told me the police had tracked Jim to the Newark airport.''

''That part I understood. You're obviously worried, and I'm sorry, but I don't know why you won't let me help you.''

''What could you have done?''

''I don't know, but you never gave me a chance. You prefer to suffer alone.''

''I'm supposed to protect you and Dan.''

''Please don't start that old story again.'' She freed herself from him. ''I'm not like your mother. I don't need a house or a car or clothes that impress our neighbors. If the business burned to the ground, I'd want to help you rebuild, but you wouldn't turn to me. You want to protect me, but Dan and I can't count on you if something goes wrong in this office.'' She spun blindly toward the reception area. She had one thought—to escape this building without him—but he kept pace with her as if she were crawling.

"Where are you going?" His stunned tone hurt most of all.

"I told you I wouldn't stay if you hid anything else from me."

"Tell me how I'm different than you, Cate. How often are you at Aunt Imogen's or Uncle Ford's houses? They don't need a nursemaid."

"They're family, and they took Caroline and me in when Mom and Dad didn't want us." Her parents, both officers in Naval Intelligence, had dropped her and her sister off at Aunt Imogen's on their way to an isolated duty station in Turkey. From there, they'd gone on to one unaccompanied assignment after another, and Cate and Caroline had remained with their maiden aunt and bachelor uncle in Leith. "They're both alone and over seventy. I look in on them." And they continued to give her the unconditional love she'd never had from either her parents or Alan.

"What about Caroline? You run to her and Shelly every time they try to change a lightbulb." Her sister had raised her daughter alone since Caroline's husband had abandoned them when Shelly was only four. Alan had never seemed to resent her attention to their extended family before, but desperation edged his tone. "You cushion them and Dan in cotton wool. I'm only trying to give you the kind of care you give our family."

His last, self-serving point pushed Cate too far. She turned on him, but momentum carried her too close to him. His familiar, spicy scent triggered a basic need whose power had always frightened her.

Wanting him so much, she felt weak and angry with herself. ''Don't look for someone to blame because you and I failed at our marriage.''

He reeled backward, stumbling into a model of the library they were supposed to refurbish. Instinctively, Cate caught his arm before she was certain whether she wanted to shove him or help him.

No, she knew what she had to do. ''I stayed for Dan, but he leaves for college in a few weeks. I don't have to pretend you and I are going to live happily ever after. Not together, anyway.''

''Cate.'' His husky plea caught her unawares. He reached for her, his wedding band glowing gold in the building's artificial light.

She arched away from him. Tears clouded her vision, but she grabbed the chrome rail on the front doors. Approaching night had strengthened the ocean breeze, and she had to lean her whole body into the door to open it.

Outside the wind whipped her hair into her eyes. She bumped into a soft figure that had to be a woman. Cate muttered a tear-choked apology and broke for the street. But she stumbled into a parking meter and fell off the sidewalk.

Her right ankle turned over. Pain nearly paralyzed her as her foot skidded through sand. Behind her, a woman's voice shrilled, but the deep blast of a car horn seemed to finish her shriek. Cate straightened, turning. A green sports car, coming fast, froze her.

''Cate!'' Alan must have followed her. He was furious, afraid and too far away.

She reached blindly into thin air, twisting back toward the sidewalk. Seconds stretched, defying the laws of nature. Alan caught her hands. She recognized the strength of his long fingers, the breadth of his palms. She grabbed at him, but she couldn't get her feet beneath her in the sand. Holding on to her husband, she peered over her shoulder at the driver.

Intensity crumpled his face. His body lifted in the seat, as if he were standing on his brakes.

They screamed, and time lost its elasticity.

Cate willed her body away from the car. Alan yanked her, but something glanced off her leg, more a jarring thump than real pain.

At first.

Alan pulled her hard against his body as a fire-edged knife seemed to slice through her thigh. Behind her, the car's tires ground into the road and chaos faded to silence.

An unnatural silence, empty of voices or traffic, footsteps or the constant whisper of the ocean. Cate knew only pain and an overwhelming nausea. Panic clutched at her. Was she sick because of the baby, or the torture of her leg? Was she going to lose her baby?

"I've got you. You're safe."

She looked up. Alan's fear fed her terror. She hadn't trusted him enough to tell him about her pregnancy, and now she didn't know how to say the words.

"Focus on me." Alan turned his head. "Somebody call 911!"

Around them, cell phones erupted in a cacophony of beeps. Somehow, Cate found a smile, but Alan stared at her, amazed.

She concentrated on his green eyes. ‘‘You’ve always wanted to save my life.’’

With his face pale as beach sand, Alan didn’t smile back. ‘‘Don’t talk.’’

People she knew, Alan’s busiest carpenter and Mr. Parker, who owned the Bucket O’ Suds, edged into her peripheral vision.

‘‘Look at the blood running down her leg, Alan.’’ Mr. Parker pushed a man-smelling apron beneath her nose. ‘‘Maybe you need this.’’

‘‘Get a damn ambulance,’’ Alan snarled, but then the muscles around his mouth worked as he fought to maintain his composure. ‘‘Cate, you’re all right.’’

A resounding roar overwhelmed her silent prayer that he’d keep holding her too close for her to look down and see the blood. Pressure, like a giant hand, seemed to push her toward the ground. ‘‘I think I’m not all right.’’

She was going to faint. First time she could ever remember fainting. Was she dying? ‘‘Alan, I— Dan— I want—’’

‘‘Dan’s fine.’’ Alan’s voice cracked. ‘‘You’re fine.’’

‘‘I have to tell you...’’ That strange pressure swathed her in darkness. Only Alan’s arms kept her from falling. She forgot what she had to tell him, but she hung on until the darkness swallowed her whole.

DR. BARTON’S CALM infuriated Alan. ‘‘After a thirty-six hour coma, we can’t know how she’ll be when she wakes up. She lost a lot of blood from that gash in her thigh, and she went into shock.’’

Each word the doctor spoke embedded itself in

Alan like a gut shot. Infuriated that he couldn't help her, he stared at his unconscious wife. Her vulnerable, wounded body rumpled the blanket on her bed. The bank of blinking monitors that surrounded her screeched persistently enough to wake the dead. Alan bit the side of his cheek.

Men didn't cry. So his father had preached, weeping into his beer or scrambled eggs or the ironing they'd both avoided after Alan's mother left. Clutching Cate's unresponsive hand, Alan alternated between an urge to bawl with unmanly pain and an acute need to break everything in the small hospital room.

"She'll wake up," Dr. Barton said, as if he saw through Alan's attempt at stoic silence. "She's healthy—no sign of infection in her wound. We just have to see where we stand. Tests, physical therapy— Excuse me, Alan, Nurse Matthews wants me."

The doctor barely cleared the doorway before Cate's twin, Caroline, slipped into the room.

She shared his wife's fragile bone structure and dark auburn hair. In the old days, only he could tell them apart until Cate had begun using a blow-dryer to straighten her hair into a sleek curtain that brushed her shoulders. She'd looked more like a bank president than a loving creative homemaker. Caroline, a pragmatic businesswoman, never bothered to tame the wild curls she used now to cover her face. Neither of them seemed to see the contradiction in their hairstyles, but maybe Cate had expressed her altered feelings about her life in a not so subtle change.

Alan rubbed his fist against his temple, annoyed

that he hadn't asked her such questions before she'd decided to leave him.

Caroline eased around the bed. "What does Dr. Barton say?"

The sisters were so close they sometimes shared each other's thoughts. If only Cate could sense Caroline's pain, she'd wake up, feeling a compulsion to help her twin.

"Barton says the same thing over and over. We have to wait." He stroked his wife's forearm, grateful for the body heat that warmed her silky skin. How long since he'd touched her? How had he not noticed she was avoiding him, even in their bed? "I'm fed up with waiting." Waiting and thinking about all the signs he should have read as he and Cate traveled to the end of their marriage.

"Where's your dad, Alan? He's the only member of our families unaccounted for in the waiting room, and I think you need him."

Richard Palmer hated hospitals. Sickness scared the pants off him. "You know his phobia."

"I thought he might have handled it for Cate."

She clearly disapproved, and Alan didn't blame her. "He calls our answering machine at home every ten minutes." Alan roused himself. Last time he'd been out of this room, the waiting area had been empty. "Is Dan out there?"

Caroline shook her head. "I sent Shelly to look for him, and she called when she found him carrying a gas can down the highway. They'll come here after she takes him to a service station and then back to his car."

He nodded, twisting his hands on the metal bed

rail. ''A full gas tank probably seems pretty mundane to him right now.'' He and Dan had stumbled blindly through the past two days. Cate anchored their family. Alan only hoped he was taking up enough of her slack to be a good father.

Caroline's eyes seemed unnaturally wide as she tried to smile. ''We're all afraid. What if she doesn't wake up? How long are we supposed to—''

''Don't think about giving up.'' Alan briefly hugged his sister-in-law. ''She feels what you feel, Caroline.'' It was ridiculous, putting such an airy-fairy notion into words, but Caroline met his gaze with Talbot determination.

''Don't you worry.'' She gripped Cate's hand. ''I refuse to lose her.''

Caroline's tenacity almost renewed his faith. But it might be too late for him and Cate. Her serious injuries and the possibility she'd never let him try to win her back lingered in his mind.

He'd wanted to make her life comfortable and easy. Instead he'd let her down, and even now, he wasn't sure what he'd done wrong.

The door swished open, and Aunt Imogen entered the room without speaking. Her bare head made Alan take a second look. She habitually wore oversize straw hats that she'd trimmed with flower displays never seen in nature. Today, only her fine gray curls clung to her temples.

Courage in her tired gaze touched Alan. He'd swear she hadn't closed her eyes since he'd had to tell her about Cate. Neither had he, but she looked fragile.

He dragged a chair to the side of Cate's bed. The

way he'd let Cate think he resented her care for Aunt Imogen shamed him. According to local gossip, the older woman had been in midheartbreak over an affair with a married navy pilot when she'd taken in Cate and Caroline. Her emotionally hungry nieces had loved their aunt back to health, and Aunt Imogen and her brother, Ford, had shown Cate and Caroline the only true family affection they'd ever known. They'd also convinced Alan he belonged to the Talbot clan from the first day Cate had brought him home. He owed them as much as Cate ever could.

Taking Caroline's hand, Aunt Imogen sat and smoothed the sheet beside Cate's hip. "I guess you spoke to Dr. Barton this morning, Alan?"

Before he could answer, Uncle Ford prodded his way into the small room with the aid of a cherry cane and his great-niece Shelly's hand at his elbow. Behind them, Dan craned for a glimpse of his mom.

Alan sidled through the others to wrap his arms around his son's surprisingly broad shoulders. Dan hugged back, to Alan's relief, but then he quickly pulled away. Dan preferred a handshake in recent years.

Alan met Aunt Imogen's questioning gaze. "Barton can't say much until Cate wakes up."

"Until she breaks out of that coma," Caroline said, as if the coma were an animal that had wrapped her sister in its vicious grip. "Let's face facts."

"I won't face that word." Aunt Imogen stood, her expression a faultless display of barely controlled fear. "Take this chair, Ford. Stop banging that cane."

Her brother gave her an annoyed glance. "Good

thing I'm not sensitive about having to use it.'' He patted his sister's hand. ''I know you're just worried.'' Bellowing at a decibel level that compensated for the hearing loss he refused to admit, Uncle Ford nevertheless took Aunt Imogen's seat. ''Maybe the racket will wake—'' he actually lifted his voice ''—Cate.''

Her foot twitched beneath the blanket. Alan went back to her bed. ''Cate?'' Could waking her be that easy?

Her eyelids fluttered. For a horrified moment, he was afraid she couldn't open her eyes.

''Cate,'' he said, ''wake up. Uncle Ford, why didn't you shout at her before?''

''Shall I try again?'' Uncle Ford struggled to his feet, maybe to lean a touch closer to Cate's ear. He might have yelled again, except Dan appeared at his side to help him—or maybe to hold him back.

Alan flashed his son a grateful smile and took Cate's hand. ''Wake up,'' he said again. ''Please, Cate.'' He didn't beg easily, and his reticence had been a sore spot between them. He'd beg pretty damn freely now. ''Cate,'' he said again, and she opened her eyes and held them open. Her steady blue gaze made him want to shout, but he knew better than to scare her.

''Are you in pain?'' He didn't dare look away. Something different in her expression bothered him—some level of detachment he'd always expected to see. Wives detached themselves, no matter what you did to keep them with you. ''Caroline, get the doctor.''

As Caroline left, Cate's gaze followed her. She

studied each person around her bed. Nothing that made her the Cate he loved was in that gaze. She eyed her aunt and uncle, her son and her niece with the same strange, dreamy look until she focused on Alan again.

"Who are you?"

The courtesy in her tone chilled him.

Trying to ask her what the hell she was talking about, he choked on his first breath. Confusion threaded the air, like a piece of twine that slipped from body to body. Strangling them all.

Aunt Imogen finally cried out, but then she covered her mouth. Uncle Ford's cane clattered to the floor. Alan reached for both older people, steadying them with hands that shook hard enough to remind him how his father felt about men who gave in to their emotions.

But even his dad would understand this. Cate had left him after all.

THE LOVELY WOMAN with copper hair had raced out of the room, and the others, except for the dark man, poured after her. Just as well. Breathing took such an awful effort, and that many people must use a lot of oxygen.

Why would a hospital let such a crowd mill around a patient's room? She stopped in midthought. She must be the patient. She was in bed.

How she'd come there escaped her, although she felt as if someone had welded a hot metal plate to her right leg. Nausea hovered, as if she were on a boat that refused to stop rocking.

She willed her queasiness away and concentrated

on the man. Watching her from wide, dark-green eyes, he was clearly waiting for her to speak. As if he knew her.

She didn't know him.

She must have been in an accident. Had she interrupted a family reunion? That many people in the same place had to be a family.

She took a deep breath that seemed to fill her head. The truth rocked her. Strangers didn't hang around a hospital bed, even if they'd banded together to rescue an accident victim.

She didn't remember what had happened to her. She remembered—nothing.

At her shoulder, a monitor's steady beep grew more rapid. The sound drew her gaze as she tried to pry her own name out of her blank memory. She didn't seem to have a name.

She knew her name. Everyone knew her own name. It was— She could feel it on the tip of her tongue. She ought to know. The monitor began to ping like sonar.

She didn't know.

Suddenly aware of the man's harsh grip on her hand, she turned toward him. "I don't know you."

"I'm your husband. I'm Alan."

He terrified her. She tried to sit up in bed, but a powerful, formless weight held her down.

"I'll help you," he said.

He wrapped his large hands around her upper arms, but his strength made her feel weak, and she pushed him away.

"I don't need your help."

Stung, he straightened, looking impossibly tall.

"What's the matter?" He reached for her again, but something in her eyes must have shown him how seriously she wanted him to keep his hands off her. He fisted them at his sides.

"You act as if you have some right to touch me," she whispered. "Who am I?" She wasn't sure she wanted to know.

"My wife," he said. "Cate…Palmer."

"Why don't I know you?" She darted a glance at the window. Low clouds hung above a sandstone building. It all looked completely unfamiliar. The glass offered a faint reflection, but she couldn't see the details of her face. "Let me see what I look like. Maybe I'll rememb—"

Before she could finish, he whipped open the top of the table at her elbow. A mirror was mounted inside. With the man's help, she twisted the table toward her, so she could see.

Wild blue eyes stared at her from beneath a mass of dark red hair. She gasped. That other woman—the one who'd gone for a doctor. She had the same face.

The mouth in the mirror opened, and a scream tore the air.

"Cate." His fear-drenched voice scared her, but he tucked her against his body, and she seemed to fit into the hard contours of his chest.

She closed her eyes. Darkness and the man's faint, spicy scent blotted out the mirror, the room, the world as far as she knew it. She didn't want to see herself. She'd lost everything, her past, her sense of identity.

Her life.

CHAPTER TWO

"ALAN, GO HOME. Get some sleep and have a shower." Dr. Barton's voice woke Cate.

She opened her eyes. She'd hardly been out of the coma for a full day, but the doctor's visits interested her. Unlike her family, he wanted nothing from her. She looked from him to the husband she didn't know.

Alan straightened in a metal-and-vinyl chair. "I don't need sleep or a shower."

She lifted her hand to him, but he shook his head, obviously aware she was going to second Dr. Barton's suggestion. She continued anyway. "You need to rest." She shouldn't have buried her face in his manly chest. Her momentary weakness had apparently convinced him she needed a bodyguard. "Nothing bad will happen to me if you leave my room."

He shot a wary glance at Dr. Barton, who nodded. Alan stood, but tension built as he hesitated. Cate didn't know how to respond to him. His deep concern touched her. She found his stubbled chin attractive, his brooding green eyes appealing. She liked the way he smelled, but Alan expected more than the gratitude and simple attraction she felt.

"Do you want me to come back?" he asked.

She'd like to remember why he seemed as uncomfortable with her as she was with him. Had their marriage been happy? "After you rest, if you feel like coming back, I'll be here."

He turned toward Dr. Barton, but his gaze lingered on her as he spoke. "You know where to reach me?"

The doctor moved to Cate's bed, an impresario, showing off his brightest talent. "Cate is awake and healthy and on the mend. We won't need to dive into that pool of phone numbers you gave us."

With a wry expression, Alan trudged to the door, and most of the pressure left with him. Cate sank against her pillows. The gruff doctor shut her door and dragged a chair to her bed.

"Let's talk," he said.

His urgency alarmed her. "Did you find something in the tests?"

"No—well, nothing new, but I've been trying to get you alone since you woke up yesterday. I have to tell you something I don't believe you've told Alan."

She attempted a smile. "Another man came forward to claim me as his wife."

He gave a slight, anxious grin that put her on edge. "We only allow one family per amnesiac." His gaze grew as intense as any of her family's. "I wish I could prepare you for this news, but I must say it quickly before someone else comes in. You're pregnant, and I've been unethical." He patted her good leg. "What a relief to say it out loud at last."

Cate grabbed her bed rails as the world seemed to open up beneath her. "I'm pregnant?"

"Just over sixteen weeks." He went on, as if they should both be ready to talk facts. "You were spotting when you came in. By the time we could leave you to speak to Alan, he should already have asked us about the baby. When he didn't, I began to worry you hadn't told him and that you had a reason for not telling him. I asked Imogen for your gynecologist's name.''

Words escaped her at first. ''How old am I again?''

''Thirty-eight.''

Pregnant, thirty-eight, with a son of eighteen, and she hadn't told anyone about the new baby. Why?

She slid her hands over her stomach. It was round all right. She hadn't thought to ask why. An unexpected protectiveness caught her by surprise, and she accepted a new first priority. ''Is the baby all right?''

''Yes. Your bleeding was light, and you stopped within a few hours. I still would have told Alan if I hadn't tracked down Dr. Davis.''

''My obstetrician?''

''Right. She said you'd decided not to tell Alan yet, so I followed your wishes. However, Dr. Davis needs to see you, so you have to decide how to tell Alan. She'll never make it in here and out again without being ambushed, considering the way your family guards that door.''

Cate's large family overwhelmed her, too. She couldn't see their constant, well-meant surveillance as a joke. ''No one else asked about the baby? Not my sister or my aunt?''

''I wish they had.''

''Did Dr. Davis explain why I've kept the pregnancy a secret?''

''She doesn't know, and I can't promise Imogen

hasn't talked to Alan since I asked her for your OB's name.'' Dr. Barton patted her forearm. ''Try not to worry. I expect Alan would have exploded by now if Imogen had told him.''

''I need to talk to Alan. What was wrong between us?''

''I'm not sure anything was wrong.''

Cate pushed her fingers through her hair. ''Dr. Barton, tell me the truth.'' She pressed her palms together, trying to look self-possessed. She didn't want or need a gentle bedside manner. ''Will I ever know these people again?''

He hunched his shoulders beneath his wrinkled lab coat. ''All I ever say to you or Alan is 'I don't know.' And I don't. Because shock, rather than a head injury, caused your amnesia, I'd say your memory will trickle back.'' Grinning, he popped his glasses from the top of his head onto his face, where they magnified his weary eyes. ''Trickle. That's a technical term.''

Cate tried to smile, but his nonanswer made her head ache. She lifted her hand between them, turning it from side to side. ''I must have seen my fingers millions of times, but I don't recognize them. I scared myself to death when I looked in a mirror and saw my sister's face. My son makes me feel anxious, because he's at an age where he won't even say if he feels let down. I'm responsible for him, but I don't feel that he's my child, and I'm more comfortable talking to you than to my husband.''

''These are the facts. You can't balance them with what you feel, because all your emotions are tied up in your memory loss.'' Dr. Barton folded her fingers between his weathered hands. "I don't know why you'd hide a child from Alan, but he cares about you. He stood a vigil at your bedside no matter how many times I begged him to go home. I thought we might end up having to treat him. That man didn't stay all this time because he felt it was his duty."

Good. She didn't want a dutiful marriage. She wanted passion and commitment, a love that made a thirty-eight-year-old woman want to tell her husband they were having a second child.

Might she have hidden her pregnancy from Alan for a more obvious and insidious reason than a marriage that had wound down to duty? "What if Alan isn't the baby's father? Would you have heard rumors if I was having an affair?"

Dr. Barton sat back as if someone had tried to yank his chair out from under him. "The Talbots have a bad habit of making destructive decisions, but not you, Cate."

"Talbots?" She found no comfort in his vehement support.

"Your father's family. Your Aunt Imogen and Uncle Ford. Before you, the Talbots have tended to live by their own reckless rules, but you've broken that mold, Cate. I've known your family a long time, and I've seen you make healthier choices than the others."

"Explain, please."

"No. You speak to Imogen or Caroline." At his nervous glance, she imagined redheaded women who ran with wolves and men who sought the company of sinners. "You need to rebuild your relationships with your aunt and uncle and sister, not with me."

"You're not hurt because I can't remember you."

He held up both hands. "You have to jump off this cliff. Think of me as a parachute if you jump and you need help getting to the ground, but talk to your family."

Outside her room, a woman's voice paged another doctor over the PA system, and some sort of heavy equipment rolled down the hall on squeaky wheels. Still, Dr. Barton waited for her to behave the way she always had.

Cate covered her face with her hands, but then flattened her palms at her sides. "I can't lie here and wait for my life to happen to me, can I?"

He slipped his hands in his pockets. "I'll arrange for Dr. Davis to see you. Figure out what to tell Alan about the baby."

Memory must shape a person's sense of self. When she tried to think how she should approach Alan, she faced a mental blank. "I think I'll try the truth." She winced a little. "The truth as we know it, anyway."

ALAN DIDN'T go home and sleep. Instead, he asked Dan to join him in an early round of golf at the country club they'd belonged to since Dan had begun to show unexpected talent for the game.

Alan kept waiting for the right moment to ask his son why he was avoiding Cate. Since his golf skills didn't measure up to Dan's, searching for lost balls usually made them talk. Today Dan helped him scour the primordial, South Georgia forest in uneasy silence. He grunted one-syllable responses to Alan's opening gambits. Finally, after they turned in their cart, Alan suggested lunch in the club's excessively Victorian grill room.

After they ordered, Dan sprawled in his wide wooden chair with a look that anticipated a firing squad. "What do you want, Dad?"

His sullen question surprised Alan. Normally, Cate handled these types of conversations. He didn't know where to go when Dan was clearly saying he didn't want to talk.

"Are you angry with your mom? Why won't you go see her?"

Dan rubbed his chin, unconsciously pointing out a little late adolescent acne. "She only woke up yesterday. I had to do some stuff for Uncle Ford and Aunt Imogen."

Was he serious? Did he really think the horses Uncle Ford boarded or Aunt Imogen's errands might be more important than Cate? "But why didn't you stay long enough to tell your mom you were glad she's okay? I know you are."

"You're talking like you think I wish she was still in the coma. I'm not a kid, Dad. I'll go see her." He sat back as their server delivered sodas and small salads.

"Hey, Dan," the girl said.

"Hey. You know my Dad?" Dan generally knew more of the people who worked at the club than Alan or Cate. He'd played enough golf here to earn a scholarship for college.

This time, the girl looked faintly familiar.

"Sure, I know Mr. Palmer. How are you?" she asked.

He was on the verge of losing his mind. ''Fine. Nice to see you.''

Nodding, she turned away. Dan's smirk mocked his father. ''Why didn't you just admit you didn't know her? I would have introduced you again.''

''To be honest, I don't have time. I need to go back to the hospital, and I wish you'd come with me.''

Dan lifted his soda for a slow sip. When he put the glass down, he wiped his mouth and looked like the kid Alan remembered. ''I'll go,'' he finally said, ''but I'm not sure why. She doesn't even know us.''

Alan studied him, taken aback. He finally understood how Cate had felt when she'd been the one Dan turned to. She'd handled their family's emotional upheavals and freed Alan to provide material support. He wanted to retire to a safe corner and wallow in his own fear, but this time he was the one who had to put his son first.

''Are you afraid your mom's not going to get well?'' He was starting from scratch with a boy he loved more than his own life.

Dan's friend came back and slid their meals onto the table. Even after she left, Dan focused all his attention on getting ketchup to come out of its bottle.

''Son, I need you to talk to me.''

''What am I supposed to say? How does she want us to feel about her? She's always been overprotective. She offered my little league coach tips when he yelled at me for rubbernecking. She's chaperoned every school trip I've ever taken. Now, she looks at me and her bottled water with the same interest.''

Dan had avoided overt affection for about four

years, but Alan dared to clip his son's shoulder with a loose fist. ''Don't underestimate how much she needs you. I don't think she's forgotten us forever, and she's still your mom. You be a son to her, and she'll follow your lead.''

Alan felt like a fraud advising Dan when he still hadn't decided what he was going to tell Cate about the business. As he'd chased her out of the office, he'd longed for a chance to start over. He had it now, but it was a bitter beginning.

''Dad, you look worried. I don't want you to keep anything from me.''

Alan shook off his indecision for Dan's sake. ''Dr. Barton promised your mom will be back on her feet in time to see you graduate.''

Dan folded a fry into his mouth. ''Will she want to come?''

Alan dropped the corner of his turkey club. ''Yes.'' Cate would have found an answer more convincing than his shocked, one-word response. He tried again. ''She'll want to see you graduate from high school.''

Dan sounded a youthful, impatient snort. ''Sorry, Dad, but I can't really take your word for it.'' He tossed another fry into his mouth and talked around it. ''I'll go by the hospital after practice this afternoon.''

Alan didn't pause to enjoy his success. ''Thanks, son. I'd better get back myself. How are your aunt and uncle?''

''I stayed at Aunt Imogen's last night after I fed the horses. Uncle Ford came over for a movie and popcorn, and then I walked Polly for Aunt Imogen.''

Imogen had recently retired Polly, her old roan mare, from farm work. She'd presented Polly with an extravagant straw hat that matched one of her own. Shocking the neighborhood, but never Cate and Caroline, who loved their aunt for her fabled eccentricity, both Imogen and Polly wore their finery for their nightly walks.

"Did you wear the hat?"

"Sure, Dad, and I took a picture so you could use it for that dorky Christmas card you send out every year."

Cate actually sent the card, but Alan had taken pride in her annual record of their family. He pushed his chair back. "Why don't you stay with Uncle Ford tonight? I'm sure your being there helps them."

"Maybe I'll pick them up after practice and take them to see Mom."

Alan got to his feet. "Sounds good. You want to sign for lunch? I'll see you later."

"Okay." Dan looked up. Strands of his longish black hair made him blink blue eyes exactly the shade of Cate's. "I'm sorry I didn't want to talk. I'm a little scared."

Alan held back a relieved sigh. He felt as if he were luring a wild animal into a clearing. He didn't want to scare Dan into running for cover. "Are you all right?"

Dan immediately thinned his smile. "I just hope Mom is. Soon."

Alan hoped male stoicism didn't run in his family, but he'd protected his own feelings long enough to recognize the steps his son was taking.

Close off. Look tough.

"Take it easy, son," he said, wanting to hug his almost grown boy. "I'll see you later." He risked a quick pat on Dan's shoulder and then crossed the black-and-burgundy dining room.

Hurrying back to his car, he checked his watch. He needed to talk to Caroline about her budgets for the medical building, but first he wanted to see his wife. Fifteen minutes took him to the hospital.

He parked in the lot and stared up at the skeletal, half-finished building that overshadowed the hospital. His work site, the new medical building.

Wind blew sand in his eyes, blurring his vision. He wiped a film of sweat off his neck as the early May sun soaked through his clothing. Work continued on the medical center despite the troubled turn his finances had taken. Thoughts of the money he'd owe his suppliers made him sweat some more.

He wanted to tell the suppliers, just as he'd wanted to tell Cate and their employees, about the damage their CPA had done. He hadn't known how to tell Cate he'd failed her by letting Jim steal from them. The other businessmen Jim had duped had decided not to tell their employees until they knew the extent of the problem. He'd argued, but he'd finally agreed to hold off. Deciding to lie to Cate had been shamefully easy.

Maybe her injuries gave him a real reason to hide the truth. Getting acquainted with her family again would be hard enough. Maybe by the time she remembered everything, the police would have found Jim and the funds he'd stolen. Cate might not have to know.

Her accusations came back to him loud and clear

and all too accurate. He'd always followed the same pattern, trying to fix business problems before he had to tell her about them.

He climbed the slight rise to the hospital entrance. Inside, he drank in the cooler air.

The guard who patrolled the lobby stepped forward. Alan knew him and the lavender-haired woman behind the information desk. Formerly kindergarten teacher to half the adults in Leith, in retirement, she volunteered at the hospital. After a curt nod to the guard and his ex-teacher, he evaded their sympathetic glances.

Their pity turned him back into the ten-year-old boy whose mother had deserted him. As his father had disintegrated in front of his eyes, Alan had cleaned and cooked and put on a "normal" face.

After he'd set the kitchen on fire for the third time, their neighbors had stepped in. A Southern staple, the casserole, had begun to show up in its endless varieties, in the hands of their well-meaning friends.

The food, he'd thanked them for. Their looks of commiseration he'd hated so much he'd begun to pretend no one was home at dinnertime. His make-believe often became the truth once his father decided to drink away his sorrows at a bar instead of in front of Alan.

The elevator doors wheezed open, pulling him out of the past. He glanced at the number painted on the pale-blue wall. Cate's floor.

At her door, he knocked lightly before he went inside. To his surprise, she was sitting up, reading a magazine. She looked up, stroking the dressing that bulged against the sheet on her thigh.

"Hey," she said, her tone lush and deep, like the dark river that ran behind her aunt's home.

"How do you feel?" *Idiot,* he thought. Idiotic question.

Cate set her magazine aside. "I want to talk to you about how I feel."

She looked younger than thirty-eight. Far younger. He still saw her as she'd been the day she'd sat in a bed on the floor above this one and held their newborn out to him.

Her wary gaze intimated this wasn't going to that kind of talk. He steeled himself. "Tell me now if something's wrong."

"You're making me nervous. Can you sit down so we can talk eye to eye?"

Wondering how hard his heart could pound before it exploded, he dropped into the chair beside her bed. "How bad is it? Just tell me."

Confronted with the threat of another injury she found hard to discuss, he realized once and for all how they'd changed. Not just because she couldn't remember their past. They'd drifted apart before her accident.

He'd tried to fool himself. He hadn't preserved their love for each other despite all his protection. He'd feared losing her for the same reasons he'd lost his mother. He'd shut Cate out, because he didn't trust her to love the part of him that felt so afraid.

"Alan, I need to know you're listening to me."

Her demand surprised him. She sounded exactly as she had the day of the accident. "You're still yourself, after all."

"Am I?" Interest filled her blue eyes as she held out her hand. "Tell me how."

"What you just said, that you needed me to listen. Just before you got hurt, you were trying to make me understand exactly what you—"

"We argued?"

"I'm afraid so." If she'd given him time, he might have tried to paint a better picture of those last seconds. "It wasn't important."

"But you didn't understand me?"

"We've been married a long time. We've learned a shorthand, but shorthand may not have covered the conversations we needed to have." Jeez, he sounded like a talk show therapist. "What's wrong with you, Cate?"

"It's not serious— I'm not— Oh, I give up." She pushed her hair behind both ears. "I'm trying to tell you gently because I'm not sure you'll be pleased, but I'm pregnant."

He heard but he didn't hear. Alan leaned forward, seeing her as a stranger. Her watchful blue eyes couldn't belong to his Cate. "How pregnant?"

"Sixteen weeks." She spread the gown over her belly, and he saw why she'd begun to avoid his touch.

He'd trusted her with his life, but she'd kept his child a secret. Her betrayal cut deep. "I thought you didn't even want me to make love to you any more." The only time they'd still communicated.

"Why didn't I tell you?" Cate asked.

Rage made him harsh. "Since you didn't, I can't explain." She'd planned to leave, but her decision hadn't been spur of the moment. She'd planned to take his child. His heart stuttered over a few beats. "I can't talk any more."

"But I need to know—"

With his own lie foremost in his mind, he met her tear-sharpened gaze. He didn't trust her tears, but he'd been no paragon of honesty.

"Why are you crying?" he asked.

"Because I don't understand. Were we unhappy?"

"I can't guess how you felt. I remember the past twenty years. I remember when you told me about Dan." They'd celebrated for nine months, until the real party started with his birth. "I would have been happy this time, too."

"JUST PARK THE CAR. Don't stop at the door, boy. I'm no invalid." Uncle Ford's orders bounced around the roof and doors of Dan's car.

Ignoring his uncle, he braked beneath the canopy at the hospital's front door. "I'm stopping here for Aunt Imogen. Will you wait with her while I park?"

"Imogen could best you in a footrace around the parking lot," Uncle Ford said.

"Glad you recognize my talents, Ford. Now get out and let the boy park. Did you bring your cane?"

Dan shot her a grateful glance in the rearview mirror, and she smiled back while Uncle Ford wrestled himself out of the car. He insisted he just used the cane to lure the ladies to his supposedly helpless side.

"We both know I don't need it," he grumbled in what he always assumed was a whisper no one else could hear. People came out of the hospital's vestry to see about the commotion. "Imogen, get out of this car. I'd like to visit my niece before tomorrow morning."

"Don't mind him." Imogen waved a bottle of vanilla-scented perfume, which she dabbed behind her ears. "He's worried about your mother, but he'd rather snap at us than admit he cares."

Thanks to Aunt Imogen, he was the only guy his age who recognized vanilla at a hundred paces. "I don't mind, but don't go up to her room without me. Okay?"

"I'll hold Ford back, but you hurry." She shoved her perfume back in her purse and followed his uncle to the curb.

Dan parked in the first spot he found and dashed through the lot. Thank God for Aunt Imogen and Uncle Ford. He wouldn't have to talk to his mom with them around. They were still arguing when he joined them.

"Don't tell me not to shout, Imogen. I never shout. Are you suggesting I'm not considerate of sick people?"

"I'm suggesting you put a sock in it before that guard throws us all out."

Trying not to laugh, Dan herded them toward the elevator. That guard wouldn't tell Ford Talbot to put a sock in anything. Uncle Ford's wild life made him a legend to every man and boy in town.

They crowded into the elevator and Aunt Imogen opened her beaded purse. With pale, pink-tipped fingers, she drew out a small brown paper package.

"Your mother's favorite cookies," she said. "Oatmeal raisin macadamia nut."

Dan made a face. Worst combination he'd ever tasted. ''She'll be glad to see you, Aunt Imogen.''

''Watch out your face doesn't freeze like that. I made some chocolate chip for you. Remind me to pack them up before you go over to Ford's tonight.'' She made a tsking sound. ''Chocolate chip. That's a plain cookie.''

''Not the way you make them.'' He meant it. He could earn a fortune off her cookies if he sold them.

Aunt Imogen looked pleased. ''You may look like a Palmer, but Cate passed you the Talbot charm.''

Yeah? Most of the time he saw himself as a stiff shadow of his inhibited father.

At his mom's room, Uncle Ford used his cane to open her door. His mom was standing at her window. Dan followed his uncle and aunt inside. Just in time to catch the way his mother's bewildered smile lingered on his aunt. When she saw him, her smile faded.

''Dan.''

She sounded different. She seemed less worried, but she still looked at him as if she barely recognized him. He'd always wanted her to put a little distance between them, but now, he needed her to know him. Even though he was eighteen—a man—deep in his heart, he wanted his mom.

''I'm glad to see you,'' she said. ''Come in. Let me ask for more chairs. Uncle Ford, take this one.'' She offered him the only seat in the room, but he pushed it toward Aunt Imogen.

''I'll go to the nurse's station and ask for more. They should have brought more chairs in here anyway. They know you have a big family. Sit down, Imogen.''

''No, I'll go with you.'' She nodded encouragingly toward his mom as she hurried after Uncle Ford. ''Dan and Cate might enjoy some privacy.''

Good thing he *was* a man, or he'd have grabbed Aunt Imogen's skirt as she passed him. Rocking on his heels, he looked at his mom. Tried to think of something worth saying. She limped toward him, and for a second, he thought she was going to try to hug him. Instead, she kept going. He lurched out of her way as she closed the door.

''I have to ask you.'' She held the door shut. ''Why does Aunt Imogen wear a strip of cellophane tape down the middle of her forehead? I swear I saw gold graduation caps and diplomas on this piece.''

Was that all? He shrugged. ''I graduate in three weeks.''

She waited. When he didn't go on, she tossed up her hands in an I-still-don't-get-it gesture.

''Oh, the tape,'' he said. ''She always wears it.'' He put his finger in the middle of his eyebrows and frowned to show her the kind of wrinkles Aunt Imogen was trying to avoid. ''Reminds her not to frown.''

''How old is she?''

''Seventy-something. No one's ever told me. Why?''

She dropped her hands to her sides. ''Well—'' she cleared her throat ''—I shouldn't say this, but she has some wrinkles. And the tape—''

Dan forgot they didn't know each other any more. ''Mom, that's rude.''

She raised both eyebrows. ''I guess it was. Sorry.''

Just like that, she looked like his mom, except laughter tugged at her mouth, and for no reason he could think of, he laughed with her.

She eased the door open. ''She was thoughtful to choose tape to fit your occasion.''

''You should see the Santas at Christmas.'' She laughed again, and he did, too, but he felt guilty about it. Aunt Imogen didn't like to be laughed at.

''I'm glad they left us alone,'' his mom said. ''I was dying to ask, but I didn't want to hurt Aunt Imogen's feelings.''

''I think she uses the tape and the hats and stuff to hide how she feels about the gossips in this town. People still spread rumors about that Navy guy.''

''Navy guy?'' She obviously didn't know. ''My whole life is on the tip of my tongue. Not remembering baffles me. I even wondered if I was imagining Aunt Imogen's tape.'' She tightened the belt at her robe and then offered her hand. ''What a relief. Good to see you, Dan.''

Dan shook hands with her. ''I'm glad to see you, too.'' For the first time since she'd come out of that coma he meant it. ''Mom?''

''Huh?''

He chewed on his lip. He wasn't a guy who clung to his mother, but he'd been so scared she was going to die. ''Can I hug you?''

She tilted her head back, startled. ''Well,'' she said, ''yes.'' She opened her arms, but he could see she felt funny about it, too. Then as soon as he put his arms around her, she hugged back. Tight.

"I'm glad you're okay," he said.

"Thanks."

They both moved to neutral corners and avoided looking at each other. But he felt better.

CHAPTER THREE

SHOCKED AT Cate's pregnancy and the fact she'd hidden it, Alan avoided his family that night. He couldn't have hidden his panic at the uncertain future of his marriage, but he realized he had to keep fighting. Dan and Cate and the new baby needed him to save the business and their family.

The next morning, Alan parked in front of Caroline's small cottage. Several miles down the beach from his and Cate's house, the cottage bore the loving stamp of the Talbot women in its neatly maintained appearance and glinting windows. Like all the Talbot homes, the cottage welcomed visitors.

Until today, anyway. He might not be so welcome once he suggested Caroline was neglecting her sister.

He opened the car door and strode up the walk to rap on the door. It swung open. Caroline peered around it and Alan got to the point. ''Why haven't you visited Cate?''

''And good morning to you.'' She stood aside. ''Come in, Alan, and tell me what makes you so surly.''

Yesterday's news about the baby gave him plenty to be surly about, but he still wouldn't discuss his growing family with Cate's twin. A new thought made him uneasy. As close as the sisters had been, she might already know. He couldn't ask. He didn't want to know if Cate trusted Caroline more than she trusted him.

"Cate needs to see everyone who might help her remember. You didn't go to the hospital yesterday."

"Maybe you didn't notice but she screamed when she looked at her own face after seeing mine."

"She's been there for you, Caroline. All your lives."

"I know. She pretended to be me when I played hooky from school. She helped me run away with my bad husband, and then she picked up the pieces when he left me. She's baby-sat Shelly when my childcare fell through, and she does more than her fair share for Aunt Imogen and Uncle Ford." Caroline paused to draw breath. "None of what she's done changes the fact that my face scares her."

"She sees your face every time she looks in a mirror." He stepped inside the small house. It wasn't so welcoming to a man. Only women lived here, and he felt too large for the narrow hall, the dainty French furniture. "Are you afraid to see her?"

She met his gaze. Not for the first time, this woman who looked so much like his wife but thought so differently disconcerted him. In silence, Caroline led him to the kitchen. She poured a cup of strong black coffee and set it on the counter in front of him.

"I'm terrified. Cate is part of me. We share so many of the same memories I'm not sure who I am without her."

Her frankness only emphasized their serious fix. Caroline had become his friend as he'd fallen in love with her sister. He'd helped her and Shelly when he could, but she'd never confided in him this way.

And now they were going through the same crisis. Who were they when Cate, the glue that had held their family together, no longer knew them?

He closed his eyes. A shout rose in his throat. Pure pain that no one but Cate could alleviate. Only his Cate no longer existed.

"I understand why you're reluctant," he managed to say. "She may not remember you, but she needs you. You are part of each other. You can tell her things about her past that the rest of us don't know."

"I don't know her better than you do, Alan." She took another coffee cup from the cabinet. "I'm only her sister. You're her husband."

Not a very good husband. He'd blamed their uneasiness on the stress of raising a teenager who was about to leave home. He'd assumed they'd find their way back to each other after Dan left.

Not that he'd resented Cate's devotion to their son. They'd both wanted to be better parents than their own. But he'd lost sight of Cate, the woman, in his reliance on her. Over the years, he'd become the provider. She'd been the mom. Had their roles divided them, or had Cate stopped loving him?

"What's on your mind, Alan? Something else is going on." Caroline's conviction reminded him of Cate after she'd seen through all his half truths. "You've never stormed in here before to point out my responsibilities to Cate."

"Help her. Make her remember."

"Make her?" Caroline blanched. "You're thinking she chose to forget? I wonder, too. Who made her so unhappy? You? Me? I've let her take care of me as if she really were older.''

''She is. She takes those thirteen minutes seriously.''

''And twenty-seven seconds.'' Caroline poured coffee in her cup and lifted it to her mouth for a wary sip. ''Don't forget those twenty-seven seconds.''

''She never meant to make you think you couldn't take care of yourself.''

''Sometimes I couldn't. I needed her, but I couldn't admit it. I always wanted to prove I knew how to handle my own life.''

Her guilt sounded too familiar. He'd needed Cate to believe he was her knight in shining armor, but he'd tried so hard to be a professional success—and then failed so spectacularly—he'd broken her ability to trust him at all.

Damn it, he'd learn how to win back her faith, but she still needed the rest of her family. ''Why don't you take care of her this time?''

She widened her eyes, as if she hadn't thought of the possibilities. That happened when guilt overwhelmed you. ''What's to stop me?'' She toasted him with her coffee cup. ''I will go. Tonight. Evening visitor's hours.''

He set his own cup on the counter. ''I have to go into the office for a few hours. Can you fax me your budget for the medical center interiors?''

''Sure. Why are you working on Sunday, Alan?''

He had no choice. He still had to save the company. Caroline and too many others depended on him for their jobs. ''I've spent so much time at the hospital I have to catch up on paperwork. How close are you to the figures we discussed when we started the project? Not over budget anywhere?''

She plucked a pair of glasses from the shelf beside the sink and slid them onto her nose. Cate didn't need glasses. ''I'll get the file now if you want. We're close on window treatments, and I hooked us up with the rugs.''

''Hooked us up?''

She flashed a grin. ''Don't you ever talk to Dan? I worked us a deal.''

Like her, he felt more at ease talking about work, a topic he and Cate rarely discussed. Lately, he'd tended to share tense silence with his wife. Silence couldn't bide easily between two people hiding life-altering secrets.

''I'M DR. DAVIS. I hear you don't remember me.''

Cate looked up from her book, relieved to quit pretending she could concentrate enough to read. A tall woman stood in the doorway, finely dressed in a beige suit that complemented her dark-mocha skin. Her looks were lovely, but the supreme confidence in her eyes brought Cate the deepest sense of assurance she remembered feeling.

''I'm happy to meet you.'' Cate took a get well card from the table and slid it into her book to mark her place. ''Come in.''

The other woman set a file on the nightstand. ''Did you tell Alan about the baby?''

''Yesterday.'' She left out the part where he'd gone and not come back.

''He didn't take it well?'' Dr. Davis reached for

the call button on the cord at Cate's shoulder. ''You can't blame him for that?''

''Maybe. Who are you calling?''

''A nurse. I'd like to examine you now that you haven't spotted for several days. Your body has endured a great deal of trauma, and I'd like to make sure the baby's perfectly healthy.''

''What do you need me to do?''

''Relax if you can.''

Cate tried to disguise her distress. ''I'm not sure I could even if I remembered how a pelvic feels.''

Dr. Davis laughed. ''Good point.''

The nurse came, and the doctor began her exam. She seemed dissatisfied with what she found. From her particularly vulnerable position, Cate still tried to be brave. ''What?'' she asked bluntly.

''Nothing to worry about.'' Dr. Davis peered over her shoulder at the nurse. ''Open Cate's file and remind me of her dates.''

The date of Cate's last cycle seemed to make matters worse. Cate fought her increasingly primitive need to remove herself from the doctor's hands. ''You're scaring me, and I really need to shove you away.''

The doctor straightened, peeling off her gloves. ''Don't be afraid. Nothing's wrong, but I need to listen.'' Taking the stethoscope from around her neck, she placed it all over Cate's belly.

''I think we need an ultrasound.''

Cate grabbed her arm, pulling her close with strength that surprised her and the doctor. ''You can't hear a heartbeat?''

Humor softened the doctor's wide eyes. "I hear plenty of heartbeats."

Her response made no sense at first. Finally, Cate remembered she was a twin. She dropped back. "Plenty?" she squeaked.

"Just two, but I don't rely on my ears this early on. Why don't we make sure before you pass out?"

"An ultrasound will tell you? Ultrasounds don't lie, do they? I mean I'm not suddenly going to come up with triplets, am I?"

"Try to stay calm. Sudden isn't the way triplets show up." Dr. Davis pulled the sheet up to Cate's waist. "Why don't I use my influence to run the test now?"

Calm? At thirty-eight, with a nearly grown son and a husband she didn't know? "Now would be perfect."

Dr. Davis picked up the large, insulated cup that stood on the nightstand. She shook the cup and then smiled as water and ice sloshed together. "Start drinking this."

LATER THAT EVENING, Cate stared at the ultrasound photo. Two babies. In another twenty-two weeks or so, she'd give birth to twins.

The two small beings on the ultrasound screen had reconnected her to the process of living. She wrapped herself in the happiness she'd felt at watching the two twisting shadows. They needed her, and she resolved to figure out who she was in time to be a good parent to all her children.

And she'd learn to be a wife to her husband. He

wanted their marriage. She must have wanted it, too. Their children deserved two healthy parents.

Someone knocked softly on her door. Cate lifted the top of her table and slid the ultrasound photo inside. "Come in," she called. She smoothed the sheet around her hips and legs and prepared to interrogate her visitor about her past.

Caroline leaned around the edge of the door. Her face still jolted Cate, but another scream seemed inappropriate.

"Do you mind if I join you?" Caroline asked.

"I'm surprised you want to. Come in and let me apologize for the way I acted. I didn't expect to see you in my mirror."

"I shouldn't have run out of here, but I love you Cate. No, don't worry—you know, you used to be better at hiding your feelings—I don't expect you to pretend you feel the way I do, but I want you to depend on me. It's my turn to be the big sister."

"Am I older than you?" Cate asked as Caroline paused to replace a lungful of air.

"By a little more than thirteen minutes, but I've needed you more than you ever needed me." She stopped again, and her face flushed a deep red. "I used to wonder if you wished you didn't have a twin, and now you don't."

"Well, don't sound sad. You're about to settle all your debts. I need a crash course in my own history."

Caroline's instant regret almost made Cate smile. "What can I tell you?" Caroline asked in a wavering tone.

With her new deadline, she had no time for subtlety. First things first. ‘‘Why are you so reluctant to talk to me?’’

‘‘I’m embarrassed. You rescued me from every jam I ever got myself into. I can’t repay you for—’’

Cate interrupted. ‘‘I know you all loved me, because my close call seems to have turned me into a saint.’’ Saints held no charm for her. She didn’t trust the tale, and she needed facts. ‘‘Tell me the bad stuff, too.’’

‘‘What bad stuff?’’

‘‘We’re sisters. You must have helped me as much as I helped you.’’

A deeper blush darkened Caroline’s high cheekbones. Cate lifted her fingertips to her own face as her twin went on. ‘‘You never needed help.’’

Not true. She probably just hadn’t asked for it. ‘‘I need help now. Dr. Barton implied our family—the Talbots—are…’’

Caroline’s discomfort eased as Cate trailed off. ‘‘Notorious?’’ she suggested.

Cate nodded. ‘‘I know our parents are deceased, but what happened to them?’’

‘‘Dad met Mom in the Navy. They were both intelligence officers, and apparently, the only thing they loved more than imminent danger was each other. They sent us here to live with Aunt Imogen when we were five. The Navy stationed them in Turkey, I think. Some remote place, but it was only their first isolated duty station. They liked the life so much they never came back.’’

‘‘Never?’’ Such parenting alarmed her. She felt for the two small girls they’d been. ‘‘We never saw them?’’

"They came for visits. Brief ones." Caroline shook her head. "But we missed them so much it was easier when they stayed away. When they tried to leave we cried—well, I cried. You pretended you didn't care."

"I did?" She couldn't picture herself as such a tough kid.

Caroline pulled up a chair and made herself comfortable. "Always. You didn't want anyone getting close enough to see how much you hurt." She stopped, seemingly amazed, and reached for Cate's water. "Do you mind if I drink some? It's hot outside."

"Go ahead."

"I never realized you were pretending until I said that just now. I always envied you because you didn't seem to need anyone, but you—"

Cate found she didn't want to know what Caroline thought of her inner workings. Plain facts mattered more. Maybe later she'd be willing to discuss her private thoughts with her sister. "How did they die?"

Caroline's expression clouded. She drank more water and set it back on the table. "In a car accident. They were driving to Nice to fly home for our high school graduation, and they took a curve too quickly. We think they had an argument before they left their hotel because the management billed us for damages."

Cate stared at her for a second and tried not to laugh at the morbid picture.

"I know." Caroline shook her head. "Aunt Imogen's attorney pointed out the tactless nature of their claims, but they still wanted to be paid. My God, how we missed them.''

''I missed them, too?''

''You wouldn't talk about it, but someone plants flowers on their graves and keeps them tended. Usually, when I go out to the cemetery, something new is blooming. You must be the gardener, but you always said you didn't know anything about the plants. Aunt Imogen has a killer thumb, and Uncle Ford's still too mad at Dad for dying to do something so kind.''

Sadness surprised Cate, knotting uncomfortable tears in the back of her throat. She'd like to see that cemetery, but she had to go by herself the first time. After that, she'd ask Caroline to help her with the flowers. She moved on to their aunt and uncle. ''How about Aunt Imogen and Uncle Ford? Dan told me a story about Aunt Imogen's Navy man.''

''I don't believe she ever had an affair, if that's what you mean, but like you, she keeps her feelings private. Maybe she'll tell you about him if you ask her in your present condition.''

Cate grinned at Caroline's prim tone. ''I wondered why she wasn't married, but it seemed rude to ask. And Uncle Ford?''

''He's never made conventional choices. None of us was conventional except you.'' Caroline swallowed. ''Actually, no one was ever sure if Grandma and Grandpa actually married each other. I mean we have a marriage certificate, but the story is, they bought it on the boardwalk in New Jersey.''

''What?''

''Don't worry. You and Alan are legal, and you've

never taken a wrong step. You've walked a tight, straight line to give Dan a sense of family you and I didn't get. You've made him strong.''

Tight, straight line? The walls started to close in again.

''In fact, you and Alan have given Shelly a good example. I want her to know someone in our family can make a marriage stick.''

A lasting marriage hardly equated with a wife who'd hidden her pregnancy. How had Alan responded to setting examples? What had she thought about such a responsibility?

''I need to ask you about Alan's father, too. Uncle Ford mentioned that I wouldn't be seeing him inside these four walls.'' She glanced quickly around the room. ''What did he mean? I don't feel comfortable asking Alan.''

''Why?''

Because she didn't trust their relationship. ''Alan's already stressed. I don't want to add to his trouble, but he's— Richard's his name?''

''Yeah, Richard.''

''He's family, too. I'd better know about him.''

''Richard has his quirks.'' Caroline grabbed the water again. ''I don't want to talk about him, either. He raised Alan alone after Alan's mom left when Alan was about ten. I'm not sure what went wrong.''

''I thought you and I were close.''

''We were.''

''I sure hid a lot from you.''

''Just the important stuff,'' Caroline said with a trace of impatience. ''I've never understood what went on between Alan and Richard, and you never told me anything. Of course there was gossip. I've heard Alan did a lot of the stuff fathers are supposed to do for their children, like laundry and cooking. I know Richard had a drinking problem. You and Alan both tried to pretend Richard was a better father than I think he was.''

Appalled and heartbroken for her husband, Cate tried to take this information in. ''Why would we cover for him?''

''Maybe for Dan, or maybe you thought he'd remind me of Ryan, my own runaway spouse. You'll have to ask Alan—or maybe Richard. He's getting married this summer. He must have finally put his first wife behind him.'' Caroline reached for her hand. ''I haven't helped you. You know my worst fears, but I only know hints of yours.''

Cate made herself accept her sister's touch. Dr. Davis and Dr. Barton had both touched her in comfort, and she hadn't minded. Family mattered more. Accepting affection she couldn't return felt false, but she wanted to love her sister so she let her hand rest in Caroline's.

''I have to ask you another question you won't want to answer.'' She felt disloyal to Alan after what Caroline had said about Richard. Imagining her husband as a lost little boy, forced to grow up, hurt her. She had to ask her sister about the state of their marriage, because she wasn't sure he'd tell her the truth. If he'd persuaded her to go along with shielding his father, he must be used to pretending things were ''normal.'' ''Were Alan and I happy?''

Caroline jerked her fingers back. ''How would I know?''

Cate held her twin's so familiar gaze with sheer will. "You're my sister. I took you at your word when you promised I could depend on you."

Caroline looked as if she'd like to run for her life. "You would no more have told me about problems between you and Alan than you would have hired a plane to list them in the sky."

"I have to know."

"You aren't yourself."

"I'm afraid not. I don't trust the way people describe me so far. I was stuffy."

"Not stuffy. Kind."

"So much circumspection sounds unnatural." Cate tucked her sheet around her waist. A walk down the hospital hall might clear her muzzy head, but weakness in her legs, combined with the deep cut on her thigh held her prisoner, and Caroline had backed away when she'd needed her most. "Thanks for talking. I appreciate your effort."

"Wait." Her expression dogged, Caroline propped one elbow on the edge of Cate's bed. "Let me try again. Alan came to my house this morning, and he insisted I see you."

Cate crossed her arms. She still possessed enough of her infamous self-sufficiency to resent Alan's intervention.

"Hold on, Cate. He wanted to make sure I took care of you."

If he knew she needed help, why had he stayed away last night? The obvious answer. She'd dropped a bomb on his head. He needed time to reconcile himself. Not the most romantic tactic, but if he showed up again soon, she'd try to understand. "Alan and I aren't your responsibility."

"Listen to me. You have to listen if you ask for advice. I don't think he'd have come to me if he didn't care." Caroline fluffed her hair. "Why are we talking about this? He loves you. He's been crazy since that car hit you."

"He doesn't act like a man in love. He acts like something's wrong."

"I noticed, but I don't believe your marriage went bad."

Cate plucked at a loose thread on her sheet's hem. "I'm glad my marriage comforts you, but I'd love to know how I felt about it."

"Yeah." Caroline sounded unsure.

And she didn't even know about the twins.

AGAIN, Alan stared at Cate's door. Someone had printed her name on a small, square whiteboard beside the metal doorframe. He brushed away a smear at the end of the *r* in Palmer. Then he went inside.

Favoring her injured leg, his wife turned from the window.

"Cate." He'd expected her to be in bed.

"I almost stopped hoping you'd come, but I didn't want to be flat on my back when we talked." A smile hovered at the corner of her mouth.

He knew that sweet shape as well as he knew his own face. He'd kissed that mouth, frowned at that mouth, dreaded seeing it thin in anger, and waited with held breath for it to smile. A real smile—not like her smile now.

"You knew you could expect me?" Somewhere

inside her remained the wife who'd trusted him to take care of her.

''If you'd stayed away again tonight, I'd have understood you'd made your decision.''

No, this Cate wasn't the wife he'd lived with for twenty years. His Cate had never tested him.

''I'm glad I passed.''

''I didn't think of it as a trial. When you didn't call or come back yesterday, I assumed you had to think about where we stood.''

A cold fist squeezed his heart. ''Is that what you've been doing?''

She shook her head. Her bright hair fell over her shoulder, tempting him to slide possessive fingers through the strands before she slipped away from him forever.

''How could I decide anything without talking to you?'' she asked in a low voice. Behind her, the night sky perfectly framed her pale skin and tense silhouette.

Her open gaze gave him hope for the first time since she'd run from the office.

''I want to go on together,'' he said. ''You're my wife.''

''Don't put it that way, Alan.'' Emotionally, she distanced herself from him. ''I don't want us to stay together because we happen to be married.''

''I get the idea you don't want me to say I love you.''

Those words didn't belong between them since he'd hidden the business trouble and she'd concealed their baby from him.

She limped toward him, but she stopped beside her

bed and flexed her fingers on the lip of her table. From her knuckles to her nails, her skin faded to palest white.

"I know something's wrong, and saying you love me would only alarm me now." She lifted her chin. "You could tell me what's wrong."

No, he couldn't. It wasn't just that her injuries had given him time to win her back. He'd never been good at admitting she'd always be his deepest need. He'd shown her in the only way he'd known how, providing a good life for her and their son.

From now on, he'd pay more attention to her, become the husband she wanted. His father's decades-old advice rang in his ears. "Give your wife the good things in life. Provide, and provide well, or she'll find a man who can."

"I still don't know why I decided not to tell you about the baby." She slid her gaze away from him. "Don't we need to know why?"

"One day I hope you'll tell me."

Frustration tightened her mouth, but she controlled it. "Tonight I have to tell you I had a test today."

"What kind of a test? Is the baby all right?" Fear nearly dropped him to his knees. Even if he couldn't provide for this child as he had for Dan, he'd love the new baby. He'd be the best father his resources allowed.

"I've scared you again. I'm sorry." Cate hurried around the bed and reached for his hand.

Her fingers felt vulnerable in his, but he couldn't let go. "I should be taking care of you," he said.

"I should have found a better way to say this. Dr.

Davis did an exam today and discovered we're having twins."

"Twins?"

She nodded. Seconds passed. He didn't know how to respond to twins. The cost, the timing. She'd never understand his panic. Distance came into her eyes. By not answering, he was losing her, the woman he'd loved since he'd learned to love, and the woman he no longer knew.

He threw a longing look at her chair. "Do you mind if I sit?"

She grinned, and he sat without her consent. Was she laughing at him? She didn't respect him for sitting?

"Not that I mind," he said. "The twins. I don't mind the twins."

"You don't have to prove how tough you are. If I hadn't been lying down when Dr. Davis told me, I might have fallen."

"Twins."

"Will you tell me how you really feel?"

"Startled." He tried hard to think how she'd want him to answer. How he should answer as a decent human being who wanted his wife back, who loved the child they'd already created, and who knew he could love two more when the shock wore off. "How are you?" he asked her.

She actually seemed to find his lack of assurance comforting. She relaxed her tense stance.

"Glad to see you." She squeezed his hand once and then let go to scoot onto the edge of her bed and straighten her leg. "I couldn't tell anyone else before I told you."

He should be the first to know. He tugged at the hem of her robe. ‘‘Do you feel anything for me?’’

Her expression was solemn, but full of regret. ‘‘I feel responsible.’’

He let her go. ‘‘I don’t know what I think about responsible.’’

She folded her hands. ‘‘Let’s just be honest and see what kind of relationship we can salvage.’’

‘‘I want a marriage.’’ He still didn’t mention the business. Eventually, she’d understand. Between the twins and her memory loss, he couldn’t add to the pressure on her.

He’d been afraid she’d leave if he admitted his lie about the company had caused all their problems. Now, he kept the embezzlement to himself because he wanted to protect his wife and their unborn children. This time, he was right to try to protect her.

CHAPTER FOUR

CATE HARDLY SLEPT the night before she was scheduled to go home. The next day's possibilities ran furiously around her mind. With Caroline's help she'd already begun to collect clues about her life. Now, to piece her past and present into one cohesive puzzle.

Lights from the nighttime traffic danced on her walls as crazily as her thoughts until she began to pick out repeating patterns that calmed her. An occasional jet roared overhead, rousing her when she was getting sleepy. She finally dozed off just before dawn.

A crack of thunder brought her straight up in bed. Its rumble slowly faded, and an early-summer downpour sheeted rain across her window.

She woke each morning, thinking the same question. Would she remember?

Not today. She sensed everything she needed to know, hanging just beyond her reach. No amount of determination brought her answers.

Impatiently, she slid out of bed, but the moment she was vertical, nausea gripped her. She clung to the table, waiting for her stomach to settle. Dr. Davis had suggested saltine crackers, but they only seemed to make her queasier.

Pushing herself to use her weakened legs, she traveled from bureau to bed to pack the small, violently floral overnight bag Aunt Imogen had brought her.

By the time she snapped the catch on her bag, the rain had begun to ease off. Cate perched on the side of her bed to wait for Alan or Dr. Barton. After a few long seconds, she crossed the room to open her door. Then she hobbled back toward her chair. Footsteps in the hall made her look over her shoulder.

Alan stopped in the doorway. His brooding expression suggested strength. His sheer size backed up the claim. He looked from her to her bag. "I came early to help you."

At the slight reproach in his tone, she wished she'd waited. She'd already learned he showed his feelings through service. "The rain woke me early." She pointed toward the hall he dwarfed with his height. "Is Dr. Barton out there?"

Shaking his head, he turned to peer down the hall to his right. His white oxford shirt lovingly caressed the strong, straining muscles of his upper back. Bracing his hand against the door frame, he twisted to look the other way. The worn shirt stretched almost out of the narrow waist of his jeans. Another shake of his head, and rich, dark strands of his hair rubbed his tanned neck. Did he know how good he looked?

"I was hoping Barton might have signed your release papers already."

"No." She tried to sound normal, but hollow, electric bursts of attraction came as a relief. If she planned to stay married, wanting her husband had to be a plus. "Do we have to wait?"

"You're all set?"

She nudged the bag. ‘‘I’ve packed everything except for the magazines and books you all brought me. The book cart lady suggested giving them to the other patients.’’

‘‘Good idea.’’ Stepping back from the door frame, he looked a touch uneasy. ‘‘Why don’t you sit and rest your leg? I’ll look for Dr. Barton.’’ Alan paused. ‘‘Dan’s waiting for us in the parking lot.’’

‘‘Dan?’’ That put a crimp in her plan. She wasn’t sure how she’d react to a home she didn’t remember, and she didn’t want to risk disappointing her son. They’d formed a tentative bond that day he’d explained about Aunt Imogen’s tape.

‘‘He thought we should take you home as a family.’’ Alan paused, his gaze pensive. ‘‘If he needs family time because he’s been worried about you, I say we all go home together.’’

She eyed him carefully. They were both Dan’s parents, but Alan knew him better. She thought back to the day Caroline had told her she didn’t share personal troubles. Her instincts hadn’t changed, but she had to take a chance for Dan. ‘‘What if he expects me to be comfortable at home? I won’t know the house. I don’t have a clue about his life or what kind of mother I’ve been.’’

Alan tapped the door frame, his gaze bemused. ‘‘You don’t have to give Dan much. He just wants you home.’’ His deep voice drew a shiver down her spine. Left unspoken in his husky reassurance was a hint he wanted her there, too. ‘‘Maybe you should try not to think of Dan as a child. He’s trying hard to become an adult.’’

Dr. Barton appeared behind him, carrying the clipboard that held her chart. Alan moved out of his way, but the doctor stopped, clearly discerning stress in the air.

''Am I interrupting?''

Cate shook her head, still digesting everything Alan had said. ''Can I go?''

''Don't rush me. How do you feel? Any morning sickness? How's the leg?''

''My leg's fine, but I feel sick as a dog.''

''Sometimes morning sickness lasts and lasts in a pregnancy.'' He flipped up a page on her chart. ''I see the nurse liked the look of your wound last night.''

Cate picked up her bag. Alan started toward her, but Dr. Barton stopped him.

''What's your hurry? Cate has to wait for a wheelchair, and you might want to bring your car around. I'll walk out with you.'' He scrawled notes on the chart. ''Cate, I believe I covered all your instructions last night?''

She nodded. ''But you can tell me anything you want to say to Alan. I'm not an invalid.''

The older man laughed. ''You're getting paranoid.'' His bland smile annoyed her. ''Once you're home, take it easy. If you want to exercise, walk on the beach, but take water along. I don't want you to get dehydrated. Call me if you have any questions. Oh, and Dr. Davis asked me to remind you about your appointment with her.''

''I have the card she gave me.''

''Fine.'' He capped his pen and held the chart to his chest as he extended his hand. ''Good luck to you, Cate Palmer.''

She ignored his hand, forgave him for his chauvinistic urge to talk about her with Alan and hugged him. "Thank you for everything."

Alan's bewildered gaze told her she rarely hugged spontaneously. She wasn't surprised after her talk with Caroline, but she didn't like thinking of herself as a woman who withheld affection.

After a brisk squeeze, the doctor released her and turned to Alan. "She's going to be fine. Better than ever. Let's go. I'll tell the nurses you're ready, Cate."

They left, and Cate felt painfully alone. What kind of woman would be better than ever because she hugged her doctor? A frightened one who wasn't sure people would return her affection? Cate shook her head and chose not to be frightened anymore.

STRIDING BESIDE Dr. Barton, Alan glanced back at Cate's door. Her concern for Dan made him feel even guiltier about their fiscal jam. He had to fix it before she found out anything was wrong. He'd made his decision to help her, not to hurt her. He hoped he wasn't kidding himself when he tried to believe she'd forgive him.

"Alan, slow down. You don't have to worry about Cate." Dr. Barton hurried, the sound of his footsteps ricocheting off the pale-blue walls.

Alan's heart thudded in time, but he shortened his stride. "You don't understand."

"I do. She's not the wife you knew, but she's charming, and she wants her life back. She'll benefit by returning to her old habits."

Barton had to be right, and yet… ''Is she more likely to remember at home?''

''Seeing the places and people she loved may stimulate her memory, but I can't promise you. Just take good care of her. If she seems down or upset, and you don't know what to do for her, persuade her to call me.''

Alan nodded. ''As long as she tells me how she feels.''

''You'll know. She isn't a complete stranger. The Cate we know is still inside her. Are you afraid you can't wait for her?''

What if he didn't know the real Cate? Maybe she'd never told him how she truly felt. How much had they hidden from each other? Alan lifted his eyebrows. ''I'll wait.'' What else could he do? Except patience had never been his strong suit. ''Cate's my wife.''

Dr. Barton's thin smile implied he shared Cate's opinion of that statement. What did they expect? He wanted the Cate he'd married. Did that mean he wasn't a good man?

A good man's wife would have told him about their unborn twins. She would have trusted him enough to share news that must have shocked her.

The day of the accident Cate had been angry enough, disappointed enough—maybe even hurt enough to believe he had no right to know about his own children. Why hadn't he realized then how far apart they'd grown?

''Alan, I wonder if I should let you leave without talking to someone. You wouldn't be normal if you weren't unsettled about your future with Cate.''

''We have to make a future. Can a stranger tell me how to do that?''

Big talk from the little man who'd been the last to know.

Alan punched the elevator button. His lie about the business was no foundation for a new life. But he cared for his family, and he'd provide for his wife.

Bracing himself to start a future he only half trusted, Alan shook the other man's hand. ''I'm grateful for the care you've given Cate.''

''My pleasure. I'll say goodbye here because I'm in the middle of rounds, but remember what I told you.''

''I will. I'm sorry if I've been abrupt.''

''You have a right.'' The doctor pulled his pen out of his pocket. ''You know my phone number, Alan?''

He frowned. ''I can find it. Why?''

''If you need to talk, call me. Don't fume about your problems alone. Dan and Imogen and Ford depend on you as much as Cate does.''

Barton's grasp of his weakness made him smile. ''Good advice. I'll remember.''

The elevator doors jittered open, and he stepped inside. He avoided looking at Dr. Barton as he pushed the lobby button. The elevator jerked once before it began to descend.

The doctor might be right. He wasn't himself, but his resolve built with every inch of space he put between himself and Cate's room. Never, in all their marriage, had she leaned on him easily. She'd always held parts of herself back as if she had to force herself to share. Now, with their past and her memories beyond her reach, even she needed him. If she leaned on him, he'd support her.

He stepped off the elevator in the lobby to find Dan sprawled in a big chair. "I thought you wanted to wait in the car," Alan said. "Why didn't you come up?"

Faint color dusted Dan's fuzz-covered, youthful cheeks. He shrugged with his mother's reserve. "I thought you'd want some privacy. Besides you had to come through here sooner or later. Where's Mom?"

"Waiting for a wheelchair. Why don't we get the car?"

Dan tossed him the keys.

Alan caught them. "You can drive if you want, son."

"I always make Mom nervous."

"You're a sensitive guy." Alan garnered a sheepish grin from his son. Side by side, they pushed through the glass doors into light, warm rain and a rumble of dying thunder. "Where did you park the car?"

"This way," Dan said and started toward the parking lot.

As he followed, Alan resisted an urge to tell his loose-limbed son not to slouch. He'd parked Cate's SUV in a spot not too far from the entrance. They got in and Alan started the engine.

He parked beneath the canopy at the hospital entrance. A nurse pushed Cate through the doors in a wheelchair. His wife's stiff posture suggested she remained a woman who accepted assistance only under duress.

"Boy, she's pissed about the wheelchair," Dan said.

"Have you ever said the word *pissed* to Mom or me before?" Alan opened his door. "Don't say it around her."

He circled the SUV. Rain had turned the air into a humid sauna that began to curl Cate's hair. Searching the buildings around them, Cate let him take her arm as she rose.

The nurse nodded. "You'll find Dr. Barton's instructions on that paperwork I gave you, Mrs. Palmer. Don't hesitate to call us if we can answer any questions."

"I think we'll be fine. Are you ready, Alan?"

He opened the door and helped her inside the front seat. When he reached for the seat belt, Cate dropped her hand on his.

"I remember how these work," she said tightly. She twisted to look over the seat. "Morning, Dan."

"Hi, Mom. How do you feel?"

"Perfect. I'm glad you came with your dad."

"Me, too."

Alan quickly joined them. He met Cate's nervous smile. At least he knew the world they were starting over in. The hospital was the only place she knew.

Her blouse trembled over her breasts. Her heart must be running like a fugitive train. "Have you guys eaten breakfast?" she asked.

"Are you hungry?" Grabbing a chance to do something tangible for her, Alan turned the key in the ignition again. "We'll take you to your favorite diner. Can you miss a couple more hours of school, Dan?"

''I'm starving,'' he said, as if that answered the question.

''Sounds like a yes to me.'' Alan pushed some telepathic reassurance Cate's way.

Her gaze lingered on him, a soft touch he'd missed as he'd miss food and drink and air to breathe. He turned his attention back to the road, the better to avoid killing his growing family.

Maybe the diner would spark a memory for Cate. It was, after all, where they'd shared their first meal together.

WIND SLAMMED RAIN against the windows, and Dan stared at the backs of his parents' heads, pretending he didn't see how scared they were. He'd like to tell them to cut the crap and act normal, but if he did, they'd work harder to convince him nothing was wrong. His mom and dad never admitted they had problems. They seemed to think his brain might explode if someone told the truth about their happy little family.

His mom went around fed up half the time, and his dad thought he was Captain Fix-it. Divorce hung in the air. He no longer doubted his mother and father would split up. Mom couldn't pick his dad out of a police line up. How could she love him?

And Dad. Big bad Palmer Construction came first. He'd kill to protect the business he'd built from scratch with his first set of tools and an ancient backhoe. How many times had Dan heard that story?

His mom turned in her seat again. ''What does this diner serve?'' she asked, her voice lighter than air.

Why couldn't she just be real? Like that day at the

hospital with Aunt Imogen and her tape? She'd talked to him that day, as if they were friends. If she was going to make a big deal out of being his mom, he'd go back to school.

He ground his teeth as he tried to answer, ignoring the spurt of fear for her that made him so angry. "It's called The Captain's Lady, and they serve the usual stuff for breakfast. Grits, eggs, pork products." Dan caught his father's stern expression in the rearview mirror and moderated his belligerent tone. "Still love bacon, Mom?"

She leaned toward him, her surprised smile startling him. "I do," she said. "Bacon, mmm."

"Even the hospital's version?" his dad asked.

"Are you kidding?" She turned to him, looking young. "They don't acknowledge bacon exists. Caroline and Aunt Imogen smuggled in a BLT. The tomatoes came from Aunt Imogen's greenhouse. She said the tomato plants in the garden are blooming already."

"You remember the garden?" Dan's voice squeaked with hope. He cleared his throat and concentrated on achieving a deeper tone. "Aunt Imogen loves having you work with her."

"Caroline said she had a killer thumb. I thought that meant she wasn't a good gardener."

His dad laughed. "That's why she likes your help."

Cate shrugged. "She told me everything about it, from tomatoes to cornstalks and all the organic fertilizer Polly provides. She gives an amazing fertilizer speech." She tossed Dan a wicked grin. "Do you suppose Aunt Imogen will make me wear one of the hats?''

''How do you know about the hats?'' He'd thought she'd pined away in her hospital bed, waiting for her memory to come back. Someone must have talked.

''Another chat with Caroline,'' she said. ''I hear you've been walking Polly for Aunt Imogen.''

''I don't wear the hat, okay?''

''Okay.'' This teasing glance didn't belong to his mom. Some other woman had snatched her body. ''But I heard Aunt Imogen requires the wearing of the hat. She must have made you the exception. I'll ask her why when I see her.''

''You do that.'' Okay, his mom was a pod person now, but he couldn't hold back a grudging laugh. He'd always wanted her to be his friend. Just not this friendly.

Suddenly she straightened. ''Look at that.'' She pointed through his father's window, her face reminding him of the time his cousin Shelly had stumbled into the locker room. The whole time he was shoving her out, she'd claimed she didn't know ''golf guys'' changed after a match.

Instead of sweaty guys switching from khakis to normal clothes, the ocean grabbed his mother's attention. At the tail end of the storm, waves slammed across the sand onto rocks that bordered the sidewalk.

''Stop the car, Alan.'' She leaned into his dad's shoulder. She was wearing a short-sleeved sweater, and her arm looked thinner.

Could she be sick on top of this amnesia thing?

Naturally, they'd hide it from him. He was "too young" to understand real bad news.

His dad hadn't stopped the car. "What about the rain, Cate? You don't want to get out?"

"I want to see the ocean. Please stop, Alan."

The second his dad parked at the curb his mom jumped out. Dan and his father sat in silence that was thick enough to cut.

"She's not her old self, is she Dad?"

"Not yet. How about you? How are you handling the changes in her?"

"I'm eighteen."

"Huh?"

"Not a baby. Don't pretend I don't get it."

"If you understand, you're a better man than I."

He meant it as a joke, but it wasn't the kind of joke they usually made. Together, they stared through the window at his mom.

The wind tossed her hair straight up into the air. She lifted her face, as if she were sniffing the ocean.

Whitecapped waves churned up blue-gray water. Low fog shortened the horizon, but the ocean looked exactly as it had during every storm of his life.

It hypnotized his mom.

Finally, she turned her head toward the wildlife sanctuary. Those trees looked taller and greener than he remembered.

Jeez.

When his Dad got out, Dan opened his door, not too sure what else his mother could change for him.

Then she moved again. Using both hands to brace herself, she leaned over the sidewalk railing and pointed her body toward the ocean.

His dad eased behind her and dropped his hands on her shoulders. He curled his fingers slowly around her arms as if he expected her to push him away.

His mother turned to his father. The wind pushed her sweater against her body and outlined the curve of her stomach. A paunch.

She'd never had one before. In fact, she'd lost weight since her accident, but her stomach looked huge.

He might not be the most observant guy on earth, but he'd seen enough pregnant girls at school to recognize the shape.

"Mom?"

Absorbed in each other, his parents ignored him.

A baby explained a lot. His mom's recent astounding ability to throw up for no apparent reason. The tension that had filled his house for the past few months.

The nearly silent arguments they never thought he'd heard. They'd argued more often in the weeks before his mother got hurt. How long had they known about this new kid?

"Mom."

And they turned.

He opened his mouth to ask what the hell were they thinking, but his voice wouldn't work. Who needed a baby? Damn fine graduation present.

"You're pregnant." His accusation shamed him almost as much as the prospect of what his friends would say. Couldn't his mom and dad have waited until everyone went away to college?

"Dan, I—we meant to tell you." His mom broke away from his dad, but he spun out of her reach.

"I'm going to school," he said.

"Dan," his father barked as if he were still twelve years old. "Talk to us."

Dan turned on his heel. What were they? Blind? Even at eighteen a guy didn't want people to know his parents had sex. He had a right to complain.

"You want to talk? Fine. When did you ask me if I wanted a kid around?"

CHAPTER FIVE

DAN SPRINTED UP the sidewalk in the direction they'd come from. Helplessly, Cate turned to Alan. His disturbed gaze made her even more worried about their son.

"Let's go after him," she said.

He hesitated, his mouth tight. "We should give him time. If we drag him back, we'll be lucky if he grunts at us." He took her hands and flicked a brief, perturbed glance toward the ocean behind her. "You're soaking wet. Let me take you home, and I'll pick Dan up after school."

"He left his books in the car. I saw them on the back seat. Are you sure he's going to school?"

Alan urged her back to the vehicle. "Don't borrow trouble."

His abrupt tone shut her out, and she resented his high-handedness. "You and I share responsibility for Dan," she reminded him. "Doing nothing can't be right."

"Try to trust me. I know him, and you don't right now. I'll take care of him."

"What if you're wrong?"

"I'm not wrong. Let me take you home."

She followed him to the car, her heart and her gaze lingering on the boy who hadn't yet reached the top of the hill. He rounded the curve in the road above them without looking back, and she lifted her shoulder to try to brush the rain off her face.

"I wish I hadn't made you stop," she said.

"He's embarrassed because we had sex, Cate."

She stopped where she stood, appalled, and Alan widened his eyes at her.

"I'd have felt the same when I was his age."

He didn't understand. What distracted her was trying to picture a world in which she had sex with Alan—made love with Alan.

The rain blurred her vision as she looked him up—up a lean, strong chest and broad shoulders. She looked down his narrow waist and long legs that stretched the faded denim of his jeans taut.

"Does that picture in your head do anything for you?" His thready voice seduced her, but his straight, thinned mouth kept his own desires a secret.

She tried to put herself in his shoes. His wife of twenty years had forgotten him. His son, who'd stepped out of character to ask for a family homecoming, disliked the idea of becoming a big brother at eighteen. Alan's family had changed entirely in the past three weeks.

Her head began to spin. Would he want her to be attracted to him, or would he want them to get to know each other again? She couldn't guess, but he was still waiting for her answer.

"The idea of intimacy with you unsettles me," she said.

He hunched his shoulders. "Lie to me once in a while, Cate." He curved his mouth in a self-conscious grin. "I can take it."

His words and his tone only strengthened her physical awareness of him, but thinking of a stranger as a lover felt a little wicked.

His sun-darkened face and arms made her wonder if his tan ran beneath his shirt. It was only May. Caroline and Aunt Imogen had told her he worked at all his building sites.

He released her hands and walked ahead of her to open the car door. ''I'll make you breakfast at home.'' He waited.

Cate looked one last time at the now empty sidewalk. What had they done to their child?

She went slowly to the car, but paused with the open door between her and Alan. He couldn't know what trusting anyone cost her.

''Tell me he'll be all right.'' Her depth of need surprised her. Terribly aware of the wall between her past and her present, she didn't want Dan to pay for mistakes she might have made.

Alan's expression softened, and he touched his fingertips to her cheek. ''I'll make sure he's all right.''

She caught her breath. She wasn't asking him to let her perch on the sidelines. ''Dan needs us both. I need you to help me be his mother again.''

Insight deepened his gaze. He nodded, and their emotional connection became as tangible as the warmth of his skin against hers. ''We'll make sure,'' he modified.

She caught his wrist and absorbed the feel of rough hair beneath her palm. His effort to understand drew her closer to him than she'd meant to go. His scent wrapped her in a fantasy of marriage with a sensual, safe stranger.

"Dan is worried about his family," Alan said. "He'll be fine if you and I are all right."

She laughed. So much for hearts and flowers and daydreams. Her heartbeat slowed appropriately. She hoped he wasn't always this practical.

ALAN STOLE a glance at Cate. The tip of her nose peeked out of the fall of her hair. If she was still worried, she hid it in a close study of the beach cottages they passed on their way home.

They might survive this crisis after all. She'd asked him to help her enter her life again, and he felt stronger because Cate needed him.

As he turned up their driveway, she drew in a quick breath and pointed to the tall, narrow white house they'd restored together. It was just home to him, or would be now that his wife was sharing it with him again. Through Cate's eyes, he saw how the bright-pink wild, rambling roses had grown to tumble across the front lawn. Bronze daylilies crowded the door.

He stopped the car. "It's beautiful." The unfamiliar word felt strange in his mouth.

Cate's hair whispered against the seat as she turned to him. "You sound as if you're seeing it for the first time."

"Maybe not the first time, but I've taken it for granted. You're in this house, the part of you I can't forget." His loving wife who'd scrubbed every separate pane of glass, who'd scraped and shaped the old plaster, who'd painted and repainted walls until she'd pronounced them perfect.

"The part you wish would remember you?" Cate prompted.

"I guess that depends on why you forgot."

"Dr. Barton didn't talk to you about shock and the amount of blood I lost?" She sounded as if she suspected the doctor might have given her a different story.

"That's what he told me." He hastened to relieve her understandable fear. "But I've researched memory loss on the Internet. I know about stress. What if Barton's wrong, and you forgot because you don't want to remember?"

"Tell me what stress I was under."

Annoyed with himself, he reached for the remote control attached to the visor above the windshield. He pressed the button that opened her side of the garage. His truck and Dan's car were parked in the other two bays.

"The usual stress. Dan's about to leave for college. You've never been home without a job of some sort, whether it was school or taking care of Dan." Another stressor occurred to him. "And you're pregnant, but I didn't know about that."

She clasped her hands in her lap. Her gaze rode him hard as he pulled into the garage.

"Why didn't I tell you?" she asked. "I can't believe I would have chosen to try to replace Dan. And I don't think I would have let myself get pregnant without your knowledge."

He tightened his hands on the steering wheel. Her tone asked him to let her off the hook. "You stopped using the Pill last year. We must have made a mistake. Don't waste time worrying about why you didn't tell me. We'll deal with the answers when they come.''

Cate slid her hand beneath the weight of her hair, leaning her nape into the palm of her hand. He rubbed his own hands together, remembering the soft texture of those dark red strands against his bare skin.

''Sometimes,'' she said, ''I feel as if you know something you aren't telling me. You don't have to protect me. I'm not fragile.''

He didn't answer. He couldn't lie to her outright.

''Alan?''

Looking at her, he knew his eyes begged her to take him on faith. She nodded slowly.

''Let's start our life again,'' she said.

Brave words. In the past weeks, he'd struggled each day for a respectable measure of courage. Hers came from sources he'd underestimated. Nodding, he pulled into the garage.

They stopped and Cate opened her door. Her leg seemed to give as she climbed out. Watching her grab for support, he felt as he had watching Dan run up the sidewalk away from them. He ought to do something before the worst happened.

''Wait, Cate. Let me help you.''

''I'm fine.'' She waited for strength to return to her injured thigh.

He got out and opened the back of the SUV to get her bag. As she pressed her hands to the car, her nervousness bounced off the walls.

''Over here.'' He opened the door and waited for her to precede him down the vine-covered, latticed walkway that led to the kitchen. Her intense concentration drew him, but he tried not to watch her. The last thing she needed was to feel like a bug under his magnifying glass.

"I'm home," she said.

He hadn't expected her to think of their house as her home already. His own legs threatened to give.

Cate flashed an apologetic glance. "I keep repeating that in my head. I thought I might be more convinced if I said the words out loud."

Reality again. He was starting to dislike it. "Do you feel up to exploring?"

"I can't wait." She plucked the keys from his hand. "Which one?"

"The brass one next to the car key."

She opened the door and walked inside ahead of him. Two years ago he'd insisted they renovate the kitchen. She stopped now at the butcher block island and revolved in a slow circle, bemused at the stainless steel fixtures, all state-of-the-art, all sturdy and useful.

"Why does this place look like a restaurant?"

He almost dropped her bag. "That's what you said the first time you saw it."

She turned her head so fast her hair swung beneath her chin. "Sorry. Am I insulting you?"

He shook his head. "I talked you into these appliances to make your life easier. You refused to hire a maid service to help you."

"Help me what?"

"Take care of the house and Dan, do the cooking, give you more free time."

"I must have had a lot of free time. Why didn't I work?"

"When you got pregnant with Dan, we agreed he

should have a stay-at-home parent. You were the more logical choice, because I'd already finished my degree.''

She tugged at the hem of her sweater, silently conceding they were about to start parenting small children all over again. ''Did I plan to look for a job after Dan left? Do I have a degree?''

How did she feel about being with the new babies? Maybe he should give her time to get used to their family before he asked. ''You majored in history, but you were working toward your teaching certificate when you left school after Dan was born.''

She turned away from the island. ''I don't recognize myself when you all talk about me.''

Alan's world slipped a little, like a foundation incorrectly laid. After twenty years, he'd believed he knew all about Cate. ''What don't you recognize?''

''Obviously, women choose to make homes for their busy husbands and teenaged sons, but how would I stay home with so little to do around here?''

Little to do? How about taking care of their family?

She laid her left hand on his forearm. He stared at the narrow band on her ring finger, at the diamond she hadn't wanted. He'd insisted, because the sapphire she'd liked hadn't said the same thing as a diamond. People might have thought he couldn't afford proper rings for his wife.

''What did I say that scared you?'' she asked.

He shook his head. ''I wonder if you were bored with me—with our life—before the accident. After all, you still think the kitchen looks like a restaurant.''

''I wish I hadn't said that.''

He twined his fingers with hers, and she didn't pull away. Did she notice she'd let him touch her? ''Say what you feel. Ask me anything. I want to help you, but I can't promise I won't be disturbed when you tell me something I didn't know about you.''

Shrugging, she gently disentangled herself from him. Her smile flirted a little. ''I hope I keep on disturbing you. I'd rather not be the only one who's confused.'' The tender curve of her lips made her look more like his Cate.

His heart responded, but he checked his involuntary response. ''Why don't we take your things to our room? I'll show you the way, and then you can explore the rest of the place while I cook.''

''Do you cook often?''

''Hardly ever.'' With his answer, he realized he should have eased more of her burden around here. ''We'll take those stairs.'' He pointed to white wooden steps tucked into the corner beside the pantry.

Cate climbed ahead of him. Her perfume drifted back from the damp strands of her hair, the knit of her sweater.

''You'll want to change out of those wet clothes,'' he suggested on the second-floor landing. ''Our room is the first door on the left.''

As she took in the narrow hallway, he saw its shadowed closeness for the first time in years. She hung back, as if she shared his unexpected claustrophobia.

''We should have discussed sleeping arrangements before now,'' she said.

A rush of resentment surged through him, but he opened their bedroom door. He was determined to be strong for her.

She followed him inside, carefully avoiding the four-poster and the overstuffed vine-printed chintz armchairs that guarded their wide bay window. A reading lamp hovered at the corner of her chair. She'd loved this room.

He also avoided the furniture they'd used all their married life. He wouldn't let his need to hold her again turn into immature anger. "You're asking me to move out?"

"No, this is your room. It's strange to me." She stopped.

Well, he probably looked stricken.

"It's comfortable," she improvised, confused about what mattered to him. "But unfamiliar. I'll move out until we know each other again."

He did know her. Some caveman instinct that startled even him suggested he ease her to their bed and remind her in all the ways he knew she loved.

"You stay here," he said and then cleared his throat. If she'd known him at all, his husky tone would have betrayed the erotic images in his mind. "I'll take the guest room."

Stubbornness she'd never shown before firmed her mouth. "Why should you sleep anywhere besides your own bed? You don't have to be a gentleman."

"I'm not," he said. "I want you to remember. Maybe, if you stay in a room you loved, surrounded by belongings you've chosen, your life will come back to you." And she'd return to him. Unless she remembered his lie about the business.

For a moment he didn't care if she remembered what he'd done as long as she remembered the rest of their lives together. The company mattered, but they had children who'd need both their parents, and he wanted Cate to remember loving him.

"I'll move my things and call the high school to make sure Dan showed up."

She relaxed her obstinate expression. "I knew you weren't being entirely straight about that."

"I'm sure he went, but it's still raining. He might need dry clothes." He was only doing what Cate would have done before. Most of what he'd done for Dan since her accident, came from a single question: "What would Cate do?"

"Can't you call from here?" Her gaze reached the telephone on his side of their bed. She picked up the receiver and held it out to him. "Do you know the number?"

"Listen, Cate, this time I could use a break. I'm willing to do what you want about our marriage, but I'm not happy about separate rooms. Let me go downstairs and call Dan's school." He stopped as she looked at him with a pinched face. "You don't know Dan any better than you know me, but you'll go the extra mile for him. I don't mean to sound jealous, but I wonder how you can care for him so much when you don't know either of us."

She twisted her neck, flexing her muscles. Once, he would have stepped behind her to massage her tension away.

"I guess I'm trying to be a mom," she said. At his lifted eyebrow, she held up her hands in submission. "All right, Dan thinks he's grown-up, and you think he's mature, but he's still young enough to look like he needs me. Dr. Barton told me about implicit memory—an emotional reaction that comes from feelings I've had before. Maybe I react to Dan because I've loved him. All I know is, he needs me.''

Alan needed her with a yearning that went so deep in his body he had to force himself not to shake like a scared child. ''I'll call the school,'' he said, unable to believe she'd want to know how he felt.

She put her hand on his arm, and he jumped, but then he stood still, meeting her gaze. Her mouth was vulnerable. Her eyes beseeched. ''I'll learn to be your wife, too, Alan.''

''I don't want you to learn.'' He bit the inside of his cheek until it hurt. ''I want a wife who loves me.'' He felt naked.

''What if I don't remember? I can't promise to fall in love with you.'' She took both his hands in hers and pulled them against her stomach where the babies they'd made together were growing. ''But I want a real marriage.'' Her dark-blue eyes glittered with life he'd never seen before. ''And I want it with you. I'm willing to believe I might come to feel love enough to make our marriage real again.''

''For the children?''

''For them. I won't lie to you, but I don't want to throw the past away just because I don't remember it. I want to know what I can feel for you if we give each other time.''

He wasn't a man who talked about maybes. He believed in reality, like concrete and steel. He carried her bag to the chair in front of his cluttered desk.

When he turned, she was still watching him. Her

soft tone and intense gaze promised a future he craved. But would she try so hard if she knew he'd failed her in their present?

He'd feared losing Cate for most of his married life. She'd always said she wanted to share the bad times, the problems he'd tried to hide as well as their successes, but he hadn't believed she'd want to be with him if he couldn't give her things—like this house, the car in the driveway.

Nothing had changed. He couldn't lose their company and keep his wife.

He needed a few more days, maybe a few more weeks. "I'll get the school's number from my briefcase and check on Dan. After I call, I'll let you know what they say."

"You don't have to handle me with care, Alan."

He held on to the desk chair to fight off another bout of shaking. She knew something was wrong. "I'm not. My dad is joining us for dinner. He said he'd like to see you now that you're home."

She lifted her chin. "What's wrong with your dad?"

He could have kicked himself. She didn't remember his father. "He can seem somewhat irresponsible before you know him well."

"Is he irresponsible?" Again, she knew something. Knowledge made her tone sound aggressive.

He nodded at her. "Who talked to you about my dad?"

"Caroline." She admitted it right away. He had to admire her courage. "I asked her about him. She didn't gossip. She said he'd had a drinking problem and that you took care of him."

He breathed deeply. "I didn't realize Caroline knew so much." He hoped Cate hadn't betrayed his family secrets.

"You think I told her?" Cate looked surprised. "She said I kept all important information to myself."

He shrugged, pretending it didn't matter. "Your clothes are in that wardrobe." It towered over the room, but her rosewood wardrobe was more delicately carved than the cherry behemoth that housed his clothes across the room.

"What will you do with your things?" she asked.

"Move them to the guest room." He paused at the door to the hall. "Settle in. You must be tired, and I can take my clothes out after you rest. We'll have to tell Dan about using separate rooms."

She opened the wardrobe door, but eyed him absently. "Why not tell him the truth?"

"After he's discovered we've had sex, we should tell him we won't any more?"

With an open laugh he'd never heard before, Cate turned from perusing her clothes. "Let's not *promise* that," she suggested.

CHAPTER SIX

CATE WOKE, gasping for breath. Her pounding heart made her reach for her chest. She listened to her own breathing, unsure what had made her wake so suddenly.

She stared at the shadows that stood sentinel duty around the dimly lit room. Furniture and memories she couldn't decode. She hadn't planned to sleep, and she wasn't sure if she'd slept through the whole day. The rain had returned, and with it, darkness.

Willing her heart to slow, she crept toward the edge of the wide bed. From somewhere outside her room, came the tinkling of dishes and the murmur of deep male voices. Richard must have arrived, because she recognized Dan and Alan, but she heard a third voice.

She bent to inspect her hair in the vanity mirror. Fluffing the flattened strands, she took stock of her makeup. Pretty much gone, but she waved her hand at her sleepy face. The Palmer men would have to take her as she was.

She hurried down the same narrow stairs she and Alan had climbed earlier. In the kitchen, her husband turned from the stove, an iron frying pan in his towel-covered hands. Dan sat alone at the table. Richard wasn't in the room.

"You didn't have to come down," Alan said. "I planned to bring you a tray."

"I'd rather eat with you."

Dan stood slowly, as if he weren't sure how she'd approach him. Painting a smile on her face, she met him halfway across the room.

"Dad told me to tell you I'm all right, and I'm sorry I ran off this morning."

His approach lacked aplomb, but she studied the circles beneath his eyes and decided there was more to him than he was letting them see. "I understand you might need time on your own, but are you really all right?"

"I just didn't expect a baby."

"We didn't have time to tell you the other unexpected news," she said, glancing at Alan. He hesitated, looking as green as she felt, but finally he nodded, and she turned back to Dan. "We're going to have two babies. Twins."

"How do you plan to do that, Cate?"

She whirled. The man who'd spoken stood at the other kitchen door. In looks, he was a mix of Dan and Alan. He shared the same tall, lean body type, but his hair was salt and pepper and resembled piano wire.

He looked her up and down. "You're a strong woman, but I don't think even you could order up a couple of kids."

His comment about her strength distracted her. Tales of her former saintliness had made her suspect she'd been something of a doormat. "They're on order already," she said. She smoothed her sweater over the mound that had begun to grow at an astounding rate.

"Mom, don't do that." Dan stared, as if he expected an alien creature to emerge from her belly.

"We're talking babies," Alan said, losing patience. "They won't hurt you, Dan."

"And two of them don't make the event more special." Dan snatched a cabinet door open and took out plates. "I'll finish setting the table. You stay and talk to Mom, Grandpa."

He disappeared down the hall, but Richard appeared to side with him. "More kids? You want more?" he asked, as if he couldn't fathom why.

"We're having more." Alan shook his head. "And Dad, we haven't asked for your advice."

"How long have you known?" Richard eyed Cate's stomach with trepidation that matched Dan's. "Not that I blame you for trying to hide your pregnancy. Aren't you two old enough to know better?"

"You love Dan, Dad." Alan's voice placated. "You'll love these babies, too. Calm down."

"I guess it's none of my business if you want to saddle yourselves at your ages." Richard held out his hand to Cate. "I probably don't need an introduction."

"You must be Richard." She shook his hand because Alan seemed to believe he possessed redeeming qualities.

"I'm sorry I didn't see you while you were in the hospital."

"Alan explained."

"My son despairs of me, but I just can't stand

being around all those sick people.'' He shuddered. ''I don't know how you dealt with them.''

''I was sick enough to fit in.''

Alan began to slice the contents of the pan he'd set on the counter. ''I don't think Dad understands how shallow he makes himself sound,'' Alan said.

Cate took a deep breath. The physical therapist at the hospital had taught her relaxation techniques. Sadly, she never could remember if she was supposed to breathe in through her mouth and out through her nose or vice versa. She tried both ways. Neither worked.

Oblivious to her surprised feelings of dislike, Richard pulled her to a chair and helped her into it. More assistance than she needed, but she reminded herself he was Alan's father. And Alan cared for him.

''I don't think I'm shallow,'' Richard said. ''I just know my limitations. Knowing exactly what you can and can't do makes you a stronger person. I just don't pretend I can be someone I'm not.''

''That *sounds* right,'' Cate said, and literally felt her husband trying to hold her back with a warning gaze.

He lifted the pan again and carried it to a marble slab on the island. ''Help me serve this frittata, Dad, and drop the subject.''

''All right, if you're determined to be foolish.''

Cate grabbed a stack of silverware from the counter, an excuse to flee the kitchen and her father-in-law. ''I'll take this to the table.''

She'd looked around the house before her nap, but she'd been so tired, it still felt unfamiliar. A narrow hall that split the living spaces ran all the way through. Two doorways down, she found Dan rearranging plates on a long, oval table in a turquoise dining room. Cate stopped in the doorway.

"These walls are bright," she said.

Dan looked up. "The paint is historically accurate. That's what you told me."

A whitewashed fireplace at the end of the room drew her. The wood flooring creaked as she crossed. She brushed her fingers against the painted plaster that bordered the fireplace. Even lit by electric candle sconces placed around the walls, the paint was hideous. Cold and unwelcoming.

"I insisted on this color?"

He nodded. "What do you think of Grandpa?"

She caught the back of a chair. "What do you mean?"

"You don't bother to hide how you feel any more. I'll take the silverware."

But she only gave him half, and then they started in opposite directions around the table. "I don't get your grandpa. Is he always so free with his opinions?"

"You'd rather he lied?"

"I guess not, but he's so cheerful, and every word out of his mouth offended me." She stopped for a careful study of her son. "And why do you and I get along better when we're alone?"

He didn't answer at first. All his attention seemed focused on the knife he arranged beside a plate at the head of the table. "I'm sorry I left this morning. I was mad. And I hate to be as honest as Grandpa, but I'm glad I'll graduate before anyone else finds out about the babies."

Cate finished her share of the silverware. How would a more natural mother respond? "You want us to keep the twins to ourselves for now?"

"Yes." He took glasses from a sideboard. "I guess I sound like Grandpa to you."

Dan might love his grandfather, and she wouldn't alienate him with her negative first impression of Richard. An impression that probably had a lot to do with what Caroline had said about the way he'd treated Alan. "I don't know the man well enough to have an opinion, but about the twins, Dan? You guessed from seeing my clothes. Your friends might be as clever as you."

"Wear something loose to my graduation," he said. "Do me that favor, Mom."

"I will, but I'm not ashamed, any more than I would have been with you."

He knocked a glass over. The sound focused her on the anger that distorted his face.

"You don't remember me," he said. "You don't know if you were ashamed of me."

She made her voice gentle, trying to ease his anguish. "I'm willing to bet I wasn't." And she'd bend over backward to prove he was important to her, whether she remembered him or not. His need was as obvious as the hollows beneath his eyes and his perpetual touchiness.

In silence, he glared at her, but she refused to be perturbed. Behind her, footsteps heralded Alan holding a serving dish and Richard carrying a pitcher of ice water. Richard smiled absently in Cate's general direction as he began to fill the glasses.

"I love breakfast for dinner," he said. "Thanks for asking me to stay, son."

Alan, more sensitive than his father, seemed to diagnose the atmosphere. "Have we interrupted, Cate?"

She hesitated. She'd be furious with Alan if he hid something as important as Dan's asking her to pretend she wasn't pregnant. But she didn't want to discuss her son in front of Richard. "Grandpa" might be as harmless as Alan and Dan seemed to think, but they loved him. Her concern for Dan was too personal to share with Richard.

"We were talking about this paint." She slapped her hand to the turquoise plaster. "I hope you're not attached to it, Alan, because Dan and I plan to change it. What color do you think, Dan?"

His open mouth expressed surprise, but he went along with her change of subject. "I like forest green," he said. "Like your truck, Dad."

"Your truck?" Cate echoed. "We're going to copy the paint from a work truck?"

"I don't think I'll have a difficult time finding a chip to pry off. They'll be able to match it for you at the paint store." Alan grinned as he set the serving dish on the table. "I made a salad, Dan. Do you want to bring it in?"

"Okay." Dan's grateful glance warmed Cate as he shot past her. He obviously loved Richard, but he must not have wanted to discuss his sibling rivalry issues in front of the older man.

"I'll get the salad dressing." Richard followed his grandson. "Did you make the vinaigrette I like, son?"

''You'll find it on the counter.'' Alan began to serve while Dan and Richard were out of the room. ''Want to tell me what really happened with you and Dan?''

''Not now. I promise I'll tell you after your father leaves. I really need to know about Richard. How much time has he spent with Dan? Is he a nice—''

Alan put his finger across his lips and glanced toward the doorway. Cate nodded, more frustrated than she'd been since she'd awakened from the coma. He was too careful with her and with Richard. His wariness hinted at a past that had begun to feel ominous.

''Let me get your chair.'' Alan pulled one out for her and she took it. She looked up at him, and his smile confused her more. She liked the curve of his mouth, the reassurance in his gaze.

''Salad, Cate?'' Richard came in, ready to serve.

''Please.''

''This is a first.'' He put mixed greens on her plate. ''Us waiting on you.''

''You like Dad's vinaigrette, too, Mom.'' Dan passed her the crystal decanter, and she poured. They all waited until Richard set the salad bowl on the sideboard and sat in a chair opposite Dan's.

Cate sliced a bite of frittata with the edge of her fork and tasted. After an experimental, ambrosial chew, she beamed at her husband. ''Delicious,'' she said as soon as she could talk.

Alan opened his mouth, but his father beat him to the punch. ''Alan did almost all the cooking when he was a boy. After his mother left us.''

This time she didn't bother to finish her bite. ''From the time he was *ten?*''

"Dad, let it go." She'd never heard the harsh note in Alan's voice before. Was he protecting his father, or did he still feel the pain of his mother's leaving?

"Do you ever see your mother?" she asked.

Again, Richard answered first. "She made no effort to stay in touch, and I began to think Alan might be better off without her. I didn't want her to leave him more than once."

Cate turned to her husband. Two broken people had raised the man she'd married. Had their neglect forced him to be strong or merely damaged him?

Tonight's conversation with Richard had told her one thing. Alan still kept his own secrets. She glanced at his lowered head. Her instincts had been right. He was holding back.

He stood up, and everyone at the table stared at him. "I forgot the bread," he said. "I'm going to the kitchen to get it, and when I come back, I'd be grateful if we could leave my past where it belongs. I'm not the one who needs to remember."

He left, and Cate looked from her father-in-law to her son. They returned her startled glance. Cate pushed her chair back.

"He can be so emotional," Richard said.

She turned on him, Caroline's information and Alan's own refusal to talk pushing her to defend her husband. "Don't try to make Alan sound less a man." She glanced Dan's way and held back on the rest of her advice for Richard. "It sounds as if he's been carrying a man's burden since he was ten years old."

Her melodramatic speech echoed embarrassingly in her mind as she headed for the kitchen. Maybe

Alan didn't need her protection, but she took their marriage and the relationship they were trying to build seriously.

She half expected to find him slumped over the counter, trying to put his world back together. But no, he was cutting slices of bread off a crusty loaf. He looked up.

"You're limping more," he said. "You should stay off that leg."

"Are you all right?"

He stopped cutting to look at her in surprise. "I understand the humiliation that drives my father. My mom convinced him he wasn't man enough to be her husband. For all I know, he may still believe her, but I don't want him to upset you."

"Do you want some butter for that?" She went to the fridge and pulled out a tub of margarine.

"You always liked garlic toast, Cate. Do you want it now?"

She grinned at him. "If it keeps us out here longer, I sure do."

His smile lingered on her face. Her heartbeat sped up, but then he opened the tub of margarine. "You're different," he said as he scooped out a dollop of margarine.

"I might be," she said. She turned toward the dining room. What really drove Richard Palmer? He couldn't be unaware he'd hurt his son as much as his errant wife had. Looking back at Alan, she lowered her voice. "I'm stunned *you* turned out so well."

He froze. An oversize blob of margarine dripped off his knife, onto the counter. "You'll have to explain that."

"Maybe I'm overreacting, but from the way your father talks, you were raised by a wolf."

Alan widened his eyes. He looked one hell of a lot like Dan when he stared at her in shock, but his shock switched to stunned laughter.

"Don't laugh. I wish you were more concerned." For himself. "Don't you ever want someone to take care of you?"

He sobered. "I'm fine. I like things the way they are."

"With my mind a blank, and your father—" She broke off. She couldn't just blurt her opinion of Richard to Alan, either.

"My dad is hardly wolflike. More a puppy you just can't train."

Cate disagreed, but she kept it to herself. "I'll help you with the toast."

"No, thanks. I don't even trust you with a butter knife in your mood." He stopped spreading margarine to glance at her. "I'd better try to stay on your good side."

THE NEXT MORNING, Dan dressed for school and started downstairs for breakfast. On his way past the guest room, he noticed his dad's pajamas on the floor.

Now, what? What happened after parents decided not to sleep together? Behind him, his mother's door opened.

"Dan?"

"Go back to bed."

"I'm tired of sleeping. Have you eaten breakfast?"

If she was going to split up his family, he'd rather she stopped talking to him as if she had to help him blow his nose. "I'll get my own."

She tugged the neck of a long T-shirt that reached almost to the knees of her pajama pants. "I'll make my own, too. Mind if I join you?"

"Sure you want to?" He jutted a thumb toward the guest room. "Looks like you'd rather be alone these days."

Her skin turned bright red. "We forgot to tell you." She wrapped her hand around her throat—also bright red. "We decided to sleep in separate rooms until I remember more. You can see I'm nervous about sharing a—room with a stranger?"

She seemed so different, he forgot he and his dad were the strangers. She was like someone he'd never known. "I guess I get it. You can come on down if you want."

He made coffee while she hunted down ingredients to make pancake batter. She didn't ask for help, and she found everything she needed. When she finished the batter, she stood over the griddle built into the stove.

"Are you sure you don't want some?"

He relented. Her cooking tasted better than his. "If you have some to spare, I'd take a pancake."

"Thanks," she said dryly. "Maybe you can find the plates. I don't remember where I saw them."

She'd opened every cabinet in the kitchen. He wasn't surprised she'd forgotten which one held the plates. He took out two and set them on the table.

"We always eat in here unless we have company," he said.

"Good. It's a long way to the dining room." She flipped the first pancake. "Thanks for going along with me on the paint in there last night."

He nodded, a little guilty for being mad at her about the separate rooms when he remembered she'd made up that story to protect him. She turned to him when he didn't answer, and he nodded again.

"Will you really help me paint it?"

Was she trying to baby him into a relationship? "You don't have to think up busywork to spend time with me."

She looked surprised, really surprised. Maybe she was faking it to trick him into a mom-son activity for old times' sake.

"I want to paint," she said, "and I thought you might help me. You're taller than I am."

"What if you like the blue-green paint when you remember everything?"

"I don't care about historical accuracy. We live here, and that room feels cold."

"Everything had to be 'appropriate' before. It was one of your favorite words."

He'd never been so up-front with his mom. She'd wanted him to look happy. He'd never been sure she wanted to know how he really felt. "You tried to convince me life runs by rules."

She twisted her mouth in disgust. "Saint Cate again. I don't necessarily want to be inappropriate, but surely you can have some fun and still follow rules. Whatever they are." Balancing the first pancake on a spatula, she carried it across the room to him.

He wouldn't have been more startled if she'd

hoisted the stove on her back and trotted it up the stairs. ''I can get you a serving plate for that,'' he said. His involuntary offer surprised him. ''You've made me more correct than you are now.''

''So lighten up.'' She looked from the pancake to him and tipped it onto his plate. ''I'll bet you'd like a couple more?''

The ''lighten up'' suggestion bugged him. ''You could try to cook more than one at a time.''

She'd already headed back to the stove, but she turned, holding the spatula as if it were a weapon. ''How do you know? Did I make you do the cooking here?''

''Grandpa really spooked you, didn't he?''

''He gave your father too much resp— Never mind.''

''You can be honest with me.''

''We didn't make you responsible for cooking and housework at such a young age.'' She flinched. ''Did we?''

''Yeah, right. You made me wait a year longer than any of my friends to get my driver's license. I'm about to leave for college, but I've never had a party without you or Dad in the house. Dad even 'supervised' me every time I balanced my checkbook for the first year.''

''How long before you leave, Dan?''

Like always, she only listened to the part she wanted to hear. Still, he was glad she didn't want him to go. ''I'm taking summer classes.''

''Why?''

''I want out of school. I'm ready to be on my own.''

She turned her back on him. She still didn't want him to see how she felt.

"Who's Saint Cate?" he asked.

"I am—or I was, and I really can't stand her." She grabbed a towel off the counter and wiped at her face.

Was she crying? If his dad found out, he was dead meat. He took her shoulders and gently made her face him.

"Why are you crying?" His voice squeaked again.

"What if you go before I remember you? I'll never really know you."

"Cut it out, Mom. You don't have to see me every day to remember who I am." He put his arms around her, but hugging her felt weird. He patted her shoulder. Girls liked that. Moms must, too. "I'll only be an hour away. If you remember, you can call me."

He felt like an idiot, so he went to the stove. She was still sniffing into the towel as he picked up the batter. "I'll do this," he said. "I've mastered the art of three at a time, and I'm going to be late for school."

She nodded. "Whatever. Listen, if I pick up the paint, we can start painting."

"Tonight? I have practice."

"Golf?" She moved out of his way. He avoided looking at her face—a real mess. "How about tomorrow night?"

His mom didn't cry, and she didn't let him cook pancakes. Why did she want to paint with him? "Okay, if Dr. Barton says you can."

"He said to rest when I'm tired. I'm not tired."

He poured batter on the griddle. "How many for you?"

"Two, thanks. Dan, are you happy here?"

"Well, yeah. This is home." What'd she think? She just pissed him off with this forgetting thing. That and he couldn't get divorce off his mind.

"You'd say if something bothered you? I know I'm not the mother I used to be, but I want to take care of you."

"I don't need you to take care of me. Mom, could you sit at the table? You're making me burn these pancakes."

She limped over to the table and pulled back her chair. As she was about to sit, the phone rang. He waited for her to answer. Damn it, this was her house. He'd cook pancakes, but he wasn't pretending she didn't know how to answer her own phone.

"I'll get it," she said.

Guilt gave him second thoughts as she made her way toward the phone on the wall beside the back door. Her leg must hurt pretty bad.

She picked up the receiver. "Hello? Oh, hi, Alan. I didn't expect to hear from you."

She turned toward the wall, as if she wanted to keep him from hearing. His dad always called home during the day.

"Tonight?" She twisted the phone cord around her wrist. "What time?" After a pause, she turned slightly. "Yes, he's still here. I'll tell him. What? We're making pancakes." She laughed, but she sounded funny. "He took over. No, I won't forget to tell him." She waited. His dad must have said something. "Okay," she said. "Bye."

She hung up the phone, and he flipped the pancakes onto a plate. ''What are you supposed to tell me about tonight?''

''Aunt Imogen and Uncle Ford asked us to dinner. We're supposed to show up with appetites at six-thirty.''

''I'll go from practice.'' He took the stack of pancakes to the table. Then he sat down and shifted his onto the plate she'd already given him.

She didn't even notice his bad manners. She just reached for syrup. ''I'll move the furniture out of the dining room today.''

''Leave the heavy stuff, Mom.''

''Don't worry.'' She looked completely unlike her old self, smiling at him as if she were about to tell a joke. ''Why break my back?'' she teased.

Her question made a lousy joke. His mom would have broken every bone in her body before she'd ask for help.

''Dad will blame me if you move the furniture.'' That should fix her.

He poured syrup on his own pancakes. At least the rest of the family would be at dinner tonight. Let someone else take a shot at this new version of his mom.

ALAN WATCHED shadows drift across his desk. He was already late getting home if he and Cate were going to make it to Aunt Imogen's in time for dinner.

The men he'd invited to meet with him and John Mabry remained stony. Each slumped in varying postures of defeat in the leather chairs that had cost him two hundred fifty-three dollars and some odd cents apiece in his company's flush days.

Howard Fisk owned the hardware center. Shep Deavers ran his family's plumbing supply business. Brian Henney had landscaped almost every project, large and small, that Alan had ever worked on.

All these men had trusted Jim Cooper with their books, and they all faced the prospect of losing their businesses. More so because they depended on Alan's jobs for many of their contracts.

''New bottom line,'' Mabry said. ''We tracked Jim to Maine. He spent two weeks with his computer and Internet access to accounts all over the States. From there, he rented a car that the Wheeling, West Virginia police found disabled with a flat tire on the side of the road. If he stayed in Wheeling, he used a false name.''

''You have no idea where he is now,'' Howard said.

''Thanks for the obvious, Howard.'' Shep also looked forward to the dependent faces of a large family when the news became public. ''I'm starting to agree with Alan. We have to tell the people who work for us.''

''No,'' the others chorused.

''Once we lose control, our businesses go under.'' Brian repeated this refrain at least three times during each of their meetings.

''How long before you catch up with Jim again?'' Alan asked.

''Hard to say.'' Mabry shifted. ''As soon as he uses a form of payment or identification we or the FBI can track, we'll find him.''

"And if we're all broke by that time?" Shep asked.

"I don't know what to tell you. The money hasn't gone out of the country yet."

"So you can still get it back?"

"Possibly. We don't know what he's done with it."

Alan disliked Mabry's answer. "How are we supposed to placate creditors with a possibility?"

"We'll prosecute Jim Cooper, but you all know where you stand better than I do. I'm doing my job, Alan."

"I wonder if you forget how many jobs will disappear from this town if the people in this office lose their companies."

"That's not fair. I know you have a lot on your mind, Alan, but I'm not sleeping any better than the rest of you."

Mabry was right. The business meant more to Alan than ever, because he'd never be able to explain to Cate now. Her concern last night had surprised and pleased him, but he could see this new incarnation of his wife going for his knees if she discovered the business problems he'd hidden.

The intercom on Alan's desk buzzed. With an eye on his watch again, he picked up the receiver. He'd promised to be home half an hour ago. "Yes?"

His secretary's voice came over the line. "Cate just called. She said she'd be happy to drive to her aunt's by herself if you're going to be late."

Already late, he was grateful she'd put it that way instead of complaining. "Can you call her back? I'd rather she waited." Dr. Barton hadn't said she shouldn't drive, but she'd slept most of yesterday. Visiting her family might tire her again.

"I don't have anything more to tell you," Mabry said, catching on to Alan's end of the conversation.

The other men stood. Alan grimaced, caught between frustration at being unable to change his business situation and relief at being able to go home to Cate. "Tell her I'm on my way," he said to his secretary.

After a round of handshaking, he saw the men out and went back to his desk to gather up paperwork he'd have to do at home. He stuffed everything in his canvas briefcase and left his office.

Caroline's door was shut. She'd already gone. Alan hurried to the front door. He should have called Cate back today, asked her how breakfast had gone with Dan. After his father'd left last night, she'd told him Dan had asked her to keep her pregnancy a secret. He'd like to know if they'd discussed it this morning.

On the street, he unlocked his truck and tossed his briefcase inside. Traffic out to their cottage was fairly light, but as he turned into his driveway, the front door opened and Cate hurried out, her limp less noticeable already.

Her filmy, pale-blue dress hid her pregnancy. She looked deceptively delicate as she draped the thin strap of her small purse over her shoulder and waved at him. He got out to open her door.

"You don't have to do that," she said, waving him off.

"I wanted to. I'm glad to see you."

She stopped at his side. "Me, too."

The shine in her blue eyes shallowed his breathing. For a moment, he believed she was going to kiss him the way she used to when he came home from work. A slight breath whispered through her lips and she curled her fingers around his forearm.

A squeeze of welcome hardly cut it, but he settled for what she offered. Ahead of him lay free time to remind her she'd married a good husband who was glad she'd come home to him.

She slid into the passenger's seat. "Aunt Imogen called a few minutes ago."

"I'm sorry I'm late."

"Don't worry. She offered to come get me, but I told her you were on your way." She reached for the door handle. "She mentioned something you and I have to discuss."

"What?"

"Get in." She closed the door and waited for him to walk around the truck. After he started the engine, she turned, curving her good leg onto the seat between them.

Something different gleamed from her eyes, a serenity he hadn't seen before. Ever. He marveled at her. Despite everything, this woman had found peace that had always eluded her.

"Why are you looking at me like that, Alan? As if I'm the stranger. Dan does the same thing."

"You're happier than I've ever seen you."

Her laugh seduced him, low and full of self-awareness that made no sense in light of her amnesia. "I finally have something to do," she said. "Unfortunately, you have to help me."

Would she respect him if he killed the truck's motor and fell outside onto his knees to beg her to let him help her? He'd grind his knees on the road for a couple more of her smiles. ''What can I do?''

''Dan's graduation,'' she said. ''How does he want to celebrate? Have we already chosen his gift? Do we need to rent a hall? I searched my desk to see if we'd made any preparations, but I couldn't find anything. We have to make decisions. Fast.''

Decisions about arrangements they probably couldn't afford, definitely shouldn't attempt right now. He'd felt less pressure facing Chief Mabry and the other gullible fools who'd trusted the CPA they'd all used for nearly twenty years.

He didn't have to lie to them.

CHAPTER SEVEN

"SHOULDN'T WE make sure we know what Dan wants?" Alan's guilt nearly choked him. Worrying about spending money on such a momentous day underscored his failure to provide. Backpedaling to keep Cate from finding out they had a problem made him feel like a slug.

"I don't think Dan will say. Aunt Imogen tried to pump him, but he won't tell her. Did we discuss a gift before the accident?"

"A golf school," he said. "I'm not sure why he wouldn't talk to Aunt Imogen, but he gave us suggestions."

They could still afford the school—barely—but they'd be foolish to spend that much money. For the first time, he wanted to tell Cate the truth about their finances. But he was still afraid to burden her with the stress of their failing business.

"What's a golf school?" she asked, somehow oblivious to his tension.

"A week of one-on-one instruction with a pro at Myrtle Beach. All the golf he can play outside of class time."

Cate sat back, so happy she made him want to give the present to Dan. "Perfect," she said. "I can't wait to see his face."

"I'm sure he knows which gift we'd choose." What a hole he'd dug for himself. Alan took her hand. "What if we had to ask Dan to wait for the school until maybe fall?"

"But isn't he starting college soon? Is the golf school full?"

"I'm actually thinking of what we can afford." Disgusted, he let her hand go. He couldn't tell her the truth yet, so he'd find a way to do what she wanted. "Never mind. I'll make the arrangements."

"If you're not sure about the cost, we should explain to Dan, but let's try to arrange the school for him, Alan."

He'd almost rather she'd argue for her own way. But Cate had never played those kinds of games, and a bad case of shock couldn't transform her completely. "I'll look at our finances again and we can talk."

"Okay," she said. "What about a party?"

"Let's leave that up to him." Alan turned off the beach road and headed across the marshy wetlands into town. An egret wafted into the air to race alongside them on the ribbon of beige road. He felt like that bird, trying desperately to keep airborne. "Dan may have made plans with his friends."

"Drinking and orgies?"

Alan stared at her. She burst into laughter. "I'll bet I looked like you do now when Aunt Imogen suggested those possibilities to me. I'm glad I was alone."

"Aunt Imogen? I can't believe she's ever heard of an orgy."

''Because she's my maiden aunt? She strikes me as a woman who made her own choices in her time.''

''I suspect she still makes her own choices.'' He reached for sunglasses as they turned into the setting sun, and their windshield framed Leith's skyline. ''Look at the town.'' He pointed toward the rounded dome of the courthouse, the church spires and the intricate Eastern design of Leith's synagogue. The sun, dropping out of sight, bathed the buildings in pale orange. Close at hand, tall pines and Southern hardwoods, maple, oak and cypress rose out of the black dirt.

''It's beautiful. I wish I could remember my past here.''

''I can't imagine how you feel.'' Asking her seemed like an intrusion, since he felt unsure how much of her life she was ready to share. He wished she'd tell him anyway.

''The frustration makes my head ache,'' she said, giving him what he wanted as if it were the simplest response in the world. ''I see the extra thought you give to every word you speak to me. Everyone treats me as if I'm about to break. I have a life to get on with, but I don't know how or where I'm supposed to start.''

''You have started. Dinner with my dad last night, and tonight with your family. You're concerned about Dan. You're attached to Aunt Imogen and Uncle Ford. You had a good visit with Caroline in the hospital.''

''And I care about you.'' She dropped her hand on his arm, her tone infused with a warmth he hadn't heard in a long time.

When she brushed her fingers over the hair on his wrist, her touch raised the skin beneath her hand. He felt like a teenager.

She tilted her head toward the window on her side of the car. ''I can't get your father's visit out of my mind. He's not even embarrassed he made you an adult so he could wallow through his loss.''

"I'm glad you came to my rescue last night,'' Alan said, slightly embarrassed. He was supposed to be his family's guardian angel. ''But Dad did the best he could. Let's not psychoanalyze him now.''

''He makes me nuts when he laughs about it. No guilt on his conscience, huh?''

''He has nothing to feel guilty for. I grew up. I'm a responsible adult.''

''And you've been one since you were ten. You don't tell me the truth, Alan.''

''Cate.'' He let his tone ask her to drop the subject. She took the hint. After a while, she leaned forward to look through his window. Her hair fell over her shoulder, soft, silky, its sweep lending her chin a vulnerable curve.

''Why are we going around the town?'' she asked.

''Aunt Imogen and Uncle Ford live on the other side, out by the Leith River.''

''They share a house?''

''No. Your aunt lives in the family home. Your uncle lives in a house he built when he left.''

''On the same property? What was his point in leaving?''

''He wanted his own place and he needed a barn. He still boards a few horses. Most of all, he didn't want to be beholden to your grandfather. He and your grandma never agreed with the way Uncle Ford lived his life.''

Cate plunged her fingers into her hair and shoved it away from her face. ''You wouldn't believe what one of the nurses told me about Uncle Ford. Don't ever mention Las Vegas or carousels to him when he's in a confiding mood. I wouldn't be surprised to learn I spring from vampires and villains.''

The old Cate had used particularly weak humor to hide her discomfort. ''Are you nervous about seeing them again?'' he asked.

''I want to see them, but they all have something to say—usually all at the same time, and everyone watches me as if they're on the lookout for the exact moment my memory comes back. Even I'm starting to expect a lightning strike.''

He braked and pulled onto the shoulder of the road. Cate faced him, her expression raw, and he curved his hands around her shoulders. At first she stiffened, but after a second she relaxed, as if she were relieved to feel human contact. With a sigh, Alan pulled her into his arms.

She smelled of Cate, some sort of spice he'd never been able to name, the soap she'd ordered from a store in town for the past several years, and the shampoo he'd left in their bathroom.

She buried her face in his throat, and he shifted in the seat to make her more comfortable. No doubt she felt his heart pounding against her. His exposed feelings made him restless. He needed her more than she needed him.

''What was wrong between us, Alan?''

''We were both afraid.''

"Of what? Didn't we want to be together?"

"We don't want to be hurt." He lifted her chin so he could look down at her. "I won't ever hurt you on purpose."

She stared into his eyes, surprising him with a hunger that might possibly match his. "We're still keeping secrets."

"If you think so, why aren't you upset?" He pressed his mouth to her forehead, a chaste kiss when his body ached from being against her soft curves. "Maybe you can learn to believe me."

"I'm trying, but you're going to have to tell me what you're hiding before I get frustrated." She twisted, until she was facing him, and she looped her arms around his neck.

Where had his Cate gone? And why had this temptress stepped into his life? She was willing to trust him until he could tell her the truth. God, what freedom that gave him.

She wriggled. "The steering wheel," she muttered.

Swallowing a groan at the pleasure of her firm breasts against his chest, he slid his hands between the steering wheel and her back, both to cushion her and to position her body away from his arousal.

"Can we stay like this for a few minutes?" She pressed a kiss to the bottom of his chin and he gritted his teeth.

ALAN'S HEART thudded against her cheek. She'd turned to him for comfort, but comfort held no attraction. Simply being in his arms, she learned each sinew that met hers, from neck to waist.

She lost track of his pulse, because she had to concentrate on holding her own respirations at a normal rate. She was drowning, swimming against a tide of overwhelming power. Her arms and legs grew heavy, languorous with delicious need.

His desire for her spoke more loudly than his silences. She had to take so much of her life on faith. Why not believe Alan would tell her what he was hiding when he learned he could trust her again?

She pulled away from him only because her family would worry if they stayed much longer on the side of this lovely road.

Alan opened his eyes, startled. His pupils were almost as large as his deep-green irises. She pressed her palm to his cheek, feeling powerful because he wanted her. ''We should go. The family will send out search parties.''

''All right.''

But he didn't move, and she didn't urge him again. She wanted more of what he'd given her, desire and human connection, a touch she might have taken for granted once. Could any woman take so much for granted?

Alan finally helped her back to her side of the seat, not bothering to hide his regret. ''We'd better move. You know who Aunt Imogen will send?''

She shook her head, mystified.

''Dan,'' Alan said with distaste.

''I'm not sure he'd approve of finding us parked in a nearly compromising situation.''

Alan's laughter came out of his throat in the low purr of a jungle cat. ''Might do him some good. He'd realize we're in this marriage for the long haul.'' He started the engine and immediately ground the gears. She jumped, and he looked at her, amused. ‘‘Sorry about that. My mind is elsewhere.’’

She laughed. ‘‘Don’t apologize to me. It’s your transmission. I’m not sure I’d have the strength to move the stick right now.’’

He stopped the barely moving truck. ‘‘I didn’t imagine you wanted me, too?’’

‘‘Imagine? You surely didn’t have to imagine.’’

‘‘Why didn’t you—’’

‘‘What? Tell you?’’ She scooped her hair off her damp nape and held it in a ponytail to cool her skin. ‘‘How could I have said it more plainly?’’

‘‘You asked for separate bedrooms, so I think you have to say the words when you’re ready for a relationship.’’

She preferred their unspoken communication. Did the strain around his mouth come from hurt feelings because she’d rejected his company in her bed?

‘‘I feel the same as I ever did,’’ he said. ‘‘I want my wife back.’’

His wife. Why did he have to claim her like a piece of furniture? ‘‘When I hear you call me your wife in that tone, I want to run.’’

The last trace of tenderness fled his expression. Remorse swept through Cate. His claims made her claustrophobic, but she might have found a kinder way to tell him.

He pulled back onto the road. His truck ate up the pavement as he pushed it to greater speed.

A concession might be in order. After all, she’d talked about working on their marriage, but she’d insisted on separate rooms. She'd put Alan off at any sign of commitment stronger than talking about it.

She stared out the window at cypress trees that seemed to hold up their skirts to avoid the kudzu vines that crawled from limb to trunk and limb again, making for the sand-rimmed road. She sympathized with those trees, but if her husband wanted her and she wanted to be his wife, she was in no danger if she reached out to him. He proposed caring for each other, not lifetime bondage.

She started innocuously. "Will we get there before dark?"

"In a few minutes. The sun will still be up." His tone was brittle, but then he cleared his throat, answering her effort with his own. "I'll show you the river behind Aunt Imogen's house."

She snatched at his compromise. "Did we spend much time at Aunt Imogen's?"

"Sure. Dan used to play in the attics and Uncle Ford's barn. He and Shelly and I built a tree house in the pines near the river."

"Is it still there?"

"Some of the floorboards, bits of the walls. The kids got too old for it about five years ago."

"I'd like to see the tree house, too."

"We'll ask Aunt Imogen to hold dinner a little longer."

"Thanks. Something will make me remember." She had to remember, because the nuances of her family relationships were killing her.

At a narrow break in the crushed shell, Alan turned onto a wide, sandy path that turned out to be a road. An arch of Spanish-moss-laden oaks embraced across the sandy drive, forming a sieve for the last of the sun's rays.

Cate peered through the squat tree trunks at a long, low white house and a red barn. Both relatively new. "Is that Uncle Ford's place?"

"Yes," Alan said. "And next we'll come to Aunt Imogen's."

Excitement made her lean forward as the road twisted in a last curve to reveal a whitewashed home. Two storys, shutters in dark blue and wide navy double front doors, sheltered in a wide porch.

Several cars sat at strange angles in the graveled driveway, but no one waited outside. Cate was glad. She wanted a few more minutes with Alan. As soon as he stopped the truck, she opened her door and jumped out, ignoring the jolt to her injured leg. She hurried around to take her surprised husband's large hands.

"Show me that river," she said. "Before the others see us."

Smiling startled agreement, he splayed his hand across her back and turned her away from the house. Glad she'd taken this chance, she leaned into the curve of his arm. At the back of a verdant yard, dotted with colorful flower beds and iron sculptures of strange animals, Alan opened the gate in a white picket fence.

Loose leaves and long pine needles scattered in front of their feet as they walked. Cate couldn't have found the path through the dense shrubbery, but Alan's step was sure. The greenery grew thickly right to the edge of the wide, dark-green river.

"How deep is it?" Cate liked the sound of the water lapping at the other bank, thirty feet away.

"This part is about twenty feet, but the current is fast. Don't swim alone."

"Is it clean enough to swim in?"

He nodded. "But it's too fast, Cate."

"Don't worry. I really asked you down here as an excuse." She draped her arm around his waist. "I wanted to talk to you for a minute more. I'm sorry I can't seem to be the woman I was."

He peered down at her, and she felt his heart again, beginning to pulse against her shoulder. "I'll try to stop pushing you."

She bumped her head against his chest. "You'd better keep pushing. I don't want to be content with the status quo until we're back to normal."

He lifted her chin and looked into her eyes. He wasn't the stranger she'd seen at her bedside when she'd awakened from the coma. He'd fathered her children, cared for her, and he was willing to wait for her. He needed her to be his wife again.

"How far can I push?" he asked on a slow, thick note that gave her courage.

Desire rushed at her with the speed of the river's current. But the kind of connection he needed required a leap of faith. Then again, if she could leap for Dan and the twins, she could leap for their father.

She breathed deeply of his musky scent. "I'm not sure...."

He leaned down, his eyes open, uncertain. Suddenly, he focused his demanding gaze on her mouth. She couldn't restrain a nervous smile. Alan's ragged groan seeped between them, and then he brushed her lips with his.

It wasn't enough. She cupped his face between hands that trembled, and he caught her fingers and deepened the kiss.

At the sweet, provocative stroke of his tongue, her legs trembled.

She was falling, but Alan's strength held her.

When he lifted his head, she freed her hands to wrap her arms around his neck. His smile, charged with erotic awareness, brushed her face like another kiss.

"Nice," he said in a thickened voice.

She pressed her face to his chest, luxuriating in the friction of his cotton shirt against her cheek. "You're a master of understatement. A talent I didn't expect."

"We'd better go inside. In a minute or two."

"We could." She ran her hands up the strong muscles of his back, exploring. This man was her husband. She couldn't guess how much she'd loved him, but his kisses implied a mutual knowledge that intrigued her.

"Dad?" Dan's voice betrayed confusion. "Mom?"

Cate turned, but Alan held her, sliding his hands down her arms.

Relief washed Dan's face at finding them together. "Sorry," he said. "Aunt Imogen saw you walk around the house. She thought you might have come down here, and she sent me to ask you to come in so everyone can say hello before we eat."

"Thanks." Alan moved to Cate's side. "She means they'll look for us if we don't go in."

Deeply aware of his long, lean body sheltering hers, Cate stayed within the circle of his arm. Together, they climbed the slight rise to reach their son.

"I brought a friend," Dan said. "Phoebe Garner. Do you remember her, Dad?"

"That girl who lives up the street from us?" Alan asked, and Dan nodded.

Cate eyed her son with interest. What did this girl mean to him? Why would he bring her to the first family function they'd attended together?

"We're all in the kitchen." Dan opened the screen door on a wide back porch.

They stepped into a jungle of tropical flowers. More fecund than sweet, the aroma went straight to Cate's unreliable stomach. She took a step backward, but Alan caught her.

"I know." He held her back as Dan entered the house ahead of them. "This porch garden creeps me out, too. Makes you think of poison."

"I just feel sick. Alan, remember I promised Dan we wouldn't mention the twins."

The crowd within the pale-yellow kitchen surged toward Cate the moment she crossed the threshold. Instinct pushed her back toward the ominous garden for safety. She put her hand behind her, hoping Alan would take it, but maybe he couldn't reach her. She held still, accepting embraces from strangers who clearly loved her.

Only one person steered clear of the throng. A willowy girl with spiked blond hair, who wore a flimsy tank top and skintight jeans. Bemused, Cate took in the barbed wire tattoo around her upper arm and the three studs and two rings that glittered in each ear. Sporting that much hardware, she must start quite a party at airport security points.

''Hello,'' Cate said when everyone else had finished their greetings and gone self-consciously silent. This girl looked like the kind of Talbot everyone had warned her about.

''Mom, this is Phoebe.'' Dan broke free from the milling crowd and took Phoebe's arm just beneath the barbed wire. ''You've met, but Mom won't remember you, Phoebe.''

''Hello, Mrs. Palmer. I was sorry to hear you were hurt.''

She wore another stud on the tip of her tongue. And she wasn't even a reckless Talbot. Cate looked from her son, whose taste ran to golf shirts and khakis to this girl, who seemed his opposite. Curious about their relationship, she tried to read the body language between them.

Dan's gaze conveyed affection, but how much, or how deeply it went, she couldn't say. Recognizing her curiosity was making her rude, Cate finally shook Phoebe's outstretched hand.

''Hi. I'm glad to meet you again.''

''Aunt Imogen, we'll walk Polly for you.'' With a smirk on his face, Dan reached for the straw hat festooned with Carmen Miranda-like fruit and flora that hung beside the door. ''Phoebe, you get to wear this.''

She planted it firmly on top of her blond spikes. ''Cool. Did you make this, Miss Talbot?''

''I did. Would you like one of your own, Phoebe?'' Aunt Imogen's tape was plain today. Kind of disappointing, but her finery couldn't have matched Phoebe's anyway.

''I'd love a hat, but I think I can show you a thing or two about decorating it.''

''Chains are too heavy,'' Aunt Imogen said in a dry tone. ''But I'm willing to learn, girl. I'd like to find out what's behind all your metal. Does it give you courage for your frank talk?'' Aunt Imogen flicked a glance at Cate. ''She pulls no punches, and she's termed us stereotypically suburban.''

Phoebe merely laughed, and Dan turned her toward the porch. ''We'll be back in time to eat, Aunt Imogen.''

''Wait.'' The older woman grabbed an apple out of a wire basket that hung above the counter. She tossed the fruit to Dan. ''Give this to Polly, and don't you two eat it and spoil your dinner.''

''Okay.'' Dan polished the apple on his shirt and opened the door for his friend. ''Don't talk about Phoebe while we're gone.''

''I doubt we'll be able to resist,'' Aunt Imogen said.

Caroline followed them to the door. Cate stared at her sister, distracted as always by the sight of her mirror image.

''Are they dating?'' Caroline asked. ''I'd die if Shelly brought home—''

''I think she's a looker,'' Uncle Ford bellowed.

Like the rest of her family members, Cate took shelter from his loud voice at the farthest edge of the small kitchen.

''Oh, good grief. I'm not that loud. You all and your delicate ears.''

"I like Phoebe." Aunt Imogen ignored her brother. "She's a wise girl, and she must have a strong sense of herself."

"If she's not covered in metal to hide from the rest of the world," Caroline suggested.

"She's probably going to be valedictorian," Shelly interjected. "Dan's lucky she's in his study group."

"She looks experienced," Cate ventured. "But I guess I'm jumping to conclusions because of the tattoo and all those earrings."

"They played together as children, Cate." Alan leaned against the counter, splaying his long legs before him as he reached into the basket for another apple.

"They aren't kids now." Aunt Imogen filched the apple from him. "We're about to eat."

He glowered good-naturedly before he met Cate's gaze. "I'm surprised Dan brought Phoebe tonight, but I've never heard you or him suggest she might be anything more than a friend."

"From what everyone says, I was overprotective."

A communal "Yes" rebounded off the walls. Even Uncle Ford flinched from the volume.

Cate took their teasing in stride. "I must have trusted her. We'd better get to know her before we prove she's right about our suburban attitudes."

They all gaped at her as if she'd sprouted a new head. This time they weren't teasing. She shivered. How to understand a former self that seemed like a figment of her family's collective imagination? Alan came to her, worry imprinting his handsome face.

"Dan's a good kid. You've been a loving mom,

and I'm not surprised you don't judge a person by her looks.''

''Thanks for reassuring me.''

With new familiarity, he pulled her close. His affection propped up her self-confidence. She hoped she hadn't been bad for Dan, but she'd try to show greater belief in his judgment from now on.

The doorbell chimed, and Aunt Imogen turned toward the sound. ''That will be your dad, Alan. He's bringing Meg.''

''Meg?'' Cate echoed as the family moved en masse to greet the latecomers.

''Meg Hawthorne, his fiancée,'' Alan said.

''Oh, yeah. Caroline told me he was getting married.''

Alan took her arm, holding her back when she would have followed the others. ''Will you be all right?''

She tilted her face to look into his eyes. He silently asked her to remember his dignity. She knew him well enough already to comprehend the question.

Girding herself for battle, she squared her shoulders. ''I remember my manners. Bring him on.''

CHAPTER EIGHT

"AUNT IMOGEN, why the plain tape tonight?" Dan's voice cut through the conversation that echoed in the dining room.

Alan waited to see how the older woman would respond. Her tape was an eccentricity, but Aunt Imogen had a few, and she might be sensitive. Seated to his left at the end of the table, she glanced at Cate on her other side before she answered her great-nephew.

"The first few days your mom was in the hospital, she stared at my tape as if I'd lost my mind." She pressed her hand to the back of Cate's head, and her tenderness for his wife swept Alan with the wide, comforting brush of her affection. "I'm not nuts, just vain, and I hate those wrinkles."

Cate allowed her aunt's hand to remain. Still flushed from the bone-shaking kiss they'd shared outside, she fascinated Alan. His awareness of her was so strong he almost believed he could feel her body heat from across the table.

He shifted uneasily in his hard chair. Memories of Cate's arms around his neck, the innocent press of her body, aroused him. He wanted to take her home, make new memories like the one they'd conjured by the river.

"I think your tape's great, Miss Talbot." Phoebe, at Dan's side, curled her index finger into the tip of her thumb, to signify a hearty okay. "I especially admired the Santas last Christmas."

"Hey, that was my favorite, too." Dan shouldered Phoebe. Her smile faded as she looked into his eyes. Startled understanding replaced her warm friendship.

Where was that relationship headed? Dan had been dating a rather timid unpierced brunette at spring break.

His judgmental thought caught Alan short. Like Cate, he'd never prejudged a person based on looks, but Phoebe provoked the protective instincts Cate's family had teased her about. He'd never been Dan's primary caregiver before, but now that he was, he'd do it right, and a young woman who looked as if she investigated alternative lifestyles alarmed Alan. He must have turned into a god-awful prude.

Looking away from Dan, he bumped into Cate's uneasy gaze. She shrugged almost imperceptibly.

Once he'd have considered the worst that could happen. So what if Dan walked on the wild side with an iconoclast? Phoebe might show him life offered more than golf. A couple of piercings—eleven or so, by Alan's count—didn't make her Mata Hari.

All the same, he'd better schedule another talk with Dan. They hadn't covered safety issues in a while. He hated those talks. Discussing such private matters turned them both into mumbling zombies.

"Dan." Alan's own father's voice boomed cross the bounty of fried chicken and fresh peas, corn on the cob and home-baked rolls. "I don't believe I've met your lady friend."

Meg, self-assured, smoothly groomed, and crisp in a linen suit that had thus far withstood the South Georgia humidity, reached across the table to shake Phoebe's hand. "I'd like to introduce myself." Phoebe and Dan had barely made it back into the house before dinner. "I'm Meg Hawthorne, and I like your look."

"My look?" Phoebe withdrew her hand, as if she didn't actually want anyone to like it.

"I do, too." From across the table, Cate stunned Alan. "You don't give in to peer pressure, do you?"

Surprisingly self-conscious in the center of everyone's attention, Phoebe appealed to Dan with a glance.

"I don't let her golf with me." His tone teased her. "All that metal glinting in the sun distracts me. Plus, I can't get her tattoo out of my mind."

"How is your golf going, son?" Richard leaned around Meg. "I always wanted your father to take up extracurricular activities."

Familiar anger tightened Alan's muscles. He pretended not to mind his dad's talk, but he slid his gaze away from Richard Palmer. Being angry with his father got him nowhere.

There was more to the story than he'd told Cate. He'd run their house, pushed himself through school and pretended nothing was wrong. One afternoon, just after he'd graduated from high school, he'd noticed Cate as she'd walked past a construction site where he'd worked for someone else.

She'd become his extracurricular activity. Being with Cate and eventually building their own family.

A mother, a father and a son who'd never had any reason to be ashamed.

Richard cupped his chin, stroking thoughtfully. "But I guess I kept Alan pretty busy at home."

"Busy how?" Phoebe asked.

Alan studied the storm gathering in Cate's eyes. She had loved his father, understood his weaknesses. She'd grown up with her own secrets, the way her parents had left her, rumors of her aunt's affair with a married man, Uncle Ford's renowned talent for chasing half the nursing staff at the hospital, because he'd chauvinistically claimed they understood a man's needs.

In an unspoken collusion, she'd gone along with Alan's tendency to hide the truth. If Richard hadn't fallen in love with confession in his middle years, no one would ever have learned the truth about his paternal failures.

Richard turned to Phoebe, glad of an audience. "My son balanced our checkbook from the time he was ten years old."

"Why?" Phoebe's irreverent expression both charmed and disturbed Alan. She was too young to be so cynical. "Couldn't you manage your own accounts, Mr. Palmer?"

"Do we have to talk about this?" Cate interrupted with deceptive softness.

"I trusted him." Blind to Cate's meaning, his dad tried to defend trusting a ten-year-old with the family finances as a mark of his good judgment. "Alan was so precise I turned that responsibility over to him."

Cate's impatience grew, and Phoebe looked uncomfortable. ''I shouldn't have asked,'' the young girl said.

Cate shook her head. ''No, you didn't do anything wrong. I should pick my times better. I apologize for—''

''Cate, I sense you're upset with me. I know I wasn't the best father, but I love my son. Don't you think the fact I can see myself as I was is penance enough?''

Alan gave Cate credit for trying not to respond. Her skin flushed bright red, and her eyes glittered as if she were holding back tears. ''You're lying to yourself if you think your behavior now makes things up to Alan. You treat his childhood as a joke, but I don't believe turning my husband into an adult at the age of ten was funny.'' She gulped a breath, and her calm voice spooked Alan as she stood up. ''Excuse me. I didn't mean to ruin dinner.''

Alan found himself on his feet at her side. She wasn't going anywhere without him. She'd been too ill to get this upset. Intent on getting her out of the house, he still caught a glimpse of his father's alarmed face.

''It's okay, Dad. You and Cate will settle this, but right now, we need air.''

With nothing except her eyes, Cate told him she didn't want company. He didn't care. He had to prove, if only to himself, that she could depend on him.

She was annoyed with his father for a few bad decisions. She'd lose her mind if she found out about the company from someone else. And he'd lose Cate.

She pulled away from him and marched through

the kitchen, to the porch. Alan followed on feet that felt like the cement blocks he'd soon not be able to afford.

Beside the screen door, he switched on the soft lights that illuminated the yard. The wooden porch steps creaked beneath Alan's feet as Cate broke away from him again, and he hurried after her.

Spanish moss dangled cool, spindly fingers through her hair. She slapped it away as she headed toward the river. Anger had conquered her limp. She turned on him.

''I don't understand why they put up with your father. How many people in this town know how he treated you?''

''It's all in the past.''

''He slaps you in the face with the past.'' She threw her hands in the air. ''Why do you put up with it, Alan?''

Her harsh question made him flinch, as if she thought him less a man because he wanted a relationship with his father. ''I love him. I'm willing to take what he can offer. That's all.''

She calmed immediately. ''I'm sorry. I didn't realize.''

''My mother took a lot of him with her. Or maybe when she left I saw him the way he really is, but he did stay, and he keeps trying to be a better father to me.''

''I still don't know how you stand it. If I believed I couldn't trust someone I loved to see to my best interests...'' She licked her lips. God, her lips had felt full and firm and pliant beneath his just an hour ago.

Had he kissed her for the last time? The marriage-breaking secret he'd kept squeezed his chest. She'd believe he'd hidden the truth for selfish reasons. And maybe he had in the beginning.

Alan shook his head. A cool night breeze off the river lifted his hair and cooled his heated skin. All of his childhood, he'd pretended life was normal. Cate alone had learned parts of the truth, but even to her, he hadn't confided the depth of loneliness that made him want to give her everything she needed. What if she still couldn't understand?

"I have to tell you something, and you're not going to like it."

"What?" Cate wrapped tight fingers around his arm, and he wondered what the hell she heard in his tone.

"A secret I have to tell you." He wanted to believe in his own courage, but fear of losing Cate forced him to say the words that might end his marriage. "When you walked in front of that car, you were leaving me because our business is in trouble, and I hadn't told you." She'd claim she was leaving because he'd lied to her, but he knew the truth. She'd been afraid of living without the good things his hard work brought them.

He didn't blame her. Women feared doing without.

She formed an O with her mouth. Only when she inhaled, did he realize he'd stopped breathing.

"I don't believe you," she said.

"I didn't want you to worry, but you'd made a special dinner, and I was late—" He broke off as he grasped what that special dinner must have meant. ''You were going to tell me you were pregnant.''

''Was I?'' She looked relieved. ''Are you sure?''

''I'd bet,'' he said, ''but you walked in when I was talking to John Mabry, the police chief, and you must have heard us. I'm losing everything I worked for, everything that was important to us.''

''What are you talking about?'' she demanded, sounding riled again. ''Why would I leave you when you needed me most? You're not making sense.''

When he needed her? She thought he couldn't handle his own problems? He fought a surge of resentment.

''How bad is the business?'' she asked. ''I'd never abandon you.''

''I don't need your help at work.''

Cate widened her eyes and he tried to backtrack. ''The business is what I do.''

''You do the business, and I run your house? I take care of your son?'' She molded her hands around her belly. ''I carry the babies?''

Cate never used sarcasm, and she never got this upset this fast. ''Have you remembered something, Cate?''

''No, but I'd give a lot to remember, so I don't have to depend on you to mete out the truth.''

A body shot. ''If you know yourself, why do you think you waited to tell me about the twins?''

She dropped her hands. ''You want the truth? From what you said about your handling the company, I suspect I thought you'd like me barefoot and pregnant. You want to be the guy on the big white horse who saves the day, and you think I'd get in your way.''

''You're wrong.'' But he couldn't admit his deepest fear, that she'd think he wasn't man enough to support her. He saw no reason to let her in on his craven cowardice now.

''I'm wrong?'' Her tone openly criticized. ''Then you tell me the truth.''

His own temper finally showed up. ''We agreed from the time Dan was born that you'd be home for him, and I'd take care of the company, but every time something goes wrong, and I do what I'm supposed to do—I protect you—you act as if I've been unfaithful.''

''Every time?'' She raked back her hair, unmistakable challenge in the familiar gesture. Known ground between them shifted.

''Let's stop now. You're still not well.'' He reached for her, but she pulled away. In the back of his mind, he'd dreaded this moment for as long as he'd known he loved her.

''I depended on you to tell me about my life, but now I think I made a mistake trusting you.''

''See it from my point of view. You're pregnant. You've forgotten me. I even wonder if I'm the reason you forgot everything. Was I supposed to tell you things that could make you worse? I just wanted a chance to make our marriage right again, to take care of my family.''

''Our company employs my sister. Think of Dan. Think of everyone who deserves a warning if the company is going to fail.''

''I agree with you, but I have to go along with the

other company heads involved, and they don't want to worry their employees or our creditors more than we have to. The police believe we're going to find Jim.''

''Who's Jim? What's happened?''

''He's our CPA, and he embezzled company funds.'' How many more times would he have to admit he'd let that scum dupe him?

''So I shouldn't worry my pretty little head? You let me babble on about starting a new marriage, and you hid the truth from me?''

''How could I drop everything on you in that hospital room?''

''I thought you might have—'' She cut herself off, her hesitation dripping discomfort. ''I thought you might have loved me, no matter what secrets we were both keeping. I don't know who I was before, but I refuse to live with a man who lies to me. Even now, you don't see me as your equal partner. Look at the way you've talked about our responsibilities—yours at work and mine at home.''

''I'm trying to protect our investments.'' He inhaled deeply. ''I believed you were too ill to know.'' And, frankly, he didn't want a marriage that felt like an extension of his business.

''Fine.'' She circled him, her hands wrapped around her belly. ''When you're ready to plan a joint solution you'll find me here.'' She turned back for one scathing moment. ''I can't believe people think the Talbots screw up their lives.''

''Meaning I have? Because we don't run our home like a business merger? When we got married we promised we wouldn't repeat history. We both made keeping our family intact our first priority.''

''You changed your mind.'' She walked away.

Fear and rage froze him. He was ten years old again, and his mother was walking out, just as graceful, just as determined, just as indifferent to pain that shredded him into small pieces.

Sheer will held his voice steady. ''I'm asking you not to do this.''

''If I can't trust you, I can't stay with you. Please don't come inside. I'll explain to Dan that you've gone home, and I want to stay with Aunt Imogen and catch up.''

''What if I don't come back?'' No woman was going to control him. If he gave up one more piece of himself, who would he be?

''Don't threaten me, Alan. You made a choice I don't respect, and now I have to trust Aunt Imogen and Caroline to tell me the truth.''

As the screen door swished shut at her back, he clenched his teeth on a groan of pain that struck from his scalp to his toes.

ON THE PORCH, in the dark shelter of Aunt Imogen's crazy garden, Cate breathed deep and willed her heartbeat to slow.

Had she just thrown her marriage away? She couldn't shake the last harsh image of Alan's stricken expression.

When she'd finally entered the kitchen, Caroline and Aunt Imogen met her with a cup of chamomile tea and a healthy helping of concern. Shelly pulled out a chair at the table.

"Where's Dan?" Cate asked.

"He took Phoebe to The Zombie Zone to listen to music," Shelly said.

"Is that a bar?" Cate shot each woman an anxious look. How tolerant were these Talbots?

"They don't serve alcohol," Caroline said. "Bands have come from all over the state to do a few nights at the zone since we were kids."

"And Richard and Meg?"

"I'm afraid we may have chased him out of the house," Aunt Imogen admitted. "I don't believe I ever saw him through your eyes before, and he appeared to dislike us looking at him tonight. Ford took him and Meg up to his house with their dinner. He asked me to tell you he was sorry."

Guilt and relief mixed in Caroline's thoughts. "I'm the one who should apologize. And Alan and I planned to talk to Dan about his graduation party when we got home tonight." A wave of nausea flip-flopped her belly. "Do we usually end an evening this way?"

"Not you, Aunt Cate," Shelly said. "Mom and I have. Remember that time I rode Polly and then didn't put her back in the barn?"

"Polly isn't a riding horse," Aunt Imogen explained.

"She was that day," Shelly said brightly. "But then she strolled through the porch door while we were eating dinner, and we had to chase her all the way to Uncle Ford's barn."

"I think the screaming made her bolt for familiar ground," Aunt Imogen said.

"And once we persuaded Polly the screen door

hadn't killed her, Mom dragged me home for a serious chat. I still say two weeks was too long to ground me for that, Mom.''

Caroline didn't say anything. She just came around the table and put her arm around Cate.

Their kindness made her self-conscious. ''I'm sorry I lost my temper.''

''No need,'' Aunt Imogen replied.

''Don't apologize,'' Caroline added.

''I'm not even sure what happened.'' Shelly balanced her hip on the chair.

''Alan and I talked about things we should have discussed weeks ago.'' Cate met her aunt's gaze. ''If you don't mind, I'd like to stay here a few days.''

''What about Alan?'' Aunt Imogen asked as all three women eyed Cate sharply.

''I need some time to myself.''

''I'd love having you. You need spoiling.'' Aunt Imogen looked doubtful, but didn't push.

''I am spoiled. I've been waiting to find out about my life, but I can't sit back any more.'' She wiped her arm across her eyes, relieved that her aunt and Caroline and Shelly were willing to be patient with her need for privacy.

Shelly looked at her watch, the canvas band barely held together by thick black thread she'd obviously used to mend it. She pushed away from the chair. ''Maybe I'll go look for him and make sure. What do you think, Mom?''

''I think it's a school night, and you need to be home at a decent hour. Do you have homework?''

''I had to translate a page of Voltaire, which I could have done in my sleep. I finished it in study hall.'' Shelly flounced toward the door. ''I'll be home by ten. And maybe I should warn you Dan's made plans for graduation. We're going to a couple of the same parties.'' She grinned over her shoulder. ''But feel free to figure out what presents you're going to give us.''

Her sneakers squeaked on the hardwood floors. Cate stared from Aunt Imogen to Caroline. ''Why does Dan always seem on the edge of losing his temper, but she looks like she's about to laugh from absolute joy?''

''I think I'm lucky,'' Caroline said.

''Maybe I should hope the next two are girls,'' Cate said before she remembered the ''next two'' were supposed to be a secret.

''What two?'' Aunt Imogen asked, frowning so hard Cate half expected her tape to eject from her forehead.

''I'm pregnant. I wasn't supposed to say anything because Dan's ashamed, but I think I'm going to be sick anyway, and you'd probably guess.''

''Or rush you to the hospital.'' Caroline hugged her tighter. ''My guess would have been concussion, not a baby. You said you're having two?''

''Twins.''

''I knew one of us would.'' Caroline let Cate go and clapped her hands together. ''This explains the green tone of your skin lately.''

Studying her sister, Cate saw where Shelly got her joy. Maybe in the next few days she'd find out why Caroline tried to hide hers.

''I hate to burst your bubble with reality, girls, but

now I have to know why you're here instead of with Alan, Cate?''

''We finally told each other the truth about some important problems we have, and I don't know if I can stay with him.'' She was too tired to paint a pretty picture, especially for her sister and her aunt.

''You don't have to be afraid,'' Caroline said. ''We're on your side.''

''Slow down.'' Aunt Imogen flattened her hand against Cate's nape. ''I can't agree with taking sides. Cate and Alan will work out their problems with each other. I love you two, but we Talbots historically run away from ugly situations, and I already helped you leave your marriage, Caroline.''

''As I recall, Ryan left me.''

''But I let you run to me, and I never suggested you fight to stay together. How many times do we have to throw love away before we learn to fight for it?''

Her unabashed passion about love startled Cate. She turned to Caroline, who quirked a smile Cate couldn't help returning. Her bond with her sister flirted at the edge of her consciousness. She felt Caroline turn toward Aunt Imogen at the same time she did.

''Laugh at me all you want if laughing makes you look like you belong together again.''

Caroline stood up and took cups from a cabinet above the sink. ''Start the coffee, Aunt Imogen, and we'll explain to Cate that my situation was different. Ryan Manning's plans didn't include marriage. And then you can tell us both if you chose to be alone because you loved someone else's husband.''

Cate stared at an echo of pain in the older woman's eyes. Aunt Imogen seemed to read Cate's mind.

"Don't worry. I've always been just as blunt with you. I should have explained the whole story a long time ago. Gossipy people in this town will tell you that Whitney Randolph and I had an affair. I don't care what they say. We didn't. When we recognized our feelings for each other, he asked for a transfer. He was a pilot out at the Naval base."

"I've been meaning to ask someone about that. I kept hearing the planes when I was in the hospital. Did you ever see him again?"

"Never." Her sadness made Cate's heart ache. "We agreed we couldn't even keep up with each other through my friendship with his wife. We both loved her too much."

"He might have been the one," Caroline said, but then snapped her mouth shut.

Cate eyed her in surprise. "Do you believe that we might have a 'one,' Caroline?"

"Not since Ryan, not for me anyway. Ryan simply didn't want to be a husband." Caroline glanced at the door through which her daughter had exited. "Or a father."

Cate shot a look at their aunt. "I hate to talk jargon, and I know our father was your brother, but don't you think Caroline and I would have made wiser choices if our parents had wanted us? I think that's what makes me so mad at Richard. I don't even remember my mother and father, but I feel abandoned because I know they chose the Navy over us. I think parents should live with their children and take care of them.''

''Cate, you have to make your peace with Mom and Dad again.'' Caroline came away from the counter to hover around the table. ''I'm sorry you have to start over, but you're a good parent and your marriage has lasted no matter what was wrong with it. You've made your choices, not Mom's and Dad's.''

''And don't measure Alan by his father or my brother. Alan wants it all,'' Aunt Imogen said. ''I haven't watched over you both all these years without seeing how much he loves you.''

Cate held her tongue. With a few words she could disabuse her aunt and her sister of their mistaken assumptions about Alan. She'd forgotten him, but he knew her enough to be sure she wouldn't be able to endure his patriarchal attitude. The damning words refused to come.

Cate bit her lip. Apart from his lie to her, Caroline had a right to know her livelihood was in danger. She'd have to convince Alan to tell her.

Her continued loyalty to Alan bewildered her. She turned toward the night beyond the kitchen windows, and her feelings remained ambiguous. She'd sent her husband home in the middle of a quarrel. She remembered the day Caroline had told her their parents died after an argument.

Why couldn't he have been honest? ''Why has he kept so many secrets from me?''

''About his father? Don't you think you might be overreacting?'' Aunt Imogen asked softly. ''Was he supposed to deliver a soliloquy on the past the moment he realized you couldn't remember? I imagine he's had other matters on his mind.''

Cate let them think Richard was her beef with Alan. ''I need to understand him.'' She smoothed her hand over her stomach, still terribly aware she'd kept an important secret of her own. Alan had learned early to depend only on himself. He'd had no choice with Richard. No one to talk to, even when he was afraid.

Aunt Imogen pulled her close. ''You've already learned something. You miss him. His answers to your questions are important to you.''

Cate agreed. ''But I resent him like crazy.''

''I'm relieved you're not really sick.'' Caroline seemed to consider the subject of Alan closed. She went to the counter and started the coffee herself. ''I knew you were hiding something from us all these months.''

''Before the accident? Why didn't you ask?''

''I told you in the hospital, some questions are off-limits between you and me because you're the big sister.''

''Being deathly ill is one of those bits of information I'd consider too personal to share?'' The incredulous question burst out of Cate. She couldn't have held it in if she'd covered her mouth with both hands. ''We're part of the oddest family, and I think we make trouble for ourselves.''

''Well…'' Aunt Imogen's astonished expression inferred it was about time Cate figured that out. ''We may be unusual, but we're lovable. Give us a chance, and you'll see.''

CHAPTER NINE

A WEEK LATER, Cate had caught up with Aunt Imogen's gardening, including a judicious trim of the people-eating plants on the porch that looked even more menacing now that she'd pruned them back. Even Aunt Imogen thought they waved their tidy little branches in search of revenge when she walked by.

Cate moved on to painting the porch, but she felt those plants behind her while she worked. When she finished, she picked up her paintbrush and the small can of paint and searched for imperfections in the walls. Finally satisfied, she entered the house, where Aunt Imogen handed her a glass of lemonade.

"You finished already? Can you change the oil in my car now, Cate?"

Cate avoided the extremely inviting lemonade and took the brush and paint to the sink. "I can try, I guess."

"Those paint fumes have gone to your head. You don't recognize sarcasm?"

"The fumes have gone somewhere." Cate grabbed her stomach and ran for the bathroom. Afterward, she hung over the sink, splashing cold water on her face. By the time she returned, Aunt Imogen had cleaned the brush and put the leftover paint away.

"All better?" she asked. "Are you hungry?"

"No," Cate groaned. "How can you ask?"

"Well, you don't have the flu or anything. I figured you might be hungry if you aren't really sick. I've never been pregnant."

Cate hugged her aunt. "You should have been. You're a loving mother to me."

"You've always said that." Her aunt beamed. "I think you're going to remember something soon. When did you last call Dan?"

"This morning." She glanced at the white clock on the wall above the stove. "I promised myself I'd call him when I finished painting."

"I'll give you some privacy. After you talk to him, have a shower, and I'll let you take me to town for lunch."

"I doubt I'll speak to him. They aren't returning my messages." Not that she'd expected Alan to call her back.

"You can't give up," Aunt Imogen said. "I'm going to choose a hat for our outing."

There was a promise that struck fear into the hearts of strong women. Cate nervously dialed her home phone and got the machine that apparently erased messages as soon as she recorded them. She was sick of hearing her own voice.

Cate hung up the phone and slumped at the kitchen table. Truthfully, she wanted to hear Dan's voice. Or Alan's. Especially Alan's. She missed them. How were they getting on without her? She secretly hoped they were just as miserable as she was.

She sagged forward until her face touched the table. The wooden surface cooled her cheek. She closed her eyes and imagined her loneliness as a dark wave of nothing that seemed to swallow her whole. She'd felt better with Alan and Dan. She was supposed to be with them, flipping pancakes and fighting for her independence.

She loved her aunt, treasured the new memories they'd made together with Uncle Ford and Polly and the houses of her youth, but her life lay in the house Dan and Alan were sharing.

"Cate? Honey, are you sick again? What's wrong?"

"Nothing." She straightened and wrapped her arm around her aunt's waist. "They'll come to Dan's graduation, won't they?"

Aunt Imogen tipped Cate's chin. Her gaze indulged her forlorn niece's. "Dan has to be there."

"But Alan will go, too, won't he?"

"You miss them?"

"I can't trim one more plant, mow one more blade of grass or paint another picket in your fence. I've been pretending I didn't feel as if I've misplaced a major part of myself. Why didn't Alan at least stay to talk when he brought my clothes over?"

"Because you told him you didn't want to live with him right now. A man takes offense as easily as a woman, you know."

"I do know." Cate rose and took the tattered phone book off its shelf. "Even Richard. I owe him an apology, too, and I won't put it off any longer."

"Do you want more privacy?"

"Yes, please. I'm humiliated that I put it off so long."

"You don't have to look up the number. I wrote it on the back page."

Cate turned the book over and opened the back page. Aunt Imogen had scrawled phone numbers at wild angles in every blank space she could find. Cate looked at the book's cover again. "1984?"

"Do you know how long it takes to transfer those numbers every year? I add any new ones in the back."

"Okay." Cate finally found Richard's number and began dialing. She put off the last digit until Aunt Imogen left her alone in the kitchen.

He answered right away, as if he kept the phone in his pocket. "Is she home yet?"

"Richard, it's me, Cate."

"I thought you were Alan. Did you forget his number?"

"I called to apologize." She suddenly recognized what he'd said. "Has he called you to talk about me?"

"Just to tell me he misses you, as if I didn't know. Do you want me to call him?"

"No," she said, too vigorously. "I want to apologize for the way I behaved at dinner."

"Don't waste another thought on that night. I'm sorry I rub you the wrong way, and I miss your friendship."

"Were we friends?"

"I thought so. Now, I wonder if you put up with me for Alan's sake. You and I should talk our problems out."

"I don't think that's a good idea until we're more used to each other," she said. She didn't see how he could explain his past away. "But I want us to get along."

"As do I."

"Next time we see each other, I'll be polite."

"And I won't say a word about my son."

"That might do the trick, Richard, but I won't hold you to your promise."

"I'd like you to promise you'll come to my wedding."

"I promise." She hoped she'd occupy a pew between Alan and Dan.

"And warn me before I annoy you so much you change your mind."

She laughed. "You've been generous about this, Richard."

"I can be, you know." He turned his head from the phone. "Cate," he whispered, reminding her of Uncle Ford's attempts to be furtive. "Meg says to tell you hi."

"Say hello for me. I have to take Aunt Imogen to lunch, but I'm glad you were home."

"Me, too. Bye, Cate-girl."

He hung up while she marveled at the affectionate pet name. She turned to find Aunt Imogen in the kitchen doorway, tying the ribbon of a peony-covered straw hat beneath her chin.

"Skillfully accomplished," Aunt Imogen congratulated her.

"Thanks. Now I'm ready to take Alan on. He might ignore my calls, but he can't duck me at our son's graduation." She squared her shoulders. "Do you mind if we make a stop in town? I noticed Shelly's watch is all beaten up, and I want to buy her a new one as a graduation present."

TEN DAYS AFTER his mother left home, Dan took his place in the line of graduating seniors. Silent, waiting in front of the Leith Community Center, he stood alone in the milling group of over a hundred. He refused to look for his parents in the crowd that streamed past to take seats in the overheated auditorium.

His mother hadn't bothered to see him. Why should he look for her? He'd be leaving in a little over five weeks, just after the Fourth of July. He'd tried to talk to his dad, who'd said the argument wasn't Dan's problem.

Right. It was only because it would have made him seem like a girl that he hadn't asked Aunt Imogen to put him up, too.

Except that would have meant rooming near his mom. He could have turned to Uncle Ford, but the horses lived in cleaner quarters than his uncle.

So he'd stayed at home with his furious father. They'd both ignored the phone. Maybe his dad thought like he did, that his mom would come home if she couldn't get them on the phone.

He'd stumbled through finals. He hardly remembered them. And he wondered why his mom didn't care how she'd screwed up their family. She couldn't remember her past. Fine, but all these years, during one silent battle of wills after another between his parents, he'd convinced himself they'd never split up.

Wrong again.

"Hey, whassup?" Floral perfume accompanied the question, a breath of fresh female that made his knees lock.

He turned. Phoebe sported a new ring today, this one through her eyebrow, gold that shimmered next to the silver ring she'd already worn there.

She followed his gaze and touched the new hoop. "Cool, huh? Graduation gift from my father's sister. He and Mom nearly collapsed over the cheese eggs."

At Phoebe's house, breakfast would never be a meat product and eggs. "I like it," he said. What he wanted to do was pull his "friend" into his arms and lick that scent off her.

"What's wrong with you?" She patted his arm, totally not getting it. "Still upset about your mom? She'll come home. Mine always does."

"But do you ever think your mom won't?"

"I think when my mom and dad decide the sex has slowed down, they pick a fight. My mom walks out, and at the exact moment they'd explode if they had to keep their hands off each other, she strolls back into the house. My sister and I have seen every movie Hollywood ever made because my mom always times her arrival so we can make the matinees."

"My mom never walked before."

"She didn't know the value of a good break." Phoebe linked her arm with his, and her perfume seemed to seep into his skin. "There she is."

"I don't give a damn. Phoebe, is that smell you?"

She pulled away, forgetting his mother. She felt

what he felt. Her eyes grew full of feelings he'd never connected with Phoebe back when they'd hunted turtles or chased crabs down the beach together.

"I told you that night when we left your aunt's, Dan, I won't let you use me to teach your parents a lesson. You know I scared them both silly, so I look pretty good to you."

"My mom liked the way you looked." He laughed at Phoebe's grimace. "You don't want someone her age to like the way you look, do you?"

She glared at him. "I don't like you letting her walk into that auditorium without acknowledging her. She was flagging you down, man."

"Mom has my dad," he said.

"No she doesn't." Phoebe eyed him curiously. "She was alone. You expected them to come together?"

"To my graduation? Yes." Damn right, he did. "I ought to walk out this time."

"Not a chance." She gripped his hand. "If I have to stand this kid stuff, you're standing it with me. You'd better be in your chair when they call your name, Dan Palmer."

"Or what?" What could she do to the Amazing, Invisible Palmer?

"Don't try me."

He'd never been a person who tried. He'd let life push him around. Why change now when it was getting so good? He took a deep breath that almost turned him into a crybaby.

Jeez, he missed his mom.

PERSPIRATION PRICKLED between Cate's shoulder blades. She arched her back as she craned to see over the whispering families around her. She'd come early, hoping for a glimpse of Dan. A glimpse was all she'd had.

Phoebe had seen her. Cate was sure she had, but she either hadn't alerted Dan, or Dan had decided to ignore his windmilling mother. She'd probably embarrassed him.

"Hey, sis. Did you see your boy outside?"

Cate forced a smile as she turned to Caroline, who must have entered the row of seats from the aisle opposite the one Cate had used. "I saw him, but I think he ignored me. How's Shelly?"

"Nervous, and so hot she put on shorts under her gown. I hope she doesn't trip. If Aunt Imogen sees her shorts, I'm a dead woman."

Caroline shook her hair away from her face, and Cate wondered why she reached for a blow-dryer every morning when her hair could look as loose and free as her sister's dark auburn curls.

Caroline slipped into a chair one seat over from Cate. "I don't believe he ignored you. He asked me to tell you hello. Phoebe was with him, and you know, I don't care if she's valedictorian. She scares me. If a guy who looked like that came calling for Shelly, I'd move."

"Because of the way he looks? That seems odd coming from you."

"Why from me?" Caroline settled a small envelope purse, more chic than anything Cate owned, on her lap.

"Look at us. I don't think anyone could tell us apart, but are we the same person?"

"No." Caroline's answer came with alacrity. "You're nicer than I am, but I'm more determined."

Cate studied her sister's slightly angular bone structure. She certainly held her faintly pointed chin at a firm angle. "I'm not that nice. I left Dan when I swore I wouldn't hurt him." She missed Alan, but abandoning Dan had been wrong. He couldn't get used to the idea of his new siblings, and now she'd busted up his life a week before he graduated from high school.

Caroline relaxed against the uncomfortable, slatted wood chair, but Cate felt the strangest sensation—her sister's confusion. After a moment, Caroline straightened again and pulled her hair off her neck, searching fruitlessly for the slightest hint of coolness in the humid auditorium.

"I thought I had us pegged. Was I wrong?" Caroline asked. "Maybe we've worked with equal single-mindedness toward different goals."

"What were yours?"

"Making a living that provided for my daughter. Shelly was only three when Ryan left us. I've been grateful to Alan for the work, and I think we make a good team, but I should have been home more."

Cate endured a slight jab of jealousy. "You and Alan work closely together?"

"I've designed the interiors for every building he's ever put up." Caroline looked proud. "We've made a name for ourselves, because we specialize in designs architects have used since Leith became a playground for the rich and famous in the late nineteenth century.''

''Sounds expensive.''

''We aren't cheap,'' Caroline said, ''but we use the money from new construction to work on projects we really love. The renovations. More and more, people buy cottages like yours. They used to be plentiful along the coast, but these days, their owners mostly have them moved here.'' Caroline laughed. ''The muckety-mucks who turned up their noses at Aunt Imogen after that whole Whitney episode are even angrier now with our family, because we don't boycott new owners who buy the land our high-and-mighty citizens sell. Then, the new people—nouveau riche, according to some of our local snobs—have the nerve to move an old cottage here, or have one built to contemporaneous blueprints. Nouveau riche cheek by jowl with old money. I like the work. I don't care how it comes to us, and I'm grateful to Alan. He's always been there for Shelly and me.''

Cate shifted restlessly. Her sister was so much more sure of her husband than she was. ''Why do you suppose Alan didn't tell me all this?''

''Did you ask him?''

Caroline's blunt response raised Cate's hackles. ''I don't know what to ask.'' And she didn't know which of his answers had been lies.

''Have you been happier without him?''

Cate didn't want to answer. Alan came to mind at times that shook her. When she was sound asleep, she woke with his name on her lips. When she thought of Dan, Alan stood with him in her mind.

She couldn't talk about the grief that swamped her at those moments.

"I've wondered about him."

"He's been a bear at work. No matter what he did, he loves you. You're better off fighting it out than pretending you don't care."

"You sound like Aunt Imogen."

"I shouldn't have taken your side against Alan." Caroline leaned into Cate's shoulder. "But when push comes to shove, you're my first concern."

Cate nodded at a stranger who spoke her name before she turned in her seat, the better to see her twin. "What if he lied to me, and I can't trust him?"

"What if he decides he can't forgive you for leaving him? I know you don't remember him. I know Alan is a grown man, but he hasn't forgotten how his mother left his father, or their agreement to not have a relationship. He's lived by that agreement. What if you remember him, and you decide you want to work on your marriage, but it's too late?"

Her relationship with her husband was too private to discuss with Caroline. "Tell me about his mother. How did they decide not to see each other? Richard implied he didn't let her see Alan."

"Maybe when he was younger, but when Alan was in high school, she came to tell him she didn't want people to know she had a son his age. She told him not to look for her when he was old enough to act without Richard's approval."

Her heart ached for an Alan who faintly resembled their gangly, almost adult son. "I told Richard I was sorry for the way I treated him, but I don't understand why Alan let either one of them get away with what they did to him."

"Do you see Alan begging anyone to love him?"

"No." Except he had begged her not to leave him. He'd let her see his pain, and it had been as real as the ache she felt now for the husband she didn't remember marrying, the father of the babies growing inside her and the son whose life passage they were celebrating separately. "Have you seen him yet, Caroline?"

"No, but when he comes, give him a chance to explain."

"I'll ask him to sit with us."

"He said he had to stop by the office on the way over here."

He must not have told Caroline about their business problems yet, so Cate had an excuse to talk to him.

"Rosalie Danvers, I was talking to you." From the back of the room, Uncle Ford's voice boomed. Cate and Caroline turned in their seats.

"He's always had a thing for Rosalie." Caroline waved at Aunt Imogen, who'd entered behind Uncle Ford.

Adorned with the cap-and-gown-embossed tape today, she wriggled between seats to take the chair between Cate and Caroline. "I thought I'd stand out with my tape, but Ford, running after that Rosalie, makes me look nice and sane. Did you arrive in time to talk with Dan, Cate?"

"He didn't see me."

"I saw him. They look as if they're about to revolt out there, where I must say they're getting a nice ocean breeze. I hope when they complete the refurbishment on this place, they take care of central air.''

''Refurbishment?'' Cate said.

Caroline leaned around Aunt Imogen. ''They gave the contract to one of our rivals. A company from Brunswick, but they've fallen behind. The renovation was supposed to have been complete by today.''

Asking if that company shared Alan's CPA might have put ideas in Caroline's head, but Alan's secret wore on Cate. She changed the subject. ''Why did you wear the tape today, Aunt Imogen?''

''For Dan. He mocks me for it, but I finally realized he was grown-up when I caught him looking at my strip of tape, and then he looked into my eyes with love.''

Cate envied Aunt Imogen a little. ''I think I understand what you mean.'' She turned back. ''I wish I'd talked to him.''

''We'll catch him after the ceremony.''

''If he wants to see me,'' Cate said in a low voice.

Aunt Imogen looped her arm around Cate. ''He wants to see you. Maybe he doesn't know how to tell you. With the twins coming, he may feel displaced. The coincidence of your being pregnant just when he's leaving home might have damaged his self-esteem.''

Cate looked from her sister to her aunt. ''Remember, he doesn't know you know.''

''You'd better tell him we know soon, or we're going to look like dopes. Have you looked in a mirror lately?'' Aunt Imogen stretched to search the crowd as Cate's ego tried to recover from her ambush. ''Where is that Alan?''

"I thought he'd be here by now," Cate said. All around them, the elderly speakers crackled with the initial strains of *Pomp and Circumstance*. "Maybe he's closer to the front."

"No, I looked for him while I was waiting for Ford to talk Rosalie into sitting with him." Aunt Imogen shook her head. "I can't believe he'd be late for this."

"You say that like he's late a lot."

"You'll have to talk to him about his punctuality."

"Or lack of it. He should be here for his son."

"You're not looking for reasons to be angry with him? I know you're wary of living with a stranger you feel has betrayed you, but you've been open with me, Cate. Give him the same chance."

"Shhh, here they come," Caroline said.

Aunt Imogen stood, and Cate followed. Caroline reached around their aunt to squeeze Cate's hand, as if they'd both worked hard for this day. Cate longed for the richness of a past, the events and images Caroline still knew.

She'd stopped on her way to the auditorium to pick up a disposable camera. She pulled it from her purse and searched each graduate's face, hoping she'd recognize Dan beneath his navy-blue cap. These young adults looked more young than adult today.

She saw Shelly, who grinned with her customary joy. Cate took Shelly's picture, and at last she saw her son. His green eyes, as large and deep as his father's, caught hers. After a long, painful second, Dan smiled a faint smile that made Cate's day. She'd begun to care for him, not just because everyone told her he was her child, but because Dan mattered. Stinging tears made her blink, and Dan looked away.

In the nick of time, she remembered the camera and snapped a picture of him walking. His serious, thin face, sober beyond his years, made Cate's decision. She had to ask Alan if she could come home and find out what kind of life they had left.

She didn't want to cause the kinds of problems for Dan or the twins that she and Alan had yet to get over. She'd like Dan to trust the woman he eventually chose to marry, not to poison their relationship with mistrust he'd learned at his parents' knees.

Dan took his place at the front of the velvet-roped seats with the other graduates. As he sat, she caught sight of Richard a few rows behind Dan. They nodded at each other. Cate divided her attention between the speakers, as they opened the ceremony, and the doors, closed now against any slight promise of coolness, as well as the threat of late-arriving guests. As seconds ticked past, she grew so anxious to see Alan burst through the doors at the back that she lost track of the goings on in the front of the auditorium.

Then a voice caught her attention.

"I remember that first day of school, my blue Tiger Woman lunch box, the terrifying home perm my mom put in my hair, and the black nail polish I insisted on."

Phoebe's voice, clear and light and flying on strength that lifted it above the audience's laughter, made Cate glad the young woman was Dan's friend.

"Since then, I've learned about reading and math, chemistry and botany and the stars. I've made new friends, lost old friends and wished I were friends with people who didn't want to be my friend. I've hurt my parents, skinned my knees and learned to drive. Most of all, I've learned how to live, and like my fellow graduates, I'll take these life lessons into the new world that opens up to me today.''

A tear surprised Cate, dripping from her cheek to the top of her hand. Dan probably shared some of Phoebe's memories. Her speech probably evoked memories in every human being in this huge room.

Not in Cate. To her, the past was empty. Why hadn't she stayed to fight for her future with Alan?

She turned away from Aunt Imogen and Caroline, unwilling to expose her loneliness. She'd been angry because Alan had lied to her, because he hadn't defended himself against his father's flip confessions. But she'd also forgotten that a man whose parents had abandoned him emotionally and physically would hurt most if his wife deserted him. She couldn't keep leaving if she meant to stay.

After Phoebe's speech, the principal began to call students to the podium for their diplomas. With each name, Cate forgot her new will to work her marriage out with Alan. How could he risk disappointing Dan?

She tapped her feet to keep from swearing at fate and Alan and her own frustration on her son's behalf. Light slashed across her face. She turned to find its source.

Alan stood just inside the door he was easing shut. Relief hit her in a wave, but Alan's intense expression changed relief to awareness.

She turned and followed his gaze to the back of their son's oblivious head. He loved Dan.

He lifted a video camera and added the whirring of its mechanisms to the low hum of the other parents' cameras. Aiming at Dan, he continued to shoot and then he turned the camera on Shelly.

"Thank God," Aunt Imogen said.

Startled at her vehemence, Cate realized she didn't quite know her aunt as well as she thought. She'd believed in Aunt Imogen's faith in Alan.

"Not that I doubted he'd get here in time to see Dan cross that stage," Aunt Imogen said.

"Does he know how good a friend you are to him?"

Her aunt's mouth curved in an acknowledgement of Cate's teasing. "I suspect he does."

"Shelly Imogen Manning," the principal called.

Aunt Imogen and Caroline linked hands, and Cate covered their hands with hers. As Shelly left the podium, she waved her cap, and they saw flowers hand painted on the mortarboard. Aunt Imogen cried, while Cate and Caroline laughed, and the principal continued calling students in a reproving tone.

"Daniel Ford Palmer," he finally intoned.

Standing, Cate found herself making a woof sound that nearly brought the whole proceedings to a halt. The room rustled as every person in it turned. From closer to the stage, Uncle Ford stood and copied Cate's approving bark. Off to her left, Alan did the same.

Aunt Imogen dried her tears to join Caroline in laughter, and the rest of the room copied them. His face flaming, Dan slouched up the stairs to take his diploma from the principal's hand, but then he turned toward Cate and woofed with her.

She subsided into her seat, tingling with pleasure. This was what being a Talbot felt like. Misbehaving in public. And not caring.

She veered her gaze from Dan to Alan and felt a sense of connection. Disturbingly undefined toward Alan. But Dan—her pride, the sheer happiness that washed through her as she studied the planes of his young face. That had to be a mother's love.

Walking back down the aisle, Dan stopped inches from his father. Alan's face seemed to crumple. His mouth tilted at a painful angle that exposed his lack of control where Dan was concerned.

She needed to believe in Alan's ability to lose control. Everything she'd learned about him told her he'd tried to peg her into a slot that made his life safe. To continue in their troubled marriage, Cate needed to believe he could care for her if she didn't fit the slot.

She lifted her camera to catch him hugging Dan, but then she lowered the camera, unable to look away from them. In her mind, she saw herself walking down the row to meet them. Before she could convince herself not to go, she was on her feet.

Neither saw her. She was two, maybe three steps away, when Alan said, close to Dan's ear, "I'm sorry I'm late again, son."

Dan laughed, but Cate's feet stuck to the floor. "It's okay, Dad. I'm used to waiting for you." He turned slightly to include Cate in the conversation. "And here's Mom, mad at you already, so at least we don't have to worry there might be an argument because you're late."

She noted Dan's sarcasm, but she'd forgotten to

be annoyed with Alan until Dan repeated Aunt Imogen's opinion of his promptness. Dan and the twins deserved a father they could count on. "Should I go back?"

Alan pulled her close. Her shoulder connected with his chest, and she felt him shiver.

"I'm tardy," he said. "I didn't miss the ceremony or commit a crime. Come on, you two. Let's go outside before they have the football team throw us out."

"I'm not sure I should," she admitted. She'd have to explain the amount of grief she planned to give him if he ever showed up late for another family occasion.

"But you want to come with me. I saw."

Dan pushed ahead of them, his ears as red as his face. "Do you have to rattle the family skeletons in front of everyone in this town? Just post the divorce papers on your Web site, Dad."

"Cool it, son."

Alan kept a firm grip on Cate's arm. Determined not to add public brawling to their sins in Dan's eyes, she gave in.

Alan leaned down as Dan shoved the auditorium door open. "I know you're upset with me, but today belongs to him. You can take me apart after he leaves for his party."

"Parties." Mindful of Shelly's announcement that ugly night at Aunt Imogen's, Cate hadn't mentioned Dan's plans in the phone calls he hadn't returned. She relaxed against Alan. "You have a deal."

Their son jerked his cap off and unzipped his

gown, ignoring interested stares from parents who'd sneaked outside to smoke or escape the heat.

"Should you go back for the end of the ceremony?" Cate asked.

"It's too hot. If you can stand each other for a whole hour, I want an ice cream cone." He tossed his cap to his father, who caught it easily. "Who knows?" Dan said. "You may never get to buy me ice cream again."

Nonsense. His school lay hardly more than an hour north on a fast road, according to Aunt Imogen.

"I'll bring all you can eat," Cate said.

A little thing like distance couldn't force her to lose touch with him now. To become his mother again, she'd yank her old life back on like a suit of clothes—even if it no longer fit.

Dan turned back, his expression baleful. "Sounds great, Mom. Don't forget my favorite bib."

CHAPTER TEN

SUNLIGHT GLINTED off his wife's dark-auburn hair. Perched as far away from him as she could manage on the bench they shared, she attacked her peach cone with zest. She'd loved Nonie's Hand Dipped Ice Cream Parlor since her Uncle Ford had staked Nonie the nest egg that put her first, small shop up on the boardwalk.

When Dan came along, their family visits had assisted Nonie with her ambition to move into larger quarters, which Alan had built. He turned to Cate, but whatever inane remark he'd been on the verge of saying about their family history with Nonie's ice cream died on his lips.

With the tip of her tongue, Cate dragged a trail through the melting, frozen treat. As if she sensed his interest, she glanced his way. A drop of peach lingered on the corner of her lip. Alan forced himself to look away.

Maybe he wasn't as bad as she thought, but he certainly had illicit designs on a woman who no longer knew him from Adam. Didn't matter. He hadn't forgotten her.

The ten days he'd lived without his wife had taught him one thing. He had no idea what his wife wanted from him, and he wasn't likely to stumble onto the key to her heart and mind. When she'd told him to leave, he'd thought he might die. He hadn't gone home, because he hadn't wanted Dan to see him in such a defenseless state.

He'd parked about a mile from their house and wandered into the dunes. He'd needed several hours to work himself from the age of ten, deserted, unloved, unwanted, back into manhood, where he had a choice about the amount of grief he took from a woman. Even a woman he loved. And how could he stop loving Cate?

Wandering their empty house, he'd realized Cate was different since the accident. She hummed now. All the time. Melodies that lingered in his head and annoyed him for days at a time.

Until she'd taken her songs away and turned him into a guy who thought with his broken heart. This new Cate made him crazy, where his Cate had tried to make him happy.

"Dad, you're melting." Dan held out his hand. "What is that? Mississippi Mud? I'll take it if you don't want to finish."

Alan bit a chunk of chocolate and nuts and marshmallow. "It's good," he said.

"Are you going to eat it?" Dan stood, digging for change in his pocket. "I think I'll get one, too."

With a bemused look on her face, Cate watched him walk away.

"Hollow leg," Alan said.

"I'm envious. Too many of these." She paused for a lick that sent his thoughts on another erotic wild-goose chase. "And Dr. Davis will fire me as her patient."

"How do you feel?"

Her stomach seemed to have grown in the past week. The mint-green dress that belted at her back draped in clinging folds around her distended belly.

"I'm fine. A little dizzy this week, and my back aches."

Peach ice cream dripped down her wrist. Once he would have eased over and cleaned that for her, but now he passed her a napkin. "Is that normal?"

"For a woman carrying twins?" She lifted her arm to her mouth and caught a small fleck of peach with the tip of her tongue. "I'm fine. I see Dr. Davis next Thursday." She glanced at him, and the lust in his gaze must have taken her aback. "What?"

He couldn't take a breath to answer. His mind filled with the ways he might show her here and now she belonged to him. They'd never been able to resist their strong attraction. He hadn't changed.

"Are you all right, Alan?"

He coughed, and then he pitched the rest of his cone into the garbage can that sat beyond the next table.

"Ice cream go down the wrong pipe?" She scooted over and pounded his back with her non-sticky hand.

"Cut it out." Her complete oblivion tried his patience, and he captured her fingers, so she couldn't return to her corner. Time to get to the point. "Are you coming home?"

As she hesitated ice cream dripped back down her wrist. This time he cleaned her arm himself.

"Phoebe's speech convinced me I was hasty. I

planned to ask you if I could come home, but your present mood scares me a little.''

Her teasing was out of character. ''You are no one I know,'' he said.

''I don't know who I am, either, but I'm trying to figure myself out. Do you want me to come home with you?''

He'd risked everything. He'd told her the truth. Now she wanted him to beg her again. ''You always said I could trust you to stay if I was honest. You left.''

''I don't know about always from before the accident, and I'm sorry I left, but I'm asking you to start over.'' She glanced toward the door, eager to finish her piece before their son returned. ''Before we agree on anything, I need to know you can change, too. I didn't like what Dan said about being used to waiting for you.''

''I was late because I met with Jim's other clients. We argued about hiring a private detective to see if we can get a quicker response than the police are giving us.''

''Did you warn Dan you had a meeting?''

''As a matter of fact, I spoke to Caroline this morning.''

Cate sat back, shocked. ''You told her about Jim?''

''No.'' But he'd have to soon. Far from improving, his business seemed to be going downhill fast. Whispers had started among the businesses that held notes he and his colleagues had to pay. ''I told her I had to stop by the office.''

"What's your priority, Alan? The business or Dan and the babies and me?"

"Without the business, how do I provide for you and the children?" He tasted panic as he realized what kind of changes they'd both have to make if he couldn't save their company.

"I'll help you," she said. "We can salvage our lives, but you have to be willing to share the problem with me."

It wouldn't come to that. "You and our family are my priority, but that means I have to take care of the business."

"Then you can't promise Dan won't have to wait for you any more?"

"What are you talking about?"

"I don't want to be his only parent." A chunk of ice cream slid off the top of her cone. With a tense grimace, she scooped up the mess in a napkin and carried the whole cone to the nearest garbage can. "I have to believe you'll be on time for family events like Dan's graduation."

"I tried. Why are you asking me to make promises I might not be able to keep? I don't want to let you down."

"Trying isn't enough." She sat at the edge of the bench. "I don't remember Dan. I don't share any of the memories Phoebe spoke of—but you didn't hear the valedictorian at your son's graduation."

She had a point that went straight to his heart. "Maybe I should have rescheduled the meeting." Especially since they hadn't managed to agree on a course of action.

"Didn't any of the others have children here today?"

"I get your point, Cate."

She wrapped her arms around her belly. "Am I nagging?"

"No." He slid to her side and dropped his arm around her. "I feel guilty because you're right."

"We have to provide for Dan and the twins, but I don't know why you want to carry all the responsibility."

He rested his chin on top of her head. "You are pregnant, not that I mean pregnancy makes you less able to work, but you don't need extra worry. Anyway, I won't be late next time."

She relaxed, as if she believed him. While he marveled at her trust, her scent climbed his body, awakening every nerve in its path. Broken only by the whispery chat of waves breaking ashore, and the distant hum of cars driving past the boardwalk, several seconds passed between them. More satisfying than any they'd shared since before she'd stormed into his office.

"We should have stayed at the community center to see Shelly," she said.

"We'll go by Aunt Imogen's before we go home."

She nodded, rubbing her face against his chest. Need for her surged through him so fiercely he had to clench his teeth to keep from groaning. He wanted her home. In their house. He wanted her to himself.

He leaned back to peer into her gorgeous, fathomless eyes. "We'll probably see my dad there, too. He tells me you negotiated a truce."

She looked anxious. "I want to understand Richard, but I feel protective of you."

Gratitude made him press his lips to her forehead. Maybe he could get used to this Cate who was so determined to take care of him. He kissed her again. Her skin, firm and warm beneath his mouth, tasted just slightly of salt. From the spray off the water or perspiration? He shouldn't have kept her in the sun this long.

"Where's Dan?" He turned, and his son came through the shop's door as if he'd waited inside for some sign they were ready for company.

Dan took a bite of his already half-eaten cone. "Are you guys ready? I have places to go."

"Yes, you do," Cate said. "Aunt Imogen's house. You can let them wish you well while I pick up my things."

"You're coming home?" A huge grin curved his mouth, but he straightened it out fast. "I guess I can go by Aunt Imogen's. I'll see if Shelly needs a ride tonight."

"Dan, you won't drink and drive?" Cate broke away from Alan to join their son as he headed for the car.

Alan allowed himself a grin that felt at least as big as Dan's had been. His Cate still lurked inside the rabble-rouser who'd possessed his wife's body.

Dan made a show of teenaged forbearance. "We made reservations for dinner, and then we'll probably end up at someone's house listening to music."

She couldn't complain about that. Of course, she couldn't remember how they'd celebrated her graduation. On a blanket in the dunes not far from where they lived now. He still had a soft spot for those dunes she'd refused to revisit.

CATE AWOKE like the dead on Judgment Day. A shrill tone had tossed her from an unusually peaceful sleep. The alarm system. She groped the tangled sheets, but she was alone. Then she remembered. She was glad to be home, but still unready to share her bed.

She scrambled to her feet and hurried to the hall. Her door squeaked a loud protest as she opened it. So much for surprising their intruder.

"It's me, Mom." Downstairs, Dan tapped out the code that reset the alarm.

Cate waited for him to climb the stairs. "Did you enjoy yourself?" she called.

"Yeah. I'm just going to watch a little TV. Night."

She waited. Was he alone? She'd noticed the way he looked at Phoebe. Dan's feelings were definitely strengthening into a more serious emotion than friendship.

What did normal mothers do in this situation? Snooping felt wrong, but what had she and Alan taught Dan about behaving responsibly with a girlfriend?

She should have asked Alan. She glanced at his door. Was he asleep or merely staying out of her conversation with Dan?

Ridiculous. Ask tomorrow. Dan hadn't said he'd brought anyone home. He probably hadn't.

"Night," she finally called.

"Are you still up?" Dan sounded amused. "Don't worry, I'm alone down here."

Busted. "Good night," she said in a crisp voice, but she laughed as she closed her door.

She crossed the room and slid back into bed. Even in the house's more than efficient air-conditioning, her bedclothes felt too heavy. She kicked the sheet down her legs, until it covered only her feet.

Lying in darkness, she recounted the day's events and she let herself hope. She and Alan had shared a quiet dinner in a house that had felt strangely empty without Dan. Ending the evening on a nearly perfect note, Dan had teased her about her uncontrollable maternal response.

Her sense of well-being should have let her sleep, but insomnia crowded her. She turned on her side and flipped on the lamp beside the bed. She saw the room as a place she'd made special for her and Alan.

She pushed her feet over the edge and padded to the bureau. Behind all the other family pictures, holding pride of place, sat a photo of her and Alan on their wedding day. She looked impossibly young, blindly adoring, as she took her husband's face in her hands.

Had she ever been a woman who could believe so completely? How could she allow herself to become that woman if depending on Alan took all her willpower?

The hope that had felt like a lifeline melted away. She searched the room for something familiar to cling to, for courage to make herself part of her family again.

Her gaze came back to the photo. Behind her stood

her sister. Caroline's gaze replicated hers, shining with pure joy, luminous with belief in the future. Caroline didn't look like that any more, either. What had happened to them?

Life, said a voice in her head, and a cool whistle of wind brushed her face. She whipped her head toward the window, but it was closed.

An image splashed in her mind, the chrome grille on a green car, anger that grabbed at her from behind. Despair reached through the fog in her mind. She gasped at a physical blow that made her grope for the lip of the tall dresser. She reached for more, the reason for such overpowering anger.

Why had Alan lied? How had he lied before that horrible day?

But all that remained of the glimpse into her own past was her certain knowledge she had to leave to protect the life she carried in her body. She couldn't force herself to live in a fabric of lies.

Her knees buckled. She caught the handle on one of the bureau drawers and sank to the floor. A groan seeped between her lips. She'd trusted Alan. She remembered accusing him. She remembered telling him she had to leave. She couldn't face raising another child in a vacuum.

She remembered the shock that had stretched the skin across his face, and his disbelief made her angry. His previous deceit remained a mystery to her now, but the truth about herself mortified her. Despite Alan's unforgivable betrayal, in some heartsick corner of her soul, she'd wanted to stay with a husband she couldn't rely on.

Cate cradled the mound of her belly. Her glimpse

of the past had literally cut her legs out from under her, but life continued to grow inside her. A connection, soul deep, never to be broken, twined between her and these two lives dependent on her.

The phone rang. Its abrasive trill screamed across down her skin. She waited through another ring before she climbed on aching muscles to her hands and knees. Finding her feet, she staggered to the nightstand and picked up the portable telephone. A female voice spoke before she brought the receiver close enough to hear the woman's words.

She muttered a sound.

"Cate?"

Caroline's urgency frightened her. Cate glanced at the clock that blinked 4:32.

"Cate, are you there?"

"Is something wrong?"

"I don't know. Are you all right?"

She slumped onto the bed. "Why did you call, Caroline?"

"I shouldn't have at this hour of the morning, but I woke up and I desperately needed to talk to you." Caroline broke off, but her shaken tone bound them.

"I remembered the accident," Cate said. "And arguing with Alan."

"You need me. I'm on my way."

"No." It was too close to the middle of the night. She didn't need that much help. "Have you always known when I was in trouble?"

"We've both always known. A lot of twins know about each other. Were you thinking of me?"

"I looked at you in the photo on my dresser, and I wondered why we've both changed."

"Do you really want me to fill in the blanks in that story?"

"I think I have to know."

"But not tonight. It takes too long to tell. You must have been looking at your wedding picture."

"Why? Because you were already cynical by the time you got married? Wasn't it just a couple of years after my wedding?" If she ever found enough strength to cross her room again, she'd look for a photo from Caroline's ceremony.

"Ryan and I married after Shelly was on the way. From the start, we chose to be together for the wrong reasons. Not like you and Alan."

"Mmm-hmm." She didn't want to talk about her own marriage. "I think I should go, Caroline. I'm exhausted, and I feel a little sick."

"I'll go, but wake Alan up. Is he there with you?"

He might never join her in their bedroom. "He's home."

"Go get him if you don't feel well."

"I'm just tired."

"You've had another shock. I'll hold the line while you ask Alan to come in."

"No, Caroline. Did I let you push me around before?"

"You were usually in charge, but I'm suggesting you wake Alan because you and the twins need him. For once, I want you to listen to me, because this time I know best."

"Good night, Caroline." Best or not, she couldn't face Alan tonight with her memory of those moments at the office so clear and painful in her mind. "Thank you for calling."

Her sister's hesitation made for thick silence. "I love you, Cate."

A roiling burst of emotion exploded in her heart. She believed in the link that had prompted Caroline to call. "I'm learning to love you, too."

"I'll call again in the morning."

Cate pulled the portable phone away from her ear and pressed the off button. Almost immediately, a knock shook her door.

She looked toward the shadowy corner, where the door led to the house's narrow, upstairs hall. Her slump to the carpeted floor must have made an awful thump above Dan's head.

"Who is it?" She'd given Dan enough to worry about. If a champion had come to her rescue, let it be her lying husband.

"Cate." Alan's tone topped Caroline's for urgency. "Did you hurt yourself?" His concern set her teeth on edge.

"Go to bed," she said.

"Can't do that. You and Dan woke me. Did you just fall?"

"I don't want to talk to you."

Naturally, he opened the door. Still in darkness, he stopped on the threshold. "What did you remember?"

She curled her fingers into the rumpled sheet to keep herself from shoving him bodily from her room. "You recognize the signs of a fight?"

"You've been angrier with me than this."

If he'd lied to her consistently, he deserved more than anger. "What about that day in your office?

Have I ever been more upset than I was then? What else have you lied to me about, Alan?''

He came a step closer. ''That's what you remembered? Not the first time we made love or our wedding day? Not the day Dan was born?''

''I only remember believing I had to leave because you don't let me trust you.''

''That night at your aunt's, I told you the truth about the business. That's the only kind of secret I've ever kept from you.'' With both hands, he pushed his fingers through his hair. ''I've kept business secrets over the years, but I never lied to you about any other part of our life.''

''How am I supposed to trust you?''

Coming into the dim lamplight, he pressed the heel of his hand against his right eye. ''The same way I trust you. A hellish amount of faith. You aren't the woman I married. I'm not the man you trusted.''

A chill raced over her skin. She imagined telling Dan she was divorcing his father. She pictured bringing two newborn babies home to a house Alan didn't live in.

She couldn't let herself remember the savage love in Alan's eyes as he'd looked at their son this afternoon.

''Are you ready to give up?'' she asked.

He clenched both fists at his sides. ''I sat by your hospital bed for nearly four full days, and Cate, I prayed you'd come back to me. I don't give up, and you never have, either. I want to find out who you are.''

''What lies am I remembering?''

''Are you asking if I was faithful to you?''

She shook her head, her stomach growing even more restless. "I didn't get that far. All I remember is disbelief that you'd lie again and dread that I'd have to leave you, because I couldn't raise the twins by myself in a marriage I didn't believe in. I don't understand what all that means. Memory is usually a building block, but only one scene in my life flashed through my mind. I don't understand what happened before that day we argued, but I know I planned to leave you." She rubbed her belly, taking strength from her need to protect the twins and Dan.

He read her gesture. "I don't want you to stay for the children. I'm vain enough to believe my wife should live with me because she wants me."

"What else might I remember?"

Tiredly, he crossed the room and sat beside her on the bed. His scent, undeniably Alan, reminded her just how badly he could make her want him, but he kept a careful few inches of distance between them.

"I can't live with any more ultimatums," he said. "I've told you everything. The last thing I want is for you to give up on our marriage, but I can't make you believe me."

Instead, his quiet declaration made her respect him. Her missing memory had felt like a fresh start that let her choose to stay married or leave her family behind. Life wasn't that simple.

"I don't have all the facts, but I can't believe leaving you was an impulsive decision." She heard her own softened voice and resented the way it betrayed her. Something deeper than memory bound her to this man.

"How do you feel about taking the biggest risk of

our lives? I'll believe you can learn to forgive me, want to be my wife again, and you'll believe I can be the husband you need.''

''Can you?'' She broached a sore subject. ''I'd like to take a job and contribute even a minimal salary.''

He swallowed. His throat worked harder, and he swallowed again. ''Why do you need a job?''

Her heart went out to him, but she wasn't selfless enough to let him control her in the interests of his mangled ego. ''I want to be with the people I used to know and learn about the town we live in and bring home wages I earn.''

''Do I have a choice?''

''I don't think so.'' She smoothed her fingertip along the frown line that ran from his nose to the corner of his mouth. ''This is what you mean about my having changed, isn't it? Before the accident, I would have given in?''

''I never realized you gave in.'' He caught her hand and held it to his chest. ''I don't care what happened before or how I felt about who you were then. I want you to stay now.''

''Please don't sound humble.'' She flattened her fingers against his T-shirt. As her palm relearned the hard muscle that warmed her skin, her breathing quickened. ''Can't we compromise?''

With his fingertips, he traced the length of her thumb. The words they spoke bore little resemblance to the conversation he effortlessly initiated with her body.

''Promise me you'll give up the job if it's too

much strain. You were twenty-one when Dan was born. You're thirty-eight and you're carrying twins.''

Cate drew her hand from beneath his, her agreement rueful. ''You're a sweet talker, Alan.''

His green eyes darkened and his mouth thinned with an almost feral intensity. ''I care about you. Meet me halfway.''

She had no choice. She wanted a life with him. ''You have to tell me if I'm going to remember anything else I can't live with.''

''I can't help the way remembering makes you feel.'' The muscles in his throat tautened again. Sliding away, he stood, as if he couldn't stand the intimacy between them. ''Uncle Ford asked me to change the lightbulbs in his barn tomorrow. Do you want to come with me?''

Exhaustion confused her, but it might be best to see him with her family around her. Their unconditional love for Alan reminded her he'd adopted them as his own. He'd found a way to help Caroline raise her child as a single parent. A good man went to such lengths. ''I'll go with you.''

She curled into the sheet she'd abandoned earlier. She was suddenly so tired breathing became an effort.

''Good night, Alan.'' Groping for bedclothes, she missed the warmth of his body close to hers. ''If we're starting our marriage over, I wonder if we should have a second honeymoon.''

He was so quiet she thought he'd left. ''Cate,'' he said at last, ''are you talking in your sleep?''

Surely she was already asleep. She must have dreamed that unromantic response.

CHAPTER ELEVEN

"MORNING, DAD." Dan breezed around the kitchen door as Alan sat down with his fourth cup of coffee and the newspaper. "Did you and Mom settle your argument last night?"

Last night? He hadn't closed his eyes since he'd left Cate asleep in the room they'd once shared. After she'd suggested a honeymoon and apparently blacked out, he'd had to curb his own ignoble need to wrap himself around her and hold her until she woke again.

He'd lied when he'd told her he couldn't live with ultimatums. He couldn't think of anything she could ask him to do that he wouldn't attempt. Had they worked out their problems? He hoped so, once and for all.

"We're together, Dan. Don't worry."

"Could you stop telling me not to worry?"

"Sorry." He hated his terse tone, but without sleep, without faith in himself, he no longer knew what kind of father he'd ever been. "Did you have fun last night?"

"Yes, I had fun. No, I didn't drink. I took part in no drug-induced orgies, and I came home without the aid of the local police force."

He left Dan's verbal gauntlet exactly where the boy had thrown it. "What's your plan for today?"

"Phoebe and I rented a sailboat. We're going over to Saint Simons, and I'll probably come back late tonight."

Alan set the paper on the table. "I don't want you sailing after dark."

"I won't, but we'll probably eat somewhere after we sail back."

"Call me when you turn the boat in." He lifted the paper again. "We'll be at your Aunt Imogen's. Maybe at Uncle Ford's." Cate's uncle usually did his entertaining at his sister's house—using his sister's food as well as her good cooking.

Dan fished a box of dry cereal from the pantry and a bowl from the cabinet. "Are you sure that's a good idea? Every time you go over there, you end up planning a divorce."

"Uncle Ford asked me to help him change some lightbulbs in the barn. Not even your mother and I can argue about how to do that." He sipped his coffee as Dan poured himself a bowl of cereal. "How would you feel if your mom took a job?"

"Why ask me? I'm leaving for school in a few weeks. I feel bad for the twins, though."

"What do you mean?" Cate's voice, from the stairwell behind them, startled Alan.

Alarmed, he kept his gaze trained on Dan. Cate, before her accident, would have disliked his discussing her plan to work with their son.

"I always liked knowing you'd be home when I got here," Dan said. "The other guys liked coming to our house, too. You made us food. You didn't talk down to us, and you got out of the way when I wanted you to. You even tried to keep up with the music we liked.'' He snickered, as if she'd failed a bit there. ''You were kind of fun, and I knew I came first with you.''

Cate came closer. Over her nightshirt, she wore a huge, faded blue sweatshirt that belonged to Alan. He sat up, intrigued at the thought of his clothing next to his wife's skin.

She hauled a chair back from the table and sat, delicately draping his shirt over her knees. ''I wonder if you two are making a big deal out of nothing? You're not used to thinking of me as someone who isn't an extension of you, and the prospect worries you.''

''Nice diagnosis, Mom.'' Dan scooped up a huge spoonful of cereal. ''I disagree. How about you, Dad?''

Her suggestion annoyed him, but she might be right. ''I'll concede your mother needs more room than we're used to giving her.''

Dan shoved the spoon into his mouth. ''Whatever,'' he muttered around the cereal, and then wiped off milk that dribbled out of the corner of his lips.

Alan tried not to laugh, but Cate whipped a paper towel off the roll beneath the cabinet. She glanced at Alan as she passed the sheet to Dan and subsided in her chair.

''Don't we own napkins?''

''Not at this moment.'' Alan tossed the newspaper onto the counter and rose from the table to fetch a cup he then set on the table. ''We'll pick up staples on our way back from Aunt Imogen's. Coffee?''

Cate shook her head. ''Can't.'' Her satisfaction with her pregnancy locked warm fingers around his heart. ''And I'd rather not tempt my stomach to turn on me again.''

Dan stood, his spoon dangling from his mouth. He opened the fridge and took out a carton of juice. The spoon still between his lips, he dropped into his chair and shoved the carton across the table.

Alan stood to catch the juice before it hit Cate, but it stopped inches from her hand. She stared as if the container had burst into a celebratory aria only she could hear.

''I remember that.'' She flashed Dan a happy smile. ''You always throw the juice at me.''

Dan finally removed the spoon from his mouth. ''Not at you—to you. Do you really remember, Mom?''

She leapt from her chair and chased around the table to wrap her arms around him. ''I remember admiring your skill at stopping the carton, as if you'd put the perfect spin on a chip shot. I love you, Dan.''

He patted her hand, the one closest to his, and leaned out of her embrace. ''Love you, too, Mom, but I'm kind of hungry. If you don't mind, I'm trying to eat breakfast.''

Humming yet another tune, Cate backed off. Crossing behind Alan, she slid her palm over the top of his head and tangled her fingers in his hair. He caught her hand and brought her palm to his mouth.

She stopped, still as a breath not taken. Could she possibly understand how much her smallest touch affected him?

With a small, faintly wicked smile that made his

heart beat faster, she slid her arms around his neck. He breathed her in, the jut of her full breasts, the mound of the babies they'd made together. Soon, she'd want him to love her again.

ALAN TURNED INTO the gravel lot in front of Uncle Ford's house, but he frowned toward Aunt Imogen's place.

"What's wrong?" Cate studied the other cars in front of her aunt's house.

"My father." He pointed at a black Corvette. "Aunt Imogen must have decided to test your cease-fire."

"I promised to be polite." Richard didn't seem as important as her relationship with his son.

"I don't care what you do to him." Alan turned off the engine. "I don't want him to upset you."

"I can take care of myself." She lifted his hand to her cheek. "But I like knowing you're behind me."

Lightning flashed in his eyes. He leaned across the seat and kissed the corner of her mouth. "Thanks."

"I mean it." She had to. This might be their last chance.

"I mean it, too," Alan said. "I won't let you down again."

"You aren't the only one who's made mistakes. I'm afraid to commit. I don't want to get hurt, and I don't remember how it feels to be completely happy." She paused, her mind on Dan. "Although this morning, when our son shoved that juice across the table…"

"That was close?"

She loved his teasing tone. Lifting his hand again, she pressed her mouth to his knuckles. Strands of sparse black hair tickled her lips. Alan's gasp rattled her composure as he cupped the back of her head and lifted her face to his.

His mouth was a whisper away when she panicked. "We'd better go in." Pictures of his hard, lean limbs wrapped around hers frightened her as much as they seduced. What if she'd forgotten how to please him? What if he didn't want her the way she looked now?

"Why are you afraid, Cate?"

She reached for the door handle. She'd leapt into this relationship as if she had faith in Alan. She thought she could learn about faith, but surely her more unnerving fears still belonged only to her. "You're misreading me."

"I know your expressions even if I can't figure out ahead of time what you should feel."

"I'd rather discuss this at home."

"No, Cate."

He couched his refusal in a tender voice that undid her. She turned back to him, aware of the rustle of her dress on the car's leather seat, the bump of an insect against the window beside her head.

"I have no memory of making love." She didn't add she was afraid to undress in front of him, afraid she wouldn't make him happy.

He wrapped her in his arms. "I won't mind showing you."

"But twenty years together—I probably knew what you liked."

His voice, low and lecherous, brushed her temple. "Lucky for you, I still know what pleases you."

"I don't want you to be dissatisfied," she said.

His body shook against her. At first, she leaned away from him, afraid he might be laughing at her. She felt no better when she found she'd been correct.

He couldn't seem to stop laughing, and once she'd seen him, he made no effort to keep it quiet.

"I've just confessed one of my deepest fears," she said.

He sobered, sort of. "I'm weak with hunger for you, and you think I'll be dissatisfied? I trembled like a scared virgin when you touched my hair this morning. What say we assume I'll enjoy—the proceedings?"

Nice of him to spare her delicate sensibilities.

Shaking his head in mock despair, he tipped her chin. Passion arced from his gaze, and Cate sank against the seat. So much desire frightened her until she realized he'd let down his guard. He wanted her to see all the way to the truth of his feelings for her.

She closed her eyes and opened to the stroke of his tongue against the seam of her lips. Anxious to return his humbling gift, she leaned into him. His groan, earthy and naked, robbed her of conscious thought.

She swam in their mutual need, but her husband's strength kept her from drowning. He caressed her shoulders, his hands restless. He mouthed her name, and for once, his possessive tone thrilled her as he slid his fingers beneath the sleeves of her dress.

With his mouth a whisper above her skin, he followed the curve of her cheek. She tilted her head to bare her neck to him. Goose bumps ran the length of her body as he suckled the pulse in her throat. Inexorably, he made his way to the rise of her breasts against her scooped neckline.

She pressed closer, her pulse pumping in her ears. He seemed too far away. She needed to be nearer. He held her body, maybe even parts of her soul, in loving hands.

"We should have tried this from the start." Alan lifted a heavy-lidded gaze that almost covered his arrogant thought.

Almost. Not quite. She touched her fingers to his lips. Still warm from hers, they melted her resistance. "Don't say anything to ruin it."

He pulled away, his smile scorching. "Come with me to the barn. I'll reintroduce you to the loft."

A tap on the window behind her head cut off her answer. She turned, and Alan leaned over her to see their intruder.

"Dad," he growled. "Naturally."

"What do you think he saw?"

"Not a thing. The man's oblivious." Alan stretched a few inches more to open her door and push it wide before he moved back to his side of the car. "We'll explore the loft some other time."

Cate prepared herself for another of Richard's inappropriate jokes as she clambered out on shaky legs, but her father-in-law grabbed her hand.

"That cut on your leg still bothering you?" Richard asked as he hauled her to his side, but he didn't wait for her to reply. "When Alan mentioned you were coming to help Ford, I asked Imogen to invite Meg and me for dinner. I've been thinking pretty hard about this, Cate. You and I can't put off our talk. I don't want bad blood to ruin my marriage ceremony.''

Positive her own marriage would be better off if she had her mouth wired shut, Cate managed an acquiescent shrug. ''I'd love to talk with you, Richard. Alan, how long do you think you'll be?''

He popped out of the other side of the car. ''Half an hour maybe.'' Doubt glittered in his eyes. ''Why don't you two wait for me?''

His concern made up Cate's mind. She could talk to the man without starting a world war. She turned to Richard. ''Why don't we walk down by the river?''

''Perfect.'' Richard offered his arm again.

She accepted his chivalrous gesture and rested her hand in the crook of his elbow. ''See you later, Alan.'' She looked back to reassure him. If Richard pushed her too far, she'd simply shove him into the river. ''Take your time, and don't let Uncle Ford climb the ladder.''

Alan glanced at his watch. ''Good Lord, I'd better get in there. If he asks for help and I'm late, he does the work himself to make me feel guilty.''

She pictured her unsteady uncle slamming the ladder around the barn. Richard tugged at her.

''Let Alan take care of Ford. He's experienced in whipping an old man into shape.''

''You always know just the right thing to say, don't you?''

''The right thing to light your fuse.''

''Let's cut to the chase.''

He braced himself, reminding her of Alan. He

pulled aside a low-hanging branch to make way for her on the path toward Aunt Imogen's house. "Hit me."

"Were you as careless with Alan as those horrible stories you tell?"

Their feet disarranged the neatly piled pea gravel. A few small pebbles shot into the grass as they walked. Cate finally stole a glance at Richard's shamefaced expression.

"I was a bad father, maybe even before Heather left. I was so intent on giving her the things she wanted, the right house, the right car, the appropriate school for Alan, that I didn't notice we'd both stopped taking care of our son."

They crossed the cement path in front of Aunt Imogen's wide porch. Cate understood some of what he said. It dovetailed with her confusion over Dan. "But why do you act as if you're proud of the way you treated him?"

"You act as if I should have been prosecuted. I didn't beat him. I stopped leaving him alone once I sobered up."

Cate eyed him with horror. Once he sobered up? Still a few yards from the muttering river, she veered toward its shore. This man deserved a dunking, and she prayed the water was icy.

Richard caught her hand, but she jerked away from him. "Does Alan know how attached you are to him?" he asked. "I don't think he believes you love him."

Love? She wasn't sure, but she cared more than she could talk about with Richard. "I don't understand how you could take his childhood from him. I hardly know Dan, but I couldn't turn him into the kind of adult you made Alan—from the time he was ten years old.''

''You went to the other extreme with Dan. How do you expect him to take care of himself when you've babied him all his life? I didn't want my son to find himself in my shoes. Abandoned. Clueless. I tried to prepare him.''

''Toughen him up, you mean?'' What if he was right about Dan? Maybe there was middle ground to cover.

''Cate, I've tried to be patient with you, but you weren't in our house, and the way I raised my son is none of your business. You Talbots think you own some kind of moral yardstick, but your uncle has slept with every married and unattached woman in this town over the age of forty. And I wouldn't put it past him to start cruising for the younger set. He'd do a lot to prove he doesn't need that cane.''

''Leave my family out of this.''

''And what about your parents? Heroes in charge of our national defense. You know what? They craved an adrenaline rush, just like every Talbot before them, and they abandoned you and your sister just as Heather left Alan and me.''

Cate's injured leg, almost completely healed now, wobbled. She struggled for a memory of her parents. She'd memorized pictures of them from photo albums during her week with Aunt Imogen, but they'd never formed in her mind as living beings.

She turned toward the river to hide tears that stung her eyes. ''Whatever my family's done doesn't excuse the way you talk to Alan or the way you talk about him. Plus, I don't want Dan to hear about it.''

Richard heaved a sigh. Broken in the middle, it almost sounded like a sob. Cate whirled to him. He quickly averted his own reddened gaze. ''How weak-minded do you think I am? I know how bad I look. I'm sorry for what Alan put up with from me, but I can't change the past.''

His dejected shoulders tempted her to put a comforting arm around him, but she held back. She didn't know Richard. He might well try to con her.

''Maybe you could stop rubbing Alan's nose in it.''

''Like I just rubbed yours?'' Richard's hand landed on her shoulder. An awkward pat that matched his tone. ''I shouldn't have mentioned your parents, but I was angry. I don't enjoy having someone point a spotlight at my faults. That's why I talk about the years after Heather left. I know I was wrong, and I'd rather say so before someone else does.''

Cate gave in, as much as she was able. ''In a way, you're right. Your family's history is none of my business until you hurt Alan. You're making it his penance, too, and that affects *my* family.''

Richard buried the heels of his palms in his eyes. Cate stared at him. Give Alan some gray hair, round his shoulders a bit, and coat him with an unfamiliar air of despair, and there he'd be in another twenty years or so.

Not if she could help it. She wanted a healthy father to raise her children. She wanted a healthy husband to live and love with.

"I apologize if I went too far, Richard."

"You didn't. Alan should have given me his side before now."

"He believes he's made his own peace with you."

"You disagree?"

She shrugged. "You aren't yourselves with each other. What kind of peace is that?"

"And who are you now, Cate? Our damsel in shining armor?"

Their talk blunted his sarcastic edge. "I'm hunting down my own identity, but I can't seem to figure out who I am until I get a feel for the people I've loved. I didn't know how I could have loved you."

He squinted at her, as if he were trying to bring her into focus. "Like I say, I think you pulled a few of your punches before."

"Maybe I've changed."

"Poor Alan." This time, he used a chuckle to soften the blow. Then he turned her toward Aunt Imogen's kitchen. "Shall we go inside? Imogen promised me a fish fry. She drove over to Thunderbolt to pick up some flounder off the docks."

"Does she ever cook healthy?"

"You've only eaten in her kitchen on special occasions." Richard patted her shoulder again, but this time the gesture felt more natural. "For instance, today, I met my daughter-in-law for the first time."

"And I began to understand my father-in-law."

"Alan owes us both. Big time."

"So does Meg, but we won't tell them anything," she said anxiously. Now that she understood Richard a bit more, she was slightly ashamed of her overprotective baiting on Alan's behalf.

"Let's show them how much we can stand each other."

"Deal."

Turning, she held out her hand and he took it. After a hearty shake, he hugged her. She stayed in the curve of his arm as long as she could. A few seconds.

DAN SAILED ALONE to Saint Simons Island. Just after his parents left, Phoebe had called to say she still hadn't recovered from "graduation revelry."

He called a couple of the guys, but they'd put together a foursome and an early tee time. He couldn't reach any of them by pager or cell phone, so he took the boat out alone.

On the island, he strolled around the lighthouse, through a cemetery he vaguely remembered. One of Aunt Imogen's favorite authors, Eugenia Price, had helped to make the island famous with her books. Aunt Imogen kept copies of them. This trip had been more fun when he'd come with her and his mom as a kid. One turn up and down the tourist-ridden sidewalks, and he was ready to sail home.

He'd really planned the trip to have a few hours alone with Phoebe. He shouldn't have come without her.

He sailed back to Leith early, turned in the boat and left a message with his Dad's secretary that he was back. At home, he called Phoebe. Her mother said she'd gone out with friends. Should he look for her? He wanted to, but he wasn't used to feeling as if he needed to see her.

He played a couple of video games, watched a

little MTV and checked the time. He could drive over to Aunt Imogen's. They'd have plenty of food for him, but his dad would probably think to bring home leftovers. Nah, he'd go. He was leaving for college in three weeks. He'd like to see his family before he left.

Just as he picked up his keys, a large tan SUV careened into his driveway. Man, another corner of his mom's precious sod, destroyed. Not that she noticed any more. He went to the door as six of his best friends piled out of the vehicle, all carrying brown paper bags.

"Hey, Palmer, whassup?"

"Kevin, what are you all doing here?" Guessing at the contents of their paper bags, he dreaded his parents' response to the party.

"We ran into Shelly and Phoebe playing disc golf. Shelly said her mom was going to a family dinner, but Phoebe said you'd be home alone."

"Are they coming over later?" He stood aside to let his friends troop in.

"No. Phoebe's going out with a friend of that guy Shelly's dating." Kevin pulled a long neck out of his bag. "Want one, angel boy?"

He'd always said no before. Tonight, he didn't feel like "no." Tonight, he was the sappy son of parents who couldn't decide whether to divorce or make *little baby siblings* for him. And he was pissed because a girl who'd once seemed like his sister preferred to be with his cousin's friend.

He reached for the bottle. "I'll take it. Come on in." Raucous laughter rose from the living room. Something made of glass shattered in the kitchen.

Dan cracked the beer open and took a long, bitter swig. He wiped his mouth with the back of his hand to hide the truth. It tasted like crap. So he drank some more.

CHAPTER TWELVE

TWO NIGHTS LATER, Alan parked in the garage and used the remote to shut the door. As soon as he got out of the truck, the scent of beer hit him. Damn. He maneuvered around his truck and Cate's SUV to lift the lid on the garbage bin.

About a dozen dead soldiers nestled in pillows of white plastic bags. Alan's gut knotted. Either Cate had craved beer, or Dan had hosted a party while they were at Aunt Imogen's.

He put his money on Dan. His fear came straight from the memory of seeing his own father disappear in case after case of cheap beer.

Alan dropped the lid and headed toward the kitchen walkway. As he opened the door, acrid smoke covered the taste of malt in his mouth. At the stove, Cate was whaling on an open fire with an ineffectual dish towel.

Alan unhooked the fire extinguisher from the cabinet door beneath the sink. Nudging Cate out of the way, he sprayed the pan flaming on the stove.

"We'd better check the fire alarms," he said as she breathed heavily behind him.

"Why?"

He nodded toward the ceiling to indicate the silence. "Don't you think they should have gone off?

Why don't you stand outside and breathe some fresh air while I open the windows and clean up this mess?''

''You don't mind?'' she asked between coughs.

''Not a bit.'' He glanced at her belly. ''I don't want you in this smoke.''

He opened the window above the sink. Should he tell her about Dan and the beer? He'd rather talk to Dan first, though hiding his son's drinking broke the strictures of his agreement with Cate.

He took a clean towel from a drawer and grabbed the saucepan's handle to toss it into the sink. His distress over Dan's dangerous choice lent him elbow grease as he cleaned the stove. He was still scrubbing as his son strolled in.

''Hey, Dad. Mom said she started a fire.''

Alan straightened. ''I'd like to start one under you. Want to explain the beer bottles in the garage?'' Dan didn't answer. His stiff expression gave nothing away. ''Don't make me wait, son.''

''Some of the guys came over.''

''Which one is old enough to buy beer?''

''I don't know how they bought it.''

''But you drank it?''

''Part of one.''

''Then the others drank your share before they left here. You think not finishing it excuses your breach of our trust?''

''Dad, it was just a beer.''

''I've heard that before, from my own father. It doesn't go down any better from you. It's against the law, Dan, and you clearly aren't old enough to handle alcohol responsibly, or you wouldn't have broken the law to drink 'part of' a beer."

"You're overreacting."

"You think? Because I don't. I should haul you and your friends down to John Mabry's office." He turned back to the stove. "I want to know who bought it."

"I don't know. I'm not lying."

"What if you'd piled into a car? You're driving, and you turn to laugh at some asinine, drunken joke one of your buddies makes. You swerve into a van, and when you wake up in the hospital, a cop's at your bed, because you've killed a two-year old girl, her pregnant mother and her favorite uncle, who happened to have taught your kindergarten class. How do you feel now?"

"Since I drank half a beer? I feel fed up with you for blasting me with this load of—"

"You damned well know who drank the beer, and you're going to write down all their names and their phone numbers. I'm talking to their parents."

"I'll talk to them, Dad. This isn't your business."

Alan stared at him. "Are you kidding me? You broke the law in my house. Now, tell your friends first if you want, so they can warn their parents, but I want the list by tonight."

The screen door opened, and Cate came inside, her gaze curious. "What's up?" she asked. "Why are you shouting, Alan?"

"Dan and his friends threw a little party." He turned to Dan. "I assume it happened while your mom and I were at Aunt Imogen's?"

He nodded miserably, avoiding Cate's gaze. At least she still had the power to shame him.

"You didn't drink?" Disappointment sharpened her voice.

Dan eased toward the other kitchen door, but Cate followed him. He stopped when he realized she wouldn't let him escape.

"I'm sorry." He flashed Alan a defensive glance. "I mean it. I had a bad day, and I was angry. I made a mistake, but it's not like I killed someone. What's the matter with you two?"

"You could have killed someone if you'd gotten in your car. We're your parents, and we're in charge around here." Cate eased toward Alan, building a united front. "If we can't trust you, your life will change."

"He did change his life." Alan said. "No driving, except for golf and school. If you aren't practicing or at school, I expect to see your keys on this counter."

"Wait a minute." Dan looked to his mom for help.

She wavered, prey to a natural need to be her son's rescuer, but Alan wouldn't bend on this.

"It was a mistake." Dan looked cornered.

"One you won't make again," Alan stressed. He'd watched his father wobble into their house too many times to take a chance with Dan.

Cate curved her fingers around Alan's. "I believed you when you said you wouldn't drink. Your father is right."

"One more thing," Alan added. "I have to ask

you to be patient about that golf school we talked about.''

Again, Cate looked as upset as Dan, but if Dan was old enough to drink, he was old enough to hear the truth. ''I'm in financial trouble with the company, and I'd like to put the school off until spring.''

''How many ways can you punish me?'' As if he hadn't heard what Alan had said about the company, Dan stalked into the hall. ''Man!''

Alan shouted after him. ''I want that list, Dan. Tonight.''

The front door slammed moments later. Cate pulled away. ''Did you do that to punish him?''

''We can't afford the school.'' She'd offered her support. He needed it. ''I have to tell Caroline and the other employees about the business. Jim's still on the run with our money. I still can't persuade the others to spend the extra money we'd need to hire a private detective, and I can't pay our bills.''

''*We* can't,'' Cate said. ''Why don't you let me tell Caroline?''

He hesitated, unused to letting her cushion him. ''Thanks,'' he said finally.

She hugged him. ''Are you all right?''

He locked his arms around her, surrounded by debris, a thin layer of smoke and an unshakable conviction his son was in trouble. ''I don't know. We need to keep an eye on Dan.''

''I'm afraid so.''

''I don't think he's done it before, but how can we be sure?''

''We'll know soon enough if it's a habit.'' Her pragmatism startled him. ''I meant are you all right about the business? Why won't the others risk the expense of hiring a detective who might help save their companies?"

"They're afraid even a detective could take months to find Jim. Add that expense to legal fees and we're sunk anyway. But I'm determined to tell our employees. I don't want them to lose anything because of me."

"Would it help if we worked on a letter to tell them what they can expect?"

He closed his eyes, breathing in the scent of her from her hair. She was asking him to become a man who let her help. "After dinner," he said. "We'll see how it goes." He nodded at the blackened saucepan. "What was this supposed to be?"

"Potatoes for potato salad."

"Maybe I won't ask how you burned boiling potatoes."

"Why don't you see if you can catch up with Dan and grill him?"

"On a spit? Good idea."

DURING THE NEXT two weeks, Alan put together a new business plan and Dan began to absent himself from home. Cate made an opportunity for her son to snub her at least once a day, as she tried to get through to him.

On the day of the beer bust, Dan had snatched up Cate's cell phone from the hall table on his way out of the house. He'd called one of his friends and arranged for a ride into town before Alan caught up with him. Since then, he'd treated his parents as if they'd tried to pass him a bad case of plague.

Cate had talked to Dr. Barton about her continuingly elusive memory, but he'd been pleased with the wisps of past that had come back to her. He'd cautioned her about building false memories based on her family's recollection of her life, but she kept thinking she might be able to reach Dan if she knew him better.

She'd asked Caroline to meet her this morning at The Captain's Lady for Saturday brunch, but first, she headed to Aunt Imogen's for a pep talk. Driving down the narrow road toward her aunt's house, she came upon her aunt and Polly in matching flower-strewn headgear, strolling down the packed-shell road. Cate eased up on the gas and pulled over behind Polly, leaving room so as not to spook the mare.

Aunt Imogen turned back with a wave of her sombrero as Cate got out of the car.

"I'll walk with you," Cate said.

"Is it too far for your leg?"

"Exercise reassures me it's all healed, and Dr. Davis told me I should walk." She locked the car and caught up with her aunt, for the first time feeling the weight of her belly as she jogged along the edge of the road.

Dr. Davis had also reassured her about the occasional cramps she'd felt. As long as she couldn't time them, they were nothing to worry about.

"I didn't expect you," Aunt Imogen said. "Something wrong?"

"Sort of. I need some more advice."

"Glad to help you." Aunt Imogen whipped a fan out of her pocket and fanned a fly away from Polly's face. "These vermin are getting thicker every day."

''I guess it goes with summer,'' Cate said. ''Aunt Imogen, why the hats?''

''I told you, this gives people something new to chew on. Besides, I like my hats, and so did the children I used to make them for at the hospital. Before children grew too cool—or groovy—whatever.'' She fanned Polly again. ''I'm hell with a hot glue gun, and neither Polly nor I like sun in our eyes.''

''Hell with a glue gun?''

''Laugh at me. I know you love me enough to overlook my eccentricities.''

''Do you know you're eccentric?''

The older woman nodded, and her silk flower petals waved up and down with the movement. ''I've cultivated the reputation. I'm alone a lot, Cate. I volunteer, but no one needs me outside my scheduled work hours.''

''So you make hats?''

''And a garden with you, and I dress dolls for the church Christmas baskets, and I read to children at the women's shelter, and I cook any time I can lure my family to come eat with me.''

''Is this because you and Whitney decided not to stay in touch with each other?''

''Well, I'm not like Ford, tasting all the flowers in the field. I guess I never found anyone I liked as well as Whitney.''

''Why don't you come to us when you need company?''

''Because you have lives of your own. Your job doesn't include baby-sitting crazy Aunt Imogen.''

As they passed between two trees into sunshine that increased the fly populace, Cate took the fan and waved it in front of her aunt and Polly. "I think Caroline and I owe you."

"I don't want love based on a debt, and I didn't mean to whine. I just don't want wrinkles, I happen to glue an attractive flower arrangement together and I believe in saying what I mean. That, along with the stories of Whitney that refuse to die, makes me unwelcome in some parts of Leith society."

Cate glanced at today's strip of tape. Clear and disappointingly bland. "I won't beat a dead—" She eyed Polly. "I mean I don't want to nag you, but Aunt Imogen, please call me or come when you want company. Did you think I took you for granted?"

"You had your own family." She paused reflectively. "I wonder if you've distanced yourself from Caroline and me because you didn't want us to see your marriage was in trouble. You never were one for sharing the hurtful parts of your life."

"That sounds right." Cate fanned again. "I hope Polly won't take this personally, but I believe she's drawing these flies."

"Shall I fan?"

"No, I don't mind. Can I talk to you about my latest problem?"

"Absolutely."

"Our business is in trouble, and I have to warn Caroline."

Aunt Imogen stopped dead still in the road. "How much trouble?"

"Alan tried to handle it, but they haven't found the CPA who embezzled from us, and we're worried the business may fail."

"Are you going to be all right?"

"Alan has agreed we'll start over together. I don't know what skills I'll bring, but I think we'll salvage a living."

"You have a history degree. If Alan can get enough renovation work, you'll know how to research materials and furniture. He likes those jobs best anyway."

Cate waved her fan with more enthusiasm, proud of her aunt's faith. "I need to suggest Caroline might want to look at another company, but I'm not sure how she'll take it."

Aunt Imogen buried her face in her hands. "I should come with you."

"What are you afraid she'll do?"

"She's a single parent, and Shelly's due to start college in the fall. She needs a job."

"We should have told her first thing."

"I can see you'd want to save her from worrying if she didn't have to, but I'm glad you're telling her now. Let's put Polly into her stall, and I'll change clothes. Do I smell like a horse?"

Cate sniffed tentatively. Smells still triggered nausea that hadn't gone away as her pregnancy continued. "Not as far as I can tell."

Aunt Imogen changed quickly, and Cate drove them both to The Captain's Lady. Caroline rose from a table for two as Cate followed her aunt inside the diner's small entryway. Caroline flagged down the server, who was quaintly clothed in a modified version of a nineteenth century maid's uniform. By the time Cate and Aunt Imogen reached her, she was moving to a table with room for all three of them.

''I'm starving,'' she said. ''I spent the morning at a fabric wholesaler's, pawing through the goods.''

''There's your opening, Cate. Don't put it off.''

Caroline looked alarmed. ''What opening?''

Cate glanced reprovingly at Aunt Imogen. ''I meant to ease into the subject, but I guess she's right. I have to talk to you about the business.'' She cast a look at the busy tables. ''I should have asked you both to my house.''

''Don't bother to go on. So the calls we've had lately from nervous creditors meant more than I thought?''

Cate tried to read her sister's mind. She sounded wary, but not frantic. Cate leaned across the table. ''Jim Cooper embezzled company funds, and he's disappeared. The police haven't found him, and Alan's creating a new business plan. I wanted to tell you before you heard it in public.''

Caroline nodded. ''I won't pretend I'm not terrified.''

Cate sensed a thread of electricity. ''You hide it well.''

Her sister looked around the room. ''Never expose your weakness,'' she said. ''Does the company stand a chance of surviving?''

''I don't know. I don't think Alan knows. He's working with the money and the bills day to day. He's arranged for a placement service to help the employees find work.''

''Can he afford that?''

''He has to. You're all family or friends. How would he sleep nights if he left you high and dry?''

Caroline nodded with an air of distraction. ''I've

considered working for myself. In fact, I've organized sample business plans of my own, but I didn't want to let Alan and you down.''

''Now you feel we've let you down?''

She shook her head vehemently. ''How could you know a man we've trusted for twenty years would steal from you? But I have to look out for Shelly. She starts classes in about ten weeks, and her scholarship only covers part of her tuition.'' Caroline waved her arm at the server again. ''May I have a glass of water?'' she called to the startled woman. Apparently, her customers rarely hailed her from across the room.

''Why not a glass of wine?'' Aunt Imogen suggested.

''I'm not ready to celebrate a new business venture yet.'' Caroline attempted a small grin that trembled on her wide mouth. ''I'll call Alan and tell him my plans.''

Cate covered her sister's hand. ''I'll warn him you're considering a business of your own, but you take your time. Talk to him Monday about what you want.''

''Thanks for telling me before I had to pretend to be calm in front of a room full of spectators.'' The server brought her water and Caroline slugged it back. ''This explains Alan's sudden interest in my budgets. I thought he'd lost faith in me.''

''In himself,'' Cate responded without thinking.

Caroline gazed at her. ''You'll help him with that.'' She clapped her hands to her enviably flat stomach. ''To be honest, I'm sort of excited about doing something completely on my own. Now why don't we put this meal off for another day?''

''Aren't you hungry any more?'' Aunt Imogen asked.

''Not particularly, and I'll bet Alan is a wreck. Cate may want to go home.''

''Alan can take care of himself,'' Cate said. ''And I came out to be with you.''

''I know how he feels about the business. I'm part of his family, and if he's not able to provide for his family, he'll see himself as a failure.''

Cate tilted her head, a touch resentful of her sister's knowledge of Alan. ''How do you know him so well?''

''After more than twenty years? I'm ashamed to admit I've wondered more than once why you married a man who's first concern is your well-being, and I chose a man who abandoned me. We're twins, after all.''

''The Talbot curse,'' Aunt Imogen interjected.

Caroline touched her arm. ''I can't afford to joke about it. I have an eighteen-year-old daughter whose choices I influence. I won't abandon her future to fate.'' She skewered Cate with pain and anger and love and frustration, all concentrated in blue eyes. ''Then I look at my identical twin. Half the time even our own aunt and uncle couldn't tell us apart. In fact, Alan's the only human being who's never mistaken one of us for the other. But why did you choose Alan, when I chose Ryan?''

''Did you want Alan?'' The suggestion weakened Cate, inside and out.

''I've resented your easier path in life, but I've

never been jealous enough to covet your husband.'' Caroline let her go, her mood lightening. ''I didn't mean to scare you, but rivalry comes with the territory. Sometimes I think it's those thirteen minutes and twenty-seven seconds. When can I stop trying to catch up?''

Cate stood, almost oblivious to their fellow diners' disapproving glances. Drawn to her sister as if forces of gravity pulled them together, she embraced Caroline and held on tight.

''I love you,'' she said against her twin's curls. ''I owe you for your comfort since I got hurt. You're a loving, accomplished woman. Why would you need to catch up?''

''I know I don't.'' Caroline's eyes glittered in wet beds of tears. ''But I'm not always sure I'm doing all right on my own. Since your accident, I've felt as if I lost my past, too. I want back what you lost.''

''It'll come.'' Cate straightened. ''To both of us.'' She suddenly noticed everyone staring at them and scurried back to her seat, to her aunt's obvious amusement. ''What's so funny?''

''You were always the decorous one. Hated my wrinkle-reducing efforts. Despaired of my millinery. You tried to persuade us to fit in, and here you are dancing around the diner, making a spectacle of yourself.''

''Could we stop discussing my stodgy do-gooding ways? My halo is now officially bent.'' She liked this less socially conscious version of herself. She turned back to Caroline. ''We're both on the mend if we can talk about rivalry. Should I tell Alan you're looking for jobs of your own?''

"But I'll be available to help if he needs me."

"You're wise to make sure you can provide for Shelly, and I'm glad you aren't angry with us for waiting to tell you."

"I wouldn't have wanted to hear this news for the first time in front of my friends at work." Caroline reached for both Cate and Aunt Imogen's hands. "I'm glad we're together again, and really, this news just forces me to make a decision I've waffled on for a year or more." She looked soberly at Cate. "I was grateful when Alan first gave me the work, and I've made a name for myself with the company, but I'm tired of feeling beholden."

"I don't believe Alan or I thought you owed us anything."

"Sometimes a benefactor's oblivion makes the gift more oppressive," Aunt Imogen suggested.

"Exactly." Caroline turned a surprised gaze on their aunt. "But how did you know what I barely recognize myself?"

"I'm Ford's sister." Aunt Imogen shrugged. "He gets into romantic scrapes. He bides by no rules, and he's crotchety, but he gets away with his poor behavior, because he's sensible in the crunch. People respect his decisions. Do you girls know he's on the hospital administration board? He's on several scholarship selection committees at the University of Georgia and Emory. He's kept our family land together, and his advice has saved me from myself more than once. I love him and resent him for the safety net he's given me."

Caroline nodded sagely. Cate looked from one increasingly beloved face to the other. She didn't always understand these women, but they were her family.

"Do you think there's a chance he's buried anything in mayonnaise jars in the yard?" she asked.

CHAPTER THIRTEEN

TWO WEEKS LATER, Alan knocked on Cate's door as she was dressing for his father's wedding rehearsal and dinner. She pulled her silk tunic maternity blouse over her head and then stepped into the matching navy skirt.

"Come in." Warily, she waited for the expression in his eyes as he looked at her. She'd put off wearing maternity clothes until she'd strained her waistbands to their limits.

Alan opened the door and came inside. When he saw her, his gaze warmed. She laughed. His wanting her made all her choices seem right.

"You like me in this?" Ludicrous shyness provoked her coy question.

"You're carrying my babies." He made no apologies for his masculine pride. "I love the way you look."

"That's a relief."

He crossed the room, his crisp white shirt rustling with each movement of the lean muscles it covered. He'd tucked his shirt into black trousers, but his collar remained open.

"I need a tie."

She met him at the closet door, opening it. "Let me help you choose."

"In a minute."

He swept her into his arms, and Cate met his insistent, seeking mouth. His tongue moved against hers, intimating a longing she felt just as strongly. Except the final commitment terrified her. She broke away.

"What's wrong?" His thick voice reminded her painfully of her own body's needs.

She rubbed her hands over her forearms. "I don't remember how to make love," she admitted again. "Knowing you better, wanting you more every day, I don't want to disappoint you." She lifted her arms to display her pregnant body. "And I don't know if you'll be so enamored of the way I look when I'm naked."

His complete disregard for her worries disarmed her. "How can I convince you I'll be enthusiastic? I could show you."

She skirted his seeking hands and turned to his tie rack. "If you do, we'll miss your father's dinner." She chose a wine silk tie. "What do you think?" It complemented his dark complexion perfectly.

"Fine." He took the tie without looking at it. "But I came to fill you in on the company, too."

She lifted both brows.

"Shep, Brian and Howard finally gave in about hiring a detective when I said we were telling our employees the truth. We're interviewing tomorrow. We don't want to waste any time on a wrong choice from the Yellow Pages."

"How did you find the ones you want to see?"

"It wasn't easy. They mostly laugh when we tell them we want an interview. Shep knows a guy who tracked him down when he was having an affair with—'' He stopped. ''Never mind that. Howard Deavers knows a couple of men he's used when he's had pilfering problems at the hardware store, but they haven't handled a job this important—as far as we're concerned.''

''Your father's getting married tomorrow.'' Alan seemed less at ease with his father since she'd begun her tenuous reconciliation with him. ''You won't miss his wedding?''

He narrowed his gaze. His unexpected hostility hurt.

''What kind of man do you think I am? I won't miss my father's wedding. I especially won't give myself an excuse to skip it just to show him I don't want to be there.''

''I'm sorry. I didn't mean to suggest you would.'' But she had wondered if some deeper reluctance lay behind Alan's flair for missing family occasions.

''I'll be home in time to take you to the wedding.''

He lifted his collar and looped his tie around his neck. Watching him, Cate suffered a powerful and peculiar pang of physical need. She wanted to prove she was on his side. Would making love strengthen their tenuous bonds?

Ironic that she'd married a man who saw his worth in his ability to provide material goods, and now the only thing that held her back from him was her fear that she wouldn't be woman enough to satisfy him. Well, maybe not that unusual. From all accounts, her previous self sounded restrained to a fault.

ALAN WISHED he'd packed his tux in the car before he'd left home for today's interviews. He pointed his truck at the tall spire that rose so high above the other buildings in town sailors had used it to steer for Leith's port on sunny days.

He swerved around the empty schoolyard and skidded into the church's parking lot. Just as the bells began to clang.

He snatched his garment bag from the hook above the passenger door and ran for the vestry. Dan shot out of the church, his forehead knotted.

"You're too late," he whispered. "They're married, and they're signing the register."

Alan dug his heels into the gravel, guilt ripping at him. "How's Dad?"

"Happy." Dan unzipped the garment bag and then glared at the grocery shoppers staring at them from the Shop and Sack across the street. "I guess you can't change out here. You'd better sneak down to the Sunday school rest rooms. Mom's going to take you apart."

"I don't doubt it." After yesterday, she would be positive he'd missed the ceremony to show his father and her just how little he valued their places in his life. "I need to see Dad first."

"Not a chance. If you show up in jeans, Meg will kill me. Her bet was, you'd forgotten your tux." Dan pulled the bag toward the front of the church, and Alan followed, trying not to wrinkle his suit.

"Let me go in first." Dan eased one side of the highly varnished doors open. He waved his father up the steps. "No one's opened the inner doors yet. They must be waiting for Grandpa and Meg. Go on."

Alan slipped inside the Sunday school wing and

bolted for the rest room. He dressed as fast as he could and packed his street clothes in the garment bag. On his way back, he tucked the bag into a closet in one of the classrooms.

Exultant voices reached him before he opened the church door again. The last of the guests had bottlenecked in the entryway. Alan mingled, explaining his absence with his weak-sounding meeting excuse.

He would have left, if he'd looked at his watch in time to see he was going to be late, but John Mabry had attended their meeting, too, giving them dire warnings about throwing away more money to find a guy who'd probably spent or squirreled away all their funds. Alan had found himself arguing the same points all over again.

He wouldn't have insulted his father or Meg on purpose. Who'd taken his place as his father's best man? Dan must not have, or he'd have been with the rest of the wedding party.

Alan finally squeezed through the doors that were propped wide-open to let guests into the churchyard. The photographer had corralled his father and Meg for pictures. At his father's other side, Cate beamed for the camera.

The hectic flush on her radiant cheeks probably came from rage at his absence. He recognized fire in her eyes.

He was tired of defending himself. He was trying with all his might to keep his friends and sprawling family safe.

"Alan, you made it." The sound of an open wound in his father's voice made him even more defensive.

"I'm sorry, Dad. I'll explain." Aware of interested gazes from the wedding guests who'd arrived on time, he paused. "Later."

"Come stand beside my best man." His dad beckoned him, but only Cate and Meg flanked him.

"Who?" Alan asked, avoiding his wife's accusing gaze.

"Cate. I've loved her as if she were my own child. When you were held up, who else should replace you? Cate, let Alan in there beside you. I know you're rattled because you think he let us down, but he'll have a good excuse when we *get him alone.*"

His emphasis on the final phrase drew laughter from the crowd and irritation from his son. Alan put his arm around Cate, his fingers sliding easily over the high-waisted sky-blue dress that draped her full breasts and silked over her growing belly. She was so stiff he was afraid he might break her.

"Smile, Mrs. Palmer." The photographer straightened to prompt her with a grin. "A couple more, and we'll adjourn to the party. What's not to like about that?"

Cate turned her head toward Richard. "Sorry."

"No problem. I'm just as annoyed."

Alan forced himself to stare at the camera, but he was far more interested in the connection he appeared to have strengthened between his father and his wife. Meg smiled his way, as if she realized he was out in the familial cold.

The photographer positioned them for a few more shots and then released them so they could go to their cars. "We'll continue at the club," he said. More of a threat, in Alan's view, than a promise.

Inside the limo assigned to them, Cate refused to look his way, much less speak. She tugged at the collar of her short jacket.

"Are you hot?" he asked. They couldn't possibly finish the conversation they needed to have before they reached the Leith Beach Club.

"On fire." She turned toward him in an effort to exclude the driver. "Where have you been?"

"With Howard, Shep and Brian. John came to the meeting and tried to persuade us not to hire the detective."

"So you had to convince him and the others all over again?"

"Yeah. John hadn't been entirely honest about the status of the investigation. Police departments all over the country are still looking for Jim, but they think he's put the money into bank accounts we'll never be able to touch."

"Why didn't he tell you before?"

"The powers that be." His stomach churned. "The police department and the D.A. are still working up a statement that won't bottom out the local economy."

Cate drooped against the seat. "I'm so glad we told Caroline."

He slumped beside her. "I wish I'd already told the others."

She touched his sleeve. "When are you going to?"

"I've scheduled a meeting for Monday. They'll probably be as upset as we are with the police. We shouldn't have held back so long."

She tugged him onto her shoulder. "You can't

backtrack now. I'm sorry I was so angry, but I still think you shouldn't have met with Mabry and the others on such an important day for Richard.''

Alan shifted so he could pull her head against his chest. Her perfume danced into his senses, stealing his power to string a rational thought out of his confusion. ''What makes you my father's new best friend?''

''He's not my favorite guy, but I'm trying because you and Dan love him.'' She shifted. ''You're probably not open to any more advice today, but you might consider meeting Richard for your own showdown. He won't hold a grudge if you stand up to him.''

''Just when I was planning to crawl on my belly. You forgive me, Cate?''

''I can't get that mad and just forget it.''

''Will it fade over time do you think?''

''Let's see how you dance.''

He pressed a kiss to her fragrant hair, not sure what he was supposed to do with this completely new side of his wife. Guiltily, he realized she excited him now more than ever before. Without effort. ''You don't like to dance.''

Stillness held her as she seemed to contemplate. ''That was when I cared whether I looked like an out-of-control Talbot.''

''You don't care now?'' Should he be surprised? Probably not, after the past few weeks.

''Do you want me to care?''

He kissed her hair again and rubbed his cheek over the strands that had curled in the humid air. ''I don't think so,'' he admitted. ''I kept thinking I wanted our old life back. Not just the company being solvent, but knowing what to expect from you. But I like the way you lose control and then reign it back in when you see the important side of an argument. I like your passion now.'' He glanced at her. ''Does that bother you?'' She'd been restrained in her passion before, saving it for the quiet of their room.

She shrugged. ''I'm all right. I don't think I can go back to being whoever I was before.'' She shrugged, and her knowing smile all but curled his toes. ''Why shouldn't you be happy, too?'' she asked.

''I can't think.''

''You'll come up with something.'' She leaned into him, brushing his upper arm with the heat and firmness of her full breast. ''I have faith in you. Sometimes shaky faith, but faith.''

She'd also become a talker since the coma. ''I literally can't think when you're like this.''

She laughed at him.

He didn't mind. The wife he hardly knew had begun to turn him into a man he didn't recognize.

''We'd better enjoy this reception,'' he said. ''I doubt they throw dances in the poorhouse.''

AFTER THE wedding dinner, Cate suggested Alan take over her best man's duties to deliver the toast. His stiff delivery made her feel guilty for lecturing him about his relationship with his father, but she anticipated a better toast at Richard and Meg's first anniversary party.

Her husband had begun to change. With new honesty in their relationship, he couldn't seem to settle for treating his own father as an acquaintance.

After the toasts, Richard and Meg took to the floor. Watching them dance with their gazes locked, Cate grew impatient for the end of the song. She wanted Alan's arms around her.

As the last strains faded, Cate took Alan's hand, but she slowed as they came to the edge of the floor. "I wish you hadn't told me I didn't dance. I feel self-conscious."

He looked down at her, his gaze totally involved. He took her in his arms, and she relaxed against him. Moving in time to the melody, Cate molded her body to his with more intimacy than she'd ever allowed herself. This moment seemed right to trust, though trust felt supremely risky.

He held her, his touch a seductive whisper of cloth and limb. As Alan tightened his embrace, she slid her hands up his forearms, testing the rough weave of the material that molded his shoulders.

They didn't speak until the song ended, and then Alan only held her close. She stood, safe and tranquil in his arms, certain in her decision to move forward.

"I'd better ask Meg to dance," he said.

She loosened her hold on him. "I'll look for Dan. He seemed to think I was going to move out again when I was upset with you. I'd like to set his mind at rest."

"You must have been angry if you couldn't hide it from him."

She met Alan's gaze squarely. "I was so upset I thought crazy things—like this might be the only way you knew how to tell me you didn't want to be with me any more. Because I'd said I needed you not to miss any more family events.''

''I'm trying, Cate.''

His honesty about the business, his willingness to share work with her, proved how hard he was trying.

''I never meant to lay all the blame for our problems on your shoulders.'' She squeezed his hand. ''Let's talk about this later. You find Meg, and I'll look for Dan.''

He held her when she would have let him go. ''He's a smart guy. He'll figure out we want to be together.''

She smoothed her dress over her stomach. ''I wish I'd stayed instead of hiding behind Aunt Imogen's skirts.''

His edgy smile transformed him into a provocative stranger. ''Go ahead. I'll find you and Dan.''

Looking down from his startling height, he seemed more male than ever and yet more vulnerable. His intensity singled them out from the other wedding guests.

Cate didn't want to leave him, but she needed to speak to Dan. She hugged the edges of the dance floor until Uncle Ford's voice stopped her in her tracks.

''Here's the best man. How about a dance, Cate? I saw you and Alan. Never knew you could trip the light whatever.''

Cate hated to point out his cane and her mission to find her son. ''I'd love to dance with you, Uncle Ford, after I chat with Dan. Have you seen him?''

''Matter of fact, I have.'' The older man prodded the floor with his cane and levered himself out of his chair. He waited to speak until he was close enough to shatter Cate's eardrums. "I saw the bartender turn him and that spiked girl away from the bar."

"He's not old enough to drink."

"A fact the barman apparently reminded him of. I'm sure they're around here somewhere."

Frustrated with his lackadaisical approach, she searched her uncle's gaze. "Why didn't you find me? You should tell me if you see Dan ask for a drink."

"The barman took care of the problem."

She shook her head. "He's not Dan's parent—or uncle. You should have told me."

"I told you as soon as I saw you."

"What if they went somewhere else?"

He pointed to the men and women, and, with any luck, one young couple, flitting around the polished dance floor. "Go out there. Check on them."

"I will." She hugged him. "Sorry I was testy."

"No problem."

She had to remember to lean away from Uncle Ford's booming voice the next time she apologized.

She wove between the dancing couples, feeling responsible for Dan's recent missteps. She didn't know what to do to reassure him.

Each face she saw raised a question in her mind. The happy couples smiled at her, or said hello or looked at her as if a woman alone shouldn't wander a dance floor.

At last, she spied Alan's head, inches above anyone near him. She backed around the couple between them and found Richard had cornered him.

"So I'm trying to tell you I'm sorry, son. I shouldn't have discussed your mother's and my divorce. I shouldn't have forced you to grow up so soon.'' Richard looked fondly at Meg, ice-blond and beautiful in her ivory gown, proudly holding his arm. ''Most of all, I shouldn't have filled you with wisdom about women from one lousy experience that frightened me so much I didn't try again for over thirty years.''

Alan's skin looked ruddy, as if he'd been out in the sun. ''That's it, Dad? You're sorry—it's over. You made a big mistake, but we've recovered at last?''

''I am sorry.'' Richard looked as if he'd expected a friendlier response.

''I've based my whole marriage on what happened with you and my mother. I almost lost my wife because I believed you.''

People stopped dancing around them. Cate wanted no one to pity Alan, and they had a bigger problem.

She moved to his side. ''I need to talk to you.''

Meg edged closer. ''What's happened?''

Too late, Cate realized her mistake if she was trying to keep her family out of the public domain. ''Not a thing.'' She plastered her best smile across her face. Dan wouldn't thank her for turning Richard and Meg's reception into an all points search for him.

Alan tightened his mouth. ''In case I don't catch you again, Meg, I want you to know how happy I am that you're officially part of my family now.''

''I'm sure we'll work things out.'' She kissed his cheek. ''Your father loves you, Alan.''

With a nod, he took Cate's arm. ''Have a good time, Dad. Call us when you get home.''

Cate welcomed his tight grip as he led her out to the club's veranda.

"What's wrong?" he asked.

"I can't find Dan, and Uncle Ford saw him ask for a drink."

"Not a soda?"

"I don't think the bartender would have turned him down for anything other than alcohol."

"You're probably right."

"Let's look in the parking lot. He and Phoebe may have taken something out to his car."

"Good plan. You go around the building, and I'll check the lot by the pro shop."

She didn't bother to answer. Alan's concern confirmed hers. The sound of the rising tide grew louder as she turned behind the building. She looked for Dan's car, but she saw two figures in a small antique-yellow sedan. Phoebe might have driven.

Cate drummed on the car's window before she made sure her son was inside. Her uncle, far older than his startled companion, twisted uncomfortably in the seat.

He rolled down the window. "Cate, did you find Dan?"

His quick conquest appalled her. "What are you doing in that car? You're going to shame the family."

He glanced at the woman who couldn't be many years older than Cate, herself. She tried to shield her face with her hand.

"That's my girl," he said. "But I don't think we've done anything shameful yet." He turned to his friend. "Do you, my dear?

"Nor will we now. Good evening, Cate. I haven't seen Dan, if you're looking for him."

"Thanks." She turned from her fast-working, careless Lothario of an uncle. She'd trust his friend to pry him out of that car.

She hurried around the front of the building. In the lot beside the pro shop, Alan had buttonholed their son outside his car. Alone.

Alan turned his head as Cate neared them. "Phoebe apparently doesn't care for underage drinking any more than we do. She gave him an earful and left after the bartender told him to go away."

"Thanks, Dad."

"You'll hear more when we get home."

Dan broke away and yanked his car door open. "This time I'm not going home. You can find me at Aunt Imogen's. She's a better cook than Mom, and she and Uncle Ford respect me."

"They won't if you keep going the way you are. Go to Aunt Imogen if you want, son, but you'll have to face us eventually." Alan gripped the car door. "And call us when you get there."

"Not a chance."

The extra strain in his voice reached Cate. "What's going on, Alan?"

He answered Dan instead of her. "I'm not eighteen any more, but I'm not naive either. You aren't going to your Aunt Imogen's house."

"I will." Dan's expression reminded Cate of a cornered animal. "After I see my friends."

"I ought to drag you home with us." Alan sounded as if he might.

"Even if you did tonight, what would you do next time? You have to trust me, Dad."

"How can I? You promised you wouldn't drink again."

"And I didn't, but I'm getting pretty sick of everyone treating me like I have more right to a pacifier than a bottle of beer."

"You do, son."

"Thanks again." He slid behind the car's wheel. "I won't drink, but I'm not going to call you when I get to Aunt Imogen's."

He slammed the door and started the car. At least he refrained from spinning out of the gravel lot on two wheels.

Alan planted his hands on his hips. "What is the matter with that kid?"

"I don't remember him. I walked out. We're giving him two new siblings and we've reneged on his golf school."

"If he's old enough to scout for booze, he's old enough to cope with his life." Alan stared over her head at the road Dan had taken. "He leaves for school next Friday."

"I feel as if I've failed him. It's too soon to let him go."

Alan turned her toward the front of the club. "You didn't fail him by yourself. Don't underestimate my contribution." He clenched his hand on her shoulder. "His whole life isn't based on the past few months, and I don't think we've done anything bad enough to drive him to drink or to feel he has to escape his home."

"Try to see through his eyes."

"I can't find empathy for Dan right now." He nodded toward the club. Lights had begun to filter the dancers' shadows through the ballroom windows. "Do you want to go back inside?"

She hesitated. "Actually, I'd love a walk on the beach, but I'm exhausted. Can we go home and burn these shoes?"

He peered at the ice-blue pumps Aunt Imogen and Caroline had somehow browbeaten her into borrowing from her twin's meticulously tidy closet.

"They make your toes look kind of sexy."

"I wish I'd worn galoshes." She almost confided the pain in her swollen feet, but a peek at Alan's strong, handsome profile reminded her no one had ever written sonnets to a pregnant woman's puffy appendages. She cast one longing glance toward the ocean. "Do you mind if we go home?"

"Best place for us, in case our son relents and comes back."

"He's in charge now, isn't he?" A way to change the balance of power escaped her.

"For tonight. We'll wrestle the reins out of his hands. That's what parents do."

She leaned into Alan's body, and he was gentleman enough to ignore the extra weight. To think, less than an hour ago, she'd felt sublimely female, a regular seductress on the prowl for her man.

Now, what she really yearned for was a wheelbarrow, so her man could more comfortably transport her to their car.

CHAPTER FOURTEEN

IN THE MIDDLE of the night, Cate woke alone in her bed. She'd been so exhausted she hardly retained any memory of getting to her room, but as she sat up, she knew beyond doubt, sleep had finished with her for the night.

She scooted out of bed. Faint light from the bay window drew her across the room. She gathered the sides of the filmy curtains in her hands and pressed her head against the window, twisting for a view of the driveway. Had Dan come home? He'd probably park in the garage.

She turned her head, and the glass cooled her forehead. Across the street, the tide seemed calmer than usual in the moon's glow.

The quiet outside threatened to lull her into her own sense of peace, but she had to know about Dan. She'd managed to turn his life upside down. Unlike those waves outside, he couldn't seem to stop churning.

She crossed her room and eased the door open, being careful not to wake Alan or Dan if he'd come home. Starting down the stairs, she came face-to-face with Alan, who stopped so suddenly on the third tread, he almost fell on her.

''I didn't mean to scare you.'' Something about her own voice reminded her of Uncle Ford.

''He's not home.''

''Dan?'' Cate peered over his shoulder, as if their son might materialize because they both wanted him. ''I guess it's too late to call Aunt Imogen?''

''Probably.'' Alan, wearing only khakis, with the waist button undone, climbed the rest of the stairs and maneuvered around her. ''I'll call anyway.''

She tried not to stare at the arrow of dark hair above his slightly parted zipper. ''I don't want to upset her.''

''She won't mind if we wake her up to find out about Dan.''

He was right. ''I'll call,'' she said. ''She'll give me extra leeway, because I'm pregnant.''

Alan grinned. ''I wonder if you've always been devious, but you were hiding it.''

She picked up the telephone and tapped out her aunt's number. ''I'm not devious.'' After three rings, her aunt answered in a sleepy voice. ''It's me, Cate.''

''He's here,'' Aunt Imogen said.

''Dan?''

''Who else? I performed a sniff test at his request. He has touched no alcohol tonight, and you all might want to lay off him. May I go back to bed?''

''Thank you.''

''Night.''

Cate pressed the phone's off button and nodded at Alan. ''She knew I was looking for him.''

''You haven't changed that much. He's there?''

''We have to talk to him.''

''We've both alienated him with talk. He's not in

a receptive frame of mind.'' Alan turned her toward her open door. ''Did I wake you?''

''I don't think so. I was exhausted when we got home. I hardly remember you helping me to bed, but I'm not at all tired now.'' She fingered her nightshirt. Not exactly the garb she'd have chosen for this moment. ''I didn't expect to sleep alone tonight.''

Alan's gaze grew watchful. ''You're absolutely awake now?''

Hardly the reaction she'd hoped for, either. ''I'm not talking in my sleep this time.''

''Maybe I should pinch you.''

''No.'' She scooted around him and returned to the moonlight at her window. Her window and Alan's after tonight. ''Come over here.''

''Okay.'' He'd already followed her, so his ''okay'' dusted her cheek with warm breath. ''What do you want, Cate?''

''You.'' She reached behind her back for his hands. He let her take them, and she pressed his palms against her belly. ''I need you to know what you're getting into first.''

''I do know. You're the one who forgot.''

''You've decided you can handle the differences I can't change about myself.'' She laced her fingers through his and stroked his hands down the sides of her stomach. ''But I'd like to know ahead of time you can make a physical commitment, too. My body can't look or feel the way you remember it.''

''Your clinical approach makes me want to laugh.'' His voice, thick and distracted, scattered her sensible intentions. He followed the curve of her tummy. Her belly appeared to protrude more each day, but Alan didn't seem to mind. With each sweep of their hands, he stretched his fingers to touch more of her skin. At last, he curved their hands around her hips, and Cate gasped.

Alan spread his fingers to free himself from her grasp, and then he reached for her shirt buttons. She tensed. Their history lived for him. All the other days and nights, all the times they'd made love, her other pregnancy with Dan.

"You're trembling, Cate." He moved on to the next button. His heart, tapping stridently against her back, belied his assurance.

She stared at the ocean, white foam riding in on dark shadows of movement. Natural motion, measurable time, but for Cate, the passing seconds built up speed. Alan nudged her hair aside with his chin.

His lips, pressed to her throat, pulled her out of her fear of what came next. Here and now, he made her feel lovely and loved. His kisses felt reverent. She only realized he'd finished unbuttoning her nightshirt when he lifted his hands to push the material off her shoulders. It dropped to the floor between them, and Alan linked his arms beneath her breasts to pull her more firmly against his chest.

She felt her nakedness in the careful distance he maintained between their lower bodies. He knew she wanted him, but he was less willing to reveal himself to her.

She backed against him and turned her head for his kiss. At last he unzipped his pants and let her slide her hands down the sides of his thighs. The khaki moved beneath her moist palms. His whole body jerked as if he weren't ready for her to touch him. She settled his hardness against the small of her back. He groaned and curved her forward, his hands in her hair as he thrust against her.

Such an intimate position startled her and yet, she wanted him more.

He slid his hands down her back and spread them over her belly again, caressing the swelling of the children they'd created together. The hunger he communicated with his seeking fingers eased her last anxiety. He wanted her, and her pregnancy definitely hadn't put him off.

A sudden fluttering he must have felt almost as strongly as she stilled them both. Cate straightened and caught her breath.

"What was that?" she said, too stunned to believe it might be one of their twins.

"Wait." He opened his mouth against her neck, but the flutter didn't repeat. "How often do they move?"

"If that was movement, it never happened before."

His breath lifted the fine hairs at her nape. "I love our babies, but I hope they settle back down and allow their parents privacy."

As he cupped her full breasts, she had to agree. His hands beneath the fertile weight gave her excellent relief. His quickened inhalation reassured her again that he found her anything but overweight and undesirable. He nudged his fingertips across her nipples. Sensitive to his slightest touch, she opened her lips and sound flowed between them.

"Did I hurt you?" She hardly recognized his ragged tone.

She rolled her head against his chest and covered his hands, inviting him to touch her with less restraint. He rolled her nipples gently between his index fingers and thumbs.

Longing buckled her knees, but when she sank against Alan, he turned her, and their legs tangled in a complicated dance that led them to the bed. Alan eased her onto her back and stood to take off his own clothes. When he stretched out beside her, he studied her face, his own thinned by desire that almost traveled through the air.

"I can't believe you're here." He dropped his hand on her thigh. "I've waited too long."

Catching his wrist, she lifted his fingers to her lips. She lost herself in his gaze as she kissed the tips of his fingers, enjoying the salty taste of him, salt that reminded her of the ocean at their doorstep. "Someday, can we make love on the beach?"

"Maybe I like this amnesia thing. We went to the beach the night you graduated, but after that, you were always too aware of being a Talbot to engage in sand dune sex. I'll find a private dune for you." He opened her mouth and stroked the pad of his thumb over the moist flesh of her inner lip.

"I wish I could remember," she said. "Alan, why did you choose me? I mean, rather than Caroline? I know you're good friends. You've been more reliable than her own husband."

"Caroline?" he said. "Why are we talking about Caroline now?"

"I have to know, I guess. The day I told her about the company, I was a little jealous of the way she talked about you, as if she believed in you more than I had.''

He shook his head at her. ''I didn't choose you, Cate. We chose each other. We fell in love, and I never saw Caroline the way I saw you. She's my sister.''

He burrowed his head into the curve of her neck. ''Can we get back to what we were talking about before?'' He made his way down the line of her shoulder, his mouth growing bolder, hungrier, and Cate forgot everything that worried her about the past.

As if he couldn't wait any longer, Alan raised himself to plant his palms on each side of her head. He kissed her, his control melting with each slide of his tongue against hers.

Need swept Cate's body and mind. She responded blindly, pulling Alan closer and closer still, when he tried to hold his weight off her. Indulging in the heady freedom of touching him, she explored the planes of his chest, the taut, quivering muscles of his belly.

Recognition quivered at the edge of her mind. Her hands seemed to know the muscles that trembled against them. As she dragged her fingertips up the muscles of his buttocks, he pressed her back to the bed and levered one leg across hers.

His concentration enticed her. He cupped her breast, holding her as if she were immeasurably precious to him. He lowered his mouth, and she watched him ring her nipple with his lips. Bathed in the heat of his mouth, her flesh tightened all the way to the pit of her stomach. She arched, begging him to take more of her.

The pleasure of his loving besieged her. A strange satisfaction spiked with aching need. He turned his head to suckle the curve of her breast. He brushed his mouth the length of her sternum, as if he were relearning her body.

She reached for him, but he held himself carefully over her, and she had to content herself with exploring the breadth of his shoulders and the strong, straining column of his throat.

''Alan,'' she whispered, and when he didn't respond, she spoke his name again.

He lifted his head. His ruffled hair lent his gaze an unfamiliar intimacy. Would they have struggled through so many problems, if she'd invited him to share their bed when she'd come home from the hospital?

''What?'' He spread his hand over her belly. ''Are you all right?''

She nodded, and even the crinkle of the crisp pillowcase beneath her head took on an erotic quality. ''I can't reach you.''

His smile brushed her lips as he kissed her. ''You can touch me later. This is like your first time.''

''I want you to feel...'' She'd insisted on communication, but she couldn't explain she wanted him to feel the way he made her feel, happy, aroused, beloved. Her emotions were too personal, even to share with him yet.

He traced the line of her throat, his mouth alternately gentle and firm. He scraped his teeth over the bones of her shoulder, but he'd finally moved within her reach.

She cupped him, and he gasped in surprise. She stroked, unsure of what she was doing, but her instinct seemed to be right. He arched above her, and his moan puckered her nipples. He took her in his mouth again. She explored his body, writhing against him, meeting his thrusts with her palm until he parted her knees.

He grazed the length of her thigh with the back of his hand. Unlike hers, his touch was sure. He knew exactly how to push her toward a culmination that almost frightened her. She wanted him with her. She wanted him to be part of her. Tonight was for connections, not selfish love.

She whispered his name, a plea and a demand he seemed to understand. Gently, he entered her, waiting for her to show him with her body when she was ready for more.

She clung to him, her faith in him complete. Alan, her husband, wouldn't take more than she could give, nor force her to beg for him.

The way he held himself above her, caring for the children they'd made in just such a moment as this intensified her joy. Their rhythm came from memories gone from her. She opened her eyes and looked into his.

He curved his mouth, but this time his smile challenged her. She held back, teasing. He adjusted to her movement. She took control, but he took it back, as if, in this one part of their marriage, he read her mind. His knowledge of her sang an emotional accompaniment to their physical joining.

Without warning, her pleasure changed. Deepened, lengthened, from her thighs to her toes, to her scalp. She raised herself off the bed, into Alan's arms. Her whole body reached for him, and he answered.

His expression tightened. His eyes drifted shut as his lips thinned. She held him, her muscles still quaking, as he collapsed and pulled her to his side. Careful to the end, to protect their unborn children.

Cate slid her arm across his chest. She pressed her mouth to his skin, smiling as his pulse raced against her lips.

"Such a worthwhile husband."

"I love you, wife."

She lifted herself on her elbow. "Are you sure your hormones aren't talking?"

He grinned, and his rumpled hair and sated eyes made her happy. "Do a man's hormones talk after the fact?"

She slid her hand down his flat stomach. "Maybe, if they anticipate being reawakened."

He caught her fingers. "I'm a little nervous. We never made love while you were carrying twins before."

"I feel spectacular, divine, ecstatic, really good." She stretched, thrusting out her breasts for effect. She was bold now that she knew for sure how he felt about her body.

Indecision entered his gaze, but he raised his head to kiss her. "Get some sleep, so I'll keep feeling spectacular." He pulled her to his side again and curved his leg over her thighs.

Nestling against him, she wondered if she'd ever

really believed her life would improve without him in it.

DAN CAME HOME the next morning as Alan opened the garage to leave for work. Alan stopped his car and got out. Dan parked on the drive as well.

"Everything okay?" Alan searched his son's face for signs of a hangover.

Dan pulled a "not again" face. "I didn't drink, Dad. I watched a movie at my friend's house, and then I drove out to Aunt Imogen's."

"What's your plan for today?"

"Start sorting out my room, so I can pack for school."

"What makes you so angry, Dan?"

"I'm not angry, and I'm not in the mood to sit through an interrogation. Aren't you late?"

By about half an hour. Holding his nude wife had proven too tempting to resist this morning. He'd left her sleeping; if she'd opened her eyes, he doubted he could have left her at all.

"I have to go, but I want to talk to you." Dan needed to know his mother and father had sorted out their problems, but their shared bedroom would tell that story. "You know your mom doesn't need any extra commotion right now. Why don't you cut her a little slack from here on? If you're angry, talk to me, but let your mother off the hook."

Dan opened his door and stood, concern blanching his young face. "Did something happen to Mom?"

Well, he still cared enough to worry about her. "No, but let's do all we can to keep her healthy. She needs our support right now."

"So you won't cut out on her when she expects you at say—a wedding?"

Dan's bitterness surprised him. "You know I've never chosen to break a promise to you or to my father."

"And to Mom?"

Maybe he'd assumed, once or twice or twenty times too often that she'd understand. "Your mother's and my marriage is our business. Not your problem, son."

"I'm not involved if my parents divorce?"

"Divorce?" Alan strode around his car and grabbed his son's shoulder. "We're about to have two babies. We have you. We've shared a lifetime together, but we haven't taught you much if you think we can throw all that away without a second glance."

"You'll never convince me Mom didn't plan to leave you that night at Aunt Imogen's."

"But she didn't leave."

"One of you will change your mind, and I plan to be prepared." He shrugged off Alan's hand. "Forget about it. Why do we have to talk about this again?"

He stomped through the garage, unfastening his keys from a ring on his belt loop. Frustrated, Alan had plenty to say to Dan's stiff back. But not one word sounded productive, even in his head. Dan wouldn't believe until he saw for himself that his parents had truly started over.

TRASH FROM last night's Fourth of July fireworks littered the road as Dan packed his car. He searched the street for some sign of Phoebe. She'd promised to say goodbye to him in person.

She was his one regret about starting classes early. He didn't want to leave her behind. In fact, he'd asked her to drive to school with him. She'd turned him down.

Behind him, his own front door opened. His mom balanced a canvas bag in front of her big old belly. A grudging smile hurt his mouth. He had to credit his parents for the honeymoon show they'd paraded past him since his grandfather's wedding.

They acted more like lovesick kids his age than middle-aged married people who were starting a brand-new family. In the old days their silences had pegged out the battle zone for him. Now, if the room they occupied was quiet, he'd learned to knock before he opened the door.

The only thing worse than your parents having sex all the time was never knowing where they'd be.

His mom peered down the street. ''I can't believe your dad's late today.''

''I'll drop by his office. Wasn't he writing reference letters?'' Forget it. He wasn't going to wait around for his dad and Phoebe.

If he hung around here much longer, his mom would start to blubber, and the last thing he wanted was his mom wailing all over him again. He'd just eaten the saltiest, soggiest grilled-ham-and-cheese a mother ever tearfully slopped onto a plate, and he'd had enough.

Besides, he'd finally begun to realize he wouldn't see her hovering over him every day. He'd miss her.

He wrapped her in a loose hug. The babies felt

funny, and her clinging arms worried him, too. "Bye, Mom. I'll be fine."

"Call me after you check in. Let me know what you think about your room." She pressed her fist to the small of her back. "I don't know why you refuse to let me drive you."

Because he'd hoped Phoebe would change her mind and come with him. "I'll survive on my own." He opened his car door and jumped behind the wheel. Why linger when the inevitable had to happen? "See you later. You and Dad can come visit in a few weeks."

"I love you, Dan."

He climbed out of the car, hugged her tight as he could and bit his lip to keep girly tears from shooting out of his eyes. "Love you, too, Mom."

This time he didn't look back. And he didn't drive by his dad's office, either.

ALAN PULLED INTO the parking lot at Whitlock College's library. He picked up the map an assistant at the registrar's office had marked for him. Myers Hall stood on the street that ran past the north side of the library. The side opposite the lot where he'd stopped.

He circled the library in the parking lot to turn onto the right road. Cate's voice spoke in his head. "Just go see him. You can take him the little refrigerator as an excuse. He must have been annoyed or he would have stopped by your office, but he's had three weeks to cool off."

Apparently, Dan had told her he was going to stop on his way out of town to say goodbye. He hadn't.

Was he annoyed or petulant? Why would Dan be upset with them now?

A sign in front of a square brick building identified Myers Hall for Alan. He parked Cate's SUV at the side of the street and trudged up the sidewalk. Tall Georgia pines and thick hardwoods sheltered the residence, accenting its exclusive atmosphere.

Would they be able to afford the tuition Dan's scholarship didn't cover if the business went as badly as he now feared? Alan scratched the back of his head.

He'd give a lot for a share of Cate's confidence. She just kept assuring him they'd manage together. He'd learned to trust the together part of her promise, but he couldn't feel as sanguine about steps they'd take to manage.

The employees he'd had to lay off had found other building firms, but their commutes had all extended. He tried to make himself feel better with the knowledge he'd helped them find something. They weren't waiting each morning on the side of a road for a chance at day labor.

Alan stopped at the stone posts at the end of the sidewalk in front of Dan's building. Dan might not be in, but Alan hadn't called first. He hadn't wanted to give Dan a chance to put him off.

He figured he and Cate would have to borrow tape from Aunt Imogen if they didn't sort out their son's problems soon.

He wove through a crowd of lounging adolescents who looked too young to drive, much less live on campus at a college. They stopped talking as one to give him a sharp once-over.

Immediately inside the loud, unoiled front door, Alan scanned the lounge for someone in charge. Not one of the inhabitants sprawled in any of the chairs or on the floor presented an air of authority. A kid about Dan's age finally looked up from his book.

"Who do you want?"

"Dan Palmer," Alan said.

"Room 324."

"Thanks."

The kid went back to his book, and Alan took the stairs two at a time. He reached the third floor about the same time he suspected he was having a heart attack. Another sign indicated which rooms went to the left and which to the right. Dan's room was on the right. Girls and boys eyed him curiously as he huffed and puffed down the hall.

He knocked on Dan's door, and his son opened up almost immediately. The second Dan saw him, wariness came into his tired expression. He stood aside and Alan crossed the doorway into chaos.

Clothes littered two beds as if a tornado had spilled them out of its spinning mouth. Books and clocks and soda cans and food wrappers added to the turmoil. Alan decided not to dig for one of the chairs.

"I hope a load-bearing beam runs beneath this floor."

"Are you telling me to clean my room, Dad?"

He ignored the sarcasm. "I brought you a refrigerator to add to the clutter. Your mother thought you might be able to use it."

Dan remained silent and sullen for a moment, but he finally twisted a reluctant smile. "Thanks. I'll help you bring it up."

He cleared a space beneath the double windows that let in the room's only light, and then they went to Cate's car. His fellow students eyed them with greater interest as they hauled the minifridge through the lounge. Alan turned toward the stairs, but Dan tugged toward the far end of the room.

"Why don't we take the elevator?"

Elevator? "Good idea."

Upstairs, Dan managed to balance his end of the refrigerator while he fished keys off his belt loop. Alan was relieved he'd remembered to lock the room. Cate would be glad to hear he followed safety procedures.

Grunting in unison, they managed to position the appliance beneath the windowsill. Dan picked up a pile of papers from the floor and dropped them on top of the fridge. When he leaned down to connect the plug, Alan glimpsed a printed schedule on top of the stack.

He frowned. Dan's name ran across the page's right corner. He was supposed to be in a Spanish class at this moment.

"Son, have you dropped Spanish?"

Dan shook his head. A hint of guilt passed through his eyes. "I slept in."

Alan waited for a less lame excuse.

"I stayed up late last night." Dan glanced around the room. "Unpacking."

"I'd laugh at a joke like that if I hadn't watched you make one increasingly serious mistake after another this summer. What's wrong with you?"

"My life."

Alan's skin crawled. "Are you depressed?"

"I'm angry."

He looked it, to Alan's relief. Angry, they'd find a way to handle. Depression opened up a whole new set of dangers.

"What makes you angry about your life?"

"Which issue do you want to lecture me on first?"

"I'm serious. I can't leave until I'm satisfied you don't need to talk to someone more skilled than I am at helping you handle problems."

With widened eyes, Dan almost seemed like the kid who'd once looked up to Alan with awe. "I don't think I've ever heard you admit anyone could do something better than you."

"Then I've been a pompous fool. What's wrong, Dan?"

"Not as much as you think, probably. Mom's accident, your arguments, golf school. The twins, when we're all too old for new babies in the house. Then I met someone I—thought I liked—a lot, but I don't know how she feels about me."

He'd met someone? Thank God that put Phoebe out of the picture. "You haven't explained Spanish."

"I honestly slept in."

"I want to be sympathetic, but you asked to start classes this summer. Sleeping through them is a waste of time and money." Dan's expression began to close again, and Alan backtracked. "Your mother and I are fine except we're concerned about you."

"And I shouldn't cause Mom any extra stress. You don't need to repeat the sermon, but I've seen how quickly you change your minds."

"If we split up tomorrow, you'd still have your own life to work on now."

"I am working." Dan turned toward the door, and Alan went with him. "Don't worry about me. I forgot to set my clock last night, but I know how tight your money is. I won't lose my scholarship."

"Hear what I'm saying to you. I'll take care of the money. I'm upset about your Spanish class because you never skipped in high school."

"And I won't again, but you have to go, Dad. I have Geology in about fifteen minutes."

"All right." Was he abandoning his son? "But call me if you need anything. Call me if you want to talk. No matter what you think about me or your mother right now, we're available to talk to you or to come here any time you need us."

Dan nodded, and Alan's spirits rose at his less belligerent gaze. "Thanks for the refrigerator." He held out his hand. "Thanks for coming."

Alan yanked him close enough for a swift hug. "Call me, Dan, if you need me."

He laughed, embarrassed, but more like the son he'd been before he'd learned to doubt. "I need to go to Geology." Then he turned and shut the door.

Alan faced the scarred white paint and discovered he shared his son's doubts. About the business, his ability to provide and his future. But not about Cate.

Since Cate figured prominently in his future, the rest, he'd handle.

CHAPTER FIFTEEN

"I'VE HEARD OF false labor, Dr. Davis, but I don't remember what it feels like, and these cramps are starting in my back. Would I feel false labor in my back?"

Dr. Davis's confidence had lost its power to ease Cate's mind today. Besides, the other woman looked concerned. Worry for her children lay lock a rock in Cate's belly.

"Let's not jump to conclusions before I do an exam. You aren't feeling pain right now?"

Cate shook her head. But she'd called the doctor's office the second Alan had left for Dan's school because the cramps had unsettled her all night. "They're never regular, but they usually go away more quickly than they have this time. Usually, I feel a few, and then they stop."

"Let's do the exam."

Cate positioned herself in the stirrups, and Dr. Davis donned fresh gloves. Cate studied her doctor, searching for any sign of trouble. The woman certainly did a thorough search of things. She smiled an apology as Cate flinched.

"I'll finish in just a moment. Everything seems fine, but you may feel more cramping this afternoon."

"Because of the exam?"

"Mmm-hmm." Dr. Davis glanced at her, looked away and then zeroed in on her again. "Calm down, Cate. You act as if you think I might keep bad news from you. I won't." She backed away. "I can't give you any bad news. Everything is normal."

Cate sagged in relief. She felt like an idiot—a reassured idiot. She should have told Alan about the pains, but she hadn't wanted to worry him when Dan and the business were on his mind.

"Just in case—you are thirty-eight, and you are carrying twins—I'd like to do another ultrasound before I send you home, and then I'd like you to limit your activity."

"Limit how?"

Dr. Davis patted her shoulder. "I'm not talking bed rest, but don't take any exercise. Don't go out of your way to do anything different than your normal routine. Let cleaning wait for another time. And no sex."

Cate blinked. She didn't care for the last part. She'd have to worry Alan with news of her visit after all.

"Just until we know everything's progressing normally." Dr. Davis plucked a pen out of her pocket to write on Cate's chart. "I guess you and Alan are back on good terms."

Cate leered dramatically. "Excellent terms."

ALAN WOKE early the next morning. By the time he'd arrived home from visiting Dan, Cate had been asleep. He rolled to his side and gazed at her, overwhelmed with gratitude for the new understanding between them.

She opened her eyes, but didn't seem startled to find him staring at her. "Morning."

"I've fixated on you."

"Good." She kissed him and then settled her head more comfortably on her pillow. "How was Dan?"

"Touchy, but he liked the fridge and we talked. I felt better when I left him."

"Did he?"

Alan shrugged, a difficult procedure when leaning on his elbow. "Hard to say. I'd never challenge him to a poker game."

"But you aren't as concerned?"

"I don't think I am. He's up and down, and he blames it on us, but you can understand when you think what a steady childhood we gave him until this spring and summer."

"I have to talk to you, Alan."

Her serious tone shook him. "Okay."

"I saw Dr. Davis yesterday. Those strange back pains came back."

He grabbed her arm. Fear took a grip on his throat. "Are you—are the babies all right?"

She nodded. "Dr. Davis said everything looks normal. She ordered an ultrasound, and the babies were active. She wants me to limit my activity for a week or two, but she says she has no reason to think anything's gone wrong with my pregnancy."

"Is she sure?"

"She acted as if she were. She said we couldn't make love."

"But the babies are all right? And you are?"

She laughed. ''I thought you'd be upset about the sex. I am.''

He ignored her teasing tone. ''I'm upset because you didn't tell me.''

''I didn't tell you because our other son needed you, and I wasn't sure I had a problem.''

''But you don't—we—don't have a problem?''

''Right.'' She snuggled into his chest, and he put his arms around her, even though her secrecy still annoyed him. ''Except we can't make love,'' she added again.

''I don't care,'' he said against her hair, but what he meant was ''I'll love you all my life.'' She just didn't respond well to ''I love you.'' Yet. Someday she'd stop looking like a deer in headlights when he told her.

''I'm relieved, but I guess you're right. I should have told you. I got scared.''

Fear still laced her voice, a sharp note that asked him for comfort. All right. He'd forgive her one secret doctor's visit. He'd kept enough secrets from her over the years. Finally, he understood how betrayed and unnecessary secrets made a person feel.

The phone beside their bed rang. Alan reached over Cate to answer it. Chief Mabry started talking before Alan put the receiver to his ear.

''Your New Jersey detective found Jim.''

A huge, killing weight hovered unsteadily over Alan's head. ''How do you know?''

''He alerted the police, and they asked me to notify all of you.''

''Why did he call the police instead of us?''

''Jim's cruising casinos, and the detective was

afraid he'd lose him if Jim decided to switch to Nevada or Europe. Apparently, New Jersey isn't lucky for our crook.''

''Great.''

''I assume you'll want to join the others on a flight to Newark?''

''I'm getting dressed. Are you coming, too?''

''Out of my jurisdiction, and besides, I'd like to shoot the son of a bitch on sight. New Jersey will send him home. Don't worry.''

''I guess I'm not allowed to shoot him on sight?''

''Not a good idea for a family man, but you'll probably have to identify him. And I figured you'd want to be there when they took him.''

''I do. Thanks for the call.''

''Your flight leaves at ten-thirty. Can you make the airport in time?''

''If I have to build myself a pair of wings.'' He hung up and turned to Cate. ''They've found Jim. I have to go to New Jersey.''

She sat up, pulling the sheet across her bare breasts. ''Why do you have to go?''

''Because he stole from me and my family and my friends. I'll be back tomorrow.'' He cupped her chin, remembering the twins. ''Unless you want me to stay? Are you still worried about the babies?''

''No.'' She kissed him. ''Go and don't worry. I trust Dr. Davis. By the time you come home, we'll know where we stand with the business.''

''Chief Mabry thinks we'll have to identify him anyway.''

''You don't have to explain. Just go—but take a cheap flight.''

"Like we'll ever fly first class again."

Cate's mouth curved, a lush invitation to heaven. "I can't remember ever going first class."

With heartfelt regret, he left her in their bed. Alone and wastefully untouched.

She dressed and made coffee while he packed. He carried his bag down the back stairs and found French toast waiting on the kitchen table.

"You didn't have to make this, Cate." But he'd eat it if he had to swallow a slice whole to make his plane on time. "Thank you, though."

He ate with rude speed and Cate walked him to the door.

"Don't drive crazy. If you miss your flight, you can take the next one."

He brushed her lips with his. So sweet. She tasted better than syrup, better than any other sweet thing in his life. "Go back to bed and rest. Don't do anything until I get home tomorrow, okay?"

"All right." She pushed her hair off her face. "I'll call Dan later."

"Don't, if you think talking to him might upset you."

"I miss talking to him. Even if his conversation is mostly monosyllabic."

"I'll miss you." He kissed her deeply and she kissed him back. This Cate gave as good as she got. On a groan, he finally pulled away.

"If I don't go, I'll have to beg you to break doctor's orders." He smoothed his thumb over her lip. "Turn around, and let me watch you walk toward the stairs."

With ego-boosting reluctance, she went. Alan

stepped into the garage walkway and locked the door behind him. Then he turned his attention to the bastard who'd stolen from him and his family and his employees.

THE DAY AFTER his dad's visit, the atmosphere in Dan's car all but choked him. Phoebe clung to the window side of the passenger seat, her face furious.

"I can't love you, Dan. You're like my brother. I kept hoping you'd get over this infatuation you have for me."

"Infatuation?" Even Phoebe treated him like a child.

"Your parents think I'm the next best thing to a card-carrying cannibal, and you think you'll show them what a grown man you are if you and I become more than friends."

"Your major is Psychology?"

"I'm angry. You're determined to ruin a friendship that matters a lot to me."

"Friendship with you no longer satisfies me."

Phoebe slowly turned her head, a fire building in her gaze. "Satisfies you?" She opened her door. "I know what you want in the way of satisfaction. My virginity in no way affects my brain function. I am not going to 'satisfy' you, just so you can annoy your parents. I'll take the bus home tonight. And don't follow me down this road. I refuse to get in this car with you again."

That being her final word, she pushed her long, mouth-watering legs out of the car and uncoiled the rest of her body to leave him in the cold emptiness of their broken relationship. She slammed the car door, and Dan sat, trying harder than he'd ever tried in his life not to cry.

He gunned the car away from the curb. Tears burned despite his strongest effort as he squealed past Phoebe. He didn't plan his trip, but he ended up at the public golf course the college used.

The dark, closed golf course.

Taking a token for the ball machine out of the change slot on his dashboard, he got out anyway. He grabbed his driver from the trunk. They didn't build fences around golf courses. Just put a wooden gate up that kept the polite golfers out.

Dan jumped over it. At the side of the clubhouse, the ball machine didn't work. He punched the front of it hard enough to break the glass that covered the metal door. Then he realized someone had unplugged it. With his bleeding hand, he plugged in the machine and got a bucket of balls. The balls kept coming even after he'd filled one of the baskets from the side of the machine.

He walked away and left the balls thumping on the cement, rolling to the grass.

By moonlight, he teed his first shot on the driving range. His aim in the near darkness wasn't expert. His third ball broke glass somewhere. He kept hitting. Another shattered piece of glass made him hesitate, but only long enough to get really angry again.

He drove a ball into the darkness. His life had about the same sense of direction. His father had believed telling him he and his mom were staying together because of him and the new babies would make him feel good.

And now, Phoebe.

He hit two more balls in quick succession. He loved her. He hadn't known he could want a woman so much, hadn't anticipated wanting Phoebe, but like everything else he wanted right now, she'd put herself out of his reach.

He hit ball after ball after ball until he emptied the basket. Then he walked back to the machine and scooped up another basketful from the pile on the ground. As he stood, blue lights slashed the night air and striped the clubhouse walls.

He turned as the officer driving the police car painted him in a spotlight.

CATE KEPT her promise to stay in bed all day. She called Dan, but no one answered in his room, and no one answered on the public phone in his building, either. In the middle of reading her second book for the day, she noticed night had fallen, but she hadn't eaten dinner.

Not particularly hungry after a day on her back, she went downstairs anyway, but as she reached the kitchen, the front doorbell rang. Cate cinched her robe and hurried through the living room. Uncle Ford stood on her doorstep.

"I heard Alan's left to find Jim Cooper, and I thought you might like some company."

Cate stood aside for him. Uncle Ford had avoided her since she'd caught him making out at Richard's wedding. "I'm glad you came."

"Have you eaten?" He produced a white sack, printed with The Captain's Lady logo. "I brought fish and chips."

"Sounds delicious. I couldn't decide what to eat."

She led the way to the kitchen where she started setting the table. "Should you be driving this late?"

"I've got a bum leg, but I gas and brake with the other foot. I'm no invalid."

She waved the plates at him. "Okay, okay, I just didn't want you doing something unsafe."

"You're still hiding my Cate in there somewhere."

She took utensils from the drawer. "You mean I can't help mothering people? Dan welcomes my efforts about the same as you do."

"I'm sorry I embarrassed you at Richard's wedding."

She laughed. It was silly now. "I don't know how you packed yourself into that car."

He flashed a self-conscious grin. "It was a tight fit." He cleared his throat. "But more importantly, I behaved with a reckless disregard for safety and public decency."

Cate stared at him. "Did you rehearse that speech?"

"I'm ashamed. I guess I saw myself through your eyes. You're a good girl, Cate."

"Woman."

"Woman, I mean, but you don't know how I feel. I'm seventy-three years old, getting older and more infirm every year—well, maybe every five years," he said with a hint of his natural personality. "I want to stay young."

"You don't have to defend your actions to me."

"I do if you don't respect me any more."

A string of pictures shuffled through her mind, tugged at her heart. Uncle Ford, with the black hair of a much younger man, teaching her to drive, Uncle Ford, with a strong proud, loving arm around Alan's shoulders—Alan in the tux he wore in their wedding photo.

Cate dropped the silverware on the table and grabbed a chair back. "I respect you." She forced her head up. "I've always loved you, Uncle Ford."

He came closer, scraping his cane over the floor. "You remember?" His rough voice matched his embrace. "You remember me, Cate?"

"You were kind to Alan. Kinder than Richard."

"I'm not scared like Richard's scared. I worry about commitment to one woman and getting old. Loving a boy who needed a father came easy."

Cate gripped his arm. "I wish I'd cooked you a nice meal."

"Why don't you slap those containers in the microwave?" He turned away as the phone rang. "I'll get that."

"It's probably Alan."

"Then maybe you should get it."

He maneuvered to the microwave and Cate took the phone off its hook. The voice on the phone gave her another shock.

The voice asked her to accept a collect call from the Devon County jail.

"Jail?" Cate whispered. She'd forgotten nothing since she'd awakened from her coma, and she knew Whitlock College was in Devon County. "I accept."

"Mom? I've tried to call Dad's office, but I couldn't reach him. I'm in trouble."

She flattened her hand over her heart, to keep it from bursting. "Are you hurt?"

"No. They haven't even arrested me yet, but I had to ask you or Dad to come up here."

"What did you do?"

A rustling sound came through the wire, and then his voice was muffled, as if he'd turned away or covered the phone. "I broke into the golf course. And I may have broken the ball machine, and then I may have broken someone's window."

How had he convinced Alan he was all right? "When did you do all that?"

"Tonight, Mom. Can you come, or can you send Dad?"

"I'll be there in about an hour. Do you know the directions?" He gave them. As she wrote the jail's phone number in case she got lost anyway, Dan spoke again. "I'm sorry. Dad asked me not to put extra pressure on you. Are you feeling okay?"

She felt desperately sick, but whether the sensation owed itself to pregnancy, shock or her son's indefensible behavior, she couldn't say. Someone shouted in the background and scared her half to death. "Be careful until I get there. Dan, what possessed you?"

"Nothing that seems reasonable now."

"Don't be afraid. We'll take care of it." Probably the wrong thing to say to an eighteen-year-old, but he was her son. She'd do anything to take care of him.

She turned to find Uncle Ford sprawled in a chair, his face pale.

"What's wrong with Dan?" he demanded.

She relayed Dan's offenses. "I have to change before I go. Will you stay here in case Alan calls?"

"He'd kill me if I let you drive up there alone."

He worked his way to his feet. ''Besides, who could strike a more sympathetic pose than a pregnant woman?''

Cate paused on the first stair. ''What are you talking about?''

''When you show up on the trembling arm of an old man on a cane, they'll send Dan home to take care of us both.''

She shook herself, like a bag full of weary bones. ''I hope you're right.''

She didn't want her son to face consequences. His pain appeared rooted in her accident and the twins Alan and she hadn't okayed with him first.

She managed to put on clothes and she yanked a brush through her hair. She hadn't dried it after her shower. It clustered in Caroline's curls around her face. She tamed it with a scrunchie and ran downstairs. Uncle Ford was waiting in the doorway, but the phone rang again.

Cate hesitated. Uncle Ford swapped a distraught glance with her. This had to be Alan. She debated letting the answering machine take his call.

''He'll worry if he thinks I'm not here.'' She grabbed the phone in the living room. ''Alan?''

''How'd you know?''

She marshaled her breathing to keep him from hearing her gasp for air. ''Who else? I've already spoken to Dan.'' Perfect opening, but the rest of the story refused to come.

''Well, we found Jim Cooper. It doesn't look good for the business. From what we can tell, he's gambled almost all the money away.'' Defeat flattened his tone, but Cate was so numb she couldn't find words to comfort him. "I have to go to the police station tomorrow, so I'll probably come home on a late flight. Do you want me to call you from the airport?"

"Yes, please. I'd like to know when you're on your way."

She paused. The truth about Dan clung to the tip of her tongue. What could Alan do from New Jersey? How could she add to his problems? Would either of them ever have conceived of Dan's being taken to a police station? Had he ever done anything like this before?

Their family life had suddenly collapsed around her feet. She'd tell Alan as soon as he returned, but she couldn't talk about it now. She could hardly face it, herself.

"Why don't you give me your phone number up there, in case I need to get in touch with you?"

"Do you have pen and paper?"

She noted the number. "Let me know what happens with the police," she said. "And, Alan?"

"Yes?"

She swallowed. Her throat constricted. "Alan, I love you." She meant it. The slow process of falling in love with her husband had finally come full circle. "I might never be the wife I was before, but I love you."

"Cate, I wish I were there to show you how much I love the wife you are now."

She glanced at Uncle Ford. He tapped his watch, and she nodded. "You can't know how much I wish that, too."

"Do you believe I've failed you?"

Pain in his voice kept her from getting upset at the conclusion he'd reached. "No. We'll work out our future, and you've already begun to help the employees." Uncle Ford tapped his cane, and she nodded again. "I just wish we were together. I'd better go—I left the shower running."

"Go back to bed. I'll see you tomorrow night, but I'll call as soon as I leave the police station."

"Thanks."

After they hung up, she couldn't take her hand off the phone. As at his graduation, Dan probably needed his father more than Cate. She still couldn't remember him. What if she let their son down?

"Maybe I should call him back."

"Why didn't you tell him?"

"We've lost the business."

"My God."

"I couldn't pile this on top of the business. He always worries he's failing us."

"I don't think you'd have been happy if he'd hidden something like this from you."

"I'll tell him tomorrow when he comes home."

"It's your choice, but I hope you don't regret it. Don't you trust him, Cate?"

"I trust him." But why bring up Dan's problems when they might be settled by the time Alan could get home? She tried to work up a smile. "I guess I'm a reckless Talbot after all."

"You chose a terrible time. Do you want to drive, or shall I?"

"I will." No need to tire him out. Besides, he might fall asleep instead of badgering her into deeper guilt.

CHAPTER SIXTEEN

THE FIRST CRAMP came more like a memory of past pain. Cate clung to the door in the surprisingly busy reception area of Devon County's police station. Pushing away, she pressed her fists into the small of her back. Had she imagined it?

"What's wrong?" Uncle Ford's lifted voice brought all police activity to an awkward halt.

"Nothing."

One female and one male officer broke away from the large reception desk. "Are you all right, ma'am?" the man asked.

"My son is here. Dan Palmer?"

"Oh, yeah." The woman beckoned with her finger, and Cate and her uncle followed her down the white hall—white walls, white tile floor, shot with threads of black paint like splashes. "Come this way. I parked Mr. Palmer in an interrogation room."

Cate stared at the woman's dark-blond chignon. Was Dan in more trouble if they considered him "Mr. Palmer?"

Uncle Ford leaned into her. "Skillful use of your pregnancy. I'm ashamed I didn't suggest it."

The woman must have heard him, but she didn't turn around. At a dirt-shadowed, closed door, she stopped.

"An official from Whitlock is with him. I've asked the golf course manager to wait in another room. I'd like you to hear what Mr. Palmer has to say, and then we'll decide whether I arrest him."

"Do you have a choice?" Cate asked. Hope shot so quickly through her body she could barely speak.

"He's a kid." The woman's dark-blue eyes coasted over Cate's figure. "Are you his stepmother?"

"Mother."

"Excuse me if I'm rude, but he's so much older than the baby you're carrying, I wondered if there might have been some trouble at home. A divorce and remarriage or something."

"I guess we have had trouble."

"Let him talk. Then you can give me your story."

Cate's hope dimmed. Her story? As in the version of events she thought most likely to get Dan off?

Who was she kidding? If she thought quickly enough, she'd try a good story to get him out of here.

The woman opened the door, and Dan bolted upright from his chair. Concern made him look older, and Cate struggled not to cry in front of the man from Whitlock and the policewoman.

Dan hugged her. "I'm sorry, Mom. I never thought this might happen. Are you okay?"

She wished people would stop asking. She nodded as she clutched at him. "How about you?"

"I feel like a jerk."

"So you should." The policewoman held out her hand to Cate. "I'm Officer Burke." She turned back to Dan. "Don't pretend this just happened to you.

You trespassed and broke private property. You caused everything that's occurred tonight.''

''Maybe he did,'' Cate interjected, ''but you don't understand.''

''I'm ready to listen. Sit down, Mrs. Palmer.'' Officer Burke pulled out a chair. ''Do you know Dr. Jared, Mrs. Palmer? Dean of Students at Whitlock College.''

''We've met,'' the tall, overly thin man said. ''Mrs. Palmer.''

She shook his hand and nodded. Not even the faintest memory of him stirred in her mind. ''Thank you for coming, Dr. Jared.''

''I've been concerned about Dan.''

''I skipped a couple of classes,'' her son admitted, ''but Dad talked to me about it, and I won't skip any more. I've always done my assignments.''

''He has.'' Dr. Jared assured both Cate and the officer. ''I've verified his performance with his professors—none of whom were that glad to hear from me at this hour, Dan.''

''I can do the work. That's not the problem.'' Dan glanced Cate's way. His face burned bright red, but he went on. ''My mother had an accident in May, and she has no memory of you, Dr. Jared, no real memory of me. She doesn't remember my father, and she didn't seem to want to remember him at first. Then came the babies—I'm embarrassed and I feel out of place, as ridiculous as that sounds. After that, we couldn't afford a golf school I need because everyone at this level plays as well as I do. Add a girl I thought would make me feel needed—who doesn't love me, and I've lost everything that mattered to me.'' He broke off on a choking sound, as if he'd used the last breath in his body. Cate reached for his hand. He pulled away. ''Mom, I'm humiliated enough. Just let me finish. I lost control of my life, and I was afraid. My past felt like a lie. I wanted Phoebe, but she didn't want me. I was throwing away school, when I knew how difficult it was for you and Dad to pay the nonscholarship part of my tuition. I'm sorry. I got extremely angry and I acted like a kid. I did some stupid things. Not just tonight.''

''What do you mean?'' Officer Burke asked.

Dan looked bleak. ''Nothing you could charge me with, but my mom understands. Whatever happens here, I'm sorry, Mom.''

Another cramp crept from her back to her groin. She concentrated on not showing how it hurt. ''I never meant to make your life look hopeless.''

''You didn't, but my 'perfect' childhood ended that day you got hurt.'' He turned to the policewoman. ''I know I have to face the consequences.''

''How much damage?'' Uncle Ford asked.

''That's my problem.'' Dan's flush deepened. ''Sorry, Uncle Ford, but I'd like to shoulder my own responsibility instead of making more for my parents.''

Cate kept her attention on the woman who held her son's immediate future in her hands. Officer Burke studied Dan, but then turned to Dr. Jared. ''What do you think, sir?''

The strongest pain yet gripped Cate's belly in a vice. She gasped, and the others looked her way. She shook her head. The pains might go away again. She needed to hear Dr. Jared's answer before she admitted she was in trouble. ''I'm upset. I can't help it. He's my son.''

Dr. Jared spoke to Officer Burke. ''I'd like to give Dan another chance. I'll make sure he attends classes. He's been a good student—surprisingly, when you consider everything he's told us. I know the golf team values him. His coach wanted to come tonight, but this is my job. What can we do to help Dan through his trouble?''

Officer Burke stood. ''I'll get Mr. Cory. He runs the golf course.'' She went away, and Cate eased in a deep breath as the tightening started again.

''Thank you for speaking up for our boy,'' Uncle Ford said to the dean. ''I'm Ford Talbot.''

''I've seen your photo in the paper,'' Dr. Jared said. ''When you used to show horses. My daughter is a big fan.''

''I didn't know you showed horses,'' Cate said.

''What did you think the barn was for, Mom?''

''My animals are old now, like me.'' Uncle Ford made himself sound pathetic, and even though Cate knew he was putting on a show, she wished she'd left him alone in that small car to prove he was still young.

Officer Burke returned. ''Unfortunately, Mr. Cory received an emergency call from home. I spoke to him and let him go.'' She smiled at Cate, appearing more human than she had before. ''His wife is pregnant, too. He left terms for Dan.'' She read from a sheet of paper. ''He has to replace the windows he broke in a resident's house. He has to help Mr. Cory repair the ball machine, and he'll have to work off the cost of repair supplies. Then he has to work off the same amount of time it would take to pay for labor to do the repairs. Finally, as I mentioned Dan seemed concerned about his tuition, Mr. Cory said if he worked well, maybe he could continue in the job and receive a paycheck."

Relief shook Cate. She wiped tears from her eyes as Dan sprang to his feet to hug her. She tightened her arms, a reflexive response to another pain, but Dan thought she was clinging and turned to Officer Burke. "Thank you. I know you went out of your way to help me."

"You looked upset enough to make me believe your story. You weren't aggressive." She shook his hand. "We don't get paid by the adolescent we slam into a cell. Besides, I'll probably see you at the golf course."

"You plan to check up on me?" His tone conveyed resignation.

She laughed. "I'm taking lessons. But, if you can handle the truth, I'd like to be sure I didn't make a mistake with you." She shook Cate's hand again. "I hope you soon recover from your injuries. Look after this boy, because I won't be so helpful if he comes back here."

"Thank you." Cate included Dr. Jared. "I'm grateful for the chance you're giving him."

The policewoman nodded. Dan thanked Dr. Jared, who cautioned him about missing any classes for the next four years. Cate restrained herself from hugging the man who'd helped save her son.

At last, she and Dan and Uncle Ford made it outside, where Cate clung to the metal pole that provided a railing on the steps to the parking lot.

"Mom, I am sorry. I hope you don't think I resent you or the twins."

She nodded. "We'll talk later about what's happened tonight. Right now, I need to go to a hospital."

Uncle Ford's cane clattered to the ground. "I knew you were hurting in there. What's wrong?"

She didn't know for sure, but she'd never been more terrified. Her son had barely escaped jail, and his siblings wanted out of her body. Her first instinct was to curl up in a small, fetal ball and shut out the rest of the world.

"I can drive, but Dan, you need to go home. Your father is going to call in the morning. He's going to a police station in Atlantic City to identify Jim Cooper, and then he'll call home."

"What's wrong, Mom?"

The latest contraction finally released her. "I think I'm in labor," she said.

"Let's call an ambulance." Dan grabbed his uncle's cane and handed it to him. "Wait with Mom."

"No." Cate straightened. "I could be wrong, and I'd rather go to the hospital in Leith if we can. I have the cell phone in the car, and if the contractions get any closer together, I'll call the closest ambulance, but I need to go now."

"Can you drive safely, Dan?" Uncle Ford asked.

"I'm scared, but I'll be careful." Dan dragged keys out of his pockets. "Let's get you into your car, Mom."

"Okay, but Dan, don't call your father tonight, and don't tell him tomorrow. I'm probably fine, and we don't have to worry him. Tell him when he gets home from the airport if I'm not home. Drive carefully. No speeding, and don't do anything reckless.''

She'd feel better when he was home safe. She didn't want a nurse to corner Dan in a waiting room and tell him something had happened to the twins. She didn't want to worry Alan long distance, when she might be suffering more false alarms.

''I'll do what you ask, Mom, but Dad will leave *you* this time.'' He took her keys and opened the driver's door on her car. He hit the lock switch and she went around to the passenger's side, while Uncle Ford climbed behind the steering wheel. ''I should go with you, Mom.''

''I'd rather you met your Dad at home to tell him. He'll understand when I explain. He has to see the New Jersey police, and I might be wrong. I was wrong before.''

She watched him run for his own car. She reached for Uncle Ford's arm. ''I didn't want him to come to the hospital in case something is horribly wrong. He shouldn't have to face it without his father.''

''If I were Alan and Dan, I'd put all your belongings on the front lawn. Do you think he'll take it better at home?''

''I don't want to believe it might be real labor. I'm barely twenty-seven weeks along. Let's not invite bad karma. I'll deal with reality later.''

Maybe Dan and Alan would understand she was doing the best she could. She acknowledged a stab of guilt.

She was trying to take care of her family, to save them from worrying needlessly, but she faced a deeper truth. Being alone to cope with her own panic felt safer.

They couldn't do anything to help her. She didn't know how to comfort her son, didn't know how to tell her husband she might be losing his children when she felt as if she might shatter in unfixable pieces.

How could she allow even Alan and Dan inside her desperate fear for her unborn children?

ALAN DRUMMED on the arm of his seat and checked his watch for the thousandth time. Two hours in the air. He'd probably reach the hospital and his wife in two more hours.

She should have called him to deal with the Devon County police. She shouldn't have asked Dan to wait until tomorrow to tell him about the twins.

Dan had called instead, waking him just after midnight. Alan hadn't tried to reach Cate from his hotel or from the plane. He was too angry. According to Dan, the doctors had stopped her labor, but at twenty-seven weeks along, she was going to be in bed for the rest of her pregnancy. As Alan had fought for control, Dan had sworn she'd thought keeping him in the dark was doing him a favor.

This favor he didn't need. He loved Cate, but had she changed so much she had to prove her independence at his expense? At their family's? How could she possibly have convinced herself Jim Cooper or the business was more important than her or Dan or the twins?

He'd been a fool. Cate wanted marriage on her terms. Either he shared everything, or she'd leave him. But she'd decided not to tell him when their family was in trouble. She seemed to think she knew best, and he should follow her wishes. Alan refused to live by Cate's double standards.

After the plane landed, he abandoned his luggage and hailed a taxi. The hospital entrance glowed faintly in six-thirty-in-the-morning light. Ignoring the security guard's curious gaze, Alan strode to the elevator.

He had to know for himself she was all right, and the twins were still safe. But he also had to tell her he didn't want to pretend they were sharing a life together.

Dan had given him Cate's room number, and he found her easily on the maternity ward. Hell of a place to put a woman in danger of losing her babies.

The sound of footsteps from the direction of the nurse's station pushed him inside Cate's room before he was ready. She opened her eyes and actually smiled at him.

"You're here." As if he'd come to the rescue. She'd denied him that privilege.

"Dan called me." He shut the door and pressed his back to it. Anger pulsed in his head, his shoulders, his fingertips.

She looked impossibly young. She'd left her hair in curls and secured it in a ponytail. Her face, bare of makeup, was pale with worry. He felt for what she'd been through, but she couldn't expect him to take what she'd done without a complaint. He felt as if she'd tricked him.

"You could have lost the babies, Cate."

Her frown carried a hint of surprise. "You're upset with me."

All around her bed, monitors pulsed and printed tapes that recorded his unborn children's condition. "You decided I didn't need to know until everything was over."

"You had the business—the police—"

"And what about the police here, with Dan? Why did you expect me to share everything? You hid an emergency concerning my children from me. Our children, Cate."

"I thought—"

"Stop. I don't want to upset you more. I don't want to cause the labor to start again, but Cate, I can't live in this kind of marriage. I'm always on probation, and you have no rules."

"I tried not to make your problems worse. I assume you'll have to go back to New Jersey now?"

"When our family is safe. How could you think the business meant more to me than Dan and the twins? More than you?"

"I planned to tell you." She held out her hands. "Dan was supposed to bring you here the moment you arrived tonight."

"You still don't get it?" His head throbbed, but he bit down on resentment that felt like a wild thing trying to escape his body. He was terrified he'd start her labor again. "Are you all right?"

"Yes. And the babies are fine. They want me to stay for a few days, and then it's bed rest at home." She shook her head slightly, but her bewilderment only made him realize how far apart they were. Had she really expected he'd understand? ''Will I be in our home, Alan?''

''That's up to you.'' He turned, and gripped the door handle. ''Do you understand you wanted to leave me because I hid business issues from you?''

''Yes, but—''

''It is different,'' he cut in, ''because it's worse. This was about our family. This was about you and Dan needing my support. I am your husband and his father—I need to be with you both when you're in trouble. Even though you were fine without me, I'm not fine.''

He had to get out of here before he voiced the threats that formed in his head, because he wanted her to hurt, too.

Threats such as she would never make decisions for him again. She would never control him.

He didn't intend to parallel the years his father had spent, slicing himself to ribbons on the shards of a marriage. He turned back to Cate before he opened the door. ''Let me know if I should pack your things or come pick you up.''

He turned away. He despised the ache that nearly rendered him helpless in front of her. He prayed she'd stop him and admit she'd made a mistake.

She didn't.

''Alan?'' a gruff, loud voice called.

He turned. Uncle Ford, on his cane, stood just in front of the waiting area. He'd probably been there all night.

''I don't want to talk to you, Uncle Ford. You should have known better. At the least, you shouldn't have saddled Dan with the responsibility of calling me.''

''I only followed Cate's wishes.''

''I thought I was also your family.''

HER OWN HEARBEAT tapped out a song of panic. Could Alan be right? Had she decided he wasn't important enough to come home and then assumed he should thank her?

No.

If Dr. Davis hadn't stopped her labor, Cate would have called him.

But what if he'd arrived too late? What if the police had put Dan in jail last night?

Why had she been so afraid to tell Alan about the children? He might be right when he accused her of wanting marriage her own way. Not because she believed she knew how to arrange their lives, but because she hadn't known how to share her deepest self, her fear for Dan and then her panic that the twins might die.

The complexity of day-to-day relationships with Dan and Alan had overwhelmed her. She hadn't seen her fear coming. Maybe it dated from before her accident, one of those implicit memories.

Caroline had told her she'd never shared the truth about her marriage. Alan implied she'd always hidden parts of herself from him. The truth was worse. She hadn't felt capable of trusting him with her grief.

A small cry that escaped her own mouth startled her. She'd hidden her deepest feelings from Alan. She hadn't meant to, didn't want to on a conscious level, but until she could be honest with him, she couldn't ask him to come back.

No more push me pull you. For the last time—for the future, she had to look into her own soul and find out if she was capable of sharing her life in a real marriage. The kind of marriage she'd claimed she'd wanted.

DAN MET Alan at the door, his expression wary but resigned. Alan's heart unclenched at the sight of him. He put his arms around Dan and hugged him as tight as he could.

"Your mother's safe. The twins are safe. I'm more grateful than I can tell you that you called, son."

"I'm glad you're home."

They'd deal with the police issue later. Right now, Dan needed to hear his little sisters—according to Dr. Davis—were still growing and thriving.

Dr. Davis had also told him Cate had asked her not to reveal the girls' sex to her. The doctor had speculated Cate might be afraid of growing that much closer to the babies.

The possibility hurt him. He wouldn't have left Cate at the hospital if he'd believed he could have helped her. She didn't want his help. She wanted to do it all on her own. How ironic that she'd persuaded him to stop being the man who hid behind his own pictures of himself as a provider.

Now he walked in Cate's old shoes. He needed her to love him without boundaries. He couldn't have produced a concept of such love before Cate had forced him to live as if he believed in it. Maybe he should be grateful.

Grateful? He felt foolish because she'd convinced him, but he hadn't noticed she didn't believe.

"YOU'RE BACK ON TRACK." Dr. Davis looked up from the strip of paper the monitor continued to feed the next day. "We'll begin to wean you off the medication. If all goes well, you can go home. To bed."

Cate nodded. "How long before I can leave?"

"I don't think I'll make you any promises." Dr. Davis dropped the strip. "Still don't want to know your children's sex?"

Cate hesitated. No, she couldn't know any more than she already knew. "Not yet." What a coward.

"Okay. When do you think Alan will come by today? I'll try to come back in case you both have questions."

"He won't come unless I call."

Dr. Davis quirked her eyebrows in apparent understanding. "You'll call?"

Cate breathed in. "I think so."

"Well, let my office know when he arrives. If I'm available I'll come back."

Cate didn't answer. Did she have the courage to call Alan? She'd spent nights in his arms. She'd shared her body with him, as naked as a woman could be.

But not quite. She'd withheld a vital part of herself, the part that needed.

"Dr. Davis?"

The doctor looked back from the door. "What?"

"Did Alan let you tell him the sex?"

She nodded. "You don't like to think he might be braver than you?"

Cate gasped. She didn't want to compete with Alan. She needed to believe he would sustain her. In all ways. And that her support, emotional and physical, had become necessary to him. She asked Dr. Davis a rhetorical question, born of her epiphany. "Maybe a married couple is as strong as their combined strength?"

The other woman thought. After a moment, she shrugged. "I guess each couple has to decide about that. You let me know, because I'm no expert."

"No, I'm right," Cate said as the door closed behind Dr. Davis. She had to be right. She reached for the telephone and dragged it to her bed, but when she picked up the receiver she lost her nerve.

She couldn't be wrong again. Not for Alan, not for Dan. This time, she had to believe. No matter who she turned out to be when she regained her memory, she refused to turn back from being Alan's wife and Dan's mother again.

She dialed home. After all her angst, the answering machine picked up.

"Alan." She willed the tremble out of her voice. "The labor terrified me. I was so afraid for the babies, I needed to be alone in case something was wrong. I couldn't let even you feel how much I hurt." She licked her lips as that pain sprang at her again. "But you were right, and I was wrong. I don't need to be alone any more. I need you. Will you come back to me?"

After a few seconds, when she couldn't think of any message more important than her confession, she hung up.

ALAN PLAYED the message several times. The wobble in Cate's voice shook him. His whole body tensed in an instinctive compulsion to do something to take care of her, but his second instinct warned him to protect himself. He'd believed her too many times since the accident, only to find she didn't mean what he thought she'd said.

Alan turned away from the phone. After he'd left Cate, he'd gone back to the airport and picked up his luggage. Then he'd spent the rest of the morning with Chief Mabry, swearing out a new statement that included information the detective had uncovered about Jim Cooper and his spending habits. They'd faxed a copy to New Jersey.

He'd called Dr. Davis's office and demeaned himself, admitting he and Cate were getting along so badly he feared he'd bring labor back on if he saw her again.

She'd taken all his numbers and essentially told him to grow up. Good advice, except he had grown. Too old to believe in fairy tales his wife spun. Even if she spun them without a conscious plan.

But he remembered how it felt to do what she'd done. In the old days, he'd shared just enough information to keep her happy. How many times had he persuaded himself she'd understand when he explained his motives?

His anger toward her troubled him when he understood the kind of rationalization she'd used.

After he played Cate's message one more time, he called the hospital again. A nurse informed him Cate had finally fallen asleep. Which probably meant she hadn't slept well the night before. She never slept during the day unless she was ill.

A memory of her soft relief when she'd seen him piled on a little more guilt. What had he done to her to relieve his own fear?

He drove back to the hospital and trekked to her room at a slower pace this time. At her door, he hesitated. She'd claimed she'd been afraid.

He understood being afraid. All his mistakes had come from his fear of losing her. Why couldn't they both learn to risk themselves for the deep and abiding bond she'd convinced him they could have?

He knocked lightly.

"Come in," she called.

He went, illogically hoping for the greeting she'd given him this morning. Instead, she eyed him warily.

"Did you get my message?" Color slid over her ashen skin.

"Did you mean what you said?"

She swallowed, and she looked so frail, he fought an urge to pick her up and take her home where he firmly believed he could shelter her from any harm.

"I meant every word, and I won't change my mind."

"What do you mean, Cate?" He couldn't soften his rough tone. She'd rubbed his emotions raw.

"I truly didn't want Dan here, but I was so frightened I forgot how to be his mother. And letting you see how terrified I was—it felt like taking my soul out and handing it over. How could I let anyone see that deep inside me?"

He'd been as frightened many times, but he'd

never told her. "Before, when we argued, we didn't explain ourselves to each other. We just made love and started fresh."

"I don't think you can start fresh until you patch up old hurts. I knew you'd be in as much pain as I was, but sharing it with you made everything too real, the babies, Dan's problems. I didn't know how to lean on you. What if you let me down?"

"But, Cate, you made me believe we were in this marriage together."

"I lost my nerve. I knew we'd figure out how to work on houses without money, but could we survive Dan being in jail? If I'd lost the twins how could we look at each other without remembering?"

"I believed we'd love each other no matter what. You gave me that, Cate. For years, I thought love came with conditions. Over the past few months, I came to think that was wrong."

"What do you want from me, Alan?"

He thought as he went to the side of her bed. "I want you to let me in. Good times and bad, I want us to be together. If I'd come home and you'd lost the twins without telling me they were in trouble, I don't believe I could have forgiven you."

Tears wet her eyelashes. "I was so afraid, I couldn't reach for you. In my mind, I've loved you a few weeks, not all my adult life."

"Can you change that, Cate?"

"You've changed. You tell me the truth even when you look as if talking at all hurts. I guess I can change, too. I won't ever take the kind of risk I took last night. For a little while, the twins belonged to me, and only I was strong enough to save them. I'm so grateful they and Dan are all right. And you're here.'' She held out her hands. ''I love our children, and I'd do anything to protect them, but I'm stronger with you beside me.''

Her hands, in his, reassured him. ''Are you sure this time? We can't go back again.''

''I'm sure I love you, and I never want to fail you again.''

He sat beside her. ''I guess I've let you down a time or two.''

''I remember snippets every so often, snippets of arguments, flashes of the love we made instead of making up.'' Blushing again, she met his gaze.

He leaned down to kiss her. He meant the kiss to be a chaste promise, but her lips stirred beneath his, and his body woke with desire for his wife. A sometimes traitorous, yet absolutely sure response to Cate's slightest touch. He pulled away, rubbing his index finger beneath her lip.

''We'd better not.''

''But you love me, Alan?''

''More than my own life.''

''This time I know exactly what kind of commitment goes with love.''

He leaned across her legs, taking care not to tangle himself in any of her monitor cords. ''I wonder when most people learn to let their lovers share their lives.''

''I hope we're slow. I'd feel sorry for a whole world full of people shoving each other away.'' She yawned. ''I'm awfully tired. Do you mind if I go to sleep?''

He took her hand and realized she might be uncomfortable under his weight. ''Do you want me to move?''

Closing her eyes, she shook her head. ''Maybe later, when I get used to knowing you're here.''

''I won't leave you.''

''Alan.'' She popped her eyes open. ''Are we having boys or girls?''

He was ridiculously glad he got to tell her instead of Dr. Davis. ''Two girls.''

She flashed a brilliant smile. ''How annoying that you're braver than I am. I was afraid I'd see them every time I closed my eyes, if something bad happened.''

''You might have, but so would I, and when you have bad days, I'll be strong. Then you can take your turn at being strong for me.''

Incredibly, she widened her smile, but tears slid out of her eyes. Alan maneuvered between the cords to pull her into his arms. He'd shelter her from everything, except life.

That, they'd face together.

''I'm thinking Mary and Melinda for names,'' he said.

''No.'' She dashed her tears off her face, the Cate he'd come to love more than he'd ever loved her before. The feisty fighter who'd hidden herself all those years. ''No alliteration. It's not cute.''

''I like Mary and Melinda.'' He snuggled closer, tucking her sweet-smelling head beneath his chin.

''We're never going to agree on anything, Alan Palmer.''

''Probably not.'' He curved a protective hand over her belly. ''Night, Mary—night, Melly.''

''That's even worse.''

Several reassuringly firm kicks mounded beneath his palm. Cate laughed, sharing his relief. ''Daddy's girls, already,'' she said.

He hugged her. ''You go to sleep. I'll wait right here for you.''

EPILOGUE

ALAN WAS ALREADY holding Mary when Melinda came into the world—screaming. Dr. Davis held their second daughter high enough for Cate to see her.

"Good work, Mom. And they're both in good shape. I'll let you hold Melinda for a second, and then they both go to the nursery. At thirty-five weeks and their weight, I think they'll be fine, but your pediatrician wants a good look. Okay with you, Pop?"

Alan nodded. "Cate?"

Deeply involved with her second daughter, Cate still had attention left for Alan, who'd shared every second of this labor. She nodded at him as she cradled Melinda against her breasts.

"Let's not ever tell her she was five minutes behind Mary, okay?"

Cate laughed, jouncing the baby. "Whatever you say, husband, but I think we'll be lying for no good reason. They'll find out anyway. They'll both want to be the older one."

"I guess we'll have to live with the consequences."

She met his gaze as she pressed her mouth to Melinda's head. Some consequences might not be as sweet as these two morsels, but they'd learned the pain, the strain and the joy of sharing.

Dan had finally begun to work for a paycheck at the golf course, and the new, downsized version of Palmer Construction worked only on the renovations Alan had loved best anyway.

"Let us have your daughters now, please." Dr. Davis nodded at the two nurses who pushed clear bassinets next to Cate and Alan.

Melinda opened her eyes. She seemed to look into Cate's, but Cate had to blink hard so she could see. Melinda uttered a soft sound that probably meant she was starving. Cate took it as a love song.

"I can't try to feed them yet?"

"After they visit the nursery."

"Can I hold Mary one more time?"

"For a second. Alan, pass Mary to Cate, and take Melinda."

Already, Cate recognized Mary's face, though she'd held her for a scant few moments before Melinda burst onto the scene. She kissed her baby's forehead and read her husband's pride in Melinda.

A love more fierce than she'd ever known unfurled from her tired body.

Melinda stretched with a squall against her father's chest, and Dr. Davis signaled the nurses.

"They won't be gone long. You can see them again in recovery."

"You should tell Dan," Cate said to Alan.

He nodded. "And Uncle Ford and Aunt Imogen, but I don't want to leave you."

"Go put big brother in the picture. By the time you come back, I'll be finished with Cate, and you can take some time for yourselves.'' Dr. Davis turned to the nurse who was passing her instruments as she stitched Cate. ''Could you scratch my nose please?''

Cate laughed, and Alan leaned over her for a brief, yet passionate kiss. ''Wait for me,'' he said.

She tried not to cry more tears of joy. As the door closed behind him, she looked wearily on her doctor. ''He's a real jokester, isn't he?''

''A proud dad. I'm proud of you both. Those girls weren't kind to you. An hour of labor for every year of your life. What do you think of today?''

Cate wrapped her arms around herself. ''I can't think. I'm too busy feeling completely happy. And a bit cold.''

Dr. Davis turned to the nurse. ''I can complete this on my own. Find a warm blanket for Mrs. Palmer. The shivering is perfectly normal, Cate. Your body's been through torture.''

''Torture?'' Cate repeated.

''A male doctor wouldn't admit it, but then, maybe he wouldn't know.''

''Melinda and Mary were worth every second. They're gorgeous, aren't they?''

''Slippery, but perfect, as I recall. We do good work together, you and Alan and I.''

''Thank you for everything, keeping the secret and all.''

Dr. Davis scooted her chair back, stood and then began to readjust Cate's bed. ''Did you ever remember why you kept them secret?''

''Parts.'' That much was true. The past and her fear of it seemed inconsequential. Maybe she and Alan had both been afraid, as empty as they'd both felt behind the walls they'd built within their marriage. "I'm perplexed now when I think of how Alan and I behaved toward each other."

"Everything worked out for the best."

A platitude that covered the truth of her marriage now, but left out the happiness that grew in her life—in her family, each and every second of every day. Some of those seconds might tick by unnoticed, but at the end of each twenty-four hours, both she and Alan could recount plenty of minutes they hadn't taken for granted.

Alan backed through the doors. "I bring gifts."

He held out the warm blanket, but the real presents streamed in under their own steam behind him.

"They're gorgeous, Cate." Aunt Imogen kissed her cheek. "Caroline and I made the attendants bring Melinda and Mary to the nursery window. They're absolutely beautiful."

"They're just red," Dan contradicted and quickly kissed Cate's forehead. "But they'll probably grow on us."

Alan leaned over her with a private smile as he tucked the blanket around her. "They were both howling. I think Melinda set Mary off."

"That's bound to happen. We'll rope Caroline in to baby-sit if the going gets rough." She looked at her sister. "Where's Shelly?"

"Running late—that new boyfriend of hers had some sort of meeting after classes, and she wanted to wait for him to drive back. She'll come by when she gets back into town."

Caroline clearly didn't approve of Shelly's Romeo. Life went on. Cate made room as Alan sat on the bed beside her. ''Uncle Ford, you're quiet,'' he said. ''Don't you approve?''

He shot a tentative glance at Alan before he answered. ''I tend to agree with Dan, but I'm so grateful to be back in the fold, I was afraid to offer my opinion.''

Alan chuckled, but stood up to pull a chair close for the older man. He wrapped his arm around Uncle Ford's shoulders. ''How am I going to convince you I was frantic for Cate and the children that day, Uncle Ford?''

''How about if we try this?'' Uncle Ford edged closer to the bed and whipped a photo out of his pocket. A small bay foal that stood about as high as his cane. ''I bought her for the girls. By the time they're old enough to learn to ride, she'll be old enough to belong to them.''

The whole family laughed, and Alan shook his uncle's hand. ''Deal. Come sit down.''

''No.'' Dr. Davis broke into the crowd. ''You all come with me. Alan and Cate need a few minutes to themselves, and then Cate goes to recovery. I'll treat the rest of you to the worst coffee ever boiled up in a public cafeteria.''

''Who could resist?'' Uncle Ford's interest sparked.

Aunt Imogen made a show of sisterly despair as she fell into the exit line. Caroline paused for a quick hug that Cate heartily returned, and Dan stopped to pound his father on the shoulder.

''I think I'll go look at them again,'' he said. ''I've still got to put one of the cribs together, so I'll probably see you tomorrow, Mom.''

“Are you sure it’s okay with your professors that you’re staying another day?”

“Jeez,” he said rather loudly over his shoulder.

Cate turned to her husband before the door closed on their son. “I love him even more when he’s impatient with my mothering.”

“Me, too, but I’m glad Dr. Davis flushed them out of here.” He smoothed her hair away from her forehead and bent until his mouth touched her ear. “My life is better because I love you.”

“Do you think we wasted time?”

“I think we got here as fast as we could. I’m sorry you had to forget the past before we could find out who we could be. Not just with each other, but as separate people.”

“I’m glad we kept on loving.”

He kissed her and then held himself above her so that their lips almost touched. “Glad we found out that where it counts most, you and I are one.”

* * * * *

0308/24/MB135

THE BABY CONNECTION

The love that binds like no other…
Two couples discover the power of a baby connection.

The Baby Bargain
by Peggy Nicholson

Little Girl Lost
by Marisa Carroll

Available 7th March 2008

THE BABY CONNECTION: TWINS!

As their beautiful twins bring them together, two couples find that they can't resist their baby bonds!

My Husband, My Babies
by Debra Salonen

Unexpected Babies
by Anna Adams

Available 4th April 2008

www.millsandboon.co.uk